Fantasy For Good:

A Charitable

Anthology

EDITED BY
JORDAN ELLINGER AND
RICHARD SALTER

PEDERSON

First Trade Paperback Edition

ISBN: 1-938644-20-4
ISBN-13: 978-1-938644-20-7

Nightscape Press, LLP
http://www.nightscapepress.com

TABLE OF CONTENTS:

PART V: WEIRD FANTASY

Dedicated to all those who fight colon cancer, whatever the outcome. For Roger Zelazny who was taken from us far too soon. For Jay Lake whose very public battle taught us so much about the important things in life. And for Richard's wife, Jennifer, diagnosed during the creation of this anthology, who made the toughest decision and is now, thankfully, cancer free.

FOREWORD

We never expected this anthology to become quite so personal...

When we started out on Fantasy For Good, we took a long time to choose our charity. We followed author Jay Lake's struggles with colon cancer, which is a disease that seems to disproportionately affect writers and yet gets very little attention, and we were inspired to do something to help out the cause. Sadly, Jay passed away recently, a loss we feel keenly. He was very supportive of this project and we will miss him terribly.

We were offered a beautiful cover, created by illustrator Paul Pederson, whose brother-in-law is currently fighting colon cancer. When writer Trent Zelazny reminded us that his father, the late, great novelist Roger, was also initially diagnosed with colon cancer, our decision was cemented.

Trent agreed to write us an introduction and we got the rights to reprint one of Roger's classic stories. We then partnered with the Colon Cancer Alliance with the intention not only to raise as much money as we could, but also to increase awareness about the disease. Colon cancer is the second biggest killer in the US and yet very few people know much about it. We wanted to help change that.

So by late 2013, the fight against this terrible disease already felt like a personal one. And then events struck even closer to home.

In October 2013, Richard's wife, Jennifer, was diagnosed with colorectal cancer. Suddenly this worthy cause became a gut-wrenching reality. We thought this was an old people's disease—Jennifer was 41 when her cancer was discovered. She got lucky and it was caught at stage one. Removal of the cancerous polyp left no detectable trace of cancer in her body, yet the doctors could give her no guarantee that it was truly gone and would not come back.

Jen wants to see her two young boys grow up, get married to the girls or boys of their dreams and have kids of their own who will look after grandma in her old age. She took the courageous step to opt for major surgery, a painful recovery, and a bag for life in exchange for a lower than 1% chance of re-occurrence. She made that heavy sacrifice for her kids. She is amazing.

So now we're really on a mission. Educate yourself, know what to look for, don't assume you're too young, and get yourself screened. **Detecting colorectal cancer early is the key to survival**. At the back of this anthology we've included a list of signs and symptoms to be aware of. We urge you to read it and talk to your doctor.

We want to thank all our contributors, from the veterans to the newcomers. We are extremely grateful for your time and creative energy, and we hope these great stories will inspire and entertain everyone who reads them. Thank you to the agents and assistants who chased after authors and poured over contracts. Thank you to Nightscape Press, particularly Jen and Bob for your support and for donating so much time and effort to this project. Double thanks to Bob in his role as editor of our predecessor, along with Mark Scioneaux and RJ Cavender. Horror For Good is still available and is still raising money for amfAR. Thank you to Trent for your moving tribute to your legendary father and for all your help. Thanks to Paul for his gorgeous cover artwork. Thanks to the go-betweens, too many to list, who put us in contact with some of the biggest names in the genre. Thanks to those authors who weren't able to write something new for us, but instead were happy to offer a reprint or words of encouragement and a willingness to help spread the word. Thank you to everyone who clicks a "like", shares a link, writes a review or blogs to their followers about us. Thanks to everyone at the Colon Cancer Alliance for your enthusiasm, your active involvement from Day One, and for the fantastic work you do to raise awareness, support patients and their families, and fund vital research. Lastly, Richard wants to thank the remarkable doctors, nurses and support staff at Toronto's Sunnybrook Hospital who took such good care of Jennifer when she had her surgery earlier this year.

It is a truly hopeful and wonderful indication of the state of the genre that, even though no one involved in this book will be paid a dime for their work, we had very few authors turn us down and those who did often offered encouragement and promotional help. We hope this anthology is worthy of the faith you put in us.

And thanks to you, the reader. Enjoy the stories, get yourself screened, live a long and happy life.

Richard Salter & Jordan Ellinger
June 3rd 2014

TRENT ZELAZNY is an award winning novelist, a playwright, an anthology editor and a short story writer. The son of famous SF and fantasy novelist Roger Zelazny, Trent has forged his own path in the publishing world. His work tends towards the darker side of fiction but is always hard to pin down in any one category. His novels include *Fractal Despondency, Shadowboxer, Butterfly Potion, Too Late to Call Texas,* and *Voiceless.*

Trent has written a very moving introduction to *Fantasy For Good* and he has also been a key supporter of this project from the start. The editors are very grateful for all his help.

Follow his blog at:
trentzelaznybloggetyblog.blogspot.com

HORSEMAN, PASS BY
An Introduction by Trent Zelazny

I lost my father when I was 18. Kidney failure associated with cancer. Colorectal cancer. Colon cancer. He was only 58 when he died. I'd known he was sick for quite some time, but he'd asked his kids to keep it quiet, not wanting the SF&F community to know about it. Also, he was foolishly certain that he would beat it.

He didn't. I wish to God that he had, but no dice. I honestly believe that a part him truly thought he was immortal. He often wrote about immortals, but he was not immortal himself. He was a human being, just like the rest of us.

For years after, I thought about something a lot, and I still think about it from time to time. What if he hadn't insisted on keeping his illness a secret? This, of course, was in the early and mid-nineties, before the Internet was in virtually every home on the planet. But news could still get around in those days. I remember, at the hospital, a few hours before he died, a close family friend and member of the community, heartbroken and pissed off that they didn't know a thing about it. "You should have told us," she said.

And so I'd ask myself, why didn't they know about it? Because they should have known about it. A lot of people should have known about it, because if people had indeed known about it, more could have been done. That, however, is the only result I can promise would have been different.

More could have, and would have, been done. This is not to say he didn't have good care. He had probably the best available. But I'm not talking about medical care here, or the few who did know, who busted their asses, going through their own utter hell to help him.

It had to be a secret, and so three Zelazny children wandered around, harboring this painful secret, instructed not to talk about it, which we didn't, or we did very little, and only in the strictest confidence. I don't recall a single conversation with my brother or my sister about it. It could have been a time for much needed family bonding, but instead it caused us all to sort of drift apart, each trapped in a personal daze with a hefty dose of denial.

It was inadvertent ignorance on my father's part, and—while unintentional—it was cruel. Cruel in that we had to walk around and pretend everything was hunky-dory, while inside, just like my father, we were being eaten alive.

I've never been angry at my father for this, however, and there's certainly no point in being angry with him now; but that question still comes along and revolves round in my head. What if his friends and colleagues knew about it? Speculative fiction is all about the question, "What if?" and so I speculate, and most every scenario I come up with is more positive than the actual outcome, whether he had lived or died. He wouldn't have hurt his family and friends so much; he would have known more fully just how deeply loved he was—by a whole lot of people. He was a well-loved man, but I'm not sure he ever really knew just how loved he was.

I loved him deeply. I still do. While I don't think he ever would have been a candidate for Father of the Year, his intentions were always good. He was a good man, a very good man, and those he touched he touched deeply.

But he kept his cancer a secret, and in my opinion, he shouldn't have. He had his reasons, though I don't personally find them to be good reasons. Well intended, maybe, but not good; and so I admire, respect, and support anyone brave enough—and compassionate enough—to let their friends and peers know that they are sick. This in no way means I didn't or don't respect my father. I did, and do, very much. But in this situation I learned what not to do. Don't keep something so important a secret.

Just as the wonderful editors and contributors did with Horror for Good, I'm thrilled beyond comprehension by these editors and contributors. And talk about the talent in this collection… well, I can't, really, as I am speechless, but I will say I'm grateful to both Richard Salter and Jordan Ellinger, as well as to every author who took the time to contribute to this collection.

In your hands you hold a book that does more than entertain, more than give the reader a little something to ponder. Like Horror for Good, this book has an additional magic power. It has the power (and the want, maybe even the need) to help, and who it wants to help most are those sick with the same thing that ended my father's life too early, because colorectal cancer is treatable. Having it does not automatically put one in the grave. Diagnosis is quite different from burial.

I could go off about healthcare in this country but I'm not going to. This introduction would be as long as the entire book, if I did. Instead I'll offer a couple of simple items that can do wonders for those diagnosed and for their loved ones: communication, openness, love, support, strength, and books like this one. Every author in this book (myself included) cares. Yes, they care about you, deeply, whether you are the diagnosed, or a family member or friend of the diagnosed. Everyone in this book cares about you.

I promised the editors that I would keep this short, so in closing, I simply want to ask three small favors of you.

First, please don't do what my father did. Don't keep something of such importance a secret. Reach out. Don't be afraid, don't be ashamed, and don't be embarrassed. I promise that you and your loved ones will be thankful, if not immediately, most certainly in the long run.

Second, enjoy the wonderful stories collected in this book, and know that the stories here were contributed out of love, compassion, and the desire to make a difference.

And finally third, thank yourself, both for buying a wonderful collection of stories, and for simultaneously contributing to a wonderful cause.

My father may no longer be with us, but wherever he is, I know he is very pleased that this book has been compiled, as am I.

Thank you.

Trent Zelazny
January 5th 2014

PART I:

Sword and Sorcery

HENRY SZABRANSKI's fiction has appeared in Beneath Ceaseless Skies, Daily Science and Lakeside Circus amongst other places. He lives in Buckinghamshire, UK, with his wife and two young sons.

Please visit his site at www.henryszabranski.com

THE EDGE OF MAGIC
Henry Szabranski

I built a tower of my own. All pearly white and twined with ever-blooming roses; erected by an army of chalk kobolds raised from the surrounding limestone cliffs. My husband Mevlish, of course, took exception to my new home, but by that time I was far beyond caring. My hastily constructed wards were enough to protect it from the worst ravages of his fury, and after a few days he grew weary of being thwarted. Perhaps the King had called him on another urgent mission, or maybe our daughter Farima had swayed his temper in favor of leniency. Either way, soon all I had to look out for were the occasional stray fireball and ragged, dust-laden whirlwinds. I assumed the worst was over and concentrated instead on nursing my anger and my grief.

Then Farima turned up at my outpost near the edge of all magic. Pale-faced and tear-streaked, she trembled with fear. The standoff was over. Mevlish would soon attack again—and this time he would show no mercy.

~~*~*

It had been, as the wine-soaked minstrels in the Admarese taverns used to sing (and probably still do), a whirlwind romance. I was just sixteen, and it was an arranged match... but one never knows what may come of these things; certainly not the plotters, my odious stepfather, and the King of Proximus himself. Luckily for them, and unluckily for me, I fell for Mevlish's superficial charms and he for my obvious ones.

Mevlish the Mighty, feared and admired throughout the Near and Far Kingdoms; Dragonmaster, Inquisitor and Royal High Wizard, official Guardian of the Source; the greatest wielder of magic alive. And so young, too: only ten years my senior. Dashing, soft-spoken, fawned on by others—how could I not be flattered when I caught and held his attention? Princess I may have been, but only of Admar, a backwater satrapy on the edge of the Farthest Lands; about as distant from the glittering heart of Proximus and the source of magic as one could get and still call it civilization.

He beguiled me with tales of high wizardry and adventure; of his duel to the death with the rebel sorcerer Feratus and his legion of fire ghouls; the time he saved a whole town from a plague of marauding she-devils; and with descriptions of his ancestral home, Cradlegate, near the Wizard's Wall.

"Come live in my tower by the Source." He grasped my hand and fell to one knee, looking up at me for the first and last time. "Kaffryn of Admar, will you be my witch wife?"

My heart skipped a beat. "Will you teach me magic?"

1

The wide smile that revealed his strong white teeth quavered for only a moment. "Of course, my dear. As long as you show some affinity, I should be able to teach you a trick or two."

It was the best I could have hoped for, I supposed. And a thousand times better than any Far Land would-be wizard could offer me. "Then I accept," I said.

He stood up, resplendent in his black and silver uniform, and beamed down at me, a dark fantasy stepped from a young girl's dream.

I rested my head against his shoulder. "Take me from here, Mevlish."

He squeezed my arm as if he already owned me, and nodded in approval. "Kaffryn. My witch princess."

~~*~*

Our honeymoon consisted of a brief layover in Proximus, the capital of the Near Kingdoms. Mevlish spent more time meeting with officials and the King than he did with me, so I was able to explore the city at my leisure. I wasn't surprised by the clamor for Mevlish's attention, but I had hoped he would make at least a token show of resistance. Still, he had made it abundantly clear during the long journey from Admar that his duty to the King and the realm came above all else, and the sooner I understood that, the happier I would be.

"Yes, darling," I had said.

Where Admar was all cobbles and slate, gulls and fishing nets, salt air and threat of storm, Proximus was turrets and colonnades, silk pennants and marbled riverbank promenades: the city closest to the Source, and hence the greatest. Its sheer scale allowed me some measure of anonymity, although whispers and stares would always follow me if I tarried too long in any one place. My abiding memory of that time is of silken bed sheets, rich with color; sumptuous feasts; and all eyes on me, Mevlish's new witch-princess. It was the dream of the life I thought I had begun.

At the grand state dinner held in my honor, whilst Mevlish was lost in discussion halfway across the ballroom, a tall, graying man with bulging eyes and a medal-encrusted military uniform detached himself from the waltz and bent his knee before me. He kissed my silk-gloved hand.

"Make my Mevlish happy." His voice was soft, barely audible above the sound of the music. I leaned forward to better hear him. "His services are worth more to me than a thousand treaties with your little seaside town." His voice lowered to a hiss and his staring eyes locked with mine. "You're to be a good wife to him, do you understand? Do as he bids. Bear him a son."

He stepped back and smiled, as if he had paid me the most gracious compliment in the world, and dissolved back into the dance. Only later, when Mevlish questioned me as to the nature of his words, did I discover it was the King himself.

And so, all too soon, even the dream was over. "We must leave," Mevlish said, expression pensive. "Cradlegate is eager for its new mistress."

The next day we were alone again, in a carriage pulled by a quartet of six-legged horses. They required no driver to give them direction.

East of Proximus, the landscape grew barren and rocky, the lush fields giving way to unpopulated foothills that wound towards the mountains. The soil here was too strange and unpredictable to grow crops, the animals too dangerous, tainted and warped by the increasing strength of the magic field, to sustain a community. There was a reason for the location of Proximus, balanced finely on the edge between maximum magic and its overdose.

Rows of wooden crosses lined the road out of the city, hung with the dead or dying. I stared at the grisly evidence of the King's justice and asked Mevlish what crimes warranted such a fate. His face darkened and he looked away from the carriage window. "Murderers, rapists," he said. "And heretic wizards practicing free magic without license."

"Free magic?" I asked. "Magic is magic, isn't it?"

"The practice of magic is proscribed within strict limits, my dear. Only spells and incantations approved by the King may be performed."

I was genuinely confused. "Why?"

He grimaced. "Otherwise it grows wild and harmful and out of control."

"I had no idea."

"You're from the Far Lands, my love." His gaze refused to meet mine. "I wouldn't expect you to."

We spent the rest of the journey in silence.

Cradlegate lay at the mouth of the mountain pass that led to the Source. The carriage stopped perhaps half a mile from the brooding tower and its low cluster of outbuildings. I was all agog, wide-eyed and nervous, my head throbbing with the intensity of the magic field. I had felt it building all day, a pressure behind my eyes, tricking occasional sparkles and strange blurs into my vision.

"Let me show you the stables first," Mevlish said.

Set into a bank of rubble near a series of tumbling cascades was a wide, single-storey stone building. At first I thought it abandoned, ash and burned stone everywhere—then I heard and felt the low rumble, and dread certainty filled me.

Dragons. At least half a dozen of them. Most slept, almost indistinguishable from the rock, but a couple extended their great wings and slithered forward to greet their returned master. Large as three tall men standing on each other's shoulders, they were all blackened slate and molten glow between thick plates of spiked armor. The air shivered before their breath, and I found myself in true fear for the first time in my life.

"Come," Mevlish said. He seemed oblivious to my reluctance and tugged me out of the carriage for introductions.

"They've been bound to my family for generations." He spoke with obvious pride, his chest puffed out, his head tilted back as he swept his hand in an arc. "It takes a king's ransom to feed them but they're invaluable for hunting down and disposing of rogue magicians."

I shuddered at the thought of being at the receiving end of these creatures' attentions. Thrax, Drax, Grax, or some such; I don't remember the litany of similar sounding names Mevlish reeled off. Instead I concentrated on not being overcome by the oily, metallic stench of them. I didn't know whether it was the heat and the smell, the altitude, or the strength of magic, but darkness threatened the borders of my vision.

Either Mevlish noticed my discomfort or he grew tired of re-acquainting himself with his pets; eventually we clambered back into the carriage and clattered on towards his home.

Like the dragons, Cradlegate had been in his family for generations. The cold stone staircase corkscrewing up through the tower's dark interior was lined with portraits of his haggard ancestors. They seemed to eye me with disapproval as I climbed and I began to feel dizzy and faint again. It finally dawned on me that this was my new home. My new life. And I had left behind the Far Lands forever.

~~*~*

Later that first night, after our attempt at lovemaking ended with Mevlish storming from the bedchamber, I had my first glimpse of the Wizard's Wall. I wandered the tower in search of my escaped husband and eventually found him on the rooftop, staring out over the battlements towards the desolate mountain pass Cradlegate guarded. Ribbons of ghostly light veiled the glittering stars, playing above the ground that rose towards the Source, and I could not help but give a soft gasp at the sight.

Mevlish did not turn as he hunkered over the edge. I approached and laid a hand on his shoulder. "Mevlish. What's the matter, my love?"

"This place," he said. "This cursed place. My head buzzes with the infernal intensity of the magic here." He hung his head, his expression pained. "I swear, sometimes it's too much."

"But this is your home," I said. *And you invited me to live here.*

"It's where I was born, yes. And my father before me, and his before him." He straightened, arching his back, and let out a pent up breath. "Do not worry, Kaffryn. It's just that I've been away too long. Eventually I'll get used to it again. You will, too."

4

I stared at the pass, all crushed slate and pulverized, glassy rock, and sensed the energy that Mevlish spoke of, a sparkling in the air. Beneath the dancing light of the aurora, to me it felt intoxicating rather than oppressive.

"There aren't any demons here?" I asked. "Like in the stories?"

Mevlish laughed, but then turned serious. "Only those we make."

"And have you made any?"

He turned away, and was silent for a time. His answer, when it came, was cryptic. "I never quite reached as far as Great-Uncle Alexandre."

I edged closer to him, curled my arm around his waist. He did not pull away. "I don't understand."

He nodded towards the pass. "Grandfather's brother. Drunk one night, challenged by some guest—the stories never agree—he marched out, determined to reach the Source." He quirked his dark brow. "He made it farther than most."

"What happened?"

"He lies there still. Along with all the other fools and madmen who have gone before and since." Mevlish pointed towards a line of black posts that meandered across the width of the valley, only just visible in the pale light. "There is the edge of magic. Beyond those markers the rise in its strength is no longer gradual: every step you take increases the power of the field by half again as much. Tarry for more than a few moments and you'll become addled; stay longer and you'll lose your sanity and die. Just a few steps beyond lies the Wizard's Wall. You can't see it, but it's there: the boundary marked by the fallen. No human has ever strayed beyond it; the weight of magic simply crushes the mind." He turned to look at me, his back to the valley. "Part of my duties here is to make sure no fools climb past Cradlegate and try to reach the Wall. Every year there are a few, bent on reaching the point of maximum magic to cast this spell or that. It's another reason the King pays to keep the dragons; they're a most effective deterrent."

I stared at the line of posts, at the aurora flickering above. "And what do you think lies beyond the Wall? How much farther is the Source itself?"

He shrugged. "Just a mile or so, the calculations suggest. As the crow flies. If one could ever survive the flight."

My brow furrowed. "Perhaps the strength of the field dips again, beyond the Wall. Like the late summer storms that sometimes wrack Admar—the winds build and build, and you think they can grow no stronger, until the breath is sucked out of your lungs… and then the wind lulls and the sky grows blue again, and you find yourself at the still centre."

5

Mevlish glanced at me sharply. "What nonsense is this?"

Stung by his rebuke, I pointed in the direction the Source must lie. "Perhaps it's like that with magic; the field mounts and then subsides, the Source at the eye of the... storm." I hesitated, no longer sure I understood my own thoughts. "If one could only push through that strongest part —"

"Kaffryn. Stop. This is just crazy talk."

I paused, my mouth moving wordlessly, and then I laughed to re-assure him and myself. I took his hand, and tried not to think of how my stepfather used to reprimand me. "It was a jest, my love."

He looked down at me, unblinking. "The Source calls those who dare listen. A siren call. Many have fallen to that fascination, believing their magic would only become stronger the closer they approached." His grip on my shoulder grew painful. "Listen to me, Kaffryn. They all fall. All. Do you understand? Never try to approach the Wall. Never."

I nodded. "Yes, my love."

But in my mind, the magic field tickled and played across an itch I knew would only grow stronger.

~~*~*

To some extent I could understand how Mevlish came to be disappointed with me, his new trophy wife. I was unpracticed in the kitchen, for one thing—my meals had all been prepared by father's staff, so I had never needed to learn to cook. In conversation he quickly became frustrated with me; I had little regard for or knowledge of the politics of the nation, and no doubt he found my stream of complaints about the dim and dank living conditions tiresome. Neither was I much use managing the household, but at least Mevlish was undemanding when it came to the tidying, sweeping and laundry; his coterie of eerie clay servants, with their hollow eyes and powdery trails of dust, were well used to coping with those duties. At first these servants disturbed me with their blank faces, incongruously formal uniforms and silent manner—but I soon became used to their ministrations. In the morning they fetched my dresses, in the afternoon and evening they served our lunch and dinner, in the evening they helped me bathe. Before long I took them for granted, an everyday miracle made possible by Mevlish's outstanding talent at magic and the intensity of the field here.

I quickly learned more than a trick or two myself. Like a sun-starved flower, I bloomed under my husband's reluctant tutelage and the strength of magic. Those times in the Mevlish's laboratory when he would deign to show me the basics of the art, and I reproduced his results, were some of my best memories of our time as a couple.

He gifted me a single slim volume from his personal library. "Elements of Approved Magic", a basic manual containing enough simple spells and mind techniques to allow me to start tapping the field. "My favorite when I was a child," he laughed. When I asked for access to the library—the door was always kept locked—he shook his head. "No, my dear. Far too dangerous." He did not say to whom.

If Mevlish was ever surprised by my latent affinity and growing skill he never mentioned it. Once or twice, after I had demonstrated some particularly elaborate technique or rite, he would give my hand a squeeze, lean close and say, "Kaffryn. My witchy wife." His condescension was unintentional, I am sure, and anyway I forgave him, since those moments soon became the only times he showed me any real affection.

Ah, the Source. Bless its ancient creators, or the passing star from which it fell, or whatever natural or unnatural process gave rise to it all those centuries ago. In the first few months at Cradlegate, when I was consumed by a growing fear I had made the biggest mistake of my life by marrying Mevlish, the vibrant energy emanating from that mysterious point just over the horizon became my one consolation, the one advantage of my move from Admar. I could feel its influence deep through my bones, a slow-pulsing potential, and each day I wondered what new aspect of its power would be revealed to me.

Despite everything, it was enough.

~~*~*

It was no surprise to learn my primary duty at Cradlegate was to bear Mevlish an heir; it was inconceivable the Mevlish name would not continue, undiminished, down the ages. To this demand I acceded, more or less willingly. As long as my study of magic was allowed to continue I could put up with the isolation and less than luxurious living conditions; not to mention Mevlish's growing emotional detachment, and the exercise of his connubial rights upon demand.

Our lovemaking was awkward and overly serious, dutiful rather than joyful; not a patch on the adventures of my careless youth, and not helped by the tinge of pity I began to feel towards him. Mighty in magic my Mevlish may have been, but meek he was when it came to the bedchamber. If I attempted to lighten the mood with humor he would become sullen and retreat; when I took the initiative he frowned disapprovingly and shrugged me away. If I had been less experienced, my confidence would have been dealt a crushing blow and I would have begun, perhaps, to blame myself for our lack of satisfaction; as it was, I knew whatever ailed our relationship, at least in that regard, was none of my doing.

Despite our problems, I fell pregnant less than a year after our move to Cradlegate. I'd always known I would end up being a mother, I suppose, but it had never been a consuming ambition of mine like it had been for so many of my serving maids and ladies-in-waiting back in Admar. I was not one to romanticize the role. To me, it was all just part of the bargain I had struck: lore of magic for child. I thought I was getting the greater part of the deal. Any young doxy down by the harbor could spawn a child or dozen: but who could exercise the skill necessary to raise the very earth to do one's bidding?

When I finally told Mevlish the news he grinned for the first time in months and almost—almost—leaned down to kiss me.

"Well done," he said. "I shall… make arrangements."

I knew better by that stage than to be affronted by his cold demeanor, even though the bodily spirits that can at times possess a woman whilst carrying child were already raging through me. I merely nodded and said, "Make sure you do."

~~*~*

Things changed once Farima was born; some for the better, many for the worse.

I'll not discuss the birth itself, save to say I took covert steps afterwards to make sure I would never become pregnant again.

To Mevlish's credit he never once expressed any disappointment, to me at least, that his first-born wasn't a son, but after a brief period of doting he became increasingly scarce. I'm sure it had nothing to do with Farima's constant crying and demands upon our time, and everything to do with the King's new crusade against the heretic territories in the Farthest Lands. On the rare occasions he returned from these distant campaigns for more than a day or two I would find him either collapsed asleep upon the bed, sitting in grim silence in his study, or striding the battlements, prone to sudden and unpredictable bouts of rage. Sometimes, behind the always locked doors of his library, I thought I heard him weeping. At night, in our shared bed, he would toss and turn and moan, his hands and jaws clenched, dark, blood-tainted things flitting in and out of existence above his sweat-slicked body as he unconsciously summoned them out of the magic field. In the mornings he would deny anything was the matter, that he was perfectly fine, that he was only carrying out the King's will, and that I should mind my own matters and tend to the babe. And so that's what I did.

I refused the aid of a nursemaid or any other help raising Farima. I'm not sure why: perhaps a sense of wounded pride. She was my responsibility, my one chance to carve out a meaningful role at last. With Mevlish's services increasingly called upon by the King, for the most part I spent the early months alone with her. I'll not lie: it was a difficult time, immensely tiring and lonely. Often I wondered if there was something wrong with me, that I did not love my child when she screamed and screamed, high-pitched and so loud for something so small, and I would wonder if she would even stop if thrown from the top of the tower. More than once I ordered the silent clay servants to take her away and I would lock my door and collapse in tears, the screams still piercing my ears. Yes, she was an unsmiling red bundle and nursing her was a painful and almost thankless task. Almost.

But over the long years spent in that dour place, taking care of her turned gradually from a labor of duty to one of love.

My formal study of magic had ended as soon as Mevlish learned I was pregnant. "Far too dangerous for you both if you continue," he muttered, and I found my copy of "Elements" mysteriously disappeared soon after—a small but hurtful slight, considering I had long since committed it to memory. I never stopped probing and flirting with the magic field, though, not even during those long stretches of exhausted, barely conscious wakefulness between Farima's feeds in the first months after her birth. And as soon as she was old enough to concentrate on small things and smile I would materialize glittering toys from the field: sparkling flowers or floating sprites she would follow with her eyes and try to grasp with her chubby little hands. Mevlish would have called it reckless free magic if he had known, but he was not there to see, and I was not one to care.

During his long absences, using a variation of the little magic I had already learned, I began to animate toys for my baby: a rocking horse whose legs cantered in the air and neighed when its long hair was pulled, a toy house full of dolls that gyrated and pirouetted when the tiny doors were pulled open, Cradlegate's clay servants in miniature. Farima loved all these, and it only encouraged me to practice more. But when Mevlish returned, invariably in foul mood, the magically enhanced playthings stilled.

Farima grew up not minding the isolation; it was all she had ever known, and of course she eased my own sense of loneliness. Not only did I love her as a daughter, but we became friends too, something I had never dared expect. She, too, began to share in my magic learning. When I would complain about lack of access to her father's library she laughed and spun around, arms upraised, and said, "But Mother, we don't need those dusty old books to learn about magic. It's here all around us; we can make it do whatever we want."

Eight good years we had; eight years during which Mevlish was an absent father and husband, too distracted to notice our growing deviation or his lack of a male heir.

Of course it could not last.

~~*~*

The playroom was dancing when he caught us.

The carriage carrying Farima's stern-faced tutor had clattered back to Proximus—Mevlish insisted she learn the rudiments of the King's Magic

9

whilst he was away and unable to teach her himself—and I was free again to see my daughter alone again for the first time in days.

"It's silly that you're not allowed to sit in the lessons," Farima said. "He even takes all my books away when he leaves. Why does Daddy make him do that?"

I smiled. "It doesn't matter, darling. Tell me what you learned."

She pouted. "Boring stuff. Repeat after me: always use the same tone and cadence during incantation, always close your eyes when making a spell, always praise the King for his tolerance, always this, always that…"

I laughed. "It does sound boring. Here: let's have some fun now!"

Farima clapped her hands at the gleam in my eye, and together we joined our minds to meld with the field. Soon we had her sizeable collection of dolls—rag, porcelain, and straw-stuffed—all marching around the floor in time to an impromptu band of floating drums, magically blown flutes and her harp plucked by dust fairies.

We didn't hear Mevlish's dragon land at the stables.

The playroom door slammed open, and such was the strength of our communion with the Source, we didn't even notice until his roar cut through our joy.

"Stop it! Stop it at once!"

The instruments crashed down to the floor. The dolls collapsed as if struck dead.

My heart jumped into my throat. I felt a wash of guilt and shame, although about what I could not explain. *For enjoying myself.* "Mevlish! What are you doing here?"

He jabbed his finger at Farima. "Bedroom. Now." Two clay servants emerged from behind him, brushed past me, and made sure Farima obeyed. She glanced over her shoulder as she was marched out, and I saw the tears gleaming in her eyes.

Mevlish strode towards me. His uniform—the same black silver he had worn the night he proposed—was covered in dirt and sweat and worse. His hair, shot through with silver too now, was all in disarray and he stank of the burned oil smell of the dragonride. "What is the meaning of this?"

"I was about to ask you the same!"

He grabbed my arm, and it was not a playful or even angry grip, but fierce, life-crushing. "I return from battle with a free magic sorcerer, barely escaped with my life, and find my own wife and child like this?" His hold tightened further and I gave a yelp of pain. "Are you insane?"

"We were just having some fun –"

"Kaffryn! This is free magic of the worst sort. I've crucified others for less."

10

My stomach went chill. He was telling the truth. Anger still got the better of me. "Then shame on you!"

Mevlish growled and thrust me away. I stumbled, but kept my feet. Behind him I could see more of his clay servants hovering. His reddened face contorted. "No more of your reckless witchery, Kaffryn. And you're to stay away from my daughter." He drew himself up. "I am the High Wizard here. I will teach her from now on."

I couldn't help myself. I jabbed out with my mind, at the servant beside him.

It cracked in two.

The pieces slid to the floor, barely contained by the starched uniform.

I stared at the shattered figure, stunned by the result of my act. I was still staring when Mevlish took two steps and slapped me hard across the face. I reeled into the wall, bounced to the floor. In that instant I felt more shock than pain; but the pain did follow, a pulsing, mounting tide of it.

"If you do anything like that ever again," Mevlish said, the words forced through clenched teeth, his hot breath washing against my face, "I swear I will kill you."

I barely noticed the playroom door slamming shut. I sat in a cloud of fine dust, left alone to mourn the destruction of the servant and the end of all my dreams.

~~*~*

There was no decision to make. It was a matter of survival.

I banged my fist against his study door until he opened it. His eyes were red, his face worn, as haggard as those in the portraits lining the stair walls. He reached out to my bruised face. "Kaffryn. This war —"

"I'm leaving," I said. "And I'm taking Farima with me."

His expression instantly hardened into fury. He stepped out and slammed the door behind him. I swear I felt the tower tremble. "You take her, and I'll hunt you down and destroy you, do you hear? Not even if you run to the farthest corners of the Far Lands will you escape."

I hesitated for only a second before realizing the battle was lost. I turned and fled.

Farima's room was empty: Mevlish must have already ordered her taken to some still-hidden corner of the tower. I used my focused anger and years of idle practice to blow apart the previously impregnable wards protecting the door to the library. I stole a few randomly chosen grimoires—not for any forbidden knowledge they may have contained (and it turned out they did not contain any)—but to spite Mevlish and demonstrate how much I could now accomplish with the free magic he so despised.

11

Despite the churning ache in my heart, I fled the tower without my daughter. I steeled myself with the thought that one day, after I had armed myself with sufficient skill and power, I would wrest her from Mevlish's possession. I almost convinced myself it was true.

His dragons waited for me further down the valley, in anticipation of my flight back to Admar, or to the Farthest Lands where the field and Mevlish's power would be weakest. He knew how much I dreaded the beasts—but they were easy to avoid.

I headed up the valley. Towards the source of magic, not away from it.

~~*~*

I took a few steps more, swayed, then stopped. My head swam with the intensity of the field, power crackling all around me. It was only a few dozen more steps to the Wizard's Wall.

I was still alive. Still sane. As far as I could tell.

I felt I could have approached closer still, if only for a few moments, but that wasn't the point. I needed to find a sustainable location, a place I could tolerate to stay in for the foreseeable future. Somewhere close to Farima, but difficult for Mevlish to approach.

This was it.

In all our years of marriage, Mevlish had never taken a step closer to the Wall than the boundaries of his tower walls. Despite his reputation and all his skill and years of practice

I think he secretly feared the power of magic.

Well I had no such fear. And standing here, so much closer now to the Source than I had ever been, I could feel how much stronger my magic was.

Don't get addled, I warned myself. *Don't become another Alexandre.*

The Wall was marked by a few dozen human skeletons, none of them fresh. I wondered which one belonged to Mevlish's apocryphal Great-Uncle. Bones gleamed pale beneath the moonlight and the faint, shifting aura crackling overhead. A few of the older remains had changed and twisted over the years, into strange, organic shapes: pale, grasping finger-bones had grown as large as ship masts, sun-bleached skulls elongated and deformed until the gaping jaws and eye sockets had grown into cavernous openings. Each an unmistakable warning to any who would dare breach the otherwise invisible Wall.

I wondered how many of the bones had belonged to males.

"Wizard's Wall," I said, and laughed. I felt drunk, bathed in warm power. "But is it also a Witch's Wall?"

Perhaps the female brain could better cope with the strength of magic here. Perhaps it was just me.

I turned my back on Mevlish's draughty tower with its cold clay servants and dusty, winding passages, and raised my hands, closed my eyes, meshing with the magic field. I made life from the chalk cliffs rising on either side; there was no need for another's seed.

I built myself a tower of my own, and there I waited, listening to the Source's siren call. Waiting for my daughter to join me. As I knew she would.

~~*~*

The ground shook me awake.

Mevlish was on his way.

"Stay inside," I ordered Farima as I led her to the lowest levels of the tower. The Lighthouse, we called it. "Hide in the deepest cellar. Whatever you do, don't try to peek out at the battle. Do you understand? One of us will come get you when it's all over."

"But Mother —"

I took her firmly by the shoulders, pushed her back through the doorway. "Please, Farima, trust me. Nothing you would see will bring you joy: today your father and I fight, and one of us must lose."

She must have seen the strain and fatigue in my face and bowed her head, dark fringe hooding her eyes. "Yes, Mother."

I had spent more than three days and nights with hardly any sleep, preparing for the coming battle; molding clay, imbuing it with the essence of life (or at least its convincing semblance), drawing on the power that flowed so strong here. I used all my hard-earned skill, and as much of my blood as I could spare.

I hoped it was enough.

I hugged Farima tight, kissed her forehead, felt an ache so strong in my heart it threatened to shatter my resolve. I pushed her away, hardly able to breathe never mind talk. "Go."

The door closed behind me, the strongest locking charms I could make sliding into place. I climbed the stairs to the tower entrance, casting protective spells as I went, erasing my daughter's tell-tale traces as best I could. Then I stepped out into the early morning light.

The ground rumbled, and I focused my attention on the threat gathering ahead of me. A yellow-brown dust cloud rose from around Mevlish's tower and swallowed the sun. The gardens that had once flourished around Cradlegate had long since faded and dried to dust. A half-mile of desolate cracked earth and dust was all that separated us now.

I tried to calm my hammering heart, but it was impossible. My husband was too skilful, too experienced with using magic in combat, for me to stand much chance against him. Despite the advantage the strength of magic here gave me, I knew I could not win.

13

Unless. Unless…

His magically amplified voice rolled like thunder towards me.

"Surrender my daughter."

"She stays of her own free will," I called out. I was pleased by how firm my voice sounded.

"You turn her against me. You've poisoned her mind with your madness and your lies." The ground shook again. "I say one last time: give her up. Give her up and I'll let you flee back to the Far Lands unharmed."

"Come and get her," I said, voice choked with returning anger. It was a challenge, not an invitation, and he knew it.

The ground shifted, left, right, like a rug adjusted. I barely kept my feet. Behind me, boulder-sized chunks of cliff clattered down beside the Lighthouse. I hoped Mevlish wasn't stupid enough to try and destroy the place with Farima still inside it.

Like some nightmarish crop, his troops began to emerge from the cracked surface of the pass. Arms and torsos made of mud and rock thrust into daylight as Mevlish molded the dirt into a shambling army. Ogres and trolls and whirling dust devils as tall as our towers advanced towards me.

A year or two ago I would have dissolved at the sight, would have submitted to whatever demands he made. But now I had some power of my own.

~~*~*

I dove my mind deep beneath the ground. Three days and three nights had been enough for me to assemble the rudiments of my own subterranean army. All I needed to do was extend myself into their bodies and pull them to the surface.

There was a moment of terrible shock as I waited for my legions to emerge, and nothing happened. Had I foolishly overestimated my capabilities? Were the hoped for results a mirage, a delusion caused by over-exposure to the Source?

But I was merely being impatient. I had never tried to control such a mass before, nowhere close.

I would need to learn fast.

The earth cracked before Mevlish's oncoming horde. His vanguard of sand spirits and soil pachyderms tumbled into the unexpected crevasse, dissolving back into the dirt from which they had come. The tide of creatures behind struggled to slow their momentum, but the cascade to destruction continued.

The approaching columns of dust wavered and dissipated along with Mevlish's concentration… but they soon solidified again, tighter than ever. They grew scythes and spun towards me, lethal twirling flowers of pulverized rock.

By this time my own army had struggled to the surface. I'd re-used the kobolds that I had first created to build my tower. Their ranks had swelled, and I'd added some new designs; the sort of nameless, dread shapes that fear and desperation give rise to in the depths of sleepless, anxiety ridden nights.

I was glad Farima would never see them.

I forced Mevlish's creations back. Despite the overwhelming force he had gathered, it was obvious he hadn't expected any effective resistance.

At last Mevlish himself pushed forward, his troops literally crumbling before him, revealed at last to be no more than a front, a show of force meant to shock and awe.

"Stand aside," he shouted at me. He was in his now familiar black and silver uniform, his cloak billowing around him.

My answer was to lift the earth beneath him, upthrusting it at a sharp angle. Surprised once more, he staggered and almost followed his minions into the pit revealed.

But two could play that game.

The ground beneath me *rippled*. A surge of mud slewed towards me. I tried to force it back, but there was no stopping it. I was moving, my legs buried ankle deep, knee deep, thigh deep, in a hot, dusty slurry that pushed me back, back. Back towards the Wizard's Wall.

"Goodbye, witch wife." Melvish's voice, shorn now of anger, distant in my head.

Pressure built in my skull. Lights danced before my open eyes, tiny explosions like stars, circular patterns, vertical streaks like heavy rain. Magic. Magic all around me. The field so strong now it was visible.

And skeletons, too. On either side, and beneath me.

I was being forced through the Wall. Beyond it.

Focus narrowed. I concentrated only on Mevlish. He struggled to stand upon the jutting shard of rock, his arms raised, thrust out towards me, his eyes closed, lips alive with some furious incantation. Blood streamed from his eyes.

Remember to use the same tone and cadence during incantation, dear husband.

The field built in intensity, blinding me. I didn't have long, if the theory it would just keep getting stronger was true. My brain would fry.

I had to do something.

So I stopped. The ground cracked as it solidified in an instant, waves of soil trapped frozen by my wish.

For a moment, standing with my back against the boundary of human magic, feeling the power coursing through my mind, my mud army dancing to my tune, sensing my husband's thwarted might—just for a glimmer of time, I hoped that I might achieve victory.

But then I heard the approaching beat of wings, the gut-shuddering roar. The air hazed with heat and not with magic, and I quailed as false hope fled.

The dragons had arrived.

~~*~*

"Take her," I said. I did not need to feign the tremor in my voice. "Anything. Just spare me."

It was difficult to see Mevlish behind the rippling curtain of hot air emerging from between the jaws of the beast he straddled. The stench of burning oil filled my nostrils, and the heat stirred my hair even as it scorched my skin. One claw of gleaming obsidian pressed me to the buckled ground, the black tip of the razor talon against my beating throat.

"Do you concede, witchy wife?"

"Spare me, Mevlish. You win."

The dragon growled, and my insides threatened to liquefy.

Mevlish dismounted. He strode towards my tower without looking at me. The dragon's talon did not shift an inch from throat.

A few minutes later he re-emerged with the girl, the one I had made. She was porcelain white, shaking, mute. Mevlish led her away.

She did not look back at me.

Mevlish paused before he re-mounted. "Kaffryn. If it were up to the King, he would have me crucify you." His face twisted, and I did not know if it was because of the heat and magic, or emotion. "But you have chosen this cursed place, so I'll let you stay here. If you ever leave or try to contact Farima again, I will return and smash your white folly apart and you along with it, mother of my daughter or not. Do you understand?"

I nodded.

"Goodbye, my witch wife. I hope never to see you again."

As my little girl, my very special and unique creation, was borne away, I felt the loss deep in my bones: a physical sensation, the pull of my blood as it was drawn from me.

I bowed my head. Smoke and dust billowed into my face as the dragon's wings eclipsed the sun.

~~*~*

When I was sure the dust had settled and Mevlish and the pale girl had returned to his tower, I staggered back to the Lighthouse—it was cracked and tottering, but not beyond repair—and made my way to the locked cellar to make sure Farima was all right. She too, was shaken, but again, hopefully not beyond repair.

"What will happen if he finds out?" she asked.

16

"He won't find out," I said, confident. The clay golem I had made in Farima's likeness would be meek and obedient: his fatal pride would protect us. The hard-won trophy daughter, who hardly spoke a word, so obedient and yet so like her mother—he would not be able to conceive she was a construct of clay and blood, fashioned by his inferior magician wife. One thing had always been true: Mevlish may or may not have been my master in magic, but I had always had the edge over him when it came to simple human understanding.

I took Farima's hand. "We are free now. At least for a time."

Free. Free to experiment with magic as never before. Free to imagine thoughts no magician had ever dared think. I hadn't had time to tell Farima yet, but during the battle I was sure I had been forced back further towards the Source than I had ever been before—further than *anyone* had been before.

And I had survived.

What had Mevlish once said, about living so near to the Source?

You get used to it.

My fate was not to be exiled here beside Cradlegate forever. Imagine what could be achieved if we were to gain true control of the Source itself, there at the calm heart of the storm? We would need never fear any man again. We would be the ones to be feared.

"Come," I said. I took hold of Farima's hand. "Let me show you something."

Slowly and very carefully, we began to walk towards the shimmering edge of magic.

KEN SCHOLES is the award-winning author of the popular *Psalms of Isaak* series, which numbers four novels so far with a fifth entry, *Hymn,* coming later this year. He has won Writers of the Future as well as France's Prix Imaginales award. His short stories have appeared in *Clarkesworld* and *Realms of Fantasy* among others, and many are available in two published collections of short fiction. He is a public speaker and frequent panelist, as well as a songwriter and musician.

Please take a look at Ken's official site: kenscholes.com

ANNUAL DUES
Ken Scholes

"So exactly why is it you've brought me here?"

I was beyond irritability, well on the way to impatient anger. Damn Gilga-Yar and his game-playing—to send me, Frewar Zej, half way across a world in the care of his minion as if I were a first year mage. And to this wasteland dung-pile, of all places.

I had been here before, back when the trade routes between Aeryé and the K'Tarii nomads hadn't been choked by the dust of war. El Ramir had been a scab of a town then, and from what I had seen before entering its only public house two hours before, it hadn't changed much. The only good memory I could find from my brief stay a quarter-century ago was of a D'an-Nubii dancing girl I had—

The demon in my pocket chortled, interrupting my re-lived pleasure."Wait. You'll see."

I looked down, my one good eye locking onto the demon's. "It'd better be good," I said. "Or you'll be very sorry."

It laughed, snorted, farted and laughed again. "I don't fear you. My master —"

"Damn you and your master both. I have things to do. I don't have time for his games—to drop everything and travel three thousand miles to this flea-infested chamber-pot just to satisfy his itch for fealty." I kept my voice low, but the ice was in it.

The demon poked his minute finger into my side, his bug-eyes narrowing. "You want to play, you've got to pay."

I had more angry words, but I swallowed them. The little bastard had me there, just like our mutual master, Gilga-Yar. After all, he hadn't sought me out thirty years ago. He hadn't asked for the contract. He hadn't said "name your price" or "whatever it takes". I had done that. And each year, as winter settled in the Northern Reaches where I made my home, my patron—or, in this case, his messenger—came calling for a "small token of my commitment".

I took a swig from the tankard before me and let the cool, fermented danaberry juice tease the back of my throat.

I could have sought another patron over the years—one perhaps more benign. But contract negotiations had never been my cup of qua'en and my focus was on the Art, not all of the politics around it. And going solo—well, why make your own flawed paints, brushes and canvases when there was such a ready, unblemished supply for the buying? I looked at the hook that pretended to be my right hand. The price thus far had been reasonable. A hand. An eye. Some toes. A soul here, a virgin there. Of course, I had preferred those years when he'd bid me kill a rival or find some artifact he craved. Still, the messenger-sprite was correct: I did want to play. And I would pay my annual dues to do so.

It began to caper in my pocket, jumping up and down in a gleeful dance. "Here she comes! Here she comes!" I looked around the room. It was crowded with an odd assortment of outlanders. A noisy band of K'Tarii freeholders, swaddled in silk robes and turbans, occupied a fair portion of the room, their heavy blades of Akiiren steel hanging from broad red sashes.Keeping a fair distance, a cluster of out-of-uniform Suranian warrior-priests, noticeable by their purple-dyed top-knots, talked quietly into their ale mugs, eyes darting around the room. Mixed in like clumps of cinnamon in wine were the natives—dark-skinned, dark-haired men and women, all dressed in a rainbow array of loose-cut pants and shirts.Most of the women sat on or near the nomads, casting playful eyes toward the Suranians but knowing better than to approach. The heavy black curtain jingled as it was drawn back, and a woman walked through.

I don't know how she came to be in this place—it was obvious she didn't belong, and yet she was dressed as any other El Ramiran. She was blond and though her skin was dusky, her eyes were a sharp blue. She looked young—maybe half my age—and she carried herself with an easy confidence. Her crooked nose marked as her part D'an-Nubii, but she had smatterings of the Northlands about her cheekbones and mouth. For a moment, I held my breath. There was a wild beauty about her that I felt guilty noticing, after all –

"That's her," it gurgled, twitching. "You see her don't you?"

"Yes," I said. "I see her. What now?"

"Master wants her soul. Give it to him."

I'd done this before. "Same terms?" I asked.

"Same terms. No magic. Use the blade. Say the words. Get another year of juice. Get juicier juice."

I nodded. Someone staggered near me and I paused. It wouldn't do to be overheard talking to my pocket, even if they couldn't understand the obscure nether-tongue I used. "Who is she?"

It shrugged. "Nobody." It paused, could have remained silent, but didn't. "A fledgling in the Art." Here my eyebrow raised.

"Does she have a patron?"

It shrugged again. "A minor devil in the Seventh Outer Ring. But…"

"Yes?" She walked over to the bar with regal grace and her smile said she knew she was turning heads. She murmured something to the barkeep and he nodded, reaching for a glass.Gods, what a woman.

"She has approached master for a contract. It's been under consideration these past three years."

The words stung me alert. "But I thought he had his allotment?"

"He does," it giggled. "Little does she know…" The double dealing bitch-whelp. Memories of my own waiting period came flooding back—years of slavish devotion to prove my intention to sign and stay signed.And now, this young woman, after three years of hard work, hoping against hope to be offered a contract, was to be snuffed out so her soul could decorate Gilga-Yar's mantle. And no doubt, her current patron wouldn't lift a tentacle to save her—her disloyalty by this time no secret. But who was I to develop a conscience? A little late in the year for such nonsense.

"Why her?" I asked suddenly but didn't know why. "Why not some king or another arch-mage?"

The demon was silent for a moment. "You do not wish to pay? You do not wish to play?" The questions were ominous probes, black fingers in my brain.

I sighed. "She's so young."

There was no response.

"Okay, damn you. Of course I'll do it." I stood and straightened my robes. I knew what *I* saw there by the counter—what would *she* see coming towards her? The great Frewar Zej, Arch-mage of the Twenty-third Order or a fifty-five year old man with an empty eye socket and thinning gray hair, who walked with a limp and sported an iron hook instead of a hand? And why did I care?

I shuffled to the counter, my one hand burying itself in travel-stained cloth to rest upon the bone knife-hilt. My fingers absently traced the runes as I pushed up beside her, my mind racing over the litany. She hadn't turned yet, the center of her slim shoulders a waiting target.

I could have done it right then—could've finished it. But I paused. Her hair smelled of apples and my eye followed its waving, broken line over her small ears, down her slim neck. In my pocket the demon poked and pushed impatiently.

Her head came up, as if hearing, and her eyes settled on me.

"Have you come far?" she asked. Her voice was music, and yes, it was D'an-Nubii—her accent proved it out.

I must have started, because she smiled.

"I can see you are a foreigner," she said. "Have you come far?"

"Yes," I said. Damn. This wasn't getting easier at all. I released the handle of the knife and rapped on the counter. "Qua-en, barkeep. And chilled, if you have it."

"Where from?"

"Erlan's Fjord," I lied. She smiled. My drink arrived and I tossed a copper regliré to the barkeep's waiting hands.

"A veteran?"A plausible explanation for my missing pieces, but she knew and I *knew* that she knew. She had turned just enough and my eye had unwittingly discovered that the left side of her chest was noticeably flat compared to the ample curve of her right breast. The demon hadn't lied—she had already begun paying her dues.

"I think you understand the reason for my condition," I stated, quickly flashing her the recognition sign that conveyed my rank and order. She nodded, her fingers quickly making her own sign. She seemed both frightened and excited at the truth, and tried badly to hide it. At this point, enough people had noticed us together. I would need a quieter place for my work now.

"My name is –"

I cut in, angrily. "I don't want to know your name."

Her lower lip jutted out. "I only…I mean –"

"I'm sorry," I said. I had to recover somehow. To turn this to my advantage. "It's been a long journey. Please. Tell me your name."

She shook her head and smiled. "No. It's not important. What I'd really like is to talk with you." Her voice lowered to a whisper. "I'm new to the Art and have never met an arch-mage before. I have so many questions."

"Then perhaps we should go someplace more amenable to our conversation." The demon in my pocket broke wind noisily and stifled a giggle.

"What was that?" she asked, eyebrows arching with surprise.

"Nothing," I said and gave my pocket a thump.

~~*~*

First-moon hung low in the sky, an evil urine-colored orb that dominated the horizon. We were silent now, watching and hearing the night around us. In the distance, desert wolves howled as we sat in the gathering dusk. Four times I had slipped my hand to the knife, and four times I had stopped myself. I knew that I would have to go through with it soon, that every moment I stalled made it harder and easier at the same time. Harder, because already I dreaded the deed. Easier, because with each word she seemed to trust me more. For hours we had sat at the edge of the oasis, gazing out over the mauve wasteland while I answered her myriad questions about my life with the Art. She seemed so innocent there, framed in the moon-light, drinking in my every word. She was a perfect woman for my ego—all rapt attention and wide-eyed wonder.

"So," I asked, breaking the silence, "Tell me of yourself." The messenger-sprite had gone to sleep two hours ago, mumbling curses and threats under its breath.

She shrugged and her fingers began to play in her hair. "There isn't much to tell. I was born here in El Ramir. I've lived here all my life. My mother was a D'an-Nubii dancer and my father was –"

The world reeled around me as a picture came into focus. "Damn and blast!" I lunged to my feet. "Damn and blast!" I repeated the words again and again, startling the demon awake with my pacing. The girl watched me. Did she know? She couldn't know. But she would if I didn't rein in my anger quickly. My hand dipped into the pocket, clutched the demon's scaly throat and hauled it out of its hiding place. I threw it to the ground.

"I won't do it!"

The girl stood up at the sight of the thing and drew near me. "Do what?" she asked.

"Gilga-Yar knows, doesn't he?"

The demon recovered its wits. "You want to play? You've got to pay!" Then, it fell to the ground and began rolling back and forth, holding itself as it shook with laughter.

"Then I don't want to play." The demon sat up, surprised.

"You—?"

I pulled the knife from my robes and hurled it at the tiny sprite. It dodged away, but I grabbed its heart between my thumb and forefinger and began to squeeze, feeling the Art give it shape and texture beneath my touch. The demon gasped and began to shriek, struggling to inflate itself to full size. It was all fang and eye and claw now, as it twisted in the dirt. With a ceremonious twist of the wrist I burst its heart like a grape and watched it collapse into itself, a puff of sulfuric smoke. Then, I turned to the girl.

She stooped over the knife, picked it up, stared at it.

"What is this about?" she asked.

"I think you know."

She swallowed, nodded. She dropped her hands to her sides. "I've known all along." It was an awkward moment and dueling visions battled over my imagination. Gilga-Yar would probably hunt me now—perhaps I would become someone else's annual dues. Gods knew I had killed his renegades before.

She stepped into my arms and I embraced my daughter.

"Father, what have you done?" What had I done? I was solo now. A free agent. And a father. I felt her shoulders shake beneath my hand and arms.

"There, there. It will be fine." Her shoulders shook even more and she said something incoherent against my shoulder.

"Besides," I said, trying to make light of it all both for her and for myself, "Gilga-Yar now has room for another contract—if you're willing to pay."

She looked up, smiling, teeth showing, and there were no tears—had never been tears.

"I am willing to pay, Father," she said, and I felt the knife slide into my back, rasp against my spine, pierce my heart. She laughed aloud now and I felt her quiver in my arms as she settled me to the ground. "I want to play."

New York Times number 1 Bestselling author,
KELLEY ARMSTRONG is best known for the Women of the
Otherworld and the Darkest Powers series. This popular Canadian
author has written adult and teen novels, as well as numerous
short stories and novellas. Her latest projects are the Cainsville
modern gothic series as well as the Age of Legend fantasy series,
which is the setting for her story here.

You can find out more at www.kelleyarmstrong.com

THE KITSUNE'S NINE TALES
Kelley Armstrong

"**D**oes he seem resigned to his fate?"

Senri stood in the small tea room over the Gate of the Crimson Phoenix as he looked down on the crowd thronging the Imperial Way below. Imperial guards led a man through the shouting onlookers in a slow march to the dungeons. The prisoner was taller than most, his dark skin shining under the summer sun, perspiration making the green eyes on his fox tattoos gleam. More sweat dripped, and blood too, where the manacles dug in. He shuffled along, his gaze down, letting the crowds pelt him with rotten fish and cries of "coward!" and "traitor!" and nodding with each, as if accepting it as his due.

"Does he seem resigned to his fate?" the man behind Senri asked again.

"He does."

"He is not."

Senri turned to the man. Broad-shouldered but not tall. Dark hair frosted with white. Dressed in a formal robe, which he'd pushed askew like a too-tight tunic. He'd shoved up his sleeves, and Senri could see battle scars dissecting the dragon tattoos that covered his arms.

Emperor Jiro Tatsu. Ruler of the largest empire the world had ever known.

"Who is he?" the emperor said, waving at the prisoner below.

Senri frowned, thinking he'd misheard. Otherwise, the question was ridiculous—there could scarcely be a peasant child who'd not know the answer, and Senri was a warrior from a line stretching back beyond the First Age.

"Who is he?" Emperor Tatsu asked again, patiently.

"Alvar Kitsune. Former marshal of the imperial army."

"More than that."

"He's a traitor. A coward who—"

"No, no." The emperor waved a hand, as if that was inconsequential. "Who *was* he?"

"As marshal? The leader of the largest army in the world. The second most powerful man in the empire after your imperial highness."

"Yes, but more. To me. Who was he?"

Senri faltered again. Was this a trick? Emperor Tatsu was not known for them. A blunt man, he was reputed to have little patience with the intricate machinations of court life.

The young warrior replied carefully. "He was, I believe, a friend. That is, you knew him well, if you would not necessarily count him as—"

"He *was* indeed a friend. The best I have ever known and, I fear, the best I ever will know. We grew up together. We won this empire together. We—"

Footsteps tripped up the stairs outside the tea room. Too light to be a warrior's tread. Too quick to be a woman's. When no one appeared, the emperor sighed.

"I would suggest, Tyrus, that you not consider a career as a court spy."

"I wasn't spying, Father." It was a child's voice and, a moment later, a young boy appeared in the doorway. "I was waiting for a break in the conversation before I intruded."

"Yet you would still intrude." The emperor tempered the rebuke with a smile as he beckoned the boy in.

The child looked about seven summers of age. He was clearly his father's son, though slighter of build and softer of face, a child more handsome than his sire, undoubtedly taking after his mother, whoever she might be. That was what Senri paused to decide—the maternity of the child before him. It was not an easy task. The emperor had two wives, three official concubines and five master courtesans, most of whom he'd fathered children on. The answer came when the boy smiled, a blazing grin that brought to mind the lovely First Concubine, Maiko. One of the bastard princes, then. Pity. Male imperial bastards had a habit of dying young, usually under mysterious circumstances.

"What is so urgent that you had to interrupt my meeting?" the emperor asked.

"I apologize." The boy bowed. "But it *is* urgent. Marshal—I mean, former marshal—Kitsune will be exiled to the Forest of the Dead tonight, and Gavril wishes to see him."

Emperor Tatsu had not shown a flicker of emotion as he named Alvar Kitsune to Senri as his dearest friend, but now, while his face remained impassive, pain flickered through his eyes.

"He isn't down there, is he? Gavril?"

Tyrus hesitated, as if considering a lie, but he nodded, and the two men walked to the window again. Senri saw the boy in a sweep. He was hanging back, dressed in a cloak with the hood pulled up. Half a head taller than Tyrus, though they seemed of an age. The boy watched his father paraded down the Imperial Way, his young face as stony as the prisoner's, until he reached up to push back a stray braid. Even from where Senri stood, he could see the boy's hand shaking. The braid fell forward again and the boy scowled, shoving it back angrily now.

"Did Gavril ask to see his father?" Emperor Tatsu asked.

"He wouldn't," Tyrus said.

"I know," the emperor murmured. "So you ask on his behalf. You're a good friend, Tyrus. Gavril will need that now."

"He will need to see his father," the boy said, his voice firm but his gaze lowered. "One last time."

The emperor sighed. "Bring him around to the prison gate. We'll figure out how to do this." He looked at his son. "Discreetly."

The boy look offended. "Of course."

"Off with you now. I'll be there soon."

Once Tyrus was gone, Emperor Tatsu turned back to Senri and seemed, for a moment, to forget why he was there, before shaking his head sharply.

"Yes, as I was saying, I know Alvar Kitsune better than I know any man alive. I am entrusting you to escort him to the Forest of the Dead and ensure he does not escape. It will be the most difficult task you will ever face, because Alvar will not meekly walk into that forest and accept his fate. You know his clan's totem?"

"The nine-tailed fox."

"Yes. The kitsune. The trickster. There are many ways Alvar will attempt to escape, and before you leave, I am going to tell you every one."

~~*~*

Their destination was not called the Forest of Exiles. Or the Forest of Permanent Imprisonment. It was the Forest of the Dead. One could claim it was so named because it had been, in past ages, used for elder abandonment, but few truly believed that. Yes, the forest itself was dead—devoid of life—but that was only another excuse for the name. Excuses for those who liked to think their empire did not practice primitive customs. They were civilized. Their criminals were not forced to kneel, head on a block, before a sword sliced it from their neck. No, their worst criminals were merely exiled for the winter to a forest… one surrounded by an insurmountable wall of lava rock, teeming with swamp fever, containing neither game nor clean water.

Senri could not recall the last time an exile had walked out of the Forest of the Dead come spring. Yet, like most, he had no qualms over the punishment. It was, in many ways, worse than a quick death, and the prospect of such exile would give even the most hardened criminals pause. Those who committed their crimes despite the risk deserved the punishment.

And Alvar Kitsune? Did he deserve it? That was the question that Alvar raised once they entered the Wastes, as Emperor Tatsu had warned he would.

Five days hard walk across lava fields separated the forest from the rest of the empire. The Wastes were a remnant from the Age of Fire, when two volcanoes had erupted, wiping out entire villages. In fact, the only thing left standing in the entire region was the forest. The lava had seemed to rise up around it, as if stopped by the force of the spirits within, later hardening into a wall that encircled the Forest of the Dead.

The armed escort and the prisoner set out into that wasteland, tramping across the uneven lava rock, peering into a landscape without a single tree or bush to enliven the view. They'd been walking half a day before Alvar Kitsune spoke his first words since leaving the imperial city four days earlier.

"You do not truly think I did it," he said, his face forward, as if he addressed the wind whipping past, burning their faces. "You seem a bright young man. I hope you understand what has happened here."

Senri said nothing. The three other guards glanced over. Alvar's voice was loud enough to carry, intentionally so. *He will single you out as the leader,* the emperor had said. *But he will appeal to all four.*

"I hope every warrior in the empire understands what happened here," Alvar continued. "Two decades of power has dulled his wits. He's so arrogant he didn't even bother to trump up plausible charges against me. Fleeing a losing battle? Abandoning my men under cover of magic? I don't know which is more outrageous: Accusing me of cowardice or sorcery." He looked at Senri. "As for the latter, I trust you are no superstitious peasant."

He was not. Yet one had only to look into Alvar's green eyes to consider the possibility. Sorcerer's eyes. Unnatural in color.

"As for cowardice?" Alvar shook his head. "You have not served directly under me, boy, or I'd remember you. But I'll presume you have served in an army I've led into battle."

"I am not yet battle-tried," Senri said. "None of us are."

The former marshal looked at the four young men, and Senri was certain he cursed under his breath. Emperor Tatsu was no fool—he'd chosen loyal and distinguished guards, but ones too young to have served in battle, ones who knew Alvar Kitsune only as a distant figure at the head of victory parades. Ones who would have no reason to believe him innocent of the charges.

Senri smiled to himself, and they continued on in silence.

~~*~*

Their second day in the Wastes brought the former marshal's second attempt to win his freedom.

It was an ice-cold morning, one that would soon turn into a blistering hot day made worse by the black lava under their feet, reflecting the sun's rays back on them. For now, Senri walked with his cloak pulled tight. One of the other men tugged up his hood. Senri grunted at him and the young warrior lowered it. Nothing could impede their vision on this journey.

He will have hired men to waylay you, the emperor had said. *But I doubt they will attack. They will see I have men of my own following at a distance, ready for trouble. Take care, though. Sleep in shifts and keep your eyes open.*

Indeed, that very morning Senri spotted a distant mercenary scout… And saw an arrow fly as if from nowhere and take the man down. No other scouts appeared. The second play had failed.

"Are you married?" Alvar asked that afternoon as they walked.

Senri shook his head. The former marshal gave a wry smile. "I presume none of you are?"

"That is correct."

"Naturally. Old enough to be trusted with my care, but not old enough to have wed. Children, then?"

"I am not wed."

A sly grin. "One is not required for the other."

"I have no children."

None of them did. Again, the emperor had taken precautions, knowing what tactic Alvar would use next.

"Brothers? Sisters?"

Senri shook his head, and when he did, he saw those green eyes gleam, the fox spotting a mouse peeping from its hole.

"You are an only child then. I know what that is like. I myself have two brothers, but only one child. My son, Gavril. Perhaps you've seen him."

Do not lie, Emperor Tatsu had said. *He will smell a lie.*

"I have. He is a fine-looking boy."

"Indeed he is." A wide grin. Then he lowered his voice. "I only wish his mother was more…capable. She was my third wife. Young and pretty, well-born, and at the time that was all that mattered. She has lived a pampered life and I fear, in my absence, my son will suffer."

"You said you have brothers."

The faintest flicker of chagrin, as if Alvar wished he had not mentioned that. "True, but neither is posted in the imperial city, and both have sons of their own. Many sons."

Senri shrugged. "They are still his uncles. Nothing is more important than family, particularly for warriors. Your brothers will watch over him and train him, and he will have a good life. The emperor has made it clear that your wife and son will not suffer for your crimes."

"And you take him at his word?"

"I do."

"Then you are a fool."

31

~~*~*

None of the other guards fell for that "think of my son" ploy. Alvar did not surrender the cause there, naturally. He had more angles, each one following exactly as the emperor had predicted. Nine tales, Emperor Tatsu had said. Like his clan totem. Each was subtly done, half a day passing between, the former marshal gradually becoming more talkative, as if not only resigned to his fate, but determined to make the most of his final days, enjoying what little company he had. He would raise topics that were simply conversational, and then take advantage of useful ones that rose naturally.

Senri was from the Inugami clan—that was obvious from his dog tattoos. But who was his father? No, Alvar admitted, he did not know him, but did his father not have a brother who'd served as a palace guard? Yes, Alvar knew *him* very well. How was his uncle's daughter? Alvar recalled that she had been ill, and his own wife had sent ointments. Had they helped? Senri had heard nothing of it? Oh, well, still, was the child well? She was? Excellent.

And another guard, Hiraku, was from the Okami clan. Did he know Goro Okami? A cousin? Wonderful. Alvar recalled the Gray Wolf fondly. They had fought side by side with the emperor at the battle of Ashawan. Ah, there was a battle. They had freed the locals from the tyranny of a mad warlord, and the people had been so grateful that Alvar, Goro and Emperor Tatsu had scarcely been able to take a step without some noble or peasant offering his pretty daughter. They'd been young then, both of them, and yes, they had indulged, perhaps more than they ought. To be so young again. Young and strong and healthy. Rich, too. Wealth and power. What every young man dreamed of. These young warriors did, did they not? No? Well, they should, and they would be wise to snatch any opportunity.

The four ignored Alvar's hints. When they finally reached the end of the Wastes, the same could not be said for one particular guard in the village of Edgewood.

As the name suggested, Edgewood guarded the only break in the wall surrounding the Forest of the Dead. It was the only settlement in the Wastes and the last stop on their journey. Traditionally, convicts spent their last night in Edgewood's livestock enclosure. Alvar seemed to expect better. He got better, of a sort. He did not need to stay with the animals. Their group wasn't stopping in the village.

Give your regrets to the commander of Edgewood, the emperor said. *But do not overnight there. Do not speak to the villagers. In particular, do not allow anyone to bring the Seeker and Keeper to bless Alvar, though he will request it. They are but children, yet he is not above using them to his advantage. Refuse his request, then move quickly or he will find a guard willing to accept a very generous bribe.*

Alvar did humbly request a final blessing from the young Seeker. The request was refused.

Then, before they entered the forest, Senri turned to the youngest warrior in their party. Odon was barely into his second decade, but a renowned swordsman and son of the captain of Emperor Tatsu's private guard.

"You will stay here. The village will deal with you."

He did not feel pity as Odon sputtered in panic, asking what he had done, please tell him what he had done. The answer was, simply, nothing. Senri had spoken privately to the commander and no punishment awaited the young warrior. Emperor Tatsu had insisted on the ruse for two reasons. First, it would put the other guards on alert, warning them not to succumb to Alvar's final pleas. Second... Well, there was another reason, more personal, and while the emperor had not given it, Senri had understood.

They paused only briefly to replenish supplies. As they prepared to part from the village guards who'd escorted them to the second tower, Senri saw one secret a dagger to Alvar.

Senri walked over and held out his hand. Alvar gave the dagger to Senri, who in turn passed it back to the village warrior. The man hesitated only long enough for Senri to draw his sword. He did not wave it in threat. That was not its purpose. When Senri withdrew it, the village guard nodded, satisfied. Then he knelt and plunged his dagger into his own gut. Senri swung his sword and cut off the man's head, granting him mercy as swiftly as possible.

They left Edgewood's guards standing—some stone-faced, others shame-faced—beside the headless corpse of their traitorous comrade, as Senri escorted his remaining two men and Alvar Kitsune into the forest.

~~*~*

When you enter the forest, he will become desperate. He will no longer attempt to befriend or bribe you. Like a fox in a trap, he will do what it takes to escape, bite any hand that tries to ease his situation. The curses will come then, as he finally admits to sorcery—true curses, against you and your family. He will rage and he will threaten, and that is the time when you must watch your men most closely, when they are most likely to break.

True. All of it. It was a two-day walk to the center of the forest, and on the dawn of the second day, when Alvar cursed their ancestors, swore his magic would damn them to eternity trapped between worlds, the stronger of Senri's two remaining comrades broke. He turned on his fellow guards and Senri cut him down with a single stroke. Then, calmly, he continued on.

~~*~*

The forest was a spirit-forsaken place. For two days, they'd tramped through absolute silence. Senri had experienced nothing like it, not even in the Wastes. This was a thick, almost sticky silence that threatened to draw the very life from their bones.

It was as they finally neared their destination that Alvar Kitsune made his eighth play for freedom. His eighth tale.

He will know what truly lies in store for him. He knows what I will do because it is exactly what he would do, and what I have learned of treachery, I have learned from him.

"He's going to kill me, you know," Alvar said to the last guard, Hiraku. He said it conversationally, more calm than he'd been since leaving the village gates.

When Hiraku frowned, Alvar nodded toward Senri. "Your silent leader there is under orders to kill me when we reach our destination. Murder me, then turn his blade on you before he takes his own life. That is why young Odon was left behind. Rescued from his fate because Jiro does not dare kill the son of his head guard. He is fond of the man, and too sentimental by far. Yet that sentimentality no longer extends to his oldest friend."

Hiraku shook his head. "Execution is not permitted—"

Alvar cut him short with a laugh. "*Public* execution is not permitted. Private, though? Oh yes. Certainly. I am a threat to your emperor. He could have had me assassinated, but that would compel my men to avenge me, to carry on my efforts and depose the despot in my stead. No, Jiro had to take away the most precious thing a warrior has. My honor. Label me coward, have me convicted as one, and exile me… then kill me here, where no one will see. The village commander has been told not to send a search party after us when you fail to return. In the spring, the Seeker will find our bodies, and it will seem that I tried to escape and we all perished in the attempt."

Hiraku turned on Senri. "Tell me he is wrong."

Senri opened his mouth to say so, but he was a moment too slow, and in his hesitation, Hiraku had his answer. Hiraku pulled his sword—he was too slow, too, and perhaps he knew it, preferring to die with his blade in his hand. He barely had time to get it from his belt before his head lay at his feet.

"Well done," Alvar said, stepping forward and clapping Senri on the back. "An admirable job all around."

"Thank you, my lord." Senri bowed, and as he rose, he took the dagger from his own belt and presented it to Alvar. The former marshal—and future emperor—took it with a grin.

"There's nothing like an empty belt to make a warrior feel naked," Alvar said, sticking the dagger into his sash. "Now tell me, because I really must ask. Did I do exactly as Jiro claimed I would? All my attempts to escape?"

All but one, Senri thought. But he'd dismissed the last. The ninth tale. So he only said, "You did."

"In the order he said I would do them?"

"Yes, my lord."

Alvar threw back his head and laughed. "I don't know if I should be flattered that he studied me so well or insulted that I was so predictable. I'll miss him. I truly will. Even as I cut the head from his neck, I will feel regret. We get few enough friends in this life, and fewer still as good as Jiro Tatsu."

"My lord, we need to—"

"Yes, yes. Stop talking and start acting. First, grab the boy's blades. I won't take your sword, but I'd like his, and you ought to have a dagger."

Senri bent to retrieve Hiraku's blades. As he straightened, cold sliced through him. A blade between his ribs, driven straight into his heart. He hung there, impaled on his own dagger, and Alvar leaned over to whisper, "There was one more tale, was there not? Please tell me there was. I would be disappointed if Jiro missed it."

Emperor Tatsu had not missed it. There was indeed a ninth tale, this one stark and unembellished. It had come as Senri had left that tea room, the emperor taking his arm and saying, "One more. The most important of all…"

Take it from one who knows—if you put your trust in Alvar Kitsune, he will put a dagger in your back. Do not ever doubt that.

Yet he had. One last tale, the gravest and the truest, and Senri had ignored it.

Alvar yanked out the blade, and the warrior collapsed to the cold forest floor.

S.C. HAYDEN's fiction has been published in journals, magazines and anthologies, podcasted, shouted from rooftops, and scrawled on bathroom walls across the English-speaking world. Authorities have recently placed him in Savannah GA, but you can find him at www.schayden.com

Hayden's story is dedicated to the memory of his father, John Francis Hayden, who was taken from those who loved him, by cancer, in May of 1992.

ELROY WOODEN SWORD
S.C. Hayden

lroy Pagan was sleeping in his father's hayloft when the barn door burst open with a crack and a bang.

"Who's there?" Elroy called out, his hair covered in straw.

"Who's there indeed," a gruff voice sounded while others snickered and laughed. "Come down from that loft, lazy boy, or we'll bar the door and set this barn a burning."

Elroy peered over the edge of the loft and recognized the plate-and-mail of the Constable Guard.

"Alright, alright," Elroy called, "I'm coming. Don't get your underclothes in a twist." Elroy shook the straw from his hair and pulled on his pants and boots. He harrumphed and coughed and made a show of clumsily descending the loft ladder. He did that to draw the guard's attention away from the heap of straw in the loft beside him. Elroy, you see, hadn't spent the night alone. Beneath that heap of straw, Gilly was lying still as stone.

A farm boy bedding a tavern wench in his father's hayloft was certainly nothing new. But Gilly wasn't a tavern wench. Gilly was a water sprite, and taking a water sprite to your father's hayloft was something else entirely.

As soon as his feet were on the ground a gauntleted fist smacked into his jaw. Elroy staggered backwards and sat down in a pile of manure.

"Me underclothes in a twist, eh?" The guard said.

Elroy spat two teeth from his mouth, looked up, and smiled red and bloody. "What's all this about, then?"

"Your father was kind enough to volunteer your services to the Crown." The guard said. "You're to be knighted soon. It's a great honor."

Elroy was dubious. If they made it sound good, it was likely going to be bad, and if they made it sound very good, it was likely going to be very, very bad.

"Knighted?"

"That's right, 'Sir Elroy, Knight of the Dung Heap.'" The guards laughed.

Elroy's father stood sheepishly in front of their cottage while Elroy was frog-marched out of the barn.

"Good luck son," his father shouted, "I know you'll make me proud."

A guard, somewhat less discreetly than Elroy's father might have liked, dropped a sack of coin at the old farmer's feet. Elroy glared, but his father would not meet his eyes.

"Miserable old goat," Elroy muttered. He wasn't surprised, a sack of the King's small coin would buy a lot of distilled potato water, and Elroy Sr. was a man with a powerful thirst.

Elroy was bundled into the back of an enclosed oxcart, which looked suspiciously like the ones used to transport prisoners. There were several others crammed into the cart already. Some were familiar, some not. All, like him, were poor. The cart bumped and rocked over pathways and lanes and thudded over ruts and ditches all the way to the High Road. Once there, he didn't need to ask where they were going, the High Road only led one place.

Elroy had been to the Capital a total of three times in his life. It was a quick-paced bustling place that stank at once of perfume and shit. It was a place where the noble and the commoner bumped elbows in the market and anything and everything could be had for a price. He'd always imagined that he'd leave the farm one day and head to the city to seek his fortune. But not like this. Not at sword point. Not locked up in the back of an oxcart.

In truth, had he not met Gilly, he'd have already left. She was the only reason he'd hung about his father's farm as long as he did. Despite her mood swings, her temper, and the not so insignificant fact that she was a green-skinned magical water sprite, he loved her. At least, he thought he did. Never having been in love before, it was difficult to tell.

At long last the oxcart passed through the gates of the city proper. Once there, despite his dire circumstance, Elroy's breath quickened. Through the splintered wooden slats of his mobile prison, he watched the hustle and bustle of the city unfold in all its wondrous complexity. Highborn Lords and Ladies dressed in splendid finery strolled haughtily past shoeless mud-stained wretches. Painted whores peered from shadowed doorways and drunkards fought in alleyways. Soldiers and constables marched to and fro while ragtag children darted hither and thither. Shopkeeps and smiths, tinkers and tailors, beggars and thieves, all plied their various trades.

Seven oxcarts containing a total of fifty conscripts arrived in the Capital that day and were corralled in the courtyard of the King's Castle. Elroy and the others were prodded out of the carts and into the open.

"Well now," said a squat, bowlegged fellow standing next to a table piled high with rusty swords, "Here we have some fighting men and no mistake about it."

Elroy felt like more of a tired, hungry, road-weary man than he did a fighting man but didn't think it wise to say so.

"Well don't just stand there catching flies," the bandy legged fellow went on, "grab a sword."

One by one they were led to the pile and given a sword. Fiftieth of the fifty, Elroy went last. All that was left was an old wooden practice sword.

"Short straw," a guard snickered.

"Right then," the bowlegged man who appeared to be some sort of captain, shouted. "By order of the King, you're all knights now. Let's go kill a dragon!"

~~*~*

The dragon lived in the northern hills just three days march along the River Althea. Slave goblins carried their provisions and Constable Guards rode horseback cracking whips and shouting orders. They marched in a shuffling irregular column, Elroy, fiftieth of the fifty, brought up the rear.

The dragon in question, Elroy learned, was actually a pygmy dragon—a half-blind, rabid, pigmy dragon, to be precise. Considerably smaller than their larger and more infamous cousins, pygmy dragons were usually quite docile. Rabid pygmy dragons, however, were another matter entirely. Even half-bind, rabid pygmy dragons could be a handful.

One of the slave goblins was, from the look of him, a northern hill goblin. Elroy sauntered up next to him.

"You're from up that way, right? Any advice on the best way to handle this dragon?"

"Well," the slave goblin muttered, "when it comes to dragons, the best thing to do is leave them alone entirely."

"Makes sense," Elroy said.

"But this particular dragon," the goblin went on, "has been munching on livestock, along with the occasional hapless farmer, up and down the countryside for months now. The Lords are in a tizzy, hence you lot. It's a brilliant plan really. If one of you actually manages to kill the dragon, problem solved, if not, who's going to miss fifty peasants?"

"Shit," Elroy said.

"Life's a bitch, eh?" the goblin said.

The next morning, just after the company had broken camp, Elroy shuffled, bleary-eyed, down the riverbank and to the water's edge. The lazy green water made him think of Gilly, but then, everything made him think of Gilly. He unhitched his pants and readied himself. Before letting loose, Elroy froze. A pair of glowing eyes stared up at him from beneath the water's surface. Without a sound, a figure rose from the water. It was Gilly. Her green skin glistened in the morning light and her hair was a tangle of riverweed.

"Oh my," Gilly said, "Is that for me?"

Elroy looked down and blushed. His pizzle was still in hand and he was sporting his morning wood.

"I…" Elroy stammered.

"Hush now," Gilly said, "there's no time." She slid two fingers into her mouth and pulled out a slick wet frond of riverweed. "Take this. Before you face the dragon, eat it. It will only work for a little while, so don't waste it."

Elroy took the weed and stared at it dumbly. He opened his mouth to say something but Gilly had dropped back into the water, leaving no more than a ripple.

Stumbling up the riverbank, Elroy stopped short when he realized his pizzle was still flopping in the breeze. He stuffed himself back in his pants and tucked the weed into his shirt. When he reached the column, an ache in his groin reminded him he'd completely forgotten to piss.

They marched and they trudged, and they trudged and they marched. Fifty knights who days before were farmers, field hands, and stable boys. On the third day the column halted at the base of a steep wooded slope. The guards tied off their horses and the slave goblins set to digging latrines and cutting firewood.

Near the top of the hill, the bow-legged captain explained, they would find a group of stony outcroppings, and beyond the outcroppings, tucked into the hillside itself, the dragon's lair. The Constable Guard was to hold the camp while the knights climbed the hill, stormed the lair, and killed the dragon. Simple as pie, he told them.

Fifty knights, men and boys who were tired and far from home, trudged up the hill. They did not march out of bravery, nor love of glory, nor loyalty to Crown and King, they marched because the guards had made it absolutely clear that any man who didn't would earn himself a spear through the gut.

The air atop the hill was foul. The scents of rotten meat and excrement commingled in a wicked brew. Old bones lay scattered, stark, white, and ominous. A foreboding place to say the least, but then, dragon lairs were not typically known for their charming ambiance.

Fifty knights stood shoulder to shoulder outside the mouth of the dark yawning cave. Each man clutched his sword. Most, prior to their speedy ascension to Knighthood, had never held a sword, some had never seen one.

Despite the danger, Elroy couldn't help but laugh. Three days back, he'd been lying in his father's hayloft with Gilly, talking idly about all the things he wanted to do with the rest of his life. Gilly, of course, had made fun of him. A silly boy with his head in the clouds, she'd called him. Well, Elroy thought, look at me now, a Knight of the Crown.

Something stirred inside the cave. Black smoke billowed forth like a thundercloud. Bursts of orange light lit the smoke from within. The stench of sulfur added its stamp to the filthy miasma. The beast emerged through choked darkness. It was smaller than Elroy imagined it would be, twice the size of a large bull, perhaps. In truth, it looked half-starved. Its thick leathery skin seemed an ill-fitting cloak, shifting over its bones as it walked. Deep furrows sagged between its ribs. It lifted its horned head and scented the wind, tiny black eyes peering round in vain, then stamped its feet in what a man could be forgiven for assuming was blind rage.

Elroy slipped the riverweed into his mouth and chewed. The moment the weed hit his belly he doubled over in pain. Saliva filled his mouth and he felt his bile rise but he willed himself not to vomit. He looked up just in time to see a plume of red orange fire sweep over him. Blinded, he stumbled backward as though pushed by a great gust of wind.

Elroy's clothing burned away, but his skin remained unharmed. River mud oozed from his pours like sweat. The mud dried and cracked and flaked away, fresh wet mud welling up in its place. Beneath it all, Elroy's skin was as cool and slick as though he'd just slithered out of a river and plopped himself down on its bank.

When the smoke cleared Elroy looked about himself. A moment ago, he had stood as one of fifty and now he stood alone. Forty-nine men lay dead or dying. The stink of charred flesh filled the air.

His wooden sword burning, Elroy let loose what he hoped was a blood curdling battle cry. The dragon stamped its feet and snapped its jaws and charged, screeching and bellowing, twin jets of fire streaming from its nostrils. The mad beast came in fast and low, swinging its head from side to side, hoping to gore Elroy with its horns, but Elroy ducked and dodged, threw his arm around the monster's neck and swung himself onto its back.

The Dragon, bucking, thrashing, and rocking, bounded down the hillside in a furry of smoke and fire. Elroy, legs wrapped tight around the dragon's neck, one hand clutching the dragon's horn, the other waving his burning wooden sword in the air, held fast.

At last the dragon reached the bottom of the hill and collapsed in a smoking heap in the middle of the guard's camp, utterly spent.

And thus, a hero was born.

~~*~*

Upon his return to the city Elroy found that in addition to being the only knight to survive the dragon, he was the only knight, period. All of the true knights had been killed on one quest or another or had simply left the kingdom altogether in search of greener pastures. The kingdom, Elroy learned, was in dismal financial straits and the Crown was inconsistent at best when it came to paying wages. Quite used to being poor, he was not deterred.

Elroy didn't know much about knights. He imagined they went around doing good deeds and helping the less fortunate. He thought they

41

were chivalrous. In truth, the knights of the kingdom, back when the kingdom *had* knights, were a bunch of stuck up peacocks who went about with their noses in the air acting hoity and superior. As such, they were roundly despised.

Knowing no better, Elroy behaved as he thought a knight *should* behave. He volunteered his time at the House of Healing, holding patients steady while the monks sawed away offending limbs, played stoolball with the foundlings at the monastery orphanage, and sat vigil with the dying at the nunnery. He spent his money, a pittance for a true knight but a fortune to him, in the taverns and bathhouses of the common folk, rather than at the gaudy balls and banquets of the rich.

Elroy took to his new role with relish. In some ways, his life was shaping up better than he could have hoped. But still, he longed for his Gilly. He hadn't seen her since the dragon, hadn't thanked her for saving his life. Truth be told, he thought he might walk away from Knighthood and all that went with it, if it meant he could be with her.

That's not to say that life with Gilly wasn't without its complications. For a human to consort with a water sprite was, of course, illegal and punishable by death. So too regarding elves, gnomes, nymphs, pixies, sylphs, and goblins, although who in their right mind would lay with a goblin, Elroy couldn't say. But customs and ways that held for city folk didn't always hold in the country. Discretion, Elroy learned, was key.

Elroy's reputation grew, a true knight who was also a man of the people. Sir Elroy Wooden Sword, they called him, Knight of the People, and later, simply, the People's Knight. One afternoon, enjoying a tankard in a tavern he'd come to frequent, Elroy heard a minstrel sing a ballad about a good knight who was beloved by all. Halfway through the song, Elroy realized it was about him.

But as many a dungeon dweller could attest, fame and fortune were dangerous possessions in the city. The King was a jealous creature. He did not like to share the center stage. The People's Knight was becoming all together too popular for the King's liking. He was, after all, nothing more than an up-jumped farm boy.

One morning, Elroy woke to find a strange woman sitting on the edge of his bed. He'd been drinking the night before, it was true, but he was quite certain that he'd gone to bed alone. She was beautiful, pale white, almost transparent, as though made of mist and air. Although he had never seen one, Elroy knew she was a sylph, a sky elemental.

"Who are you? Where did you come from? How did you come to be in my bed?"

The sylph remained silent. Her gaze was fixed not on him but on some distant point in space, as though, in her mind, she was far away. The morning sun shafted through the open window and the sylph shimmered like lake water. She was nude. Elroy moved to cover her with his blanket. With her gaze fixed at last upon him, he saw that she was crying.

"What's wrong?" Elroy asked.

With a crack and a bang, Elroy's chamber door burst open. A troupe of stone-faced guards marched into the room followed by the King himself.

"Sir Elroy Wooden Sword," the King bellowed, "you are hereby charged with amalgamation and miscegenation most foul and unnatural."

The sylph buried her face in her hands, a statue of ice weeping in the morning sun. "I'm sorry," she whispered. Her tears smelled like storm clouds and summer rain.

~~*~*

While the People's Knight, publicly denounced as a race traitor, languished in the deepest of the King's dungeons, something remarkable was afoot in the great courtyard.

A mysterious woman arrived astride an enormous painted elephant wrapped in colored silks. Her hair was black obsidian and her skin burnished copper. She entered the King's castle courtyard at the head of a procession of servants bearing litters piled high with exotic fruits, jewels, and spices. Trailing the procession, two more elephants pulled a wheeled cage containing a striped saber toothed beast that could have leapt from the pages of a storybook.

After a screeching fanfare a golden-cloaked herald announced the arrival of Queen Nayada the Wise and Beautiful. Queen Nayada, it was explained, hailed from faraway in the East and had traveled widely in search of a worthy King to share her wealth and maidenhood. Chests of gold were emptied upon the courtyard ground as tokens of the Queen's wealth. Garlands of perfumed flowers were dropped on top of the gold as symbols of the queen's considerable feminine assets.

She would, the herald announced, marry the King whose champion bested her saber-toothed Liger in mortal combat.

It was, of course, too good to pass up. Both an influx of money to jumpstart the beggared kingdom and a beautiful and exotic maiden to share his bed. Indeed, it was as though the answer to all the King's problems had simply fallen from the sky.

But first, he would need a champion. The closed counsel bandied about names. Someone mentioned Sir Elroy Wooden Sword, but that was quickly dismissed. As the kingdom had no true knights available, they went down the lists of the Constable Guard.

They talked and drank, and drank and talked. The King, being the King, drank and talked more than anyone. Whenever his goblet was empty, his chamber slave would rush to refill it. The King's chamber slave was a forest sprite. Her skin changed color every few seconds, first

43

yellow, then orange, then red, then brown, then yellow again, as though she were the leaves of autumn. It was really quite dizzying to watch, had anyone actually bothered watching, but because she was a slave girl, she was ignored almost completely.

She set the King's goblet on the table and, with a deftness few could match, pulled a small black pearl from behind her ear and dropped it into the King's wine. The pearl dissolved instantly, but even if it hadn't, the King would have likely swallowed it whole without noticing. He was a prodigious wine-drinker.

Before too long, the King was slurring drunk, however, what happened next couldn't be explained by mere drunkenness. As they were discussing the merits of holding a tournament to choose a champion, the King stood up abruptly, knocked his chair to the floor and said, "Well it's perfectly clear we aren't going to find any champions in this rotting carcass of a Kingdom. I know what you're all thinking, you're thinking this is a job for the King."

The council members squirmed in their seats and coughed in their hands. No one, of course, had been thinking anything like that. The King, while once a formidable presence on the tournament fields, was well past his prime. In fact, it was all he could do to battle a flight of stairs. Battling saber-toothed monsters seemed exceedingly ill advised.

"*Ahem.* Your Majesty, if I may," the senior counselor said. "Doubtless you would defeat the beast, but perhaps that would send the wrong message. After all, a King is busy dealing with the important matters of the State, too busy by far to battle every beast that lumbers into the Kingdom. That's why kings use champions."

"Nonsense," the King roared, splashing wine down the front of his doublet. "The people need to be reminded just who it is that rules them."

"But your Majesty —"

"Silence!" The King shouted. "I'll hear no more of this nonsense. Where are my squires?"

The city was abuzz. The news was trumpeted from every tower. The King himself was going to battle the gnarly beast and marry the beautiful and exotic Queen. It was easily the coolest thing happening anywhere and a welcome distraction from the daily grind so everyone, rich or poor, high or low, noble or common, flocked to the great courtyard to watch the show.

The King marched out in gilded armor. His long sword glinted in the sun. His jewel-covered crown added a stately and noble flourish to, had he not been short, fat, and visibly tipsy, what would have been a dashing figure. Slowly, the cage door was lifted and the enormous cat stalked out.

~~*~*

In the dungeon, the People's Knight, head hanging between his knees, pondered the inscrutable nature of fate. To what purpose had he risen from peasant farm boy to noble knight, only to fall to this? Surely fortune's vassals danced to some master tune. Perhaps not, he mused, perhaps it was all random after all. Perhaps fate was no more real a thing than a conjurer's illusion, a trick of smoke and mirrors.

Elroy was, as far as he could see, the only human prisoner in the King's dungeon. Most of his fellow inmates were goblins. There were a few wood sprites, a gnome, and one individual so old and emaciated it was difficult to say for certain what he was, although he appeared too small to be a human man.

One of the goblins, a grizzled creature with a great hooked nose, was staring at him from a dank shadowed corner, eyes glowing dim red in the darkness. All at once, the hook-nosed brute stood up and started walking toward him.

"All right then," Elroy said, readying himself for a fight.

The goblin stopped short, glared, and spewed a mouthful of water into Elroy's piss bucket.

"What in blazes?" Elroy started.

The goblin raised his gnarled finger to his fleshy lips. Elroy hushed as he was bid. The goblin pointed to the piss bucket. The piss and water swirled as though stirred by an unseen ladle. A strange sheen of shifting color spread across the surface. It flashed as bright as flame, before fading completely. With the colored lights gone, Elroy could see a shape at the bottom of the bucket. It was a key. It hadn't, he was certain, been there before.

Elroy wasted no time. He reached into the piss, snatched up the key, and sprinted to the dungeon door. He pressed his ear against it. Silence. Holding his breath, Elroy slipped the key into the lock. The bolt turned with a heart-thrumming squeak. The door pushed open. Beyond the door the jailer lay snoring on the flagstone floor. There was a goat's bladder wineskin hanging from a nail by the doorframe and an overturned goblet on the floor beside the jailor's head. Elroy tiptoed through.

The jailer's chamber slave, a small wood gnome, sat smiling on a footstool. The gnome pointed at the wall to Elroy's side. There, on a set of hooks, hung a wooden practice sword very much like the sword he'd earned his name by.

Elroy lifted the sword and tested its balance and heft. It felt good in his hand and despite all, his sprits lifted.

"You'll need this," the gnome said, tossing him the wineskin.

Elroy started to ask why, but the gnome bade him hush and led him through a series of dark and narrow passageways. Finally, they emerged into a long open space where Elroy was greeted with the familiar stink of manure.

"These are the Constable stables," the gnome whispered, "at the far side you'll find a small plank door. The door will take you to the great courtyard. From there you're on your own."

"Thank you," Elroy said

"Just go!"

Elroy located the door in question quickly enough but he couldn't open it. The wood was swollen tight inside the frame. It looked as though it hadn't been used in quite some time. Elroy backed up a few steps, took a deep breath and threw all his weight at it. The door burst open and Elroy went careening, arms flailing, into the courtyard. He spun around in confusion, blinking his eyes at the sun.

He found himself surrounded by a roaring crowd. Huge painted elephants lumbered about the courtyard and a beast unlike any he'd ever seen or heard-tell of, was swatting a man about the way a cat swats a mouse. A dented crown rolled and bounced across the ground and stopped at Elroy's feet. Elroy looked up in time to see the beast disembowel what was left of the King.

In the very next instant, the beast was charging. It was impossibly fast. Elroy threw himself to the side and rolled out of the way. By the time he found his feet, the monster was rounding on him again. Without thinking, Elroy threw the wineskin at the big cat's head. The Ligra snatched the bladder from the air with a snap of its jaws and batted Elroy aside with a massive paw in a single fluid motion.

The wind knocked from his lungs, Elroy sputtered and hitched, trying to catch his breath. His vision dimmed. It was all he could do to push himself to his knees. Standing and fighting were well beyond him.

Leisurely, gracefully, the giant cat circled. Sensing its prey was past a struggle, it took its time. Elroy, his wooden sword broken, was resigned. I'm going to die now, he thought. Not a bad run though, for a farm boy.

The beast came in close, arched its back, curled up in a massive striped ball, and was still.

Now what? Elroy wondered.

As if in answer, the cat began to snore.

Elroy laughed. It hurt like hell, but he laughed just the same. Slowly, carefully, and with a great deal of pain, he pushed himself to his feet. Still clutching the hilt of his broken sword, he raised his arm to the crowd.

"It's Elroy Wooden Sword," someone shouted, "The People's Knight!"

"We have our King!" someone else shouted.

"The People's King! The People's King! The People's King!" the crowd chanted.

~~*~*

And so it came to pass that Sir Elroy Wooden Sword, the People's Knight, became King Elroy Wooden Sword, or simply, the People's King.

First there was a coronation, then a royal wedding, and then a great celebration. The streets were filled with revelry till the wee hours. Later that night, in the King's chamber, alone together for the first time, Elroy sat down with his bride.

"I don't even know you," he said.

The strange woman threw her head back and laughed out loud. "Oh, but you do know me, silly boy."

She rose, dropped her robes to the floor, and stood before him completely nude. Ere he could speak, her features began to change. The air around her shimmered and her copper skin blushed every color of the rainbow, settling at last on green.

Elroy's jaw dropped. "Gilly!"

Gilly laughed again, wild eyes flashing. Beautiful and seductive, she walked to Elroy's desk, where she made a show of bending over and opening the draw. She removed a rolled parchment and spread it across the desktop.

"And here," she said, "King Elroy, is your first royal decree."

Elroy followed her to the desk. Poorly lettered, he read slowly, sounding out the words as he went. Gilly helped him along when he had trouble, whispering the words in his ear, soft and breathy.

From this day forward humans and magical creatures, including but not limited to, sprites, elves, gnomes, nymphs, pixies, sylphs and goblins, shall be considered equal under the law.

No human may enslave any magical creature nor shall any human have the right to confiscate any magical creature's possessions or lands, provided those possessions or lands were come by lawfully.

Furthermore, all contacts and transactions between humans and magical creatures including but not limited to marriage shall be considered legal and lawful.

Elroy looked up at Gilly and down at the parchment again. "Everything," he whispered. "You made it happen."

"Did you think you'd done it all yourself," Gilly said impishly, "Elroy, Knight of the Dung Heap?"

"All for this?" Elroy said, rustling the parchment.

"What, you thought I was with you for that little worm between your legs?" Gilly said, snaking her arm around his waist. She lifted a candle from the desktop and poured a dollop of wax onto the bottom of the parchment.

"My Gilly," the king whispered, and pressed the royal seal into the wax.

GEORGE R. R. MARTIN is the author of the international bestselling *A Song of Ice and Fire* series and the co-executive producer of the hugely successful HBO TV series based on those books, *Game of Thrones*. For a decade he worked in television, including work for *Beauty and the Beast, Max Headroom* and *The Twilight Zone*. He has written fantasy, science fiction and horror, but it is his stories of the Seven Kingdoms that have propelled him to international acclaim.

Find out more at www.georgerrmartin.com

IN THE LOST LANDS
George R R Martin

You can buy anything you might desire from Gray Alys.
But it is better not to.

~~*~*

The Lady Melange did not come herself to Gray Alys. She was said to be a clever and a cautious young woman, as well as exceedingly fair, and she had heard the stories. Those who dealt with Gray Alys did so at their own peril, it was said. Gray Alys did not refuse any of those who came to her, and she always got them what they wanted. Yet somehow, when all was done, those who dealt with Gray Alys were never happy with the things that she brought them, the things that they had wanted. The Lady Melange knew all this, ruling as she did from the high keep built into the side of the mountain. Perhaps that was why she did not come herself.

Instead, it was Jerais who came calling on Gray Alys that day; Blue Jerais, the lady's champion, foremost of the paladins who secured her high keep and led her armies into battle, captain of her colorguard. Jerais wore an underlining of pale blue silk beneath the deep azure plate of his enameled armor. The sigil on his shield was a maelstrom done in a hundred subtle hues of blue, and a sapphire large as an eagle's eye was set in the hilt of his sword. When he entered Gray Alys' presence and removed his helmet, his eyes were a perfect match for the jewel in his sword, though his hair was a startling and inappropriate red.

Gray Alys received him in the small, ancient stone house she kept in the dim heart of the town beneath the mountain. She waited for him in a windowless room full of dust and the smell of mold, seated in an old high-backed chair that seemed to dwarf her small, thin body. In her lap was a gray rat the size of a small dog. She stroked it languidly as Jerais entered and took off his helmet and let his bright blue eyes adjust to the dimness.

"Yes?" Gray Alys said at last.

"You are the one they call Gray Alys," Jerais said.

"I am."

"I am Jerais. I come at the behest of the Lady Melange."

"The wise and beautiful Lady Melange," said Gray Alys. The rat's fur was soft as velvet beneath her long, pale fingers. "Why does the Lady send her champion to one as poor and plain as I?"

"Even in the keep, we hear tales of you," said Jerais.

"Yes."

"It is said, for a price, you will sell things strange and wonderful."

"Does the Lady Melange wish to buy?"

51

"It is said also that you have powers, Gray Alys. It is said that you are not always as you sit before me now, a slender woman of indeterminate age, clad all in gray. It is said that you become young and old as you wish. It is said that sometimes you are a man, or an old woman, or a child. It is said that you know the secrets of shapeshifting, that you go abroad as a great cat, a bear, a bird, and that you change your skin at will, not as a slave to the moon like the werefolk of the lost lands."

"All of these things are said," Gray Alys acknowledged.

Jerais removed a small leather bag from his belt and stepped closer to where Gray Alys sat. He loosened the drawstring that held the bag shut, and spilled out the contents on the table by her side. Gems. A dozen of them, in as many colors. Gray Alys lifted one and held it to her eye, watching the candle flame through it. When she placed it back among the others, she nodded at Jerais and said, "What would the Lady buy of me?"

"Your secret," Jerais said, smiling. "The Lady Melange wishes to shapeshift."

"She is said to be young and beautiful," Gray Alys replied. "Even here beyond the keep, we hear many tales of her. She has no mate but many lovers. All of her colorguard are said to love her, among them yourself. Why should she wish to change?"

"You misunderstand. The Lady Melange does not seek youth or beauty. No change could make her fairer than she is. She wants from you the power to become a beast. A wolf."

"Why?" asked Gray Alys.

"That is none of your concern. Will you sell her this gift?"

"I refuse no one," said Gray Alys. "Leave the gems here. Return in one month, and I shall give you what the Lady Melange desires." Jerais nodded. His face looked thoughtful. "You refuse no one?"

"No one."

He grinned crookedly, reached into his belt, and extended his hand to her. Within the soft blue crushed velvet of his gloved palm rested another jewel, a sapphire even larger than the one set in the hilt of his sword. "Accept this as payment, if you will. I wish to buy for myself."

Gray Alys took the sapphire from his palm, held it up between thumb and forefinger against the candle flame, nodded, and dropped it among the other jewels. "What would you have, Jerais?"

His grin spread wider. "I would have you fail," he said. "I do not want the Lady Melange to have this power she seeks."

Gray Alys regarded him evenly, her steady gray eyes fixed on his own cold blue ones. "You wear the wrong color, Jerais," she said at last. "Blue is the color of loyalty, yet you betray your mistress and the mission she entrusted to you."

"I am loyal," Jerais protested. "I know what is good for her, better than she knows herself. Melange is young and foolish. She thinks it can be kept secret, when she finds this power she seeks. She is wrong. And when the people know, they will destroy her. She cannot rule these folk by day, and tear out their throats by night."

Gray Alys considered that for a time in silence, stroking the great rat that lay across her lap. "You lie, Jerais," she said when she spoke again. "The reasons you give are not your true reasons."

Jerais frowned. His gloved hand, almost casually, came to rest on the hilt of his sword. His thumb stroked the great sapphire set there. "I will not argue with you," he said gruffly. "If you will not sell to me, give me back my gem and be damned with you!"

"I refuse no one," Gray Alys replied.

Jerais scowled in confusion. "I shall have what I ask?"

"You shall have what you want."

"Excellent," said Jerais, grinning again. "In a month, then!"

"A month," agreed Gray Alys.

~~*~*

And so Gray Alys sent the word out, in ways that only Gray Alys knew. The message passed from mouth to mouth through the shadows and alleys and the secret sewers of the town, and even to the tall houses of scarlet wood and colored glass where dwelled the noble and the rich. Soft gray rats with tiny human hands whispered it to sleeping children, and the children shared it with each other, and chanted a strange new chant when they skipped rope. The word drifted to all the army outposts to the east, and rode west with the great caravans into the heart of the old empire of which the town beneath the mountain was only the smallest part. Huge leathery birds with the cunning faces of monkeys flew the word south, over the forests and the rivers, to a dozen different kingdoms, where men and women as pale and terrible as Gray Alys herself heard it in the solitude of their towers. Even north, past the mountains, even into the lost lands, the word traveled.

It did not take long. In less than two weeks, he came to her. "I can lead you to what you seek," he told her. "I can find you a werewolf."

He was a young man, slender and beardless. He dressed in the worn leathers of the rangers who lived and hunted in the windswept desolation beyond the mountains. His skin had the deep tan of a man who spent all his life outdoors, though his hair was as white as mountain snow and fell about his shoulders, tangled and unkempt. He wore no armor and carried a long knife instead of a sword, and he moved with a wary grace. Beneath the pale strands of hair that fell across his face, his eyes were dark and sleepy. Though his smile was open and amiable, there was a curious indolence to him as well, and a dreamy, sensuous set to his lips when he thought no one was watching. He named himself Boyce.

Gray Alys watched him and listened to his words and finally said, "Where?"

"A week's journey north," Boyce replied. "In the lost lands."

"Do you dwell in the lost lands, Boyce?" Gray Alys asked of him.

"No. They are no fit place for dwelling. I have a home here in town. But I go beyond the mountains often, Gray Alys. I am a hunter. I know the lost lands well, and I know the things that live there. You seek a man who walks like a wolf. I can take you to him. But we must leave at once, if we are to arrive before the moon is full."

Gray Alys rose. "My wagon is loaded, my horses are fed and shod. Let us depart then."

Boyce brushed the fine white hair from his eyes, and smiled lazily.

~~*~*

The mountain pass was high and steep and rocky, and in places barely wide enough for Gray Alys' wagon to pass. The wagon was a cumbersome thing, long and heavy and entirely enclosed, once brightly-painted but now faded so by time and weather that its wooden walls were all a dreary gray. It rode on six clattering iron wheels, and the two horses that pulled it were of necessity monsters half again the size of normal beasts. Even so, they kept a slow pace through the mountains. Boyce, who had no horse, walked ahead or alongside, and sometimes rode up next to Gray Alys. The wagon groaned and creaked. It took them three days to ascend to the highest point on the mountain road, where they looked through a cleft in the mountains out onto the wide barren plains of the lost lands. It took them three more days to descend.

"Now we will make better time," Boyce promised Gray Alys when they reached the lost lands themselves. "Here the land is flat and empty, and the going will be easy. A day now, perhaps two, and you shall have what you seek."

"Yes," said Gray Alys.

They filled the water barrels full before they left the mountains, and Boyce went hunting in the foothills and returned with three black rabbits and the carcass of a small deer, curiously deformed, and when Gray Alys asked him how he had brought them down with only a knife as a weapon, Boyce smiled and produced a sling and sent several small stones whistling through the air. Gray Alys nodded. They made a small fire and cooked two of the rabbits, and salted the rest of the meat. The next morning, at dawn, they set off into the lost lands.

Here they moved quickly indeed. The lost lands were a cold and empty place, and the earth was packed as hard and firm as the roads that wound through the empire beyond the mountains. The wagon rolled along briskly, creaking and clattering, shaking a bit from side to side as it went. In the lost lands there were no thickets to cut through, no rivers to cross. Desolation lay before them on all sides, seemingly endless. From time to time they saw a grove of trees, gnarled and twisted all together, limbs heavy with swollen fruit with skin the color of indigo, shining. From time to time they clattered through a shallow, rocky stream, none deeper than ankle level. From time to time vast patches of white fungus blanketed the desolate gray earth. Yet all these things were rare. Mostly there was only the emptiness, the shuddering dead plains all around them, and the winds. The winds were terrible in the lost lands. They blew constantly, and they were cold and bitter, and sometimes they smelled of ash, and sometimes they seemed to howl and shriek like some poor doomed soul.

At last they had come far enough so Gray Alys could see the end of the lost lands: another line of mountains far, far north of them, a vague bluish-white line across the gray horizon. They could travel for weeks and not reach those distant peaks, Gray Alys knew, yet the lost lands were so flat and so empty that even now they could make them out, dimly.

At dusk Gray Alys and Boyce made their camp, just beyond a grove of the curious tortured trees they had glimpsed on their journey north. The trees gave them a partial respite from the fury of the wind, but even so they could hear it, keening and pulling at them, twisting their fire into wild suggestive shapes.

"These lands are lost indeed," Gray Alys said as they ate.

"They have their own beauty," Boyce replied. He impaled a chunk of meat on the end of his long knife, and turned it above the fire. "Tonight, if the clouds pass, you will see the lights rippling above the northern mountains, all purple and gray and maroon, twisting like curtains caught in this endless wind."

"I have seen those lights before," said Gray Alys.

"I have seen them many times," Boyce said. He bit off a piece of meat, pulling at it with his teeth, and a thin line of grease ran down from the corner of his mouth. He smiled.

"You come to the lost lands often," Gray Alys said.

Boyce shrugged. "I hunt."

"Does anything live here?" asked Gray Alys. "Live amidst all this desolation?"

"Oh yes," Boyce replied. "You must have eyes to find it, you must know the lost lands, but it is there. Strange twisted beasts never seen beyond the mountains, things out of legends and nightmares, enchanted things and accursed things, things whose flesh is impossibly rare and impossibly delicious. Humans, too, or things that are almost human. Werefolk and changelings and gray shapes that walk only by twilight, shuffling things half-living and half-dead." His smile was gentle and taunting. "But you are Gray Alys, and all this you must know. It is said you came out of the lost lands yourself once, long ago."

"It is said," Gray Alys answered.

"We are alike, you and I," Boyce replied. "I love the town, the people, song and laughter and gossip. I savor the comforts of my house, good food and good wine. I relish the players who come each fall to the high keep and perform for the Lady Melange. I like fine clothes and jewels and soft, pretty women. Yet part of me is only at home here, in the lost lands, listening to the wind, watching the shadows warily each dusk, dreaming things the townsfolk never dare." Full dark had fallen by then. Boyce lifted his knife and pointed north, to where dim lights had begun to glow faintly against the mountains. "See there, Gray Alys. See how the lights shimmer and shift. You can see shapes in them if you watch long enough. Men and women and things that are neither, moving against the darkness. Their voices are carried by the wind. Watch and listen. There are great dramas in those lights, plays grander and stranger than any ever performed on the Lady's stage. Do you hear? Do you see?"

Gray Alys sat on the hard-packed earth with her legs crossed and her gray eyes unreadable, watching in silence. Finally she spoke. "Yes," she said, and that was all.

Boyce sheathed his long knife and came around the campfire—it had died now to a handful of dim reddish embers—to sit beside her. "I knew you would see," he said. "We are alike, you and I. We wear the flesh of the city, but in our blood the cold wind of the lost lands is blowing always. I could see it in your eyes, Gray Alys."

She said nothing; she sat and watched the lights, feeling the warm presence of Boyce beside her. After a time he put an arm about her shoulders, and Gray Alys did not protest. Later, much later, when the fire had gone entirely dark and the night had grown cold, Boyce reached out and cupped her chin within his hand and turned her face to his. He kissed her, once, gently, full upon her thin lips.

And Gray Alys woke, as if from a dream, and pushed him back upon the ground and undressed him with sure, deft hands and took him then and there. Boyce let her do it all. He lay upon the chill hard ground with his hands clasped behind his head, his eyes dreamy and his lips curled up in a lazy, complacent smile, while Gray Alys rode him, slowly at first, then faster and faster, building to a shuddering climax. When she came her body went stiff and she threw her head back; her mouth opened, as if to cry out, but no sound came forth. There was only the wind, cold and wild, and the cry it made was not a cry of pleasure.

~~*~*

The next day dawned chill and overcast. The sky was full of thin, twisted gray clouds that raced before them faster than clouds ought to race. What light filtered through seemed wan and colorless. Boyce walked beside the wagon while Gray Alys drove it forward at a leisurely pace. "We are close now," Boyce told her. "Very close."

"Yes."

Boyce smiled up at her. His smile had changed since they had become lovers. It was fond and mysterious, and more than a bit indulgent. It was a smile that presumed. "Tonight," he told her.

"The moon will be full tonight," Gray Alys said.

Boyce smiled and pushed the hair from his eyes and said nothing.

~~*~*

Well before dusk, they drew up amidst the ruins of some nameless town long forgotten even by those who dwelled in the lost lands. Little remained to disturb the sweeping emptiness, only a huddle of broken masonry, forlorn and pitiful. The vague outlines of town walls could still be discerned, and one or two chimneys remained standing, jagged and half-shattered, gnawing at the horizon like rotten black teeth. No shelter was to be found here, no life. When Gray Alys had fed her horses, she wandered through the ruins but found little. No pottery, no rusted blades, no books. Not even bones. Nothing at all to hint of the people who had once lived here, if people they had been.

The lost lands had sucked the life out of this place and blown away even the ghosts, so not a trace of memory remained. The shrunken sun was low on the horizon, obscured by scuttling clouds, and the scene spoke to her with the wind's voice, cried out in loneliness and despair. Gray Alys stood for a long time, alone, watching the sun sink while her thin tattered cloak billowed behind her and the cold wind bit through into her soul. Finally she turned away and went back to the wagon.

Boyce had built a fire, and he sat in front of it, mulling some wine in a copper pot, adding spices from time to time. He smiled his new smile for Gray Alys when she looked at him. "The wind is cold," he said. "I thought a hot drink would make our meal more pleasant."

Gray Alys glanced away towards the setting sun, then back at Boyce. "This is not the time or the place for pleasure, Boyce. Dusk is all but upon us, and soon the full moon shall rise."

"Yes," said Boyce. He ladled some of the hot wine into his cup, and tried a swallow. "No need to rush off hunting, though," he said, smiling lazily. "The wolf will come to us. Our scent will carry far in this wind, in this emptiness, and the smell of fresh meat will bring him running."

Gray Alys said nothing. She turned away from him and climbed the three wooden steps that led up to the interior of her wagon. Inside she lit a brazier carefully, and watched the light shift and flicker against the weathered gray wallboards and the pile of furs on which she slept. When the light had grown steady, Gray Alys slid back a wall panel, and stared at the long row of tattered garments that hung on pegs within the narrow closet. Cloaks and capes and billowing loose shirts, strangely cut gowns and suits that clung like a second skin from head to toe, leather and fur and feathers. She hesitated briefly, then reached in and chose a great cloak made of a thousand long silver feathers, each one tipped delicately with black. Removing her simple cloth cloak, Gray Alys fastened the flowing feathered garment at her neck. When she turned it billowed all about her, and the dead air inside the wagon stirred and briefly seemed alive before the feathers settled and stilled once again. Then Gray Alys bent and opened a huge oaken chest, bound in iron and leather. From within she drew out a small box. Ten rings rested against worn gray felt, each set with a long, curving silver claw instead of a stone. Gray Alys donned them methodically, one ring to each finger, and when she rose and clenched her fists, the claws shone dimly and menacingly in the light from the brazier.

Outside, it was twilight. Boyce had not prepared any food, Gray Alys noted as she took her seat across the fire from where the pale-haired ranger sat quaffing his hot wine.

"A beautiful cloak," Boyce observed amiably.

"Yes," said Gray Alys.

"No cloak will help you when *he* comes, though."

Gray Alys raised her hand, made a fist. The silver claws caught the firelight. Gleamed.

"Ah," said Boyce. "Silver."

"Silver," agreed Gray Alys, lowering her hand.

"Still," Boyce said. "Others have come against him, armed with silver. Silver swords, silver knives, arrows tipped with silver. They are dust now, all those silvered warriors. He gorged himself on their flesh."

Gray Alys shrugged.

Boyce stared at her speculatively for a time, then smiled and went back to his wine. Gray Alys drew her cloak more tightly about herself to keep out the cold wind. After a while, staring off into the far distance, she saw lights moving against the northern mountains. She remembered the stories that she had seen there, the tales that Boyce had conjured for her from that play of colored shadows. They were grim and terrible stories. In the lost lands, there was no other kind.

At last another light caught her eye. A spreading dimness in the east, wan and ominous. Moonrise.

Gray Alys stared calmly across the dying camp fire. Boyce had begun to change.

She watched his body twist as bone and muscle changed within, watched his pale white hair grow longer and longer, watched his lazy smile turn into a wide red grin that split his face, saw the canines lengthen and the tongue come lolling out, watched the wine cup fall as his hands melted and writhed and became paws. He started to say something once, but no words came out, only a low, coarse snarl of laughter, half-human and half-animal. Then he threw back his head and howled, and he ripped at his clothing until it lay in tatters all about him and he was Boyce no longer. Across the fire from Gray Alys the wolf stood, a great shaggy white beast, half again the size of an ordinary wolf, with a savage red slash of a mouth and glowing scarlet eyes. Gray Alys stared into those eyes as she rose and shook the dust from her feathered cloak. They were knowing eyes, cunning, wise. Inside those eyes she saw a smile, a smile that presumed.

A smile that presumed too much.

The wolf howled once again, a long wild sound that melted into the wind. And then he leapt, straight across the embers of the fire he had built.

Gray Alys threw her arms out, her cloak bunched in her hands, and changed.

Her change was faster than his had been, over almost as soon as it begun, but for Gray Alys it lasted an eternity. First there was the strange choking, clinging feeling as the cloak adhered to her skin, then dizziness and a curious liquid weakness as her muscles began to run and flow and reshape themselves. And finally exhilaration, as the power rushed into her and came coursing through her veins, a wine fiercer and hotter and wilder than the poor stuff Boyce had mulled above their fire.

She beat her vast silvery wings, each pinion tipped with black, and the dust stirred and swirled as she rose up into the moonlight, up to safety high above the white wolf's bound, up and up until the ruins shrunk to insignificance far beneath her. The wind took hold of her, caressed her with trembling icy hands, and she yielded herself to it and soared. Her great wings filled with the dread melody of the lost lands, carrying her higher and higher. Her cruel curving beak opened and closed and opened again, though no sound came forth. She wheeled across the sky, drunken with flight. Her eyes, sharper than any human eyes could be, saw far into the distance, spied out the secrets of every shadow, glimpsed all the dying and half-dead things that stirred and shambled across the barren face of the lost lands. The curtains of light to the north danced before her, a thousand times brighter and more gorgeous than they had been before, when she had only the dim eyes of the little thing called Gray Alys to perceive them with. She wanted to fly to them, to soar north and north and north, to cavort among those lights, shredding them into glowing strips with her talons.

She lifted her talons as if in challenge. Long and wickedly curved they were, and razor sharp, and the moonlight flashed along their length, pale upon the silver. And she remembered then, and she wheeled about in a great circle, reluctantly, and turned away from the beckoning lights of the northlands. Her wings beat and beat again, and she began to descend, shrieking down through the night air, plunging toward her prey.

She saw him far beneath her, a pale white shape hurtling away from the wagon, away from the fire, seeking safety in the shadows and the dark places. But there was no safety in the lost lands. He was strong and untiring, and his long powerful legs carried him forward in a steady swift lope that ate up the miles as if they were nothing. Already he had come a long way from their camp. But fast as he was, she was faster. He was only a wolf, after all, and she was the wind itself.

She descended in a dead silence, cutting through the wind like a knife, silver talons outstretched. But he must have spied her shadow streaking towards him, etched clear by the moonlight, for as she closed he spurted forward wildly, driven by fear. It was useless. He was running full out when she passed above him, raking him with her talons. They cut through fur and twisted flesh like ten bright silver swords, and he broke stride and staggered and went down.

She beat her wings and circled overhead for another pass, and as she did the wolf regained his feet and stared up at her terrible silhouette dark against the moon, his eyes brighter now than ever, turned feverish by fear. He threw back his head and howled a broken bloody howl that cried for mercy.

She had no mercy in her. Down she came, and down, talons drenched with blood, her beak open to rend and tear. The wolf waited for her, and leapt up to meet her dive, snarling, snapping. But he was no match for her.

She slashed at him in passing, evading him easily, opening five more long gashes that quickly welled with blood.

The next time she came around he was too weak to run, too weak to rise against her. But he watched her turn and descend, and his huge shaggy body trembled just before she struck.

~~*~*

Finally his eyes opened, blurred and weak. He groaned and moved feebly. It was daylight, and he was back in the camp, lying beside the fire. Gray Alys came to him when she heard him stir, knelt, and lifted his head. She held a cup of wine to his lips until he had drunk his fill.

When Boyce lay back again, she could see the wonder in his eyes, the surprise that he still lived. "You knew," he said hoarsely. "You knew… what I was."

"Yes," said Gray Alys. She was herself once more; a slender, small, somehow ageless woman with wide gray eyes, clad in faded cloth. The feathered cloak was hung away, the silver claws no longer adorned her fingers.

Boyce tried to sit up, winced at the pain, and settled back on to the blanket she had laid beneath him. "I thought… thought I was dead," he said.

"You were close to dead," Gray Alys replied.

"Silver," he said bitterly. "Silver cuts and burns so."

"Yes."

"But you saved me," he said, confused.

"I changed back to myself, and brought you back, and tended you."

Boyce smiled, though it was only a pale ghost of his old smile. "You change at will?" he said wonderingly. "Ah, there is a gift I would kill for, Gray Alys!"

She said nothing.

"It was too open here," he said. "I should have taken you elsewhere. If there had been cover… buildings, a forest, anything… then you should not have had such an easy time with me."

"I have other skins," Gray Alys replied. "A bear, a cat. It would not have mattered."

"Ah," said Boyce. He closed his eyes. When he opened them again, he forced a twisted smile. "You were beautiful, Gray Alys. I watched you fly for a long time before I realized what it meant and began to run. It was hard to tear my eyes from you. I knew you were the doom of me, but still I could not look away. So beautiful. All smoke and silver, with fire in your eyes. The last time, as I watched you swoop towards me, I was almost glad. Better to perish at the hands of she who is so terrible and fine, I thought, than by some dirty little swordsman with his sharpened silver stick."

"I am sorry," said Gray Alys.

"No," Boyce said quickly. "It is better that you saved me. I will mend quickly, you will see. Even silver wounds bleed but briefly. Then we will be together."

"You are still weak," Gray Alys told him. "Sleep."

"Yes," said Boyce. He smiled at her, and closed his eyes.

~~*~*

Hours had passed when Boyce finally woke again. He was much stronger, his wounds all but mended. But when he tried to rise, he could not. He was bound in place, spread-eagled, hands and feet tied securely to stakes driven into the hard gray earth.

Gray Alys watched him make the discovery, heard him cry out in alarm. She came to him, held up his head, and gave him more wine.

When she moved back, his head twisted around wildly, staring at his bonds, and then at her. "What have you done?" he cried.

Gray Alys said nothing.

"Why?" he asked. "I do not understand, Gray Alys. *Why?* You saved me, tended me, and now I am bound."

"You would not like my answer, Boyce."

"The moon!" he said wildly. "You are afraid of what might happen tonight, when I change again." He smiled, pleased to have figured it out. "You are being foolish. I would not harm you, not now, after what has passed between us, after what I know. We belong together, Gray Alys. We are alike, you and I. We have watched the lights together, and I have seen you fly! We must have trust between us! Let me loose."

Gray Alys frowned and sighed and gave no other answer.

Boyce stared at her uncomprehending. "Why?" he asked again. "Untie me, Alys, let me prove the truth of my words. You need not fear me."

"I do not fear you, Boyce," she said sadly.

"Good," he said eagerly. "Then free me, and change with me. Become a great cat tonight, and run beside me, hunt with me. I can lead you to prey you never dreamed of. There is so much we can share. You have felt how it is to change, you know the truth of it, you have tasted the power, the freedom, seen the lights from a beast's eyes, smelled fresh blood, gloried in a kill. You know… the freedom… the intoxication of it… all the… you know…"

"I know," Gray Alys acknowledged.

"Then free me! We are meant for one another, you and I. We will live together, love together, hunt together."

Gray Alys shook her head.

"I do not understand," Boyce said. He strained upward wildly at his bonds, and swore, then sunk back again. "Am I hideous? Do you find me evil, unattractive?"

"No."

"Then what?" he said bitterly. "Other women have loved me, have found me handsome. Rich, beautiful ladies, the finest in the land. All of them have wanted me, even when they knew."

"But you have never returned that love, Boyce," she said.

"No," he admitted. "I have loved them after a fashion. I have never betrayed their trust, if that is what you think. I find my prey here, in the lost lands, not from among those who care for me." Boyce felt the weight of Gray Alys' eyes, and continued. "How could I love them more than I did?" he said passionately. "They could know only half of me, only the half that lived in town and loved wine and song and perfumed sheets. The rest of me lived out here, in the lost lands, and knew things that they could never know, poor soft things. I told them so, those who pressed me hard. To join with me wholly they must run and hunt beside me. Like you. Let me go, Gray Alys. Soar for me, watch me run. Hunt with me."

Gray Alys rose and sighed. "I am sorry, Boyce. I would spare you if I could, but what must happen must happen. Had you died last night, it would have been useless. Dead things have no power. Night and day, black and white, they are weak. All strength derives from the realm between, from twilight, from shadow, from the terrible place between life and death. From the gray, Boyce, from the gray."

He wrenched at his bonds again, savagely, and began to weep and curse and gnash his teeth. Gray Alys turned away from him and sought out the solitude of her wagon. There she remained for hours, sitting alone in the darkness and listening to Boyce swear and cry out to her with threats and pleadings and professions of love. Gray Alys stayed inside until well after moonrise. She did not want to watch him change, watch his humanity pass from him for the last time.

At last his cries had become howls, bestial and abandoned and full of pain. That was when Gray Alys finally reemerged. The full moon cast a wan pale light over the scene. Bound to the hard ground, the great white wolf writhed and howled and struggled and stared at her out of hungry scarlet eyes.

Gray Alys walked toward him calmly. In her hand was the long silver skinning knife, its blade engraved with fine and graceful runes.

~~*~*

When he finally stopped struggling, the work went more quickly, but still it was a long and bloody night. She killed him the instant she was done, before the dawn came and changed him and gave him back a human voice to cry his agony. Then Gray Alys hung up the pelt and brought out tools and dug a deep, deep grave in the packed cold earth. She piled stones and broken pieces of masonry on top of it, to protect him from the things that roamed the lost lands, the ghouls and the carrion crows and the other creatures that did not flinch at dead flesh. It took her most of the day to bury him, for the ground was very hard indeed, and even as she worked she knew it was a futile labor.

And when at last the work was done, and dusk had almost come again, she went once more into her wagon, and returned wearing the great cloak of a thousand silver feathers, tipped with black. Then she changed, and flew, and flew, a fierce and tireless flight, bathed in strange lights and wedded to the dark. All night she flew beneath a full and mocking moon, and just before dawn she cried out once, a shrill scream of despair and anguish that rang and keened on the sharp edge of the wind and changed its sound forever.

~~*~*

Perhaps Jerais was afraid of what she might give him, for he did not return to Gray Alys alone. He brought two other knights with him, a huge man all in white whose shield showed a skull carved out of ice, and another in crimson whose sigil was a burning man. They stood at the door, helmeted and silent, while Jerais approached Gray Alys warily. "Well?" he demanded.

Across her lap was a wolfskin, the pelt of some huge massive beast, all white as mountain snow. Gray Alys rose and offered the skin to Blue Jerais, draping it across his outstretched arm. "Tell the Lady Melange to cut herself, and drip her own blood onto the skin. Do this at moonrise when the moon is full, and then the power will be hers. She need only wear the skin as a cloak, and will the change thereafter. Day or night, full moon or no moon, it makes no matter."

Jerais looked at the heavy white pelt and smiled a hard smile. "A wolfskin, eh? I had not expected that. I thought perhaps a potion, a spell."

"No," said Gray Alys. "The skin of a werewolf."

"A werewolf?" Jerais' mouth twisted curiously, and there was a sparkle in his deep sapphire eyes. "Well, Gray Alys, you have done what the Lady Melange asked, but you have failed me. I did not pay you for success. Return my gem."

"No," said Gray Alys. "I have earned it, Jerais."

"I do not have what I asked for."

"You have what you wanted, and that is what I promised." Her gray eyes met his own without fear. "You thought my failure would help you get what you truly wanted, and that my success would doom you. You were wrong."

Jerais looked amused. "And what do I truly desire?"

"The Lady Melange," said Gray Alys. "You have been one lover among many, but you wanted more. You wanted all. You knew you stood second in her affections. I have changed that. Return to her now, and bring her the thing that she has bought."

~~*~*

That day there was bitter lamentation in the high keep on the mountain, when Blue Jerais knelt before the Lady Melange and offered her a white wolfskin. But when the screaming and the wailing and the mourning was done, she took the great pale cloak and bled upon it and learned the ways of change. It is not the union she desired, but it is a union nonetheless. So every night she prowls the battlements and the mountainside, and the townsfolk say her howling is wild with grief.

And Blue Jerais, who wed her a month after Gray Alys returned from the lost lands, sits beside a madwoman in the great hall by day, and locks his doors by night in terror of his wife's hot red eyes, and does not hunt anymore, or laugh, or lust.

~~*~*

You can buy anything you might desire from Gray Alys.
But it is better not to.

New York Times Best-selling author DAVID FARLAND has penned dozens of science fiction novels as David Wolverton, including hugely successful Star Wars titles and The Golden Queen series. As Farland, he created one of fantasy's most beloved series, The Runelords, which spans eight best-selling novels with a ninth coming in 2014. His Ravenspell series for younger readers began last year, and he has won awards for his historical fiction and YA novels. He is also a creative writing instructor, an editor, a writing competition judge, a videogame designer, a screenwriter and a movie producer.

Visit his official site for more info: www.davidfarland.net

WORMS RISING FROM THE DIRT
David Farland

We're all destined to be beggars at one time or another...
—A saying among dwarves

The village of Monkshood did not seem like much when viewed while flying above it on a dragon's back: a few stone houses with wheat-thatch roofs, clustered on a lonely road beside a river that was no more than a band of silver, snaking among barley fields.

Rath would have flown past, but from the seat at his back, the dwarf Sir Bolgrum made a deep crooning sound. "Ah, the inn down there has a *fine* reputation. Beer as brown as a doe's eyes, and so stout, it can stand up on its own!"

Rath eyed the village again. Rich farms, surrounded by berry thickets. Trails down in the fields and thickets were too small for human feet, too *purposeful* for rabbits. *House brownies*, Rath decided, industrious folk who had a magical knack for gardens...and brewing.

After the blood and massacre of the past week, Rath needed something to ease his nerves, so with a kick he urged his dragon to ground.

~~*~*

"Grimmsberry wine," a fat innkeeper shouted, "aged for seven years!" The man shoved a large mug into Rath's hand, filled with a wine that flowed like syrup, the color of molten copper. The innkeeper grinned, displaying teeth beneath a braided moustache that hung down into his blond beard.

Rath had never been able to afford Grimmsberry. He'd only been hoping for stout ale, but it had only been ten days since *the dark god's fist* had struck the world. Cities had crumbled, monsters awakened. Rath had almost died in the aftermath, but a god had saved him, denied him the chance to die, even when he longed for it, and given him a dragon to ride. Now, for the first Dragon Rider to appear in the realm in two thousand years, the innkeeper offered only his best.

Rath sniffed the sweet wine, sipped, and felt the fruitiness explode on his tongue even as his mouth burned. He gulped more down, savoring it.

The inn began to fill. Eager peasants had seen Rath's dragon, Shofarun, and many gathered outside to admire it. They were shouting and gesticulating. In truth, as Shofarun squatted in the road, he didn't seem to be much more than a large, sluggish green lizard with wings, basking in the afternoon sun.

People marveled anyway. If he stretched his neck, he was fully as tall as the inn.

Peasants soon came tumbling through the door, fresh from the field. It was spring, and they smelled of sheep from shearing, or rich barley from the field, or freshly turned soil. Green-bottle flies spun lazily behind the bar, drawn by the odor of ripe peasants. Soon, a pair of server wenches weaved among the patrons, never spilling a drop from the mugs on their wooden serving trays despite the occasional slap or pinch.

A sad little band began playing—pipes too shrill, drums too eager. The inn became a madhouse, as busy as on Midwinter Feaste.

So much for a quiet drink, Rath thought. He hefted his mug, tried to savor the Grimmsberry wine. But the putrid odor of ogre blood on his sleeve ruined the taste.

Across the bar, a serving lad peered up, eyes shining in admiration, while the crowd pressed against his back.

"Give a man some room!" Sir Bolgrum roared at Rath's back. There is a saying, "The shorter the dwarf, the louder he grumbles." It was certainly true in this case. The dwarven mercenary threw an elbow, which clubbed a merchant in the gut. Then Sir Bolgrum grasped the haft of his ancient dwarven ax and cast a baleful glare, as if daring any peasant to take a swing.

"See that?" someone in the crowd whispered. "He just thumped the constable's son!"

The constable's son stood holding his belly, more shocked than hurt, but Rath worried that this was only the beginning of trouble. Sir Bolgrum could be an angry drunk.

The room went quiet as Sir Bolgrum wiped ale from his long brown beard. "He's lucky I didn't aim lower. I'd have gladly cracked his precious chestnuts!" The dwarf glared about, inviting a fight, as if he'd love to take on the whole town.

"Peace, my friends," Rath pleaded. *This day I want nothing more than peace.*

At that moment, the outside door swung open on rusty hinges, and a small gasp ushered through the crowd, a sound like breakers in a distant surf.

Rath glanced over his shoulder to see the cause: an old man with stringy gray hair and a beggar's dirty robes was crawling across the threshold.

Just a drunk, Rath thought, *hoping to lick up any ale that spills.*

But the beggar's appearance brought whispers of surprise from the crowd, and Rath felt hair begin to rise on the back of his neck, as if a cold wind suddenly slithered through the room.

Rath recognized that sensation. *Something* else had entered the room with the old man: creatures from the spirit realm. What they wanted, Rath could not begin to know. He only knew that they were there, shadowy things that slipped into the room, sensed only as a chill that ran down the spine.

Rath could feel their eyes upon him, as if a stare was a heavy thing.

Sir Bolgrum peered down, *tsk*-ed at the beggar. "Everywhere *you* go, Rath, beggars appear—just like worms rising from the dirt."

It was a singular moment. Rath realized that this was no common beggar. It was a personage of great power, to have spirits surrounding him so, perhaps a sorcerer even.

There was a loud gasp nearby, and people began to back away from the beggar.

Rath did not mind the constant petitions. The world was full of need. But this one would be different, he could tell.

Rath gulped his wine and turned to get a better view of the old man. The crowd began to part. The man's gray hair was ratty, and he dressed in robes of sackcloth, but with each lurch of his hand, there was a small thudding upon the wooden floor, and Rath saw that he wore rings of gold and silver on every finger—rings too valuable for a beggar. Indeed, one fat ring was set with a small pixie's skull, fangs protruding, and a fiery sprite inside made its eyes flame violet. The townsfolk were staring at the beggar in awe, and one maid dropped to her knee.

The old man suddenly peered up at Rath, with eyes of clearest green, lush as sea jade. He was not old at all. He was an elf, with silver hair worn in dreadlocks. His skin was pale bluish-white, as is common among the fair folk. He had a red griffin tattooed at each temple, a sign of royalty.

"Dragonrider," the elf pleaded. "Though I am king of this realm, and your king in name, I come to you now as a beggar, seeking aid."

Rath had never met a king, and had never wanted to—especially this one. King Seloniss ty Valtur, it was whispered, leaned toward the philosophies of the Argent Elves, some of whom thought that humans were but animals, to be used as servants, or slaughtered when they were of no use.

King Seloniss ty Valtur was the one who levied taxes, sent men to the gallows, or ordered them to war. Rath didn't know whether to stand, or kneel, or piss his pants.

"Wha, what do ya want?" he managed.

"My daughter, Arriannis," the king said. "She has been kidnapped. She is held in an orcs' prison. Only you can save her."

"Surely you have better swordsmen," Rath objected, picking the king up from the floor. "I'm no hero."

"Oh, I have men who can dance with a blade as if it were a lover," the king said, "but none have a *dragon*. I need it. My daughter is held in a prison that flies…"

The peasants in the room had been jubilant only moments before. Now their faces grew pale. The music died completely; the laughter ceased. Even the simplest farmer realized the import of this.

In the past ten days, the earthquakes had broken the Lightwall, and orcs had finally breached it for the first time in four hundred years, taking three of Shandrual's northern kingdoms.

The realm needed more defenders and weapons than ever. But their elven blades were forged by Argent Elves in the north. Their leader, Prince Gavar of Glamdower, was betrothed to the princess. The two had taken sacred vows, binding the kingdoms, almost as if they were married, for it was said that they were bound at the spirit.

But if Rath could not return the princess, the alliance would become void. Gavar would be forced to make another alliance, and the weapons Rath's people needed would be lost.

If Rath failed to rescue Arriannis, everyone in the village of Monkshood, perhaps everyone in all of Shandrual, might well be doomed.

"You say she's on a prison that flies?" Rath asked, wondering how much had changed since the dark god's fist had slammed into the world. "How can that be? Does it have wings?"

The king's eyes lost color, as happened when elves shielded their feelings, and he answered hesitantly, as if he did not want to discuss such matters in public. He peered at the peasants, then shrugged, as if he realized that secrecy could no longer be maintained. "There was a great storm in the southern reaches, my rangers tell me, just two days after the god's fist struck the land. It was a storm like no other."

The king raised both hands, palms facing Rath, thumbs spread, and nearly cupped Rath's face. Then the king "sent" him a vision, in the way of elven mages. The things that Rath saw could not have come from just one witness, but had to have been seen by dozens of elves.

Rath saw a storm roiling toward him. It came like a towering wall of blackness, four thousand feet high, with colored lightning blasting through its midst in shades of green and purple, flickering like serpents tongues. It roared as if in rage at the world.

Sandstorms in the desert were said to sometimes appear like this, but there were no black sands within this storm. The blackness was something else, some other "substance" that had no name.

The winds howled like beasts, beating at Rath, and he saw the storm bear down upon the dwarven kingdom at Cor Wurm, and upon the human habitations near the Ondruil Sea. The storm tore through the land, bowling over trees, sweeping houses away like so much dust, flattening strong fortresses.

Those caught above ground were simply swept away, like straw in the wind, never to be seen again. Some managed to hide beneath the ground, yet even they did not escape. For Rath saw as if from the keen eyes of an elven ranger, as a family took refuge in an underground fruit cellar. The vision shifted, and after the storm a ranger leaned down to open the cellar door, after the house had been swept away.

Upon pulling the door upward, he saw frightened human children huddling with their mother. Their skin was ragged, yellow, and blotched with rot. Their eyes had turned a dull green, as if infected.

The children growled at the light, baring pointed fangs.

The vision ended abruptly, and Rath blinked in surprise to find himself back in the inn.

The peasants stared at the king, dread plain on their faces, and no one spoke, though some shifted uneasily.

Sir Bolgrum gave a derisive snort. He had not seen the vision. "Changed how? No little storm could frighten a dwarf. I should like to see one of these storms. I'd piss into its winds!"

"Dwarves have stout hearts," the king admitted, "but this was not a storm from this world. My rangers call it a 'chaos storm'."

The king reached into a fold of his robe, pulled out a small vial made of cut quartz that seemed to be filled with an inky liquid. "Here is some air from that storm," King Seloniss whispered. "It is like no substance we have ever seen. It seems thicker than any mist. It is the very essence of corruption. Watch!"

He lowered the vial to the bar, and pulled off its crystalline stopper. Black air flowed down like a fog, then began to surround a stoneware mug. But it did not spread as a fog would. Instead, the inky darkness moved like an animal, coiling like a snake, filled with unknowable purpose. As soon as it touched the mug, the ink rushed around it, gripped it, and then began to seep into the stoneware as if it were a sponge.

The mug suddenly...shifted. The stoneware turned into a crablike creature with three claws, seven legs, and a single great eye upon its back.

"By my father's beard!" Sir Bolgrum shouted. He pulled his ax from its sheath, and swung at the tiny monster.

It leapt sideways, fast as a jumping spider, and then scuttled across the table. It leapt onto a peasant's arm, ripped with a claw, and tore open the peasant's hand. Blood flooded out of a ragged wound, and the man screamed. He hurled the monster back onto the bar, and it landed with a sound like a mug thumping down.

The innkeeper's tabby cat had been sitting upon an ale keg behind the bar, apparently napping, but now like any fine mouser upon seeing something small scuttling about, it pounced upon the creature.

The strange crab grabbed the cat's legs with three separate claws, and bones snapped. The cat yowled, and tried to bite down upon the creature's head, but the stoneware crab was too hard to pierce.

The crab's claws kept working, snipping into the cat's flesh like shears, crunching through bone.

Sir Bolgrum slammed a fist on the crab, and it shattered into several pieces that skittered across the table and went still.

The crab lay dead, broken, in two dozen pieces.

Rath could see no proper guts or innards or muscles in the monster. Instead the thing's broken limbs were white inside, like baked clay, covered with a brown glaze, like mere crockery.

The innkeeper's wife grabbed her cat, and instantly wrapped it with her apron, trying to staunch its bleeding wounds.

"I'm sorry," the king told the innkeeper's wife. "I had no idea what that damned air would do. Ever it is thus: that which it does not destroy, it alters. There are new things in the world, new races of creatures, new plants. From the far north to the distant south, these storms have begun to rage. What news I have is as sparse as it is grim. If we do not find the source of this evil, I fear what might become of us."

Rath pondered what the king had told him, and what he hadn't. Saving the princess was one thing, but the people of this realm needed so much more. He would need to solve this mystery—discover the source of the chaos storms.

Rath was hardly more than a boy. Solving such mysteries seemed beyond him. This was a worthy work for the king's wizards, and even they might not be equal to the task. Yet he longed to find an answer.

"You said that the orcs have your daughter in a flying prison. But how did she get there? Did the orcs that take her sprout wings?" He asked the question half as a joke. With what he'd just seen, flying orcs sounded quite...possible.

"The creature that took her was no orc," the king said, as he held his palms out, a sign that he was giving all the answer that he could. "Her guards heard her scream two nights ago. They burst in and saw... *something*—a creature of shadow, bearing her away. It wore armor beneath robes of black, and it held Arriannis in its arms as it floated out an open window, and into the clouds. That was two nights ago, in the dark of the moon.

"We have searched the bestiaries to learn the creature's name, but have done so in vain. This is nothing from our world."

Rath pondered. A shadow, like the black ether that the king had freed from the jar? Could it be that the substance in that storm really did have a consciousness, a will?

"Mystery piled on enigma," Sir Bolgrum mused. "There is some deep sorcery here..."

The king eyed Rath, clutched his hands together in supplication. "Please, Dragon Rider, the prison has floated into the canyons above Griffinal."

Rath glanced about at the peasants in the inn, wishing that he could take someone to support him. But none of them would be of help. He felt that chill creep down his spine again, and felt of a surety that he was stepping into a larger world, one more dangerous and terrifying than he'd ever dreamt.

A god had made him a Dragon Rider, stepped in after his death, granted him a new body. Rath suspected that the god had his reasons, that Rath had been called to fight some foe that was beyond the understanding of mortal men.

But this inky darkness unnerved him. Could even a Dragon Rider hope to face it?

Legend said that ancient Dragon Riders were immortal. *Right*, Rath thought, *that's why they've all been dead for more than a thousand years.*

Fear knotted his guts.

The king raised his hands, once again, and sent an image forcefully: an elven girl with skin of bluish white, and hair the color of spun silver. She was a tiny thing. If she'd been human, she might not look more than thirteen. She peered up from the floor of a dark cell, while shadows surrounded her. There was a light coming from her, as insubstantial as starlight. Outside her barred room, True Orcs paced—monsters eight feet tall, even hunched as they were, with yellowed tusks protruding from their lower lips.

Rath's heart pounded. He had never seen a girl so beautiful. In the sending, the king also sent his love for Arriannis, as pure and hot as the heat from a forge. In that instant, Rath loved her, too.

He grabbed a small loaf of brown bread from a basket on the table, and a hunk of goat cheese, so that he could eat as he flew.

"I'm on my way," he announced. Without another word he raced out to the street, leapt onto Shofarun's back, and urged the beast into the air.

People poured out of the inn behind him, shouting in surprise, some begging to come with him, others crying "Fare thee well." Loudest of all he heard Sir Bolgrum, in his gruff voice, demanding, "Come back, you fool! You can't do this without me."

He did not need them. His heart was pounding too hard. This was not a job that a common mortal could handle. He would return for the dwarf later. He dared not keep Arriannis waiting.

JAMES ENGE is the author of *Blood of Ambrose* (which was nominated for the World Fantasy Award), *This Crooked Way*, and *The Wolf Age*. His current project is the trilogy *A Tournament of Shadows*, which is about to see completion with the forthcoming publication of *The Wide World's End* (slated to appear in winter 2015). His short fiction has appeared in Black Gate, at Every Day Fiction, in Swords and Dark Magic, and elsewhere. He is a lecturer in classical languages and literature at a medium-sized public university in northwest Ohio. He's on Facebook as james.enge and on Twitter as @jamesenge.

SNOW WOLF AND EVENING WOLF
James Enge

There was a man called Evening Wolf. No one knew his parents. He came out of the east and settled at Ulfstad in Iceland. Iceland was newly discovered then and there was plenty of good land. Evening Wolf worked hard, dealt shrewdly and became rich. He would rise early each morning to go out and direct his workers. He worked all day himself. Toward evening when people began to grow sleepy, he would become bad-tempered and snarled at anyone who spoke to him, his eyes red as blood. People left him alone and he would go to bed. Some said this was why he was called Evening Wolf; some said there were other reasons.

~~*~*

There was a man called Snow Wolf. His father was Iron-Grim Hvitason, who farmed at Hvitaness in Westfarthing. Iron-Grim is not named in *The Book of Land-Taking*, and the reason is this: men say that the Hvitasons were already settled in Iceland when the first people from Norway arrived.

Snow Wolf was illegitimate; his mother was a concubine that Iron-Grim brought back from a viking-raid into Ireland. Iron-Grim had no other children, and when he and his ship were lost at sea Snow Wolf took Hvitaness as the only heir.

Snow Wolf was a capable and friendly man, well-respected by his neighbors. He was something below average height; he had a round head and dark hair, as the Irish do. There was one strange thing about him: toward winter, his hair would turn white. Then he would leave his stead in the hands of his wife and a steward and go away. Men said he travelled in southern lands, for when asked he would say he had been "chasing the sun." Otherwise he never discussed his travels, but he often returned from them with gold.

~~*~*

One morning, not long before dawn, Snow Wolf awoke with the feeling it would soon snow. He left the sleeping closet quietly, that he might not disturb his wife, and stepped almost as carefully around his henchmen who were sleeping in the central hall, along the pit where the embers of last night's fire still smoked. He went out the front door and, standing before the house, looked into the sky. Light was beginning to rise in the east, but the sky was still the dark radiant blue of predawn.

The sky was clear, but Snow Wolf's feeling became a certainty. It would snow soon. He must leave, or he would change.

Suddenly he had another feeling—as if a spirit standing behind him had whispered, *You will not escape the change this year.*

75

Then he did hear someone behind him. Snow-white hairs rising on the back of his neck, he turned. His wife was standing at the door of the house.

"I'll be leaving today," he told her.

She looked at him sadly. "I knew it would be soon. Your hair has been foam-white for a week."

From among the things he might have said, he said this: "You were to tell me."

For a moment she said nothing. Then she whispered, so low he could hardly hear her words, "Stay with me this year. Don't go away. I miss you so."

He knew that she took other men while he was away. But, though this hurt him, he did not blame her. He knew it made her unhappy, too. And: he had loved her because her blood was hot, like summer, like the south. That was why he had chosen her.

It was his blood that he blamed: the blood that brought the change.

"It's for you I go," he said, knowing she would misunderstand. (No one who had witnessed the change had ever survived.)

"We don't need the gold," she said desperately, misunderstanding. "It's you that I need."

If he could have sung to her, as he sang when the change came upon him, then he might have explained. But he could not sing, he could not explain: all he could do was say.

"I will leave before nightfall," he said.

She turned and went back into the house.

Before sunset, he said to the spirit standing behind him.

Too late, the spirit sang. *Too late: you will not escape the change.*

Snow Wolf knew the spirit, which he recognized as his own, was right. But the man within him was still stronger than the other. He might fail. He would still try.

~~*~*

Snow Wolf left Hvitaness and went to a place among the Westfjords. Trading ships were still there and he took passage on one to Norway. But a storm blew out of the south and east, driving the ship against the lee shore of Snaefells Strand. The ship broke on the rocks and the dark blue sea poured in. But Snow Wolf was taken up by the waves and thrown alone onto the shore. If any others from the trading ship survived, they do not come into this story.

Snow Wolf lay on the shore for part of a day. He had broken one leg and a shoulder in the wreck of the trading ship and could hardly move. Before sunset some people came down from Ulfstad to the shore. They found Snow Wolf and carried him back to Ulfstad between them. They put him to bed in a servants' sleephouse and tended his wounds.

Evening Wolf was displeased when he found what his servants had done. He did not like strangers or beggars, he said, nor servants who wasted his stores and spent his money. (Because it was clear the shipwrecked stranger would have to stay the winter.) And when he heard Snow Wolf's name his face became terrible to see and he snarled like a dog.

His servants knew it was no use talking to him in his evening mood so they left him alone. The next day Evening Wolf grudgingly gave out that the stranger could stay. But his eyes were red as blood as he spoke, and it was obvious he would have preferred it otherwise.

From that day Evening Wolf became increasingly bad-tempered with his own people, prone to sudden rages and little given to useful work. He spent much of his time pacing around the garth of the stead, and especially around the sleephouse where Snow Wolf stayed. He sniffed the air constantly and complained many times of a stench, but people paid no attention to this.

One day, about two weeks after Snow Wolf's arrival, Evening Wolf was in the main hall of Ulfstad talking with a neighbor who had come to get some advice. (Evening Wolf was shrewd and capable; he was always ready with advice or any kind of support for those he considered his friends.)

The neighbor, Nord of Nordstad, was sitting in the hall before the open front door, for it was one of the last really warm days; Evening Wolf was opposite him. They were discussing the matter in hand when suddenly Evening Wolf looked out the door with an expression of sheer hatred.

"He stinks," snarled Evening Wolf.

Nord looked out of the door also. He saw a small well-knit man with snow-white hair and beard taking a few limping steps in the yard. He guessed this was Evening Wolf's unwelcome guest, of whom he never ceased to complain.

This was the first time Snow Wolf had walked since his bones were broken, and his skin was beaded with sweat in the cool sunlight. But his face was calm. He walked from the sleephouse to the garth, then walked slowly along the garth, supporting himself with one hand. Nord admired his determination (the exercise was obviously causing him great pain) but did not say so to Evening Wolf.

"His sweat stinks," the red-eyed man continued. "His piss stinks. His shit stinks."

Nord did not say anything to this.

"I go out and piss by the sleephouse every night," Evening Wolf said confidingly, "but it does no good. It still stinks of him. I think he's been pissing around the yard. If I catch him at it, I'll kill him."

Nord began to think he had better go. It seemed as if the evening mood were coming over his host, though it was hardly past midday.

"You know why he came here?" Evening Wolf asked.

"Men say he was shipwrecked," Nord replied.

Evening Wolf laughed derisively. "He came to take my bitches and kill my cattle. Kill and eat, kill and eat, that's all he understands, all he wants. And he wants my followers, too. There's many a man of them capering at his heels already. The young ones, the stupid ones. They'll find out. I'll rip his throat out, and then they'll know the bark and the bite and the blood like never before. Kill and eat. Kill and eat. Kill and eat. They'll kill 'til they're sick of killing, eat 'til they're sick of eating—"

He was shouting by this time, having risen to his feet. Nord rose also, but could do nothing other than stand and stare.

Then Snow Wolf approached. He limped over to the front door of the house. Evening Wolf fell silent. It was the first time they had faced each other. Snow Wolf spoke through the open door.

He greeted Evening Wolf and Nord politely and by name. "My name," he added, "is Snow Wolf, but I would be only a dead dog were it not for the hospitality of Evening Wolf the magnificent. I am indeed grateful. I shall not trouble him any longer, now that I can keep to my feet. My humblest thanks to Evening Wolf the magnificent, whose wisdom, courage and generosity are famous throughout Westfarthing." And he held out his hands and lowered his head in an odd gesture of submission.

He did all this seriously, without the slightest trace of mockery or sarcasm. But it was not, Nord thought, as if he were really being humble. That proud white head was incapable of real humility, of real submission. To Nord it seemed rather as if he were being magnanimous, trying to allay Evening Wolf's insane anger for his host's own good, no matter what it cost Snow Wolf in the esteem of those standing nearby. (For Evening Wolf's raving had drawn quite a crowd of open-mouthed workers.)

But the gesture of submission seemed only to increase Evening Wolf's rage. He advanced through the open doorway in curt deliberate steps. "*Get* out! *Get* out!" He was shouting in short staccato bursts. "Go! Go! Go! *Get* out! Go!"

Snow Wolf bowed his head even lower and backed away slowly.

Evening Wolf screamed, like a hunting bird or a berserk. He leapt at the retreating man as if to attack him. But Nord and many others rushed after Evening Wolf and held him down as Snow Wolf retreated to the sleephouse.

Evening Wolf was screaming and snarling and snapping with his teeth like a mad dog. Then towards evening he grew more quiet, and they left him alone as usual.

Nord stopped by the sleephouse before he left to return home. Snow Wolf had fallen unconscious on returning to the sleephouse and had not awakened yet. His broken leg was bent at an odd angle that reminded Nord of a dog's leg.

"Tell him when he wakes," Nord said to the servants who slept there, "it will be better for him if he leaves here—better for him and for your master. Bring him to Nordstad when he wakes; he can winter with my people there."

Riding home, he almost regretted this offer. For there was something strange about Snow Wolf, a sanity stranger than Evening Wolf's insane fury. But he owed much to Evening Wolf; if he could keep his old friend from the crime and shame of having murdered a guest, it would be a very small repayment. So he was well content by the time he reached the garth of Nordstad. But his meditation and his content came to nothing in the end, for Snow Wolf never went to Nordstad and Nord is now out of this story.

~~*~*

When Snow Wolf awoke it was already long after dark. He woke to the heavy complex rhythm of the servants' breathing in the dark sleephouse. He felt his broken leg and decided it was strong enough to carry him. It would have to...

Evening Wolf's jealous rage proved that the change was very close upon him now. Indeed, Snow Wolf could feel it himself; he had almost forgotten why he had ever wanted to escape the change. He no longer wanted to.

But, if the change came upon him here, it would destroy many of those who had so foolishly saved his life. He did not want that. His kind and their kind were enemies; one would prevail and the other would be destroyed. But Snow Wolf did not want to destroy them. So he had to depart and go into the unpeopled lands, before the snow fell and the change came.

Carefully stepping over those sleeping by him, he walked over to the door, unbarred and opened it. The darkness outside was radiant with moonlight and the air was bitterly cold. He drank down the deadly air like beer and felt the change almost start within him in response.

Then he became aware of the other; a hot feral stink rode the air. He glanced to one side and saw a hunched animal shape slinking toward the sleephouse. Its narrow doglike face was just visible in the half-shadows and its eyes in the moonlight glowed red as bright fresh blood. Then, without a single sound, Evening Wolf leapt.

Snow Wolf slammed the door and threw his weight against it. Instantly the door was shaken by the impact of the leaping wolf. Snow Wolf, feet braced, managed to hold it shut and when the attacking wolf had retreated to strike again he lowered the bar and set it against the door.

He was safe. A wolf's strength is to pursue or flee; its ferocity is to rend and feed; its cunning is to seek out the hidden. No wolf or werewolf is fitted to carry out a siege operation against a house with locked doors and shuttered windows.

Snow Wolf returned to his pallet and slept. He was still unsteady on his feet and he guessed he would get little rest tomorrow. As he dropped off he could still hear the wolf, snarling in frustration at the barred door.

~~*~*

Snow Wolf awoke before dawn and before anyone else. He made his way quietly to the door, unbarred and opened it.

Evening Wolf, in human form, lay naked across a threshold thick with morning frost. His eyes were open, bloodshot and staring, but he was obviously not awake.

He was not dead, either; Snow Wolf knew that from his smell. It would take something chillier than a morning's frost to kill one such as Evening Wolf. He stepped over his naked senseless host, speculating on what the servants would say when they found him there. Would there be surprise? Or had it happened before? Would it be an occasion for retelling old stories, remembering old rumors, asking old questions?

It was not his business, anyway. He climbed over the garth and walked away from Ulfstad, north and east, toward the stony unpeopled lands.

~~*~*

Steam and the comforting sheeplike reek of his people surrounding him, Evening Wolf awoke at noon. He was warm. The dry bitter stink of his rival, the cold heavy presence of an alien wolf in his territory, was gone. He sighed in content. Perhaps it had been a dream. Or perhaps he had killed Snow Wolf last night and had not remembered it yet.

He sat up. He was naked in bed. Several of his servants were standing nearby, with stiff expressions on their faces.

Then he knew. Without a word spoken he knew. They had found him naked and unconscious, scratch marks on the door of the servants' sleephouse. The last he remembered was lying in front of it, snarling and whining.

"Where is he?" he shouted.

There was no need to explain whom he meant. "He left sometime during the night," one of the servants said.

"Gone?" Evening Wolf snarled. "Escaped? No!"

That *no* was a hunting call, a howl that would gather his kin so that they could hunt the stranger, the victim, the prey. But the servants were not his kin. They stared at him in sheeplike confusion. They neither wagged their tails nor offered to touch noses. They must be insane.

"Bring me clothing!" he barked.

They paused and glanced at each other. Their master was clearly ill. Nord had been sent for, as well as other respected men of the region, who might be able to tell them what should be done. But these had not yet arrived.

The servants brought him clothing, blue as death: tunic, trousers and cloak.

He dressed in front of them, pulled on his boots and walked out of the house. He took no weapons and no provisions. He leapt over the garth and loped away, east and north, toward the stony unpeopled land.

He had good hunting that day. The dry cold stink of his prey clung to the blue bitterly cold rocks, the thick dry turf, (gray with apprehension at winter's approach). The wind, too, was rich with the scent. The blue clouds covering the sky threatened snow; he remembered that his prey was crippled and laughed.

In late afternoon the trail crossed a scrub wood; the thick dankness of the scent proclaimed that his quarry had rested there awhile. Some of the wood had been cut and broken and he found a few scraps of torn cloth. He guessed that Snow Wolf had fashioned a brace for his hurt leg, so that he could travel more quickly. Evening Wolf laughed again. He liked a clever rival. Snow Wolf was clever, in a way. But he was not clever enough. It was stupid to be weak, clever to be strong.

He continued the chase. Not much later he spotted his prey, hobbling among the upthrust rocks and ice-sheer slopes of the broken land.

He shouted. He saw Snow Wolf's white head bow down. The prey scurried even harder into the wasteland of broken stone. But it was too late for him, Evening Wolf told himself happily. Dusk was rising into the sky; the sun had set behind the dense blue clouds. Evening Wolf felt his mortal veins pulse with the magic of the change.

There was always a brief emptiness when the change came. Evening Wolf had been running on two human feet among the high shattered stones of the waste land. Now he was rolling on his back, paws stretched out imploringly toward the dark starless sky, a human scream dying in his wolfish throat. His blue clothing lay in rags about him.

He rolled to his four feet and tested the air. His prey had made some headway while the change was on him, but not much. He loped off in pursuit, soon catching up with Snow Wolf.

Evening Wolf began to sing, that music of the werewolf more demanding than the strictest skaldic discipline, where word and music are one, the kennings as intricately complex and radiantly clear as polished gems. He sang readily, with practiced skill, as his padded feet traced a subtle shifting path among the rocks that lay roughly parallel with the gasping Snow Wolf's course. But he broke off his song with dismay when he found he had abruptly lost Snow Wolf's scent.

The wind had steadily risen, driving hard through the broken passages of rock. But this was not a trick of the wind. Evening Wolf still caught the trace-scent of Snow Wolf's path, the places he had passed. But the live smoking scent of the prey now eluded the predator.

Evening Wolf leapt forward, running a swift arcing path ahead and around the end of Snow Wolf's path. But the prey still hid from him. Grimly Evening Wolf continued the arc until he came almost full circle, crossing Snow Wolf's trail. He abandoned the arc and followed the trail step by step. As he ran, nose to the ground, he kept his eyes with human cunning on the high broken pinnacles of rock on either side.

Suddenly he was assaulted by a still pool of prey-scent, thick in the air, smoking with life. His eyes snapped down to the ground, where a pit yawned blackly before him. Two white hands were scrabbling scrabbling feebly at the verge.

Evening Wolf snarled and lunged. The hands let go their precarious grip and disappeared in darkness. Evening Wolf heard Snow Wolf fall gasping to the ground.

This was the answer, then: blind with fear, the prey had run straight into this pit and was now trapped there. Evening Wolf laughed and, laughing, wove his laughter into a wolfish song of triumph. He knew his prey could not survive a night's cold in the pit. It would remain there and die. It would come out and fight. Either way the victory was his. He would kill and eat. He sang on.

Meanwhile the wind was still rising. Dark shapes moved among the clouds.

~~*~*

Snow Wolf lay at the bottom of the pit. His improvised brace had come apart on his first fall and his leg had broken again on the second. Clearly he could flee no more: this business was almost over. A cold turbulent peace, not unlike a winter storm, began to settle on his heart.

But there was one more chance. Evening Wolf was not now fully wolf any more than he had been fully human by day. If that lingering human part could be reached, perhaps he could convince Evening Wolf to go away. It was a feeble hope, but the one remaining to him now.

"Listen," Snow Wolf shouted to his enemy, "listen to me. I am a shape-changer, like you. You have guessed this. When the snow falls I'll change—"

You are not like me, Evening Wolf sang. He went on to observe, in precise ululating syllables, that he himself was a master wolf, proud and unconquerable, whereas Snow Wolf was a pale castrated dog that the pig-tenders used as a woman every ninth night.

"The human creatures," Snow Wolf continued, "they have legends of ice giants... in the shape of wolves. My ancestors are such. They run now in the sky, hunting the sun and the moon. You cannot expect... you cannot expect..."

He was struck dumb by the enormity of the explanation he was trying to make.

Evening Wolf interrupted, in fine voice, suggesting that it was not necessary for Snow Wolf to keep squeaking; it would be easy enough to locate him by the scent of his relaxed bowels.

Snow Wolf made no retort to this, though Evening Wolf paused for him to make one. There was no point in talking anymore. The human in Snow Wolf felt weak, very weak. But all the time he was stronger and stronger.

~~*~*

Evening Wolf, weary of abusing his passive enemy, began to expound on his own virtues. He allowed that Snow Wolf might have stood high among such white dog-sheep as were native to Iceland. But he himself was a different breed. Descended in long line from the gigantic dire-wolves who reigned pre-eminent in Europe before it was known to humankind, Evening Wolf had many illustrious ancestors and he named a few of these to Snow Wolf and to the snowthick night sky.

He told of his own heroic birth, during the collapse of Roman power in Central Europe. Those were good times, rich in blood, in action and in food. But the chaos simmered down to a long wasting anarchy–without war and its harvest of carrion, without peace and its rich preyable increase. Famine came, and after it plague. Humans and other cattle grew thin and scarce; live ones were not worth killing and the carrion was not safe to eat. Those were the bad times and many of Evening Wolf's people died in them.

Then Evening Wolf had the courage to rise up and go alone, far from the familiar paths and the known hunting grounds, sacred from thousands of centuries of slaughtered prey. He fed among the steppes of Russia, and won names of terror from the free farmers around Novgorod. Then he went north and west, drawn by his destiny, and hunted among the dense woods of the Scandinavian Peninsula. After many lifetimes of cattle he heard of a new land in the northern sea. People were fleeing there to escape the conqueror, King Harald, the first king to unite all Norway.

Evening Wolf followed them. King Harald was waging war ceaselessly, and that was good. But he promised peace, and that was bad. Evening Wolf followed the Norse to Iceland and established himself as a great landholder and chieftain. It was a land of opportunity and Evening Wolf made the most of his opportunities.

Now he had great herds of cattle: sheep, pigs, humans, cows. He killed among them when he chose. He rewarded them when he chose. They knew their lives and their deaths rode in the corners of his jaws. That was why Snow Wolf had been a fool to challenge his supremacy. They feared him and loved him. They would never leave his rule.

I am a god among them, Snow Wolf! Evening Wolf howled, throwing his head back exultantly to hurl his voice straight up into the wind-driven snow. *I am a god to my people!*

Likely, likely, very likely, Snow Wolf sang in the pit. *Gods are good eating,* he added reflectively.

~~*~*

The man in Snow Wolf had died a seasonable death, as the snow settled down like a shroud around the boasting Evening Wolf. Snow Wolf's pity for his enemy was equally dead; he would be merciless, soulless, bloodless for a long bright season until summer returned, if summer ever returned. His jaws clamped and clamped again in ecstasy at the thought of tasting the sun's golden blood.

~~*~*

Evening Wolf shifted his stance uneasily as he looked down into the pit. There was light there now, two circles of ice-blue light that were Snow Wolf's eyes. The rest of the white wolf's appearance was oddly unclear, shifting in outline constantly like a cloud or a snow-drift. The voice, too, was oddly disconcerting. It was a wolf's voice, clear and true... too clear, too bell-like. It hardly differed in sound from the voice of the winter storm, singing on the rocks around him. It had breath but no blood in it; it did not have the hot meaty tone of a voice from a living throat.

Snow Wolf sang.

A god, a god, a god, he sang, with mockingly curt barks. *Very likely. Gods come from the south and east, like the sun. Many have come, from the south and east, to Iceland. We were here before. We were here when the sun itself first crossed the sea. The Firbolgi came, the Vanir came, the Aesir came, the Coranians came: we were here. We killed and ate them all.*

Evening Wolf began to back away from the pit, but it was too late for him. Snow Wolf—a wolf-shaped patch of blizzard with blue burning eyes—leapt out of the pit and seized Evening Wolf by the throat with teeth the color of lightning. Snow Wolf's jaws clamped shut and Evening Wolf died. Snow Wolf's jaws opened and Evening Wolf fell to the ground and shattered like glass. The dead wolf's body had been frozen solid by Snow Wolf's wintry touch.

Snow Wolf stepped into the air and ascended swiftly to the sky, his howling indistinguishable from the winter winds.

84

The others had already begun to gather in the appointed place beyond the clouds: his brothers and sisters, his ancestors, those cold inimical spirits of nature, eternally hostile to gods and other mortals. The snow wolves formed two great packs to continue their perennial quest: to hunt down and kill the sun and the moon, so extinguishing all light and hope for mortal life.

Snow Wolf ran west and south, beyond the horizon, baying after the sun that had already fled the winter sky.

~~*~*

It was a long winter and a hard one for Hvitaness. Snow and storms and bitter cold did much damage; many animals died and the planting was late. It was late, too, before Snow Wolf returned, his hair still streaked with winter's white. He seemed weary and dispirited when he surveyed the damage done to the stead, but said nothing about it. Perhaps this was because, on his travels, he had won a great wealth of raw red gold (which he poetically referred to as "a few mouthfuls of the sun"), and this was of more value than the dead animals or the poor crop that summer promised.

His wife had fallen in love with a great chieftain who lived nearby. She often went to visit him, and one day she did not return again to Hvitaness. That day, in early evening, Snow Wolf sat alone in his darkening hall. He wondered if a god would ever come across the sea that he and his kindred would be unable to kill and eat. But if one ever did, it is not part of this story.

JANE LINDSKOLD is a New York Times best-selling, internationally published author of over sixty short stories and twenty-some novels. Her most famous works include the acclaimed "Firekeeper" fantasy series, which began with *Through Wolf's Eyes* and concluded with *Wolf's Blood*, and the "Breaking the Wall" series.

Jane was living with the late, great Roger Zelazny, when he died in 1995 after a battle with colorectal cancer. Our cause is very close to Jane's heart.

KNIGHT'S ERRAND
Jane Lindskold

The worst thing about taking out sorcerers is the clean-up afterwards. Seriously, during a fight you have some idea what to expect—it might be fireballs or lightning strikes or bolts of ice; they might summon demons or elementals or maybe a host of undead—but the basics are the same. They're going to try to make sure the one who dies isn't them.

My job is to make certain their heartfelt desire doesn't come true, that, instead, they are the ones who end up as bleeding corpses or heaps of earth (some of the ones who've played around with longevity magics skip the dead body and go directly to dust) or get transformed into ravening insane monsters (which I then have to kill all over again).

It's the aftermath that always makes me regret taking up this job. There's a good feeling to finishing off someone whose goal is global domination or some other ambitious bit of cultural reform which—no matter how grandiloquent the speech—always boils down to "my world, my rules." Even when I was a boy, I didn't like bullies. That didn't change when I got older and their rationalizations got fancier.

But, as I said a moment ago, it's the clean-up that makes the job unpredictable. Site inspection and survey became a part of the job back when I was just getting started as a knight errant. There had been too many instances when something nasty crawled out of the ruins of a collapsed stronghold or seemingly deserted castle. If it wasn't something animate, then the trouble came from enchanted items left about the place. No matter how fraught with evil the history of the location, it didn't take many years for the brave and the bold—or the stupid and the greedy—to start poking around. They'd emerge wearing a ring that turned them into a berserk ogre when the moon was a waning crescent or brandishing a sword that demanded the blood of a virgin every fortnight. Or they'd turn loose the dragon that had been sealed in the caverns deep below the sorcerer's retreat or unbottle the djinn or…

You get the idea, right? It isn't pretty.

So there I was, high up in a tower, sorting through the alchemical lab and magical research facility owned until very recently by Myron the Magnificent.

(Why do sorcerers always live in towers anyhow? Is it from a deeply buried sense of inferiority? I can understand the desire for isolation. If you were doing the sort of things they like to do, you'd want to be isolated, too. And anyhow, it's easier to believe you're lord of all you survey if there aren't that many people around, outside of those who work for you. But towers? Even for the ladies?)

I hadn't brought my assistants along with me for this part of the job. Myron the Magnificent had actually been a rather mild type as sorcerers go, more into research and fabrication than the usual grandiose power dreams. If it hadn't been for his liking of such unsavory ingredients for his potions—and how many of those ingredients came from living creatures, including humans—he might have been left undisturbed to work away in the highest reaches of his porphyry tower amid his chosen desolate mountain fastness.

(If you're wondering, it was the incident with the four newborn infants and the basket of kittens that got me called in. Nasty stuff.)

Even though I'd left my assistants getting some well-earned rest and repair, I wasn't exactly alone. I had ridden out on my dark chestnut warhorse, Biter, as nasty-tempered a mount as ever decided to take out his resentment over being gelded on anyone he could get his hooves and teeth into. I also had brought along Spike and Tyke, a pair of war dogs who, in addition to being two of the fiercest hounds to wear spiked leather collars, had also been trained to sniff out magic. The final member of my entourage was Turbulent, a gyrfalcon who was both battle-trained and a remarkably intelligent message carrier.

Spike and Tyke had already done their part, discovering at least one hidden door I would have missed and a staff concealed as one of the supports of a canopy bed. They found a lot of other stuff, too. I'm just giving them credit for what I would have missed.

They didn't miss the little box that would turn out to be the source of all my troubles. I didn't miss it either. I just had no idea that what it held would be such a pain to deal with.

But I'm getting ahead of myself. Let's get back to that room at the top of the tower. I was there, not wearing my armor, because it's really easy to break things when you're encased in bulky steel clothes, and there was a lot of glassware, mirrors, ceramics, and other breakables in that round-walled room. I might not be wearing armor, but I was hung with enough amulets and talismans that I was nearly as well-protected—at least against the sort of threats I expected.

I was holding a box in my left hand. It wasn't much bigger than what you'd use to hold a deck of playing cards. The box itself was wood—teak, I think—but it was so heavily inlaid with slivers of mother-of-pearl and ebony set in complex geometric designs that you could be forgiven for missing the underlying reddish-brown. I'd just finished saying a series of disabling charms over the box and had undone the lock with a bone key that on a ring I had removed from Myron's body before it was consigned to the fire. Next I tilted back the lid and looked inside. I wasn't really surprised to find that this box contained another box. Sorcerers like things like that. Not only do the layers frustrate thieves, they keep the contents from rattling about and getting scratched.

Again I went through the routine necessary to open this box (which was of ebony, inlaid with teak and mother-of-pearl)without getting myself burned or electrified or whatever nasty curse had been left for those making unauthorized entry. This time, I selected a different key from Myron's ring, a tiny one, delicate as a soap bubble, carved from alabaster. Despite its apparent fragility, the key turned in the lock without snapping. I lifted the lid, worried I'd find yet another box— Myron seemed to be a box-within-a-box-within-an-eggshell-within-a-kernel-of-grain sort of fellow. To my relief, I found instead a piece of plush green velvet wrapped around something irregular enough in shape that I was pretty certain I wouldn't find another box.

I bet myself that it would be a ring—a ring set with a dark emerald that had been carved into the semblance of something reptilian and nasty. What I saw when I unfolded the last bit of velvet was a white stone so brilliant that it was almost translucent. It wasn't set in a ring either. Instead it was shaped into a small, not very well-crafted carving of a duck. At least that was my first impression. There were wings sweeping back and meeting at a point, just like those of a duck or swan when it takes to the water. The head was all wrong for a duck. Instead of a beak or bill or whatever it is that ducks have, there was a bulky head with what appeared to be small horns. The area around the tail was wrong, too. There was something frothy there that I took to be a representation of the water this mutant duck was swimming on.

Striding over to the window, I held the carving up to the light. Just like that, my perspective changed and I saw the carving for what it really was. It wasn't a duck at all; it was a winged horse. The carver had rendered it with its legs folded under it as if it had lain down to sleep. The neck had a proud arch and the head—now that I wasn't trying to make it into a duck's—was fine-boned and delicate, with flaring nostrils. What I'd taken for horns were actually small ears, pricked and alert. The frothy stuff was the winged horse's tail.

Awed by the craftsmanship in this tiny carving, I inspected it more closely. The stone seemed to be some sort of marble, lightly veined with ivory and palest grey. The unknown sculptor used these veins to suggest shadows and bring out highlights. The end result was that the stone looked more purely white that it would have if it were all one color. Even though the winged horse was not painted in any way, it looked so realistic that I wouldn't have been surprised if it unfolded its wings and rose to its hooves at that very moment.

For a fleeting second, I considered withholding this piece from the roster listing all the goodies, dangerous or not, that I had found. Usually, my contract stipulated that my fee included my pick of what I'd found, but there are restrictions. If something was ruled too dangerous, too unpredictable, or too valuable, then I must graciously make another selection or take compensation in currency. I didn't need to have been at this job for as long as I had to know that this little carving was going to be ruled too valuable. Just the skill with which it was made would raise the price, but I could also feel the magic shivering off it in waves.

I was about to rewrap the carving in its green velvet shroud when I noticed that the sky, which had been perfectly clear when I took the carving to the window so I could get a look at it in sunlight, was darkening. Roiling clouds in shades of storm grey and blackest night were swirling, creating a whirlpool current that was moving to center—no great shock– on Myron's purple porphyry tower.

At the same moment, I felt motion in my hand. The tiny winged horse was stirring. I know I said that the carving was so realistic that I wouldn't have been surprised if it unfolded its wings and got to its hooves. That's just a figure of speech. The fact is, sophisticated as I was in a wide variety of magics, I *was* surprised, so surprised that my hand opened of its own accord. I would have dropped the carving, except that it spread its wings and glided to the floor. As it did so, it began to grow. When I recovered from my shock, I wasn't looking down at a tiny white carving of a winged horse, I was looking up into the face of the full-sized animal.

The winged horse was muscular and powerful in a manner the carving had only managed to suggest. Its muzzle shaded to bluish-grey, as did the tips of its ears. Otherwise, it was a study in white on white with one striking exception. The eyes that now met mine were dark brown and so typically horsy that they seemed all the more exotic.

"Are you the knight for whom I have waited?" asked the winged horse in a voice that resonated like trumpet calls on the field of battle. "Then don your armor of silk and spider webs. Equip yourself with the Lance of True Valor and the Sword of Righteous Might. Then leap astride and we will sally forth to win the day from darkness."

"Whoa!" I said, somewhat unwisely, for those pricked ears flattened as if I'd spoken an obscenity. "I mean, prithee, slow a moment. I am indeed a knight, sword-kissed near twenty years ago, and hardened in many battles. Yet I know not of what you speak."

The winged horse snorted. "This is no time for talk! The dark clouds swirl. The celestial portal will gape wide and my enemy will be upon us!"

I'm still not sure how he managed what he did next. I mean, the room had windows, but they were by no means large enough for even a pony to pass through, much less this magnificent destrier, even without the added breadth of his white-feathered wings. But somehow he worked it so that in one breath he was in the tower room, a threat to shelves of delicate crucibles and retorts. Then, in the next breath, he was outside, flapping his wings only enough to hold his position, while angling his head so that he could better inspect the ominous windstorm above us.

"Before he set me in safe haven," the winged horse said, "the wise mage Myron showed me the demon horse who would threaten the free skies, not too far in the future. He promised to find me a knight who would join me in battle, and that he himself would use his magics to properly armor and equip my rider. Thrice he has woken me so that he might do some further enchantment. Each time he showed me what he had created to assure me of his good faith."

"Uh... Why did you let him shrink you and lock you in a box if you weren't certain of his good faith?" I asked.

"I did not doubt him," the winged horse replied. "However, he needed to draw some of my power from me to assure that what he created would be sympathetic with my essence. I believe he desired to reassure me that the pain was not for naught."

This was beginning to sound very bad, especially given what I knew of the sort of magics Myron the Magnificent had specialized in. This winged horse reminded me of certain bone-headed knights I'd known, the sort who still believed in fighting an enemy head on, or letting him reclaim his wand after you'd gone to all sorts of effort to knock it from his hand, or other such chivalric nonsense.

I knew that sort all too well. I'd been like that as a young knight, my shoulder ever tingling with the press of my liege lord's blade, my ears ringing with his exhortation to be a noble knight and true. I'd held on to my idealism through my first few quests, right up until the day my devotion to chivalry had gotten my best girl and three knights, including my mentor—in those days I'd have called them my "lady love" and "boon companions"—killed in a particularly ugly way. Now I still fight and I like to think I fight for the right, but I'm a lot more cynical and a lot harder to fool. I'm also not terribly inclined to trust, but there was something about this white winged horse that made me trust him—even as I was suspecting that his idealism might get us both killed.

From the base of the tower, I heard Spike and Tyke barking wildly. Biter was bugling. Fighting against increasingly wild winds, Turbulent soared up unbidden to request orders. My animals didn't speak—not like this winged creature I'd unwittingly freed—but they understood both me and each other.

"Take cover, all of you," I commanded Turbulent. "The stable is stone-walled and secure. Get in there and don't come out until I come for you or you know I'm dead."

Turbulent shrieked what might have been agreement or might have been protest. Like I said, I didn't understand them, though they do me. Then she spiraled down and I heard the barks and whinnies cease. I hoped they'd gotten into safety.

I looked over at the winged horse who had been observing the exchange with lively interest. "I just realized," I said, "we can talk to each other. Is that more of Myron's work?"

The winged horse snorted in mild disgust. "Are you not aware that the first winged horse, the legendary Pegasus, was associated with poetry? Indeed, the spring that was created when his hoof struck the rocks of Mount Helicon released the fountain Hippocrene that gave those who drank from it poetic inspiration. How would any of that make sense if he and his kind could not speak?"

I hadn't thought about it, and I wasn't sure the question actually bore thinking about, not with the storm clouds growing darker and the winds more ferocious with every instant.

The winged horse continued, "I am called Halite, son of Skyvaster, of those herds that roam the Impossible Reaches. And you are?"

"Sir Gilroy of Pearl Cove, sworn vassal of King Yeats. I am also called the Lord of Iron," I said, using my full titles for the first time in many years. Knights errant don't usually bother with long introductions. I was about to ask what sort of enemy Halite expected when the center of the windstorm swirled tight, like the pupil of the eye shrinking against sudden light. In the time it took for three fast beats of Halite's wings, the eye of the storm swirled wide again, emitting from its center what at first glance seemed a winged horse as storm-stained and tainted as Halite was white and fair.

Halite bugled an equine challenge and would have risen to do battle, but I nearly fell out of the window, grabbing at his mane to hold him back.

"Take care!" I bellowed against the rising wind. "That's not a normal creature!"

Nor was it… The head was distinctly equine, as were the four slender legs. The remainder was a rising firestorm. The flames were what created the illusion of wings where, in reality, there was nothing but heat eddies, fire, and smoke.

Shaking loose my grip on his mane, Halite continued to rise to the attack. Frantically, I called after him, "You idiot! Weren't you supposed to have a knight with you? Isn't that what Myron told you? Would he have spent all that time creating magical weapons if they weren't important? Don't –" I knew the words were ill-chosen, but they tumbled out all the same, "Don't put the cart before the horse!"

Halite backed air, slowing his advance. "Are you my knight, Sir Gilroy of Pearl Cove, called the Lord of Iron?"

"I certainly am. Get back here. Let me grab…"

I cast my gaze around the heaps of things I'd been sorting and classifying—had it only been a few minutes before? There were several swords, none of very good quality. I chose the flashiest, one with bright diamonds set not only on the hilt but inlaid into the blade as well. I'd already tested it and knew its magics to be of the most minor sort—mostly charms for brilliance and shine. Still, it should impress my idealistic future steed.

I was at a loss for a lance until I remembered the bedpost Spike and Tyke had sniffed out. It lacked the flaring cuff that protected the user's hand on a true lance, but it was sturdy enough. Again, the magics on it were not of much use in and of themselves. A wizard's staff is a versatile item, meant to store magic for future use. This staff had been prepared and strengthened, but the reservoirs were empty.

The armor of silk and spider web provided more of a challenge. I'd seen nothing at all that fit that description, nor did I have time to put on my own plate armor—even if I'd brought it along, which I hadn't, since it takes a squire or two to bolt the stuff on. Moving quickly, I tugged a length of greyish fabric off a table top, slashed a hole for my head, then belted it with one of the sashes that held the window curtains. I thrust the bedpost staff sideways into my makeshift belt. Since the staff was much slimmer and lighter than a true lance, I could just about manage.

So armed and attired, I hoisted myself onto the broad windowsill and, without taking time to think about it, dropped onto Halite's back. I had no saddle or stirrups, of course, but I discovered that I could throw my legs forward in the general area of the withers, where the feathered wings met the equine body. When I bent my knees slightly, I had a fairly secure seat that didn't seem to restrict Halite's ability to use his wings in the least.

The storm-born flame steed had not taken advantage of Halite's retreat to press its own attack. I wondered why until I noticed that during the interval it had acquired a rider—a man-shaped specter built from its own storm stuff and tatters of flame. It was attired as a knight in wispy armor, and bore a lance and long sword. I felt troubled. Despite the rider being almost as ill-defined as its steed, something about it was vaguely familiar. As Halite beat his wings and mounted the air to confront the flaming demon horse, the pair turned to face us.

That's when I recognized other rider as the absolutely, certainly, without-a-doubt, dead—after all, I myself had slain him and put his body to the torch—Myron the Magnificent.

Instantly, I comprehended the sorcerer's plot. He had gulled Halite, imprisoned him under the guise of protecting him, and then drawn from the winged horse the power to destroy him. Nothing calls to like like like, stupid as that sounds. Weapons imbued with a creature's own essence are the most dangerous.

I had no doubt that the lance born by the spectral knight was the actual Lance of True Valor and the sword was the Sword of Righteous Might. I had no idea how armor made from silk and spider web would offer any useful protection, but I had no doubt it would do so.

And here I am, I thought, *bearing the Sword of Shininess, carrying the Lance of Empty Dreams, clad in armor made from a dirty tablecloth. I wonder if I can convince Halite of the wisdom of that old proverb: "Those who fight and run away, live to fight another day?"*

I most sincerely doubted it. Certainly the young man I had been all those years ago wouldn't have been convinced. He'd have spouted words like "coward" and "weak of heart," not to mention "lily-livered" and "unworthy of one's shield."

What to do? Right now I didn't have many options. Halite was charging to the attack, so I'd better get ready to defend. My makeshift equipage lacked a shield. I wished I'd thought to grab one. Still, there was one thing in my favor. I wouldn't be the spectral knight's target. His goal would be to hit Halite as many times as possible, for each strike would do not only bodily damage, but also drain away the winged horse's inherent magic.

(Do I need to stop here to note that, of course, winged horses have magic? There's no way they could fly without it. Graceful as they look, they're just too heavy and bulky.)

Based on what I knew about Myron's magical specializations, I had a pretty good idea what the end result would be. That still insubstantial duo would gain more and more substance until they transformed into some eldritch horror suitable for world domination. Halite would plummet to the earth as nothing more than a drained husk. What would happen to Halite's unscheduled rider would be even less amusing, since he—that is, me—would likely hit while still able to feel the impact.

Beneath me, I could feel the pounding of Halite's mighty heart as he surged upward. The flame-cloud steed was making wide circles as it descended. The specter had readied his lance. I considered matching him, then decided that would be stupid. These weren't lists where we would be barreling toward each other, aiming for shield or breastplate. There would be no dramatic shivering of lances while crowds cheered. Instead there'd likely be a shaft of pointed wood impaled in shining white hide.

The image was so real I could almost see the blood fountaining forth, feel the shudder as my steed staggered in mid-air, wings beating unevenly.

Our opponents swooped upon us in eerie silence. Not even a crackle of flames or the whoosh of raging fire could be heard. Halite was banking, probably so he could snap at the other equine's throat, since he didn't have enough elevation to effectively kick. He seemed oblivious to the threat the lance offered—and maybe he was. If I'd been Myron, I'd have tossed in a charm to make the weapons invisible or at least to seem unimportant to their intended target.

That damned lance was going to go right into Halite's chest if I didn't do something. So I did, even though it was close to suicide. Leaning hard to my right, I grabbed a handful of Halite's long mane. Keeping hold, I tightly wound it around my wrist for good measure. I knew from experience that horses didn't feel as much pain when their manes were pulled as humans do when hair and scalp are involved. I had to hope the same was true for winged horses.

I leaned far out, yelling to Halite, "Turn to the right! The right!" I thought my winged steed might refuse, since that would mean giving up his part in the fight, but apparently my speech about his needing a knight in order to conquer had gone home. He looped far more tightly than I had dared hope. My butt in the air, my hold on my steed maintained by a heel, a leg, and my hand on the mane, I brought the Sword of Shininess down on the Lance of True Valor.

The impact shuddered up my arm. I felt something give and wondered if it was my shoulder. Then I realized it was my sword's blade. Diamonds might be the hardest thing there are—the hardest natural thing, I should say—but they aren't known for flexibility. The blade shattered into myriad sparkling dewdrops, but the one strike had done what I hoped. The tip of the Lance of True Valor had been neatly sliced off. From the severed end spilled a bloody mist that ate its way down the shaft until the lance was gone.

For the first time, our opponents made a sound. The specter shrieked with inarticulate anger as the flame-cloud steed burned the air, rising to where they could regroup.

I found myself wondering if they'd even been aware of me before that. After all, my presence had not been part of the plan—no matter that Halite had been told to expect a knight. The undead—especially those recently alive—are not the smartest or most observant creatures. Likely the specter was running on some pre-set imperative. I had my doubts as to whether that horse of flame and cloud was even really "alive." I suspected it was more akin to a partially created magical item.

I couldn't count on being overlooked to help me next pass. My sword's remaining blade was useless; its brilliance only a glittering memory. I stuffed the remaining length back into the sheath and pulled my lance—really, more of a staff—from my window sash belt.

"Myron only showed me that horrid facsimile of a horse in his scrying mirror. He didn't show the rider," Halite complained indignantly.

This was not the time to tell him that Myron had tricked him in more dangerous ways. I needed my steed strong, his confidence intact—though if I could instill some caution, that wouldn't hurt, either. Clearly, Halite had not recognized Myron's features in the specter. Did he even know the sorcerer was dead?

"Perhaps," I offered, "Myron's vision was less than perfect. He did tell you would need a knight. He may have been aware of the facsimile's rider on a subliminal level. They do blend together as if they are one creature. Do you wish to retreat and reassess?"

I didn't know which I'd prefer. Pulling back was safer, certainly, but taking out Myron had been my assigned task—and that included if and when he returned as something other than a mousy researcher. Still, Halite was the one taking the bigger risk, even if he had no idea just how great. And if I let Halite retreat now, how could I keep him safe in the future? Myron would certainly not give up. Even if his undead self did not remember precisely why, the imperative to pursue and destroy the winged horse and suck away his power would remain.

Guilty relief flooded me when Halite trumpeted indignantly, "Retreat! By no means! This is my battle and you are my true knight."

"Then be guided by me, noble one," I said. "My sword is ruined, but so is his lance. We have the advantage of reach—he of sharp steel. Prithee, do not charge in. Close combat does not offer the victory you crave."

Halite considered. The flame-cloud demon was swirling above, as the specter clumsily substituted the Sword of Righteous Might for the destroyed lance.

"Like the smoke and fire of which it is made, that parody of beauty rises more easily than do I," Halite admitted. "If we could draw it into a dive and I could get above it, I could fight with my hooves, as well as my teeth."

"That plan has potential," I agreed. "As long as you don't get skewered in the belly."

"I'll keep to one side. Here's how I think I can get him to dive…"

Halite's idea was a good one, if rather terrifying for his rider. We were well above Myron's porphyry tower. Halite's intention was to make as if we were fleeing for shelter within. That meant a dive of our own, directly toward one of the too-small windows in that wall of reddish-purple stone. Halite had been able to get in that way before—Myron had given him some enchantment—but we both knew we couldn't count on it working now.

I gripped my knees hard, wrapped my fingers in the silky white mane, and tried to decide if waiting to smash was better with my eyes open or shut. Shut would be worse, I decided. So it was with wide-open eyes that I watched the purple wall loom closer and closer. Our enemies took the bait. Much like a striking hawk—if a hawk trailed fire—the flame-cloud horse swept down, the specter leaning forward, long sword glittering in its grip.

Halite swerved at the last moment, cutting a tight spiral around the tower. The flame-cloud horse plummeted past us. Halite beat his wings so that we could close in while keeping the advantage offered by our greater elevation. The plan was working beautifully. I had my makeshift lance set to knock the sword from the specter's smoky hand when I noticed the bats.

Their leathery wings were of a stormy darkness that blended well with the tormented skies. Their eyes were preternaturally bright and held ruddy flames. Eldritch as they appeared, I wasn't terribly worried. I've never been afraid of bats. Then I heard what they were whispering.

"So, Gilroy, leading another innocent to his doom, and all for your own glory."

"Get the job done at any cost, is it? You'd think you'd have learned by now."

"How bloody are your hands anyhow, Sir Knight? Your fights now aren't honorable battles. They're assassinations."

On and on they went, voicing every doubt I'd ever felt about myself, about my choices, about the deaths I'd been responsible for—of both of the innocent and the guilty. I heard the voices of fallen comrades, of those who died because their lives were sustained by some evil magic. I saw my lady love, as she had been so long ago and far away. She turned away from my lined and grizzled self, shielding her pretty face with her hands.

"I know you not, Sir. Gilroy, you say? Nay, my Gilroy is a youth, pure and fair, terrible in his innocence and valor."

I heard a scream and believed it was her own dying scream, come to my ears again. Then I realized the one who had screamed was Halite. While I had been ensorcelled by those all too true, oh so false, words, the specter had risen to stand upon the back of his steed. When I say he stood balanced there, I only say what my eyes told me. In truth, he was yet part of his demonic mount. His sword streamed red and I realized that he had sliced a long furrow across one of Halite's forelegs, then up into the muscles on the underside of his barrel. The distance had been too great for the specter to penetrate to the organs. Nonetheless, blood rained down, bathing specter and steed in a red rain that made them more solid with every shining drop.

"Up!" I screamed to Halite. "Up! Get clear! Your blood gives them strength."

The winged horse obeyed, though his wing beats were already less powerful. As I had suspected, injury from that sword did more damage than a mere bloodletting.

The specter chortled a horrid triumph and readied the sword for another slice.

"Away, Halite!" I cried. "Your life depends on it! Up!"

And that faithful heart strove to obey, I think, largely because Halite felt responsible for me, as ever does a good warhorse for rider. As the surge of his wings took him up, I decided to make it easier for him to get away. Pulling my legs free of their grip on his withers, I leaned. As my winged companion went up, I went down.

I wasn't planning on suicide—though I knew that was definite possibility. I figured that Myron and his awful steed were solid enough now that they could take another passenger. Holding my staff in one hand, I let myself fall. The flame-storm creature tried to dodge, but that armor of silk and spider web the specter wore proved tougher than I had imagined possible. I snagged one edge as I went by, then hauled myself up.

Turns out I had been wrong when I told Halite that close quarters fighting was out. As soon as I landed, I battered at the specter with my staff. He cut at me with his sword. The flame-storm horse couldn't join in without pitching his rider off.

In a staff against sword contest, I usually give odds to the sword. Staffs, after all, are wood. Swords can cut them up easily. In this case, though, my staff had been magically hardened to resist attack. Moreover, my opponent's sword had been created to eviscerate a relatively defenseless creature. Though very sharp, it wasn't the best balanced sword and the specter wasn't much of a swordsman.

Still, he had the edge, there was no doubt about it. My footing wasn't the best. I felt as if I was standing in mud that was simultaneously sticky and slick. Time came when Myron backed me to where I could back no further—not unless I wanted to see if I'd learned to fly. Worse, that armor of silk and spider web was providing good stuff. Many a solid blow I thought would sweep the specter into the abyss bounced off.

My tablecloth wasn't much shakes as armor, but the assortment of charms I'd put on before starting to triage Myron's goodies offered some protection. Thing is, they weren't meant to last long—more to ward off a single fireball if I set off a trap, than to soak up repeated slices from a sword. As the battle wore on, I accumulated cuts and bruises all over. At least my blood didn't feed the monster as Halite's would have done.

I realized that I probably wasn't going to live through this battle, but I didn't feel all that much regret. I was dying as a knight should, protecting the innocent, punishing the wicked, saving the world from yet another power-crazed lunatic.

And that's when I heard the voices. Figuring it was the bats again, I tried not to listen, but the words got through anyhow.

"We never blamed you."

"We've been proud of you."

"Knight errant… What's wrong with that? More work. Less glory."

"You hold the Lance of True Valor, Sir Knight." This from a particularly beloved voice. *"Use it."*

So I did. I stopped swinging that bit of bedpost like a staff. Shifting my grip, I thrust out as if I held a lance, imagining that the most powerful charger in the universe carried me through the lists, joining his strength to mine. Believing in my weapon, believing in myself, believing in my cause, I felt my blow meet, then pass right through, the center of the specter's chest.

My opponent didn't scream, though he opened his mouth as if to do so. He vanished before the sound could come out. In less time than that, his steed became a memory. I was falling. Around me, storm clouds shredded and white doves flew where bats had been.

Haloed in sunlight, my boon companion, the winged horse, Halite, rose to catch me upon his broad back. The impact knocked the breath out of me and sent fire through my myriad wounds.

Aching and bleeding though I was, I felt better than I had for many long years.

PART II:

Fairy Tales

FRANCES SILVERSMITH writes computer software for a living, and science fiction and fantasy stories for fun. She lives in a small town in Germany with her husband, seven guinea pigs, and an Icelandic horse. Her fiction has appeared in *Daily Science Fiction* and the *Grantville Gazette*.

Please visit her website: www.francessilversmith.com

LANGUID IN ROSE
Frances Silversmith

Lilia I, Queen of Roses, reluctantly opened her eyes to yet another perfect day, courtesy of the Enchantment. The briar rose outside her windows threw moving shadows on the salmon-colored curtains of her four-poster bed. What a disgustingly lovely sight.

Lilia forced her heavy limbs to a sitting position. Instantly, her maid appeared with a cup of hot chocolate—as she did every morning. When she was younger, Lilia had often tried to trick the Enchantment, getting up in the middle of the night, or staying prone in bed until long past her usual hour—to no avail; the maid always appeared on time.

Lilia sipped the cocoa, wishing that she could decline the too-sweet drink. But Queen Rose I, Lilia's great-great-grandmother and the Great Benefactress of the kingdom, had decreed that the queen should have a cup of hot chocolate upon awaking. And so the queen did.

Queen Rose I had made a Great Sacrifice a hundred years ago when she cast the Enchantment to protect the kingdom and give its citizens peace and prosperity. Disobeying the Great Benefactress' commands could not be risked, because nobody alive knew which of those commands were vital for the protective spell's stability.

After Lilia had forced down the last of the cocoa, her maid helped her into a silk gown of pale rose. Thus dressed, Lilia descended to the Fuchsia Parlor, which was decorated true to its name. The Great Benefactress had loved all shades of pink.

Lilia's aunt and uncle waited for her in the parlor.

"Old Wartir passed away last night," Uncle Ikan said as the servants put overfull dishes of food in front of Lilia. "He was the one to put you on your first pony, wasn't he? I thought you might like to know."

Lilia's eyes filled with tears. Wartir had always had time for a lonely princess, told her stories over his tack cleaning chores. She had not been down to the stables to visit him in too long, and now he was dead.

"But—he wasn't that old, was he? He was healthy, and still able to work. I thought he had many years left!"

"His knees were starting to act up lately, and he often nodded off over his chores. So I suppose it was his time. The Enchantment gave him a peaceful end—he never woke from his sleep."

"But…"

Aunt Bryonia interrupted her. "People die when they grow too old to work anymore. You know that, child."

Lilia sighed inwardly. Aunt Bryonia had reared Lilia from birth and would probably always treat her as a child.

Lilia kept her voice carefully even. "So you taught me, Aunt. But Grandmother abdicated because she couldn't even stay awake through a Court Day anymore, and she lived on for years afterwards."

"The Royal Family is different. You know that, too, Lilia. Now please stop being difficult and eat your breakfast."

There was no point in trying to argue, Lilia knew that from experience.

Lilia's grandmother had made her daughter-in-law Bryonia Lilia's guardian. Aunt Bryonia was also the one Grandmother had told the secret of the Enchantment to, with the behest to pass it on to Lilia when she turned five-and-twenty. Lilia had another five years to get through, five long years of choosing her battles carefully and being meek and obedient at all other times.

So she swallowed her tears and dug into her sumptuous breakfast. It tasted like ashes.

~~*~*

Today was an Open Court Day. Lilia sat erect on her throne and tried to concentrate on the problems her rose-clad subjects brought to her attention. Not that there were usually many important matters to deal with–the Enchantment took care of that. On a normal day, only a few people attended Open Court, bringing her minor squabbles to judge.

Today was different. A stray wolf had made its way to a village in the outer reaches of her kingdom and had killed three sheep in the last two weeks. A farmer in the same village had broken a leg in a fall from a ladder, and a freak storm had destroyed several grain fields, again not far from that village.

"The Enchantment's been severely weakened in our region, Your Majesty," said the mayor of the unlucky village. He'd brought several of the village's elders along, as well as three sturdy-looking fellows who kept close watch over a frail youth. "We've caught the culprit, though. Bring him forward!"

Two sturdy men grabbed the youth by the arms and yanked him toward the throne.

"Your Majesty, this is Peitir. He's always been a good-for-nothing dreamer, but lately, he's turned to evil. Just look at this!"

The third sturdy fellow brought forward a flat object covered with a blanket. He pulled the blanket away to reveal a painting. A scandalized gasp ran through the court, and several people turned their eyes away from the abomination.

Mesmerized, Lilia stared. The painting showed her castle, bathed in purple light, with a raging storm sending lightning from the sky all about it. The picture blazed in vivid colors, making Lilia's heart sing. The piece was wild, dark, and threatening. Judging by every standard she had ever been taught, it was evil.

It was also marvelously, heartbreakingly beautiful.

Behind her, Uncle Ikan cleared his throat. Lilia tore her eyes away from the masterpiece, and faced its doomed maker. "Did you create this painting?"

He gave her a defiant look. "Yes."

"Do you have anything to say in your own defense?" she asked, for formality's sake. There was nothing he could say that would save him now.

Peitir squared his shoulders and met her gaze, but said nothing.

Lilia hesitated. Maybe she could exile him from the kingdom? She'd gotten away with that solution twice in the three years since she had nominally taken over the rule of the kingdom.

But this time, Aunt Bryonia intervened before she could voice her decree. "Lilia—Your Majesty—there can be no question as to the judgment you need to make. This abomination and its creator need to burn, to protect the Enchantment and the kingdom."

Most of the courtiers nodded, and a murmur of "Abomination!" and "Burn him!" ran through the court.

Lilia took a deep breath and yielded to the inevitable.

"So be it. This is my judgment:

You have succumbed to the dark and created a work of evil that might spread your darkness to others, thereby endangering the Enchantment and treating with contempt the Great Sacrifice Queen Rose the First made to create it.

You have the rest of this day and the night to contemplate your sins. Tomorrow at dawn, you will burn at the stake, along with your evil painting."

Peitir did not react. He stared at her with such blazing contempt, she had to look away. But there was nothing she could do. Such a blatant attack on the Enchantment was unpardonable, especially in light of the recent disturbances.

~~*~*

Several hours later, Lilia was finally back in her chambers. She sent the maid away, pleading a headache. For a moment, she leaned back against the closed door, fighting tears. This morning had been too much like that fateful day three years ago, when she had condemned the love of her life to burn at the stake.

Oh, Theiran.

She squared her shoulders and pushed away from the door. Slipping out of her gown, she dug deep in the back of her wardrobe and came up with a set of clothing that nobody knew she possessed: A frayed shirt and a pair of linen trousers. She must find a way to replace these clothes soon, she thought as she slipped them on. They were growing so ragged they might call attention to her.

She paused for a moment to recall the first time she had put these clothes on, to go on an adventure with their former owner. Theiran had always been there for her when she needed a break from being the kingdom's well-behaved heir.

Smiling wistfully, Lilia opened her bedroom shutters and climbed into the enchanted briar rose, which adorned the castle walls. The plant was part of Queen Rose's protective spell, made indestructible by the Enchantment. Its branches easily held up under her weight.

As a member of the royal family, Lilia was somewhat protected from the briar rose's wicked thorns, but by the time she reached her destination two stories down, her arms and legs were bleeding, and her clothes had acquired several more tears.

She slipped through a window into an empty store room, which held one of the more mysterious aspects of the Enchantment. No servant ever came here, and Lilia was the only person in the kingdom who knew about the trap door in the corner of the room. Even Theiran had been unable to see it, unless Lilia held his hand.

Wondering once again why the Great Benefactress had needed a secret entrance into the dungeons, Lilia opened the door, slipped in, and silently closed it behind her.

~~*~*

They'd added a third guard. The men kept a close watch on the exit, unlike the last time she'd been down to the dungeons. Fortunately, they still had no inkling of the secret passage, which ended in a small chamber at the back of the dungeon. They were all in the guard room next to the exit.

Next time she might not be so lucky.

Staying out of the guards' sight, she slipped into the corridor and went over to the one occupied cell. The prisoner came to his feet and opened his mouth as if to say something, but at her frantic wave for silence he closed it again.

Keeping a wary eye on the guard room, Lilia slipped a hair pin into the cell door's lock. It took an eternity, but finally the lock sprang open.

She beckoned for Peitir to follow her. He frowned, but obeyed in silence, thank the Enchantment. Once they were safely back in the store room, he demanded, "Who the *chance* are you, and what do you want from me?"

Lilia turned to him and removed the piece of cloth she had used to hide her distinctive golden curls.

"Queen Lilia? What the...!" He stopped himself in time to avoid a second expletive.

"We don't have time for explanations," she said, but he was not content with that.

"What do you want from me?" he repeated, crossing his arms.

"I want to save your life," Lilia snapped. "There is no time to lose. The guards might raise the alarm any moment. Do you want to escape, or not?"

"What's your price for my freedom? And what about my painting? You're not going to burn it, are you?"

"There is no 'price'. And yes, your painting will be burned in the morning, I can't prevent that." She frowned at him. "Please don't make a fuss that would cost your life–and my freedom to ever help anyone else ever again–over a painting, magnificent as it may be!"

He did not look convinced, so Lilia put on her best imitation of Aunt Bryonia.

"Please stop arguing now. You need to climb out this window. The briar rose will bear your weight–but beware its thorns, they have a will of their own." She had once seen the remains of a man who had attempted to climb the trellis without royal blessing. It had not been pretty.

She walked over to Peitir and put her lips to his forehead before he could flinch back. "This will protect you from the worst of it, but the rose will still do its best to scratch you bloody. There is no other safe way out, though. Climb straight down and swim the moat to the other side. There's a little hut where you can hide for the day. Nobody goes there any longer."

He touched his hand to the spot she had kissed and frowned at her. She could see his stubborn distrust fight with dawning curiosity. Curiosity won. "How do you know all this?"

"I've been down that route before, many times." She smiled at the memories that thought evoked.

The smile seemed to be infectious–Peitir returned it. "I would like to know the story behind that statement. Maybe I'll paint the scene one day. *The Queen Climbing the Briar Rose.*"

Lilia had to grin at that. "You do that, as long as you do it outside the kingdom's borders. Now please leave, before the guards catch us in here."

Peitir hesitated for a moment longer, but then he bowed to her. "Thank you, my Queen," he said, and was gone.

Lilia made her way up to her chambers, again paying a tribute in blood to the briar rose. Once there, she busied herself washing out her cuts and hiding all other evidence of her excursion. Thank the Enchantment that long sleeves and gloves were all the rage at Court this season.

~~*~*

There was a tremendous outcry over the prisoner's escape. Rumors sprang up in droves, some telling of evil sorcerers having spirited the delinquent away, others attributing witch powers to Peitir himself. Still others told of a conspiracy inside the castle, bent on destroying the Enchantment and sending the kingdom into chaos.

Tidings of little accidents, minor storms, and other disturbing incidents trickled in. The Enchantment seemed to be weakening, might even be on the brink of breaking. Lilia sat in the Fuchsia Parlor, picking at her breakfast while her aunt and uncle discussed the disturbing news.

Is the Enchantment really breaking? Would that be such a bad thing?

She was startled out of her thoughts when the door flew open with a crash, and a pair of castle guards rushed into the room.

"There is an intruder in the castle!" The guard sounded breathless, and his face was the color of a well-ripened tomato. The other guard didn't look much better.

"What?" Uncle Ikan exclaimed. "No intruder can make it past the briar rose. The Enchantment has always prevented such a thing!"

"I know, my lord, but somehow, an evil sorcerer has made it past our protections. We must keep the Queen safe at all costs."

The guard walked up to Lilia and urged her to her feet. "Come, Your Majesty, we will take you to your chambers. Nothing must happen to you."

Not for the first time, Lilia secretly cursed her ancestress for tying the Enchantment, and with it the kingdom's fate, so closely to the queen's life. The guards marched her up the stairs to her room, and urged her to lock the door. One of the men stood guard outside.

Once she was alone, excitement surged. She was going to find out who the mysterious intruder was. She felt more connected to life than she had in months. For the second time this week, Lilia changed into her old trousers and climbed down the briar rose to the store room. She changed back into the gown she had carried in a bag on her back and made her way through empty corridors to the Throne Room. Where was everyone? Just a few minutes ago, the place had teemed with guards, and now there was nobody in sight.

The answer to that question became clear when she entered the Throne Room, where she found her courtiers and guards assembled. All stared spell-bound at a figure clad entirely in stark, uncompromising white. What an unthinkable breach of etiquette in her rose-colored kingdom.

Lilia stopped in the doorway and joined her courtiers in staring at the intruder. He turned his head to look at her, and her heart did a somersault. For a moment her surroundings faded, swallowed in the warm glow of his dark brown eyes. Was there a twinkle in those eyes? She couldn't tell.

"Theiran? What... why... how did you get into the castle?"

Now the courtiers stared at her instead of the intruder.

"My Queen." He made her an elaborate bow. "It seems the kiss you gave me three years ago still has some effect."

Her gaze rose to the spot on his forehead that she had kissed that day. The first and only kiss she had ever given him. He smiled.

"Lilia, do you know this man?" Aunt Bryonia asked. Her voice sounded weak, as if she was forcing the words out against an obstruction in her throat.

"Yes, Aunt. This is Theiran. He was condemned to death three years ago, for composing a maleficent song for my birthday. He escaped from the dungeons the night before the burning was scheduled."

Now there definitely was a twinkle in Theiran's eyes. A mischievous one. Curse the man, he was going to betray just who it had been who had helped him escape.

"What did you do to my court?" she asked hastily. She had thought at first that her people were just stiff with surprise, but they were all still frozen in place after several minutes–silent and unmoving save for their heads.

"That evil sorcerer put a curse on us," her aunt said. "Don't stand there and make chitchat with the villain, Lilia!" Bryonia's face was red with the effort of speaking. Even so, her voice barely rose above a whisper.

Theiran spoke over Aunt Bryonia's protest. "I took temporary control of the spell your ancestress put on the kingdom. I condensed that spell in the castle and used it to paralyze your people."

"What are you talking about? The only spell any ancestress of mine put on the kingdom is the Enchantment of Eternal Peace."

"That's exactly what I'm talking about. The *Enchantment*, as you call it, is a diffused Curse of Stagnation–blood magic at its worst."

"Blood magic? Don't be ridiculous. Queen Rose sacrificed her Great Love to power the Enchantment. She was no blood magician."

Theiran grimaced. "Queen Rose didn't sacrifice her *love*, she sacrificed her *lover*. Got herself pregnant by him, and then killed him in a ritual to bind the curse to the unborn child, your great-grandmother Rose II."

Lilia swallowed against the sudden tightness in her throat. "That can't be true."

"Just look what the curse has done to your kingdom. You have no art to speak of, and there haven't been any technical inventions in a hundred years. Lilia, you *burn* people who dare to think for themselves!"

"There hasn't been a burning in years." Her protest sounded feeble in her own ears.

"I know," Theiran replied, face sardonic. "Your aunt was not exactly happy with you for that, was she?"

Aunt Bryonia made a strangled sound, but Theiran ignored her. "In fact, that lack of burnings is one of the reasons the spell has weakened enough for me to make my way here. The curse feeds on the old and feeble, of course, but that is not enough to keep it strong without the burnings."

No. Please, no! "Are you telling me the Enchantment kills people?"

He lifted his brows at her. "That's how the kingdom pays for the extraordinary amount of good fortune its people have had. Not to mention the little luxuries Queen Rose built into the castle."

Lilia blinked furiously. She did not have time for tears. "What can I do to stop that?"

"Lilia!" Aunt Bryonia managed to take a single step towards them. "You cannot mean to let that–person–trick you into destroying the kingdom's protections."

"But Aunt, what if it's true that the Enchantment kills people?"

"Of course that's true, silly girl. The old and decrepit would only be a burden on the rest of us. Who'd want to live like that? The Enchantment does these people a favor, giving them a peaceful death before they can become useless parasites."

Lilia stared at her aunt, speechless. So did the rest of her court, including her uncle, she noted. At least she hadn't been the only one who was naive enough not to have known.

Turning back to Theiran, Lilia repeated: "What can I do to keep the Enchantment from killing people?"

"As long as the spell remains in place, there's nothing you can do. You need to break it. That means your kingdom will lose its unnatural good fortune. Your people will once again have to deal with the vagaries of life."

There'd be storms, and sickness, and other calamities large and small. Calamities her people had never known. Lilia closed her eyes and took a deep breath. Looking up at Theiran, she said, "Tell me how to break it."

Theiran studied her. "Are you sure you want to break the Enchantment?"

Lilia met his eyes and nodded.

He walked up, folded her into his arms, and kissed her. For a moment, she was too startled to react. But the kiss felt right, just as if he had never left her. She wrapped her arms around him and kissed him back.

Lightning flashed outside the windows, followed instantly by a deafening thunderclap. Lilia took a step back. "What was that? Did we just break the Enchantment? Was that why you kissed me?"

"A kiss was the fastest way to break the Enchantment." The mischievous smile was back, laced with tenderness. "Besides, I've dreamed of kissing you for the last three years."

Warmth suffused her. She, too, had dreamed of kissing him. She walked back into his arms. Behind her, murmurs rose as the paralysis fell away from her courtiers.

"Guards!" Her aunt's voice had regained its strength. "Arrest this intruder!"

Lilia sighed, and turned to face Bryonia.

"Aunt…"

"Your Majesty, this man obviously is a black sorcerer. He has enchanted you. Step away from him, please." Waving for two guards to follow her, Aunt Bryonia strode towards them.

Lilia shrank back, then caught herself. The enchantment was gone, that much was obvious from the storm that raged outside–the first one to touch the castle in a hundred years. For the first time in her life, Lilia was free to oppose her aunt without fear of the consequences.

She took a step forward and raised her hand. "No," she said.

Her aunt stopped to stare at her, as did the guards.

A panicked cry interrupted the tense scenario. "My queen, the castle is on fire!"

Lilia looked up to see flames licking at the window frames. Now that she was paying attention, she caught a whiff of rose-scented smoke. Running over to a window, Lilia saw that the briar rose was burning, flames blazing brightly against a gloomy sky.

She took a deep breath and turned to face the room. "I declare emergency rule," she said. Rose I had decreed that in an emergency, the queen would have absolute control over the court for two weeks, no questions asked.

The courtiers all snapped to attention. Thankfully, nobody seemed to realize that the author of that rule had just been exposed as a black sorceress and a fraud. She must not give them time to think.

"Uncle Ikan, please organize the courtiers into groups and have them find out what damage the breaking of the spell did to the castle. Guards, Lady Bryonia is under house arrest. Please escort her to one of the guest chambers and place her under guard."

She turned to face the majordomo, who looked back and forth between her and the flames outside the windows, hands wringing. "Rolvo, please have the servants form bucket lines to the windows and douse the walls so they do not catch fire. Theiran, please follow me."

She turned and walked out of the room, Theiran at her heels. They checked the windows on every side of the castle and found that the fire encircled the walls completely, though it did not touch them. Only the briar rose burned.

It took all day for the flames to die down. Theiran stayed at her side, placating upset courtiers, talking to distraught servants, and helping in other small but significant ways. Whenever there was a brief spell of calm in the chaos, he told Lilia about the wonders of the world outside the kingdom's borders.

By the time she made it to her bed, Lilia was exhausted. Even so, sleep was a long time in coming.

~~*~*

Lilia woke in her four-poster-bed and stared up at a faded and lusterless canopy. No leafy shadows played on the bed curtains. The air reeked of smoke.

She walked over to her window and looked out at a gray, cloudy sky. Rain fell, the raindrops creating little rivulets down the soot-stained wall. The briar rose was gone—burned down to the roots.

Turning away from the window, Lilia pulled the string that would ring the servants' bell in the kitchen. A few minutes later her maid appeared, out of breath and looking dismayed to find her queen already out of bed. The usual cup of hot chocolate was conspicuously absent.

Half an hour later, Lilia stepped into the Fuchsia Parlor clad in a threadbare dress. The formerly splendid parlor looked run-down and faded, as well. Her uncle waited for her, without his wife, his face drawn and unhappy. Lilia's throat constricted. What was she going to do about Aunt Bryonia?

And she had destroyed the protections her people had come to depend on.

For a moment, she almost wished yesterday's events undone. But then she membered old Wartir, who might still be alive but for the Enchantment. Her resolve returned. She would find a way to steer her kingdom through the troubled times to come.

A second person waited in the Parlor. He rose from his seat, smiling at her. Lilia walked into Theiran's open arms and hugged him. He kissed the top of her head. When they let go of each other, Lilia caught her uncle watching them. A small smile lit his care-worn face.

ALAN DEAN FOSTER's career spans over forty years, during which time he has novelized a host of movies from *Star Trek* to *Transformers* to *Terminator*. George Lucas may have his name on the 1976 novelization *Star Wars: From the Adventures of Luke Skywalker*, but it was Foster who wrote the book. He's also well known for the *Humanx Commonwealth* series of SF novels, dozens of standalone books, anthologies and collections, various trilogies and the fantasy series, *Spellsinger*.

Visit his official page: www.alandeanfoster.com

GREEN THEY WERE, AND GOLDEN-EYED
Alan Dean Foster

The moon was near to full, the rain was falling unheavy and warm, and Weipo thought it an altogether fine night when he heard the crash.

At first he thought it was a tree falling, because falling trees were generally what made crashing noises in the forest. But the more he considered it, the less it reminded him of a tree falling and the more it suggested something else. Since he could not think of anything else that could cause such a loud crashing noise, he decided to set off and see for himself. This he did by vacating the branch he had chosen for his evening perch with a most prodigious leap.

As he neared the origin of the sound he began to advance more cautiously, every sense alert to the natural noises of the forest around him and the possible presence of food. Once, he struck at a dragonfly, but missed. Disappointed, he continued on, until he came to a place where there was a hole in the canopy. Palm fronds and vines were strewn about the ground, forming a damp green halo in the moonlight around the object which had brought them crashing down from the heights.

It was a twice-peculiar sight. Attached to a large boxy object, obviously man-made, were eight... no, nine... of the strangest creatures Weipo had ever seen. They resembled nothing so much as skinny-legged wallabies with horns. Each was attached in harness to the boxy affair.

A very large, very rotund human was going from one creature to the next and disengaging each in turn from its harness. As he did so, the animal would stagger and stumble a little ways into the forest, where it would pause, collapse, and be violently ill. Being a naturally sympathetic sort of fellow, Weipo felt sorry for them. He also felt sorry for the man, who clearly was more than a little tired and frustrated.

Something told him that it would be safe to approach. If he was wrong, he was certain he could dodge any human so large.

The man was seriously overdressed in a heavy red suit with black belt and white trim. As Weipo drew near the tall figure was exchanging a white-trimmed red cap for a rich red, wide-brimmed rain cap. He observed silently as the human drew a matching red slicker over his plush red suit. At about that time the man noticed him.

"Well, hello there. What are you grinning at?"

"I am a golden-eyed green tree frog," Weipo replied evenly, more than a little surprised at the man's ability to converse. "We're always smiling."

"I see." The large human pursed his lips, which were nearly hidden by a vast, flowing white beard. "And I suppose it's always raining here?"

Weipo blinked. "That's why they call it a rain forest."

"I know, I know." The man sighed. "You don't have to state the obvious."

Weipo nodded in the direction of the nine horned wallabies, who were busy being sick all over the place. "You seem to have a problem."

"You don't know the half of it." The man consulted his wristwatch. It was a very unusual watch. Most watches are based on Greenwich Mean Time. This one was calibrated according to Christmas Mean Time. It ran slow, oh so very slow, but it still ran.

"My busiest night of the year," he said, "and look at this." He indicated the horned wallabies, who if anything were certainly more unhappy than their driver.

"What happened?" asked Weipo solicitously.

"Some kind of food poisoning, I think." The man flicked a drop from his bulbous nose. "They have a very special diet, but no matter how careful you are this sort of thing is going to happen from time to time. It's just that it's never before happened on this particular day." He glanced down at Weipo. "I am badly in need of some temporary assistance." He hastened to explain.

So warm and needful was his expression that Weipo felt compelled to do what he could. As he confessed, that wasn't likely to be much.

"I'm sorry. I'd like to be of assistance, but as you can see, I'm small enough to fit in the palm of your hand."

The man nodded resignedly. He was sitting on the lower part of the boxy vehicle, his hands on his knees. "No harm in asking. There aren't likely to be any reindeer within several thousand miles of here, either."

"Is that what those things are?" Weipo regarded the unhappy horned creatures with interest. "I'm afraid not. I have, however, been giving the matter some thought, and there is one who might be able to help."

The man raised his head, a hopeful look on his face. "If you can do anything, anything at all, I promise you all the flies you can eat for life."

"That's all right." Weipo's smile grew even wider than usual. "I can manage. I'd just like to help someone who's in trouble. You stay here and I'll be back as quick as I can."

The man sighed and gestured toward the dripping Alexandra palms, from which rangiferian retching noises continued to come. "As you can see, I'm not going anywhere soon."

Weipo took off back through the forest, trying to remember where he'd last seen Mullgarra. The king of the tree-frogs moved around a lot, checking on his kingdom, but Weipo had encountered him not two days earlier, exploring the billabong which had formed from a branch of the big creek.

Conscious of the sense of urgency inherent in the human's plight, he traveled as fast as he dared. Once, an amethystine python nearly got him, its sharp teeth nicking the webbing of his right foot. Another time an insomniacal emu tried to catch him by the head, but he darted left just in time and left the huge flightless bird spitting out a beakful of moist dirt.

The billabong was beautiful in the moonlight. Above the soft patter of the rain striking the glassy water the sounds of night-birds and insects could be heard, as well as the deeper-throated calls of his relations.

He found Mullgarra sitting on a flat brown rock that protruded only an inch or so above the surface. There was nothing about him to indicate that he was the king of the tree-frogs, provided one discounted his slightly larger size and the small jeweled gold crown that occasionally winked into existence out of the Dreamtime and onto his head.

"Bother this thing," Mullgarra groused as he reached up to straighten the crown. "I wish it would stay or go as destiny sees fit. This coming and going is downright frustrating." Gold eyes regarded Weipo, who floated patiently nearby. "Well don't just lie there; get up here on this rock and state your business."

"Yes, your Greenness." Weipo crawled out on the cool wet stone and settled his legs beneath him. "It's about..."

"Excuse me." Mullgarra had spotted a juvenile salt water crocodile approaching. It was about three feet long and at the anxious frog-hunting stage. The king performed some quick calculations and parted his mouth. His tongue struck the startled croc square in its left eye, a not unimpressive feat considering that they were still some twenty-six feet apart. The croc paused, its dim reptilian mind attempting to make some sense of this impossibility, and then turned and with steady sweeps of its muscular, armored tail, swam away, squinting.

"Sorry about that." Mullgarra returned his attention to the supplicant. "What can I do for you?"

"Not for me, your Omnipotent Greenness. It's a human who needs your help."

Mullgarra blinked. "A human? Why should I do anything to help a human? Their children catch us and put us in jars and sometimes they dissect us. As if their own insides weren't sufficiently interesting."

"I don't think he's an ordinary human. He came crashing down into the forest in a big red boxy affair pulled by nine flying horned wallabies, only they're not wallabies, and they're not in any kind of shape to pull their own tails right now. That's his problem. He promised that if I helped I'd have all the flies I could eat." Weipo paused, thinking if there was anything else he could add. "I don't think he'd ever put one of us in a jar," he finished.

The king mulled this over. "First time I ever heard of a human showing a gourmet interest in flies. He sounds interesting, your acquaintance." Mullgarra glanced skyward, rain running down his bulging golden eyes and green back. "Too nice a night to sit here and do nothing except bedevil crocs. This sounds like it might be interesting. Where is he to be found, your human?"

Weipo turned and gestured with his tongue. Mullgarra nodded. "You say there were nine of these pulling wallaby-be-likes?" It was Weipo's turn to nod. "Very well. There's me and thee already. Go and round up seven of the guys and meet me at the place." Before Weipo could say anything more Mullgarra was on his way with a leap that carried him clear across the billabong and well into the trees beyond, the moonlight sending a pellucid shaft of light glinting off his crown.

He found Boomooloo, Nirra, and Tug in the next billabong, and Girrarree in the little stream that fed it. Ngamalgeah and Widbagar were sharing a fat grasshopper beneath a fallen fern tree, and they picked up sleepy Mauk on the way back.

They found King Mullgarra and the big round human engaged in earnest conversation by the side of the man's open-topped vehicle. Mauk was reluctant to continue, having once had an uncle smushed by an errant four-wheel drive, but Weipo convinced him it was safe by pointing out that the vehicle had no wheels.

"Greetings," said Weipo cheerfully as he hopped forward. "These are me mates." The six behind him ribbetted in chorus. "I see that your situation isn't much improved."

"I'm afraid it isn't," the man admitted. "Donner is flat on his flank, Blitzen is downright hoarse, and Prancer is nearly as green as you are. The rest aren't much better." He glanced down at Mullgarra, who was sitting on his knee. "You really think you can help?"

"Well now, as I see it, and I see quite well out of these eyes, what we have here is a little problem of spacetime. If you are telling me true that you can handle the time, I believe we can assist you in doing something about the space."

The man's lips tightened. "Believe me, I would be grateful, as would a great many children. But I don't see how you can do much."

"There are nine of your horned pullers. There are nine of us."

"There is some difference in size," the man said politely.

"You underestimate us. People are always underestimating frogs." Mullgarra turned to his subjects. "I am going to teach you the puffing trick. It's a very old trick, a Dreamtime trick, and it hasn't been used in quite a while. Now's as good a time as any.

"What you must do is inhale and puff yourselves up, only instead of chirruping as you normally do, just keep holding and puffing, puffing and holding."

"'Scuse me," said Boomooloo, "but there's the little matter of breathing."

"Vastly overrated," sniffed Mullgarra. "Don't worry about it and it won't bother you. I'll make certain of that." He hopped off the man's knee to confront the green semicircle of others. "Just watch me and do as I do. And don't breathe until I tell you to or all will be for naught. Now then… inhale!"

The heavyset man had seen many impressive sights in his time and his travels, but he had to confess that what he witnessed that night there in the rain forest ranked right up near the top.

"Bless my jolly old soul," he murmured in astonishment when Mullgarra and the rest turned to face him. Then he moved to set them in harness, placing Weipo in front in the position of honor.

When all was in readiness he climbed back into his vehicle and surveyed his remarkable new team. No need presently for a lambent red nose at the front because those great golden eyes shone like searchlights in the glow of the full moon. He sat down heavily and chucked the reins. "Ready whenever you are. We've a lot of stops to make." He spared a glance for the sickly quadrupeds off to his left. "And while we're gone, the lot of you might try eating some grass."

Mullgarra glanced around and because he was king, managed the difficult task of speaking without breathing. "She'll be right, mate. Ready then? On three, mates. One, two, three… breathe!"

The people who lived in the rain forest were used to thunder. Besides, it was late and most of them slept through it anyway. But in Ayton and Wujal Wujal a few were still awake and they heard, and where more than one sat or lay together they discussed the noise. Very peculiar sounding thunder it was, they allowed. Not a crrraash, or a brrrooommm, or even a sharp crack. Most decidedly, yes, more like an enormous, reverberant, echoing Buuurrr-aaaarrrrppp!

After deciding that, they went about their tasks or back to sleep and forgot all about it.

Down the coast the sleigh shot, making haste along a time-line stretched out like an infinite rubber band. Over the tablelands, disturbing the flying foxes. Into the small towns of the Outback and back over the larger towns of the Inback. Criss-crossing New South Wales and the big cities, thence west to Adelaide and beyond.

Skimming low over the Spencer Gulf, a patrolling Great White Shark lifted its pointy snout out of the water long enough to latch onto the sleigh's left rear runner. It hung on grimly, slowing it down, as the driver dumped whatever lay on top of his bottomless bag onto the persistent fish. Eventually it became tangled up in a knot of flashing, blinking Christmas lights and let go, allowing the sleigh to regain some altitude.

Being waterproof and self-powered, the lights remained lit. Frustrated, the Great White cruised the surface, blinking and winking cheerily as it made its way across the Gulf, the laughing-stock of every Great White for two hundred miles around until the integral batteries in the light strand finally ran down.

On up through Andamooka and Coober Pedy, swinging sharply through Alice Springs and south once more, over the Nullarbor toward Perth. Then north all the way to the Kimberlys and the Bungle Bungles, turning east through Arnhem Land, the great golden-eyed frogs pulling the sleigh and its load in leaps large and bounds bitty.

It was when the Down Under circuit was nearly complete that the sleigh's driver grew, just for an instant, the slightest bit careless. It was over Burketown, still very late indeed, when Mr. Paddy Wheaton and his friend Theos happened to look up at precisely the propitiate moment. They had been spending the night engaged in a serious debate over the merits of Foster's Lager versus Four EX and while their perceptive abilities were qualitatively reducio, the absurdium manifested itself only when Paddy happened to glance skyward.

His mouth dropped and his eyes bulged, though not as much as those of the creatures he saw.

"Gawd help us! There be frogs in the moon!"

Whereupon he set to running madly, and it was two days before Theos and the rest of his friends found him cowering in a bog beneath a giant lily pad, giggling at nothing in particular and stone cold sober.

Over the Top End then, descending rapidly, even at that critical moment not forgetting the children at isolated stations like Strathgordon and Merapa and Sundgrave. Back to the rain forest with its luxurious warm drizzle and night sounds, where nine anxious and extremely embarrassed reindeer waited in the unfamiliar woods.

Touch-down was, as it had been on rooftops and in farmyards, abrupt but tolerable. At a word from Mullgarra the frogs in harness exhaled relievedly, and rapidly shrunk down to their familiar, palm-sized dimensions.

"You did well," declared Mullgarra.

"Because of you a great many good children will not wake up tomorrow disappointed," the man told him. "If there's anything I can do for you, anything you need…"

"Bwarp. Don't need a thing. I'm a tree-frog, and a tree-frog's life isn't such a bad one, fair dinkum." Whereupon Mullgarra turned and vanished into the surrounding leaves.

"I'm hungry," Murk announced, and promptly hopped off into the forest. He was followed by the rest of his mates, all bounding off in different directions. All except one.

"What can I do for you?" the man asked as he worked busily to re-harness his recovered (but still slightly bilious) team. "I did promise you all the flies you could eat, didn't I?"

"And if I recall correctly, I declined," said Weipo. "There is one thing, though."

The man paused and bent over, smiling the most wonderful wide smile at the bright green amphibian. "Name it."

Weipo looked slightly embarrassed, a difficult thing for a tree frog to bring off. "It's just that I've watched men and some of the things they can do, and while a tree frog can't hope to match them... no hands, for example... I thought maybe there might be a way I could do this." He beckoned and the man bent way, way over to put his ear close to the frog's mouth.

The beetle was big, fat, and bright yellow with black spots. It sat on its branch and rubbed its antennae together, confident it was safe despite the presence of the frog in the bush nearby.

Weipo gauged the distance, tensed his tongue, and flicked. The thin, sticky-tipped organ shot out, bent ninety degrees around one branch, ducked beneath another, described a french curve through a hole in a palm leaf, and in defiance of every known rule of amphibian physiology, whacked the startled beetle smack on the head. It retreated, following the same quite impossible path, to conclude coiled back up in the tree frog's mouth.

That was interesting, Weipo mused as he munched on his snack. Later I'll have to see if I can manage a Mobius strip.

He turned on his branch, securing a new grip with his oversized feet as he settled down to regard the moon. Around him the creatures of the tropical night scuttled and crawled and sang. Taking a quick breath he added his own bwarp to the chorus, smiling with satisfaction.

Hot and sticky and steamy the rainforest might be, but it was still alive with the music of Christmas.

TODD MCCAFFREY is the youngest son of legendary author Anne McCaffrey and is best known for his collaborations with his mother for the *Dragonriders of Pern* series. Todd has written or co-written multiple novels in the *Pern* series and continues his late mother's timeless legacy to this day. He has written many short stories and even a *Choose Your Own Adventure* type novel.

In addition to his novel writing, Todd is a mechanical engineer, a pilot, a screenwriter and an artist.

For more about Todd, please visit his site: pernhome.com/tjm

GOLDEN
Todd McCaffrey

"How does this sound? 'It can never be stressed sufficiently: to anger a dragon is to die. To steal a dragon's gold is to die, to covet a dragon's mate is to die. Death by dragon is swift but not painless, usually involving flames which can melt steel.'"

"I think you could have stopped with the first sentence, Daddy," Golden said. "The rest are merely illustrations of how to anger a dragon."

"And you forgot to mention challenging a dragon to a joust," Elveth said.

"If I mention that then you'll get fewer jousts and less gold," Simon replied. "I thought the idea was to create more challenges."

"The *idea* is to get more gold," Elveth corrected testily. She smiled at her daughter, adding, "Golden isn't getting younger and she'll need a horde of her own." Her smile faded as she added pointedly, "You're certainly not getting any of mine."

"Of course, mother," Golden said demurely. When Elveth wasn't looking, she shot a look toward her father who shrugged sympathetically.

"Your mother left you quite a nice pile, if I remember," Simon said.

"That's because I killed her," Elveth reminded him waspishly. She flicked a finger at her daughter. "You're not to get any ideas, little miss gold scales."

"Yes mother," Golden replied, dipping her head and avoiding eye contact. Elveth was the sort of mother who would *literally* rip your head off if she got too angry: Golden had seen it once and needed no reminders—in this she was like her mortal and human father.

In most other things she was the exact replica of her mother. Only where Elveth was a mottled copper color when a dragon, Golden was pure gold—hence her name. Even when born, she had a beautiful head of fine golden hair and there was no contention over her name.

"She is Golden because she is my gold child," Elveth had said and Simon had wisely kept silent, particularly as, according to his studies, he was the first human dragon-mate to survive through the rigors of childbirth with a head still upon his shoulders.

Simon and Elveth had often conversed on their daughter's coloring: Simon was convinced that it was protective in nature while Elveth held to the old dragon lore that color predicted flame.

"A pure gold like that will mark the hottest of fires," Elveth had declared with much warranted maternal pride.

At the time, Golden had yet to have her first molt and was still clinging to the forlorn hope that she was not a dragon but, rather, a normal human child. She loved her father as fiercely as all girls—perhaps a bit more so because of her dragonish heritage. Simon, because he loved his daughter, hoped that her wish would come true but deep down he was convinced—and secretly relieved—that she would molt and turn into a dragon when she was of age.

There were tears all around when that day finally came and Golden found herself molted into the slim body of a young dragon princess.

"Oh, my dear, you are so beautiful!" Elveth had cried with tears of joy.

"I'm a dragon!" Golden had cried with tears of despair.

"You shall live forever," Simon had said with tears of relief.

"As a dragon!" Golden had wailed. "I don't want to be a dragon!"

"Well, you are," Elveth had snapped, her copper color eyes warming dangerously.

"Ixnay on the agon-dray," Simon had muttered warningly to his daughter.

"But it's true!" Golden cried, flouncing out of their small house and accidentally destroying the staircase, the good dining table, and three large iron pots.

When they had found her later, she was lying on her mother's horde in the deep cavern that was hidden behind their house.

Elveth growled and looked ready to change but Simon put an arm on hers. "She must have a terrible headache."

"Golden, how do you feel?" Elveth asked, primed by her mate.

"My head feels like it's going to explode!" Golden had cried.

"Oh, dear! It's all the magic going around," Elveth had said sympathetically. She turned to Simon. "I should go out and kill more mages to ease the pain of my poor little girl."

"Now, dear, we've had this conversation before," Simon told her soothingly. "The evidence is that magic flows from the sun. The mages merely tame and use it. Ridding yourself of them leaves more magic to pain you."

"At least I've got my gold," Elveth said, moving to join her dragon daughter in the huge pile that spilled from its mound in the center of the cavern. She turned back to smile at her mate. "And I've got you to thank for it."

Simon blushed but said nothing.

"How's that, mother?" Golden asked, her talons digging deep into the pile and spilling it over her like a torrent of pebbles—although these pebbles were mostly gold doubloons mixed with the occasional broken crown or necklace.

"Well, it was your father who realized that knights and princes would wager much to fight against a dragon," Elveth said, glancing slyly at her mate. "And so he arranged it and I've been successfully ridding the countryside of useless knights and worthless princes."

"But I thought Daddy was —"

"Your father, a knight?" Elveth asked with a laugh. She eyed Simon thoughtfully. "Well, he *is* of the nobility or he would not be a suitable consort for one such as myself but he was a squire when we met and much more scholarly than most." She smiled at him. "The bashful boy was completely taken with me after I'd scorched that useless knight of his into mere ash."

"Sir Girwhed was noble and brave," Simon said in defense of his long lost knight, "but he would not listen to my counsel."

"And that was?" Golden prompted, lifting her snout through a pile of treasure and letting it spill to either side.

"I told him if he fought the dragon, she'd burn him to a crisp," Simon said with a shrug.

"See!" Elveth cried, giving her mate a look of adoration. "He's one of the smartest humans I'd ever met."

"Of course it took a while for our courtship to mature," Simon reminded her.

Elveth laughed long and brassily. "Yes, I recall telling you every night that while I enjoyed our conversations, I was never going to be foolish to transform into a woman just so you could kill me."

"Actually," Simon said, "I seem to recall endless nights of your telling me how quick and painful my demise would be."

"Only after you beat me at chess!" Elveth said, her expression slipping.

"And then she changed into human form," Simon said with a smile that bordered on a leer. To Elveth, he added, "I always knew that you'd be the most beautiful of women."

"Flatterer!" Elveth chuckled. "And, of course, well, Golden dear, you came along."

"And now I'm a dragon!" Golden cried. "And I'll horde gold and flame useless knights to ash just to build my horde!"

"And it had never get bigger than mine, missy," Elveth added warningly.

"Of course, momma," Golden replied shyly.

"How's your headache?" Simon asked.

"Better."

"Then maybe you can change back," Simon suggested.

"Change back?" Golden repeated in wonder. "How do I do that?"

"Close your eyes," Elveth told her. "Close your eyes and think your wings away. Think your pretty scales gone and your beautiful slitted eyes turned back into small golden round orbs. Feel your hair on your shoulders and your body shrink as you become a mere human shape."

It took more coaxing but in twenty minutes, Golden was once again in human form.

"Later, dear, we'll teach you how to build clothes," Elveth promised as Simon lent his daughter the jacket he'd worn just for the occasion.

~~*~*

That had been the beginning of dark days all around.

"Well, I'm learning a lot," Simon had quipped when challenged to find the good in theemotional stew that was two dragon-queens in the same house—one daughter of the other.

Golden would wail about her mother, Elveth would shriek about her daughter and Simon would spend most of his time trying to perfect his flameproof armor and—naturally—work on creative ways to keep one or the other from escalating things into a firestorm.

"The house is made of wood!" Simon had cried hopelessly at the beginning of their first mother-daughter, dragon-dragon spat.

Not long after the ruins were made of ash.

A year later, Simon was saying, "I didn't know your flame was hot enough to melt brick."

It had been Golden's flame which had reduced their second home to glowing glass slag—much to the surprise of all.

Simon had taken to spending much time in the village tavern—they knew nothing of his home life; thinking him merely a farmer with a wife and daughter but to no avail. It had ended the night Golden had run into the inn crying and a copper dragon had flamed off the roof.

Simon had, at least, earned much respect from the villagers when he'd stood up to the copper dragon and had sent it packing.

Of course, as he knew, the whole family was shortly packing to find some new dwelling—not just because of Elveth's flame tantrum but also because the villagers decided that they were better off without the services of a farmer who spoke to dragons.

They settled many hundreds of miles away in an entirely new kingdom far in the south where, after not too much time, Simon had begun convincing princes in other lands that their greatest glory lay in challenging a flaming dragon in a duel to the death.

Simon also learned much of the ways of daughters and mothers from those willing to share their knowledge—and there were many—and grew more and more despairing for the survival of not just his dwelling and his hide, but his family.

It seemed like it would all end when Golden, just barely fifteen and far too young for a dragon to go a-roaming, fled the house in a flaming huff which set the far mountains aflame.

With the flames marking a clear path, Simon knew that he and Elveth would also have to move or face uncomfortable questions and other such things—like pitchforks.

"Pitchforks won't hurt me!" Elveth had exclaimed when Simon brought them up.

"I, on the other hand, am not so sturdy," he reminded her. She had not been so distracted by the loss of her daughter to consider the impending loss of her husband unworthy of her concern and so, as Simon had urged, they fled for healthier parts.

Fortunately, Simon was a wise man and had their destination long-planned—when living with two strong-minded dragons, it was practically inevitable that one way or the other they would find themselves relocating—so, even her family fled in her wake, Simon had the comfort of knowing that Golden would know where to find them.

They were settled into the cold, wet north that was safely far away from their other homes for over two years before Elveth started pining for her missing daughter.

"She's old enough to take care of herself, dear," Simon had staunchly assured her—trying to believe the words that he'd been telling himself for the past twenty-four months.

"A dragon isn't mature until her fiftieth year!" Elveth cried.

"You were forty-five when you ate your mother," Simon reminded her.

"Exactly!" Elveth said. "I'm glad you take my side in this, Simon. If only you had been quicker, she would still be with us."

Simon wisely kept silent. The only result of his reminding his dragon-wife of her part in their daughter's departure would be to have her grieving over the ashes of her husband... and, doubtless, complaining that *that* was her daughter's fault.

When Elveth had finally dissolved into a flood of heart-broken tears, Simon said, "There, dear, we'll find her. She'll be back, you'll see."

"She'd better," Elveth hiccupped, pushing herself away from her husband, her eyes slitting as she speared him with her gaze. "After all, it's all *your* fault."

"Yes dear," Simon had said wisely. He then excused himself on the grounds that he needed to get some water. He did not say that he intended to douse himself in it for protection. He was away long enough that Elveth was asleep when he returned, her human body slumped in her chair, head on the table. With a sigh, Simon gently pulled the chair back, lifted her up, and carried her to their bed.

He was still drying himself off, having covered her in their blankets, when he heard wings rustling. He dropped the towel and tore out the front door.

Out of the darkness a golden-haired girl emerged hesitantly.

"Daddy?" Golden asked in a small quiet voice.

Simon raced to her, grabbed her and twirled with her in his arms, his head pressed firmly against her shoulder, his tears flowing unabashed. "Baby!"

They stood, entwined, for the moment that was forever. Then, because even eternity must end, Simon pulled away from her.

"Are you staying?" he said, glancing back to their newest home and wondering how to manage the re-union and its aftermath.

Golden shook her head and her fine blond hair shimmered around her like a gold waterfall. "I can't."

Simon heard another noise rustle in the darkness and quickly pushed her behind him, ready to defend her with his life.

A small, dark-haired, green-eyed woman shrank back from his motions.

"This is Erayshin," Golden said, grabbing his arm and pulling her to a halt. She beckoned with her other hand for the girl to approach.

"Is she –?" Simon asked, his eyes wide in fear.

Golden shook her head.

"Does she –?"

"Yes," Golden said. She gestured again for the girl to join them. The girl stepped forward. She was smaller than Simon, short, and lithe. Her eyes were on his daughter. They flicked to him with worry and then back to Golden with determination. Golden's voice hardened as she said, "They wanted her to marry a prince and she didn't."

"She saved me," Erayshin said, her voice fluid with words learned far away.

"He brought a dowry," Golden said, her voice filled with the sharpness and longing that Simon had first heard so many years before from his dragon wife—the voice of dragon lust.

"There have been twelve more," Erayshin said. An impish look crossed her green eyes and gave Simon the distinct impression that the foreign girl was just as devilish as his daughter.

"I've got a rather nice horde," Golden agreed.

"I asked to come here," Erayshin said, giving Simon a frank—and somewhat terrified look.

Simon had rarely seen that look but he knew all the muscles that caused it. He waved to his daughter. "Why don't you let me talk with your friend for a bit, Golden?"

"I need to stretch my wings," Golden said agreeably.

"There are some nice places to the north—the far north," Simon suggested.

"Thirty minutes?" Golden asked.

"That would be plenty," Simon agreed. His daughter smiled at him, waved at her friend and walked off into the dark. Not long after a beautiful gold dragon erupted into the skies above them and raced away northwards.

"She's been gone two years," Simon said in the silence.

"I met her about six months after," Erayshin said, moving closer to him so that she could look up into his eyes in the gloomy dark.

"My wife—her mother—is inside, sleeping," Simon said, waving toward the house. "I'd invite you in but… well, Elveth is jealous."

Erayshin smiled. "So is your daughter."

"She learned it from the best of teachers," Simon told her with an answering smile. A moment later he said, "Will there be a prince who claims your heart?"

"Will there be a woman who claims yours?" Erayshin responded. When Simon shook his head, she nodded. "I came to ask you how you managed."

"It will be easier for you," Simon told her. "Without a daughter to argue with, all you'll have to –"

"There will be a child," Erayshin said, her hand going to her belly. "I wanted to know –"

"A child?" Simon interrupted in amazement. "How?"

"Golden told me: 'Where there is a heart, there is a way'," Erayshin said. "It took her many months but we found a way."

"The child is *hers*?" Simon cried.

"Ours," Erayshin said. Her smiled turned inward for a moment. "Just once, she became a male."

"I must write of this," Simon said, nearly running back to the house for pen and paper.

"Please," Erayshin said, reaching forward and touching his arm for the first time. "I must know—how, what, how –?"

Simon put his other hand over hers. "You have to say yes if you say anything," he said, glad to have this one chance to share his hard-won knowledge with someone. "You must be silent when you want to scream, be obeisant when you want to fight –"

"I can do that," Erayshin said, trying to sound certain.

"You should be ready to move often," Simon warned.

"She has a horde, we know where to go," Erayshin affirmed.

"And you must never stop loving the both of them," Simon said finally.

"How do you do that?" Erayshin said as they heard wings in the distance flapping back toward them. "She's been gone all this time—how did you –"

"And you have to love them more than life itself, love them enough to let them go when they need, love who they want," Simon told her. He moved and brought her close against him, wrapping her into a tight embrace.

Erayshin looked up at him, her ears wet with tears. "Will you forgive me? For taking her love from you?"

Simon shook his head, his lips quilting upwards. "You could never do that. I will honor you."

"For what?"

"For the courage to love her."

The wings hovered near the forest, stopped, and Simon turned them to face the darkness.

Golden rushed out into the light, paused fearfully, and then rushed into their open arms.

While PIERS ANTHONY is most famous for his long-running novel series set in the fictional realm of *Xanth,* he has written more than 160 books in various genres. He's been a New York Times bestselling author over twenty times and has won The British Fantasy award for *A Spell for Chameleon.*

See more of his work here: www.hipiers.com

MOUNTAIN SPIRIT
Piers Anthony

Part One: Background, dull but necessary

The Village of Mire was not much of a place, as its descriptive name indicated, but its denizens liked it because it had one outstanding asset: Mt. Miracle. When the villagers had a problem, they could appeal to the mountain, and the mountain would solve it. It had done so many times in past centuries. Once there had been a killing drought, and the mountain had brought copious rain. Once there was an invasion by a foreign power, and the village had been directly in the path of the marching enemy army, certain extinction. But the mountain had spewed out major rivers of lava that encircled the village, causing the invaders to hastily detour around it; later when the lava cooled and weathered it became fertile soil, another benefit. Once the king was going to set aside Mt. Miracle as a tourist attraction, moving all the villagers out and razing their houses; kings were like that. The mountain shook the ground warningly and blew out volcanic dust and clouds of villainous looking gas, satisfying the king's men that this was no safe place for a resort. Once the village had gotten in a bad financial bind, so had asked for money; the mountain issued a lava stream of solid gold that forever solved that problem. When there was a crop blight, the mountain gave them access to blight-resistant plants on its lower slopes. The mountain always came through without stinting.

But there was a price: a lovely sacrificial maiden. She had to be the prettiest nubile virgin available, and of good mind and character, a perfect young woman. What the mountain did with her no one knew; she was never seen again. That meant there would be one or more heartbroken young men, not to mention her family. So the villagers were cautious about asking the mountain's favor.

Now they had a crisis: almost all their marriage-eligible young women were gone. A recruiter had come and lured them away with the promise of fabulous notoriety and wealth as showgirls in the big city. Only homely women remained. Rather than marry them, the young men were about to go off to the city themselves to seek their fortunes. That would effectively wipe out Mire, which would slowly fade as the older citizens died out. Something had to be done.

The Village elders cogitated and finally, by dint of much discussion facilitated by several kegs of ale, came up with the answer: they would have to appeal to Mt. Miracle. But how could they meet the mountain's price, when there were no remaining pretty girls? It was not possible to pass off any ugly one; the mountain knew the difference and would only be annoyed if they tried. They could not risk that.

But there was one saving grace: the recruiter had taken only girls of the age of consent, planning to return a year later to pick up some more as they came of age. There were some promising prospects, for the village was known for its lovely women. One outstanding girl had been one day short, and so was left behind, to her immense frustration. She would have to wait another year. This was Faire, smart, talented, sweet, virginal, and so lovely that mirrors brightened in her presence. Unfortunately she was also honest, so had refused to lie about her age, to the recruiter's considerable disappointment.

The village men clustered about her, each eager to marry her. But Faire had been bitten by the bug of fame, and no longer wanted to settle for life as the dull wife of a dull farmer, miller, or mechanic. She wanted excitement and fame, plus maybe a really hunky rich young man who would forever dote on her. Nothing like that offered in Mire. So when the Village elders approached her, she agreed to become the Mountain Spirit. That at least would give her celebrity for a day, and who knew what surprises the mountain might have for her thereafter?

Thus it came to the ceremony of sacrifice: the village elders stood on the designated foothill of the mountain and made their case. "We beseech you, Mt. Miracle, to solve our problem: we need a coterie of nubile attractive young women to become loyal hardworking village wives. We offer in exchange Faire."

Some of the older denizens shook their heads. It seemed impossible for the mountain to grant this particular wish, assuming it even wanted to try. What could it do? Advertise for immigrants? Girls of that description were notoriously fickle, and were unlikely to settle for the backwoods life. In fact, that attitude was the cause of the problem.

Faire stepped forward. If the mountain accepted her, it would grant the beseechers' favor. And it did: a delicate gust of wind ruffled her skirt to show her marvelous legs, and tousled her lustrous hair, and the Spirit of the Mountain infused her. Suddenly she was twice as beautiful as before, a manifest impossibility, with an expression of rapture on her face. "Farewell, friends," she said. "My destiny calls." Then Faire spread her arms and floated up into the air and on over the forested slope of the mountain's base. She glided up to the steep rocky faces, and disappeared in the swirling mist of the peak.

The elders visibly relaxed. They had known their offering was lovely, but there was always a bit of a fog of doubt when dealing with the mountain.

There was another part of the ceremony. If any man were able to climb the mountain to the top within two days, he could claim the girl and bring her home, and the mountain still would grant the favor. This was a compromise worked out in the mists of antiquity, so that the villagers could maintain hope that the sacrificial maidens could theoretically be rescued, though it had never happened. So there were a number of husky young louts eager to join the chase, the more fools they.

Part Two: Challenge, as it starts to get interesting

Heroe considered. The other young men were forging ahead, following the route that the Spirit Maiden had taken, albeit on the ground. This was bound to be mischief. So Heroe chose to walk around the base of the mountain, studying its avenues. He had two days, and a straight climb could be done in one, if unimpeded. That of course was the rub. He knew the reputation of Mt. Miracle: it did not like to be climbed. It tolerated birds on its higher reaches, and ants, but not much else. Finesse was required.

Heroe didn't hurry. He was passing a turnip field, careful not to step on the plants. He had a sense that there was something here for him, if he just let it catch up. What he needed was not the fastest route, but the right route. That was not necessarily purely physical.

A mature villager fell in beside him. "You're not from Mire," the man said.

"I believe the challenge is open to all," Heroe said.

"Oh, sure. But I've seen you before, somewhere."

"The sister village of Bog."

"That's it! At their Challenge two weeks ago, petitioning their mountain spirit. I was there delivering a load of turnips. Hi; I'm Tunsley, turnip farmer. This is my acreage. I saw you crossing my field and thought I'd check."

"Heroe, adventurer."

"In fact you were one of the entrants. Bog had the same problem we did: their pretty girls getting raided. My daughter was one of them, here in Mire; we couldn't hold her back. I had to get on home before dark, so I didn't see how that turned out. You gave up on the chase?"

"No. I won it."

Tunsley stared. "But nobody ever won against a mountain!"

Heroe shrugged. "Believe what you will."

"But if you did, what are you doing here? I mean, you would have the prettiest girl of your village to love, cherish, and marry. I saw her take off; she was almost as lovely as our Faire."

"No. I did not take her."

"Now I'm not the brightest man extant, which is why I'm a farmer; turnips are easy. But this doesn't make any sense to me."

135

"She was a closet lesbian. She enlisted with the mountain so that she wouldn't have to fight off the men any more. The mountain doesn't care about sexual orientation, just beauty and dedication. She confessed that, in tears, when I won her, knowing that she had no further choice. But I didn't want to do that to her, so I let her go. It would be like forcing me to marry a man; I'd never be happy, and knew she wouldn't. I spoke to the mountain, and it allowed her lady lover to come up so they could live together in privacy, protected by the mountain."

"You did a decent thing," Tunsley said, amazed.

"I try to be a decent guy. But it left me without a bride. So I came here to try for this mountain spirit, who I think is even more lovely than the other."

"My daughter knows her," Tunsley said. "She's no lesbian. She just doesn't want to settle for the backwater village life. Can't say I blame her. She could've been a star, if she'd lied one day about her age. I have to respect that."

"I have to respect it too," Heroe said. "If I win her, I'll do what I can to enable her to shine."

"I'm curious, as there has been no news from Bog. How did your mountain solve your village's problem?"

"I can't tell you that. It put a magical geis on me forbidding me to tell until after Mt. Miracle has been dealt with. But I can say the mountain came through. So will yours, if I win through to the peak."

"You know that no one in centuries has ever made it to the peak?"

"Yes. But I hope to be the first. It's a tough but honest challenge. The mountains don't like to be bothered by weaklings any more than they want imperfect girls as offerings."

Tunsley considered briefly. "I like you, Heroe, and hope you will succeed, though I fear you will die as so many have before you. Therefore I will help you, to the extent I can."

"I had a premonition that there was something good for me here at the turnip farm. I suspect your help will be invaluable."

"I have spent many years exploring the mountain slopes, admiring Mt. Miracle, and it has come to tolerate me in a manner it does not do for strangers. It allowed me to make a map of its features, some of which are beautiful, some dangerous. I will show you that map so that you may be guided in your challenge. But I must warn you that there is no way to the peak that does not pass by one or more threats. The odds are still against you."

"I thrive on challenge," Heroe said. "It gives my restless life meaning."

Tunsley reached into his shirt and brought out a hide parchment. On it was drawn a crude but accurate map of the mountain, as seen from above. "This is it."

Heroe studied it briefly. "This is exactly what I need. Thank you."

"You may take it with you."

"There is no need. I have memorized it."

The farmer pursed his lips. "You are remarkable."

"Not really. The mountain I conquered gave me certain gifts, such as premonition, minor magic, and eidetic memory. I did not appreciate the need for the third until you showed me the map."

"Your mountain is helping you with this one?" the farmer asked, surprised.

"Yes. I believe it concluded that none of your local boys will succeed in ascending to the peak, and since I did not take the woman I won, it is helping me win another. It's a matter of mountainly honor."

"I am still learning things about mountains," Tunsley said.

"They are to be sincerely respected."

"They are indeed." Heroe glanced up the slope. "I must get moving. I have another premonition."

"But you're heading right for the avalanche area!" Tunsley protested.

"Yes, as your map informs me. Thank you muchly for it." He strode onward.

The turnip farmer watched him go, bemused. The challenge he faced was formidable. Was he a hero, as his name implied, or a fool?

Part Three: Adventure, self-explanatory

Heroe forged directly to the avalanche area. This was a moderately steep slope strewn with rounded rocks. It did not look too bad. But he knew better than to trust it. He stood at the edge, waiting.

Another young man arrived, walking an intersecting path. He had a hiking staff and a loaded backpack. He was clearly one of those challenging the mountain. "Get out of my way, jerk," he snapped.

Heroe stepped aside. "By all means. But I feel it only fair to warn you that this is an avalanche area, not to be treaded lightly. It is better to bypass it."

"Too bad for you, chicken. I have to make it to the peak before some other lout does, and this is the shortest route. You can wait forever for all I care."

"I will wait," Heroe agreed.

The man tromped on across the slope. When he got fairly into the zone, there was a warning rumble, as of stones being jarred loose. Instead of sensibly retreating, he hurried on forward. Heroe, watching, winced.

The rumble increased in magnitude. Rocks began to roll.

The climber broke into a lumbering run, but there was too far to go. A rolling slide of rocks came down, catching the man and burying him.

His hiking staff flew up into the air, then clattered on the stones as if marking the place of burial.

The motion slowed, and the stones settled into their new places. The avalanche was over.

Now Heroe started across himself. The rumble resumed, but was powerless to restart the avalanche; the rocks were already moved. He came to the staff and took it; its owner would no longer be needing it.

He made it safely across the zone, thanks to his timing. He regretted the fate of the other climber, but the lout had refused to heed common sense.

Beyond the zone the slope developed a thicket of small dry bushes. Heroe paused again. His mental map indicated that this was a region of chronic fires. If he got in the middle of it, he could be trapped by a spontaneous blaze. But there did not seem to be an alternative route. How should he handle this?

He explored the mental map more carefully. Beside the dry bushes was a steep river channel that was now dry, the water diverted to an adjacent channel. The mountain could probably switch them back and forth to catch unwary climbers. Could he somehow make use of this? Maybe.

Heroe returned to the avalanche to fetch some rocks. He carried several to the stream bed and dropped them in, blocking it somewhat.

Now he went to the channel. "I'm going to climb through this to get around the burning field," he announced. He wedged his feet in crevices and started climbing.

The water shifted. In a moment the stream was pouring along this channel, soaking him. Heroe scrambled out of it. "Or maybe not," he said.

The water continued to pour, making sure he couldn't change his mind. It coursed to the more level river bed below, encountered the block, and quickly overflowed, spreading across the dry field and sinking into the earth.

Heroe started across the slope. Fire sputtered, trying to ignite, but couldn't get properly started, because of the water. One menace had canceled out the other. He could feel the mountain seething, but it was unable to get him.

Now he came to a jagged crack, a small chasm, too wide to hurdle, too deep to navigate. He would have to bridge it. Naturally there was no loose wood nearby for construction.

Heroe took down his backpack. He brought out heavy gloves and a length of stout cord with a small anchor on the end. He stood at the brink and whirled the anchor around and around in widening circles, crossing the chasm, until at last it caught against the trunk of a tree on the other side and wrapped around it, the anchor catching on the cord. Then he put his pack back on, tied the near end of the rope around his waist, and dropped into the crevasse. He smacked into the opposite wall, then hauled himself up hand over hand until he reached the ground and the tree. He was across.

The mountain rumbled angrily. Enough with this passive resistance; it was time to get serious. A vent opened not far up the slope. Brightly burning lava welled out and flowed like the liquid fire it was directly down toward Heroe. He dodged to the side, but the advancing tongue changed direction to follow. The mountain was no longer trying to make it seem like coincidence; now it meant to dispatch him directly.

But Heroe had an inkling of a notion, knowing that sort of thing could happen here. He ran in a circle, and the fire followed. He completed the circle, leaping over the stream of lava, and ran on. The lava intersected itself, took itself for an enemy, and fought itself. In a moment it was a whirling column of fire, as each part of it tried to surmount the other.

Heroe did not stay to watch the fray. He got out of there quietly but swiftly. Another threat evaded.

His next challenge was a sheer icy rock face leading toward the summit. It was almost vertical, impossible to climb barehanded. He opened his pack again and fetched metal pitons and a small hammer. He hammered in the first piton, then a second. The mountain shivered with ire, as if its flesh were being punctured, but it couldn't stop him from making his slow climb, piton by piton.

But Mt. Miracle was hardly through. A wind came up, becoming a storm that blasted sleet at him and tried to dislodge him. He hung on, and when there was a pause, hammered in another piton. The storm raged, but could not stop him.

Finally, cold, tired, and hungry, he made it to the top of the ice face. Not far beyond he saw Faire, hovering just above the rock, eye-splittingly lovely, beckoning him. From there it was relatively simple to mount the peak itself. He had made it.

But he paused, suffering another premonition. This was too easy. So he got down on his belly and crawled toward the gesturing mountain spirit. Sure enough, there was a ledge, concealed by illusion. Had he walked straight ahead he would have fallen off it and been killed. As it was, he was able to navigate it by feel, get beyond it, and make it to the peak. Now he had truly won.

Part Four, conclusion, satisfying

"You made it!" Faire exclaimed, kissing him ardently. "You have won me. I feared you would not. I hated having to beckon you, but it was part of the challenge. Who are you?"

"I am Heroe, from Bog Village, some way distant. I will love you passionately, and cater to your slightest whim. I will take you on a tour around the world, so that everyone may see and envy your beauty."

"This interests me," she confessed.

"But first there is a detail we must attend to."

"A detail?"

"Lead me to the mountain fastness."

"As you wish." She took his hand, and the pair of them flew gently down to the rock face he had so effortlessly navigated. She touched it, and a door opened. They entered.

Inside the mountain was a chamber wherein floated dozens of lovely maidens in suspended animation. These were the sacrificial girls of all the prior occasions, locked in forever as they had been in life, not aging at all. All were pristine, but many had clothing and hair styles that bespoke prior ages. In fact some were centuries old, by exterior reckoning. It was like a historical museum. Faire had expected to come here herself, if not rescued. The mountain had assured her, non-verbally, that it was not an arduous confinement; it would seem like only an instant before she woke. The maidens were merely being saved.

"Wake," Heroe said, and clapped his hands.

Immediately all the young women snapped out of stasis. "Oh!" they exclaimed almost together. "Have we been asleep long?"

"A decade at least," Faire said. "Millennia at most."

They were amazed. "It seems like only an instant."

"Exactly," Faire agreed.

"Listen up, girls," Heroe said. "I am Heroe. I have conquered Miracle Mountain. But before I depart with my phenomenally lovely bride I must assist the mountain in solving the village problem. They desperately need lovely, talented, and obliging young woman to marry their farmers, millers, and mechanics and bear their children. Women who will not be tempted to flee to the big city for show business."

The women looked confused. "What is show business?" one asked.

"That is where pretty women don revealing garb and prance around a stage, inciting leering men to pointless lust, as they are not allowed to touch the women."

"Eeuu," the girl said.

"What's a big city?" another asked. She wore a dinosaur hide robe and evidently dated from a time before cities evolved.

"A huge collection of people, far away from here."

"Ugh!" the girls chorused in horror. Then one explained: "We are Mountain Spirits. We must remain near the mountain, and commune on its slopes daily, for it sustains us. If we go away from it, our true ages will quickly manifest, and we will become old crones, age 28 at least. So we wish only to make loving families close by, and raise our dear children to be mountain spirits too."

Heroe saw that the mountain had indeed solved the village problem. These girls would remain here, and so would their children. "But what of you, Faire?" he asked his new beloved.

"I have not yet become a full Mountain Spirit, though I have felt the passionate lure of it," she replied. "You rescued me too soon. I still want to travel and see the sights. But once I get with child, which should not take long considering the sustained effort we will make, I will want to return here to stay. I am no longer interested in show business, just in fulfilling my natural destiny as a wife and mother."

Heroe liked that answer. "You shall have it," he said, kissing her.

"Oooo," the maiden spirits ooooed, jealous. "We want men of our own to kiss and fondle and support."

"This way," Heroe said. He led them out the stone doorway. Then they all spread their arms and floated gently down toward the village, where a number of louts were about to become happier than they perhaps deserved.

Once again, Mt. Miracle was responding in full measure. There would of course be future crises, when it would resume its collection of sacrificial spirits. The mountain took the long view, having plenty of time.

MEGAN MOORE is a writer and artist based out of her native north Texas. She is currently working on numerous projects, including a YA novel. Megan made her writing debut in the shared-world anthology *World's Collider*, with a second story featuring in *Nightscapes: Volume 1*.

MOON GLASS
Megan N. Moore

The moon is made of glass. Everyone knows this. See the way she glimmers, starlight shining from her sides as the sunlight cascades over our earth and catches in her body, sending fractal patterns through the cracks within.

See, on darker nights, how this world is imitated on her surface, as if she were a twin planet. See the dead, cold, glassy reflection of satellites and cityscapes.

~~*~*

A long time ago a meteor collided with the surface of the moon and sent down sparkling showers, spinning in circles around the world in a shimmering orbit until they collided with the earth to be ground up into sand. Very few have seen moon glass. Even fewer have touched it, or held it in their hand.

I own a piece of moon glass.

"What would happen if something bigger hit the moon?" asks my daughter. Earlier she saw a tumbler shatter into a thousand-thousand pieces as it fell from the kitchen counter. She is afraid. We are all afraid, when we are young.

"It would take something very large to shatter the moon," I tell her as I take the piece of moon glass from my own neck and place it around hers. She fondles the piece in her pudgy, small hands. It is the color of rose, cut through with shimmering green streaks. Sometimes you can see starlight reflected from deep, deep inside.

It glistens against her funereal black dress, already streaked with dirt and mud. She refused to change when we returned home from the church. There are even streaks of green sand across her nose. I try to brush it off and she struggles with a small, pitiful whine.

"Can I go now?" she asks.

"Not until Granddad gets back. Don't you want to see him?"

"I guess," she says. Then, in a quieter tone, she adds, "I wish Grandmamma was still here."

~~*~*

On the day my heart was first broken, my mother wound a piece of cord three times around the narrow end of the glass and hung it around my neck. A boy who had told me he loved me decided that he loved someone else instead.

"It makes your eyes sparkle," she told me. "You're such a beautiful girl."

I wasn't; I was gangly and awkward and sixteen. She knew that as well as I did. But when I looked into the mirror I thought that perhaps my eyes did sparkle a little brighter, and it made me smile, and when I saw the boy he had decided he loved me again. But I no longer loved him.

When my mother was sixteen all the boys in her town said they loved her. My father said he would do anything for her love and my mother asked for impossible things. She wanted to hold starlight in her hand. When he offered her a diamond, she said, "I want the moon."

My father left their town that night. He rode to the edge of the earth and he sailed the sea in search of moon glass, even though it was impossible. He danced with the Priestesses of the Moon, and was forced to flee them when he denied the High Priestess a kiss. He studied ancient scrolls in the library of an ancient land, and he climbed a mountain so high that at its peak it was impossible to breathe—but love makes people do impossible things.

From there, he could see the moon's shattered surface. The mounds of moon dust swirled across her surface, caught up in the gravitational pull. My father dropped to his knees and prayed for the moon—or perhaps he prayed for my mother's love. Maybe he asked for both.

As he stood on the mountaintop, two shining points of light began to descend from the moon's glimmering surface. The first sliced into the earth at his feet. The second sliced into his chest, where it was embedded in his heart, and where it still remains. He picked up the glass and climbed down the mountain, and sailed across the sea back to a small and inconsequential town, where a small and inconsequential girl dreamed of holding starlight in her hands.

I'm told that on their wedding night there was a moon shower — glittering specks of dust filled the nighttime atmosphere and made the whole world glow with celestial light.

They say that moon dust is a blessing. I hoped for moon dust on my own wedding day, but there were only clouds and shadows. "We don't need starlight," my husband said.

He was the boy from two houses over. We skinned our knees together, and practiced fumbling first kisses. He broke my heart, and I broke his, time and time again.

I would have climbed the highest mountain for him—I would have sailed a river of stars just to pluck a piece of moon glass from the moon's surface. Instead, I asked for the impossible. I asked for the moon, and I asked for starlight, but he found his true love on the other side of the sea.

After he was gone I had the moon glass, and my daughter, to remind me of the existence of love that defies all impossibilities.

~~*~*

She looks very much like my mother, and not at all like me. She has pale yellow hair and a spray of freckles across the bridge of her nose, which is still dotted with dust. The moon did not shine for my wedding day, but the sky was flooded with dust on the night that she was born.

When she smiles, her eyes do more than sparkle—they are kaleidoscopic in the way they catch the light. Her thrilled shrieks reverberate throughout the empty house and I sit at the kitchen table, waiting for my father to walk through the door.

He has been restless since my mother died. The emptiness of the house they built together eats away at him. He says it is as strange and dark inside those walls as it would be if the moon were to vanish from the sky.

Although it is still not night, I can see the moon shimmer in the pale blue light preceding dusk. I can almost see the glimmer of my mother's eyes in the near-translucent sphere, and I imagine that her soul has been caught up inside the glass.

~~*~*

My father comes through the door. He pauses at the threshold, and half-smiles as he sees my daughter, his hand involuntarily clutching at his chest. Then there is an excited squeal and my daughter sails into the room. "Granddad!" she calls out, and as she skids to a stop the cord of the moon glass necklace comes undone and slips from around her throat.

It falls to the floor and breaks. The three of us stand and stare at the shattered glass, and without a word I lean down to brush it all up, ignoring the sting as the most minute of pieces embeds itself in my palm.

"I'm sorry," says my daughter, breathless, repeating the phrase over and over again until it becomes meaningless.

All I do is smile at her, like my mother smiled at me every time she promised broken hearts don't last forever.

I hand the shards of moon glass to my father, and he places them into the box that holds my mother's ashes. And I know now where he will go. He will cross the sea, and climb the highest mountain. Once, when they were young, he promised her the moon and returned with a piece of glass. Now he will give her the moon itself.

~~*~*

Someday, I know, the time will come that something large enough to break the moon invades our atmosphere. The moon will shatter into a thousand-thousand pieces, sending brilliant shards showering to the earth to be ground to multicolored, iridescent dust.

The night will be streaked by starlight as pieces of the moon rain down, and for one brief instant all of humanity will marvel at her beauty and her grace as the sky lights up with one last celestial ballet. Then they will crash down, and down, and everything will be ended.

Someday, my daughter will learn. We are all afraid, when we are young. Afraid that we will never find love, or afraid that we will find love

145

and lose it. Someday, someone will promise my daughter the stars and he will climb the highest mountain for her, or sail the sea just to find an impossible piece of glass. Someday I will die, and she will die, and all these memories will be forgotten.

But there will always be moon dust, and moon dust is a blessing. It holds all our hopes and dreams, even those that seem impossible.

"Tell me the story, Granddad," says my daughter, the matter of the broken glass already forgotten. My father lifts her up onto his knee and wipes the smudge of green dust from her nose.

"Which one?"

"You know which one!" she says.

I move to the window, listening as my father begins a tale I have heard too many times to count. The night sky shimmers with dust.

The late ROGER ZELAZNY is the legendary author behind the much-loved *Amber Chronicles*, which began in 1970 with *Nine Princes in Amber*. The series is considered by many to be one of the finest ever written. During his career, he was awarded with six Hugos and 3 Nebula awards (after being nominated a staggering 14 times for each), as well as a host of other awards. He wrote around 50 novels, 150 shorts and 3 collections of poetry, and he also edited multiple anthologies.

Roger left us too soon in 1995 after being diagnosed with colon cancer. We are honoured and delighted to include one of his classic stories in this volume.

THE GEORGE BUSINESS
Roger Zelazny

Deep in his lair, Dart twisted his green and golden length about his small hoard, his sleep troubled by dreams of a series of identical armored assailants. Since dragons' dreams are always prophetic, he woke with a shudder, cleared his throat to the point of sufficient illumination to check on the state of his treasure, stretched, yawned and set forth up the tunnel to consider the strength of the opposition. If it was too great, he would simply flee, he decided. The hell with the hoard; it wouldn't be the first time.

As he peered from the cave mouth, he beheld a single knight in mismatched armor atop a tired-looking gray horse, just rounding the bend. His lance was not even couched, but still pointing skyward.

Assuring himself that the man was unaccompanied, he roared and slithered forth.

"Halt," he bellowed, "you who are about to fry!"

The knight obliged.

"You're the one I came to see," the man said. "I have—"

"Why," Dart asked, "do you wish to start this business up again? Do you realize how long it has been since a knight and a dragon have done battle?"

"Yes, I do. Quite a while. But I—"

"It is almost invariably fatal to one of the parties concerned. Usually your side."

"Don't I know it? Look, you've got me wrong-"

"I dreamt a dragon dream of a young man named George with whom I must do battle. You bear him an extremely close resemblance."

"I can explain. It's not as bad as it looks. You see—"

"Is your name George?"

"Well, yes. But don't let that bother you—"

"It does bother me. You want my pitiful hoard? It wouldn't keep you in beer money for the season. Hardly worth the risk."

"I'm not after your hoard—"

"I haven't grabbed off a virgin in centuries. They're usually old and tough, anyhow, not to mention hard to find."

"No one's accusing—"

"As for cattle, I always go a great distance. I've gone out of my way, you might say, to avoid getting a bad name in my own territory."

"I know you're no real threat here. I've researched it quite carefully—"

"And do you think that armor will really protect you when I exhale my deepest, hottest flames?"

"Hell, no! So don't do it, huh? If you'd please—"

"And that lance… You're not even holding it properly."

George lowered the lance.

"On that you are correct," he said, "but it happens to be tipped with one of the deadliest poisons known to Herman the Apothecary."

"I say! That's hardly sporting!"

"I know. But even if you incinerate me, I'll bet I can scratch you before I go."

"Now that would be rather silly—both of us dying like that—wouldn't it?" Dart observed, edging away. "It would serve no useful purpose that I can see."

"I feel precisely the same way about it."

"Then why are we getting ready to fight?"

"I have no desire whatsoever to fight with you!"

"I'm afraid I don't understand. You said your name is George, and I had this dream—"

"I can explain it."

"But the poisoned lance—"

"Self-protection, to hold you off long enough to put a proposition to you."

Dart's eyelids lowered slightly.

"What sort of proposition?"

"I want to hire you."

"Hire me? Whatever for? And what are you paying?"

"Mind if I rest this lance a minute? No tricks?"

"Go ahead. If you're talking gold your life is safe."

George rested his lance and undid a pouch on his belt. He dipped his hand into it and withdrew a fistful of shining coins. He tossed them gently, so that they clinked and shone in the morning light.

"You have my full attention. That's a good piece of change there."

"My life's savings. All yours—in return for a bit of business."

"What's the deal?"

George replaced the coins in his pouch and gestured.

"See that castle in the distance—two hills away?"

"I've flown over it many times."

"In the tower to the west are the chambers of Rosalind, daughter of the Baron Maurice. She is very dear to his heart, and I wish to wed her."

"There's a problem?"

"Yes. She's attracted to big, brawny barbarian types, into which category I, alas, do not fall. In short, she doesn't like me."

"That is a problem."

"So, if I could pay you to crash in there and abduct her, to bear her off to some convenient and isolated place and wait for me, I'll come along, we'll fake a battle, I'll vanquish you, you'll fly away and I'll take her home. I am certain I will then appear sufficiently heroic in her eyes to rise from sixth to first position in her list of suitors. How does that sound to you?"

Dart sighed a long column of smoke.

"Human, I bear your kind no special fondness—particularly the armored variety with lances—so I don't know why I'm telling you this... Well, I do know actually... But never mind. I could manage it, all right. But, if you win the hand of that maid, do you know what's going to happen? The novelty of your deed will wear off after a time—and you know that there will be no encore. Give her a year, I'd say, and you'll catch her fooling around with one of those brawny barbarians she finds so attractive. Then you must either fight him and be slaughtered or wear horns, as they say."

George laughed.

"It's nothing to me how she spends her spare time. I've a girlfriend in town myself."

Dart's eyes widened.

"I'm afraid I don't understand..."

"She's the old baron's only offspring, and he's on his last legs. Why else do you think an uncomely wench like that would have six suitors? Why else would I gamble my life's savings to win her?"

"I see," said Dart. "Yes, I can understand greed."

"I call it a desire for security."

"Quite. In that case, forget my simple-minded advice. All right, give me the gold and I'll do it." Dart gestured with one gleaming vane. "The first valley in those western mountains seems far enough from my home for our confrontation."

"I'll pay you half now and half on delivery."

"Agreed, be sure to have the balance with you, though, and drop it during the scuffle. I'll return for it after you two have departed. Cheat me and I'll repeat the performance, with a different ending."

"The thought had already occurred to me. Now, we'd better practice a bit, to make it look realistic. I'll rush at you with the lance, and whatever side she's standing on I'll aim for it to pass you on the other. You raise that wing, grab the lance and scream like hell. Blow a few flames around, too."

"I'm going to see you scour the tip of that lance before we rehearse this."

"Right. I'll release the lance while you're holding it next to you and rolling around. Then I'll dismount and rush toward you with my blade. I'll whack you with the flat of it—again, on the far side—a few times. Then you bellow again and fly away."

"Just how sharp is that thing anyway?"

"Damned dull. It was my grandfather's. Hasn't been honed since he was a boy."

"And you drop the money during the fight?"

"Certainly. How does that sound?"

"Not bad. I can have a few clusters of red berries under my wing, too. I'll squash them once the action gets going."

"Nice touch. Yes, do that. Let's give it a quick rehearsal now, and then get on with the real thing."

"And don't whack too hard…"

That afternoon, Rosalind of Maurice Manor was abducted by a green-and-gold dragon who crashed through the wall of her chamber and bore her off in the direction of the western mountains.

"Never fear!" shouted her sixth-ranked suitor—who just happened to be riding by—to her aged father who stood wringing his hands on a nearby balcony. "I'll rescue her!" and he rode off to the west.

Coming into the valley where Rosalind stood backed into a rocky cleft, guarded by the fuming beast of gold and green, George couched his lance.

"Release that maiden and face your doom!" he cried.

Dart bellowed, George rushed. The lance fell from his hands and the dragon rolled upon the grounds, spewing gouts of fire into the air. A red substance dribbled from beneath the thundering creature's left wing. Before Rosalind's wide eyes, George advanced and swung his blade several times.

"…and that!" he cried, as the monster stumbled to its feet and sprang into the air, dripping more red.

It circled once and beat its way off toward the top of the mountain, then over it and away.

"Oh George!" Rosalind cried, and she was in his arms. "Oh, George…"

He pressed her to him for a moment.

"I'll take you home now," he said.

~~*~*

That evening as he was counting his gold, Dart heard the sound of two horses approaching his cave. He rushed up the tunnel and peered out.

George, now mounted on a proud white stallion and leading the gray, wore a matched suit of bright armor. He was not smiling, however.

"Good evening," he said.

"Good evening. What brings you back so soon?"

"Things didn't turn out exactly as I'd anticipated."

"You seem far better accoutered. I'd say your fortunes had taken a turn."

THE GEORGE BUSINESS ~ ZELAZNY

"Oh, I recovered my expenses and came out a bit ahead. But that's all. I'm on my way out of town. Thought I'd stop by and tell you the end of the story. —Good show you put on, by the way. It probably would have done the trick—"

"But—?"

"She was married to one of the brawny barbarians this morning, in their family chapel. They were just getting ready for a wedding trip when you happened by."

"I'm awfully sorry."

"Well, it's the breaks. To add insult, though, her father dropped dead during your performance. My former competitor is now the new baron. He rewarded me with a new horse and armor, a gratuity and a scroll from the local scribe lauding me as a dragon slayer. Then he hinted rather strongly that the horse and my new reputation could take me far. Didn't like the way Rosalind was looking at me now I'm a hero."

"That is a shame. Well, we tried."

"Yes. So I just stopped by to thank you and let you know how it all turned out. It would have been a good idea—if it had worked."

"You could have hardly foreseen such abrupt nuptials. You know, I've spent the entire day thinking about the affair. We did manage it awfully well."

"Oh, no doubt about that. It went beautifully."

"I was thinking… How'd you like a chance to get your money back?"

"What have you got in mind?"

"Uh—When I was advising you earlier that you might not be happy with the lady, I was trying to think about the situation in human terms. Your desire was entirely understandable to me otherwise. In fact, you think quite a bit like a dragon."

"Really?"

"Yes. It's rather amazing, actually. Now—realizing that it only failed because of a fluke, your idea still has considerable merit."

"I'm afraid I don't follow you."

"There is—ah—a lovely lady of my own species whom I have been singularly unsuccessful in impressing for a long while now. Actually, there are an unusual number of parallels in our situations."

"She has a large hoard, huh?"

"Extremely so."

"Older woman?"

"Among dragons, a few centuries this way or that are not so important. But she, too, has other admirers and seems attracted by the more brash variety."

"Uh-huh. I begin to get the drift. You gave me some advice once. I'll return the favor. Some things are more important than hoards."

"Name one."

"My life. If I were to threaten her she might do me in all by herself, before you could come to her rescue."

"No, she's a demure little thing. Anyway, it's all a matter of timing. I'll perch on a hilltop nearby—I'll show you where—and signal you when to begin your approach. Now, this time I have to win, of course. Here's how we'll work it..."

~~*~*

George sat on the white charger and divided his attention between the distant cave mouth and the crest of a high hill off to his left. After a time, a shining winged form flashed through the air and settled upon the hill. Moments later, it raised one bright wing.

He lowered his visor, couched his lance and started forward. When he came within hailing distance of the cave he cried out:

"I know you're in there, Megtag! I've come to destroy you and make off with your hoard! You godless beast! Eater of children! This is your last day on earth!"

An enormous burnished head with cold green eyes emerged from the cave. Twenty feet of flame shot from its huge mouth and scorched the rock before it. George halted hastily. The beast looked twice the size of Dart and did not seem in the least retiring. Its scales rattled like metal as it began to move forward.

"Perhaps I exaggerated..." George began, and he heard the frantic flapping of giant vanes overhead.

As the creature advanced, he felt himself seized by the shoulders. He was borne aloft so rapidly that the scene below him dwindled to toy size in a matter of moments. He saw his new steed bolt and flee rapidly back along the route they had followed.

"What the hell happened?" he cried.

"I hadn't been around for a while," Dart replied. "Didn't know one of the others had moved in with her. You're lucky I'm fast. That's Pelladon. He's a mean one."

"Great. Don't you think you should have checked first?"

"Sorry. I thought she'd take decades to make up her mind—without prompting. Oh, what a hoard! You should have seen it!"

"Follow that horse. I want him back."

~~*~*

They sat before Dart's cave, drinking.

"Where'd you ever get a whole barrel of wine?"

"Lifted it from a barge, up the river. I do that every now and then. I keep a pretty good cellar, if I do say."

"Indeed. Well, we're none the poorer, really. We can drink to that."

"True, but I've been thinking again. You know, you're a very good actor."

"Thanks. You're not so bad yourself."

"Now supposing—just supposing—you were to travel about. Good distances from here each time. Scout out villages, on the continent and in the isles. Find out which ones are well off and lacking in local heroes..."

"Yes?"

"...And let them see that dragon-slaying certificate of yours. Brag a bit. Then come back with a list of towns. Maps, too."

"Go ahead."

"Find the best spots for a little harmless predation and choose a good battle site—"

"Refill?"

"Please."

"Here."

"Thanks. Then you show up, and for a fee—"

"Sixty-forty."

"That's what I was thinking, but I'll bet you've got the figures transposed."

"Maybe fifty-five and forty-five then."

"Down the middle, and let's drink on it."

"Fair enough. Why haggle?"

"Now I know why I dreamed of fighting a great number of knights, all of them looking like you. You're going to make a name for yourself, George."

PART III:

The Paranormal

NEIL GAIMAN is one of the most beloved authors working today. He is the internationally bestselling author of *Neverwhere, Coraline, Good Omens* (with Terry Pratchett), *American Gods, Stardust* and, most recently, the highly successful *The Ocean at the End of the Lane*. He has won every major award in the field of science fiction, fantasy, horror and children's literature, including the Hugo, the Nebula, the Stoker and the Locus. He is the creator of the hugely popular *Sandman* comics, and has written two episodes for the television series *Doctor Who*.

For more details see his official site: www.neilgaiman.com

ONLY THE END OF THE WORLD AGAIN
Neil Gaiman

It was a bad day: I woke up naked in the bed, with a cramp in my stomach, feeling more or less like hell. Something about the quality of the light, stretched and metallic, like the colour of a migraine, told me it was afternoon.

The room was freezing—literally: there was a thin crust of ice on the inside of the windows. The sheets on the bed around me were ripped and clawed, and there was animal hair in the bed. It itched.

I was thinking about staying in bed for the next week—I'm always tired after a change—but a wave of nausea forced me to disentangle myself from the bedding, and to stumble, hurriedly, into the apartment's tiny bathroom.

The cramps hit me again as I got to the bathroom door. I held on to the door-frame and I started to sweat. Maybe it was a fever; I hoped I wasn't coming down with something.

The cramping was sharp in my guts. My head felt swimmy. I crumpled to the floor, and, before I could manage to raise my head enough to find the toilet bowl, I began to spew.

I vomited a foul-smelling thin yellow liquid; in it was a dog's paw—my guess was a Doberman's, but I'm not really a dog person; a tomato peel; some diced carrots and sweet corn; some lumps of half-chewed meat, raw; and some fingers. They were fairly small, pale fingers, obviously a child's.

"Shit."

The cramps eased up, and the nausea subsided. I lay on the floor, with stinking drool coming out of my mouth and nose, with the tears you cry when you're being sick drying on my cheeks.

When I felt a little better I picked up the paw and the fingers from the pool of spew and threw them into the toilet bowl, flushed them away.

I turned on the tap, rinsed out my mouth with the briny Innsmouth water, and spat it into the sink. I mopped up the rest of the sick as best I could with washcloth and toilet paper. Then I turned on the shower, and stood in the bathtub like a zombie as the hot water sluiced over me.

I soaped myself down, body and hair. The meagre lather turned grey; I must have been filthy. My hair was matted with something that felt like dried blood, and I worked at it with the bar of soap until it was gone. Then I stood under the shower until the water turned icy.

There was a note under the door from my landlady. It said that I owed her for two weeks' rent. It said that all the answers were in the Book of Revelations. It said that I made a lot of noise coming home in the early hours of this morning, and she'd thank me to be quieter in future. It said that when the Elder Gods rose up from the ocean, all the scum of the Earth, all the non-believers, all the human garbage and the wastrels and deadbeats would be swept away, and the world would be cleansed by ice and deep water. It said that she felt she ought to remind me that she had assigned me a shelf in the refrigerator when I arrived and she'd thank me if in the future I'd keep to it.

I crumpled the note, dropped it on the floor, where it lay alongside the Big Mac cartons and the empty pizza cartons, and the long-dead dried slices of pizza.

It was time to go to work.

I'd been in Innsmouth for two weeks, and I disliked it. It smelled fishy. It was a claustrophobic little town: marshland to the east, cliffs to the west, and, in the centre, a harbour that held a few rotting fishing boats, and was not even scenic at sunset. The yuppies had come to Innsmouth in the Eighties anyway, bought their picturesque fisherman's cottages overlooking the harbour. The yuppies had been gone for some years, now, and the cottages by the bay were crumbling, abandoned.

The inhabitants of Innsmouth lived here and there in and around the town, and in the trailer parks that ringed it, filled with dank mobile homes that were never going anywhere.

I got dressed, pulled on my boots and put on my coat and left my room. My landlady was nowhere to be seen. She was a short, pop-eyed woman, who spoke little, although she left extensive notes for me pinned to doors and placed where I might see them; she kept the house filled with the smell of boiling seafood: huge pots were always simmering on the kitchen stove, filled with things with too many legs and other things with no legs at all.

There were other rooms in the house, but no-one else rented them. No-one in their right mind would come to Innsmouth in winter.

Outside the house it didn't smell much better. It was colder, though, and my breath steamed in the sea air. The snow on the streets was crusty and filthy; the clouds promised more snow.

A cold, salty wind came up off the bay. The gulls were screaming miserably. I felt shitty. My office would be freezing, too. On the corner of Marsh Street and Leng Avenue was a bar, 'The Opener', a squat building with small, dark windows that I'd passed two dozen times in the last couple of weeks. I hadn't been in before, but I really needed a drink, and besides, it might be warmer in there. I pushed open the door.

The bar was indeed warm. I stamped the snow off my boots and went inside. It was almost empty and smelled of old ashtrays and stale beer. A couple of elderly men were playing chess by the bar. The barman was reading a battered old gilt-and-green-leather edition of the poetical works of Alfred, Lord Tennyson.

"Hey. How about a Jack Daniels straight up?"

"Sure thing. You're new in town," he told me, putting his book face down on the bar, pouring the drink into a glass.

"Does it show?"

He smiled, passed me the Jack Daniels. The glass was filthy, with a greasy thumb-print on the side, and I shrugged and knocked back the drink anyway. I could barely taste it.

"Hair of the dog?" he said.

"In a manner of speaking."

"There is a belief," said the barman, whose fox-red hair was tightly greased back, "that the *lykanthropoi* can be returned to their natural forms by thanking them, while they're in wolf form, or by calling them by their given names."

"Yeah? Well, thanks."

He poured another shot for me, unasked. He looked a little like Peter Lorre, but then, most of the folk in Innsmouth look a little like Peter Lorre, including my landlady.

I sank the Jack Daniels, this time felt it burning down into my stomach, the way it should.

"It's what they say. I never said I believed it."

"What *do* you believe?"

"Burn the girdle."

"Pardon?"

"The *lykanthropoi* have girdles of human skin, given to them at their first transformation, by their masters in hell. Burn the girdle."

One of the old chess-players turned to me then, his eyes huge and blind and protruding. "If you drink rain-water out of warg-wolf's paw-print, that'll make a wolf of you, when the moon is full," he said. "The only cure is to hunt down the wolf that made the print in the first place and cut off its head with a knife forged of virgin silver."

"Virgin, huh?" I smiled.

His chess partner, bald and wrinkled, shook his head and croaked a single sad sound. Then he moved his queen, and croaked again.

There are people like him all over Innsmouth.

I paid for the drinks, and left a dollar tip on the bar. The barman was reading his book once more, and ignored it.

Outside the bar big wet kissy flakes of snow had begun to fall, settling in my hair and eyelashes. I hate snow. I hate New England. I hate Innsmouth: it's no place to be alone, but if there's a good place to be alone I've not found it yet. Still, business has kept me on the move for more moons than I like to think about. Business, and other things.

I walked a couple of blocks down Marsh Street—like most of Innsmouth, an unattractive mixture of eighteenth century American Gothic houses, late nineteenth century stunted brownstones, and late twentieth prefab grey-brick boxes—until I got to a boarded-up fried chicken joint, and I went up the stone steps next to the store and unlocked the rusting metal security door.

There was a liquor store across the street; a palmist was operating on the second floor.

Someone had scrawled graffiti in black marker on the metal: *just die*, it said. Like it was easy.

The stairs were bare wood; the plaster was stained and peeling. My one-room office was at the top of the stairs.

I don't stay anywhere long enough to bother with my name in gilt on glass. It was handwritten in block letters on a piece of ripped cardboard that I'd thumbtacked to the door.

LAWRENCE TALBOT.
ADJUSTOR.

I unlocked the door to my office and went in.

I inspected my office, while adjectives like *seedy* and *rancid* and *squalid* wandered through my head, then gave up, outclassed. It was fairly unprepossessing—a desk, an office chair, an empty filing cabinet; a window, which gave you a terrific view of the liquor store and the empty palmist's. The smell of old cooking grease permeated from the store below. I wondered how long the fried chicken joint had been boarded up; I imagined a multitude of black cockroaches swarming over every surface in the darkness beneath me.

"That's the shape of the world that you're thinking of there," said a deep, dark voice, deep enough that I felt it in the pit of my stomach.

There was an old armchair in one corner of the office. The remains of a pattern showed through the patina of age and grease the years had given it. It was the colour of dust.

The fat man sitting in the armchair, his eyes still tightly closed, continued, "We look about in puzzlement at our world, with a sense of unease and disquiet. We think of ourselves as scholars in arcane liturgies, single men trapped in worlds beyond our devising. The truth is far simpler: there are things in the darkness beneath us that wish us harm."

His head was lolled back on the armchair, and the tip of his tongue poked out of the corner of his mouth.

"You read my mind?"

The man in the armchair took a slow deep breath that rattled in the back of his throat. He really was immensely fat, with stubby fingers like discoloured sausages. He wore a thick old coat, once black, now an indeterminate grey. The snow on his boots had not entirely melted.

"Perhaps. The end of the world is a strange concept. The world is always ending, and the end is always being averted, by love or foolishness or just plain old dumb luck.

"Ah well. It's too late now: the Elder Gods have chosen their vessels. When the moon rises…"

A thin trickle of drool came from one corner of his mouth, trickled down in a thread of silver to his collar. Something scuttled down into the shadows of his coat.

"Yeah? What happens when the moon rises?"

The man in the armchair stirred, opened two little eyes, red and swollen, and blinked them in waking.

"I dreamed I had many mouths," he said, his new voice oddly small and breathy for such a huge man. "I dreamed every mouth was opening and closing independently. Some mouths were talking, some whispering, some eating, some waiting in silence."

He looked around, wiped the spittle from the corner of his mouth, sat back in the chair, blinking puzzledly. "Who are you?"

"I'm the guy that rents this office," I told him.

He belched suddenly, loudly. "I'm sorry," he said, in his breathy voice, and lifted himself heavily from the armchair. He was shorter than I was, when he was standing. He looked me up and down blearily. "Silver bullets," he pronounced, after a short pause. "Old-fashioned remedy."

"Yeah," I told him. "That's so obvious—must be why I didn't think of it. Gee, I could just kick myself. I really could."

"You're making fun of an old man," he told me.

"Not really. I'm sorry. Now, out of here. Some of us have work to do."

He shambled out. I sat down in the swivel chair at the desk by the window, and discovered, after some minutes, through trial and error, that if I swiveled the chair to the left it fell off its base.

So I sat still and waited for the dusty black telephone on my desk to ring, while the light slowly leaked away from the winter sky.

Ring.

A man's voice: *Had I thought about aluminum siding?* I put down the phone.

There was no heating in the office. I wondered how long the fat man had been asleep in the armchair.

Twenty minutes later the phone rang again. A crying woman implored me to help her find her five-year-old daughter, missing since last night, stolen from her bed. The family dog had vanished too.

I don't do missing children, I told her. *I'm sorry: too many bad memories.* I put down the telephone, feeling sick again.

It was getting dark now, and, for the first time since I had been in Innsmouth, the neon sign across the street flicked on. It told me that Madame Ezekiel performed Tarot Readings and Palmistry. Red neon stained the falling snow the colour of new blood.

Armageddon is averted by small actions. That's the way it was. That's the way it always has to be.

The phone rang a third time. I recognized the voice; it was the aluminum-siding man again. "You know," he said, chattily, "transformation from man to animal and back being, by definition, impossible, we need to look for other solutions. Depersonalization, obviously, and likewise some form of projection. Brain damage? Perhaps. Pseudoneurotic schizophrenia? Laughably so. Some cases have been treated with intravenous thioridazine hydrochloride."

"Successfully?"

He chuckled. "That's what I like. A man with a sense of humour. I'm sure we can do business."

"I told you already. I don't need aluminum siding."

"Our business is more remarkable than that, and of far greater importance. You're new in town, Mr Talbot. It would be a pity if we found ourselves at, shall we say, loggerheads?"

"You can say whatever you like, pal. In my book you're just another adjustment, waiting to be made."

"We're ending the world, Mr Talbot. The Deep Ones will rise out of their ocean graves and eat the moon like a ripe plum."

"Then I won't ever have to worry about full moons anymore, will I?"

"Don't try and cross us," he began, but I growled at him, and he fell silent.

Outside my window the snow was still falling.

Across Marsh Street, in the window directly opposite mine, the most beautiful woman I had ever seen stood in the ruby glare of her neon sign, and she stared at me.

She beckoned, with one finger.

I put down the phone on the aluminum-siding man for the second time that afternoon, and went downstairs, and crossed the street at something close to a run; but I looked both ways before I crossed.

She was dressed in silks. The room was lit only by candles, and stank of incense and patchouli oil.

She smiled at me as I walked in, beckoned me over to her seat by the window. She was playing a card game with a tarot deck, some version of solitaire. As I reached her, one elegant hand swept up the cards, wrapped them in a silk scarf, placed them gently in a wooden box.

The scents of the room made my head pound. I hadn't eaten anything today, I realized; perhaps that was what was making me lightheaded. I sat down, across the table from her, in the candle-light.

She extended her hand, and took my hand in hers.

She stared at my palm, touched it, softly, with her forefinger.

"Hair?" She was puzzled.

"Yeah, well. I'm on my own a lot." I grinned. I had hoped it was a friendly grin, but she raised an eyebrow at me anyway.

"When I look at you," said Madame Ezekiel, "this is what I see. I see the eye of a man. Also I see the eye of a wolf. In the eye of a man I see honesty, decency, innocence. I see an upright man who walks on the square. And in the eye of wolf I see a groaning and a growling, night howls and cries, I see a monster running with blood-flecked spittle in the darkness of the borders of the town."

"How can you see a growl or a cry?"

She smiled. "It is not hard," she said. Her accent was not American. It was Russian, or Maltese, or Egyptian perhaps. "In the eye of the mind we see many things."

Madame Ezekiel closed her green eyes. She had remarkably long eyelashes; her skin was pale, and her black hair was never still—it drifted gently around her head, in the silks, as if it were floating on distant tides.

"There is a traditional way," she told me. "A way to wash off a bad shape. You stand in running water, in clear spring water, while eating white rose petals."

"And then?"

"The shape of darkness will be washed from you."

"It will return," I told her, "with the next full of the moon."

"So," said Madame Ezekiel, "once the shape is washed from you, you open your veins in the running water. It will sting mightily, of course. But the river will carry the blood away."

She was dressed in silks, in scarves and cloths of a hundred different colours, each bright and vivid, even in the muted light of the candles.

Her eyes opened.

"Now," she said. "The Tarot." She unwrapped her deck from the black silk scarf that held it, passed me the cards to shuffle. I fanned them, riffed and bridged them.

"Slower, slower," she said. "Let them get to know you. Let them love you, like... like a woman would love you."

I held them tightly, then passed them back to her.

She turned over the first card. It was called *The Warwolf*. It showed darkness and amber eyes, a smile in white and red.

Her green eyes showed confusion. They were the green of emeralds. "This is not a card from my deck," she said, and turned over the next card. "What did you do to my cards?"

"Nothing, ma'am. I just held them. That's all."

The card she had turned over was *The Deep One*. It showed something green and faintly octopoid. The thing's mouths—if they were indeed mouths and not tentacles—began to writhe on the card as I watched.

She covered it with another card, and then another, and another. The rest of the cards were blank pasteboard.

"Did you do that?" She sounded on the verge of tears.

"No."

"Go now," she said.

"But—"

"*Go.*" She looked down, as if trying to convince herself I no longer existed.

I stood up, in the room that smelled of incense and candle-wax, and looked out of her window, across the street. A light flashed, briefly, in my office window. Two men, with flashlights, were walking around. They opened the empty filing cabinet, peered around, then took up their positions, one in the armchair, the other behind the door, waiting for me to return. I smiled to myself. It was cold and inhospitable in my office, and with any luck they would wait there for hours until they finally decided I wasn't coming back.

So I left Madame Ezekiel turning over her cards, one by one, staring at them as if that would make the pictures return; and I went downstairs, and walked back down Marsh Street until I reached the bar.

The place was empty, now; the barman was smoking a cigarette, which he stubbed out as I came in.

"Where are the chess-fiends?"

"It's a big night for them tonight. They'll be down at the bay. Let's see: you're a Jack Daniels? Right?"

"Sounds good."

He poured it for me. I recognized the thumb-print from the last time I had the glass. I picked up the volume of Tennyson poems from the bar-top.

"Good book?"

The fox-haired barman took his book from me, opened it and read:

"Below the thunders of the upper deep;
Far, far beneath in the abysmal sea,
His ancient dreamless, uninvaded sleep
The Kraken sleepeth..."

I'd finished my drink. "So? What's your point?"

He walked around the bar, took me over to the window. "See? Out there?"

He pointed toward the west of the town, toward the cliffs. As I stared a bonfire was kindled on the cliff-tops; it flared and began to burn with a copper-green flame.

"They're going to wake the Deep Ones," said the barman. "The stars and the planets and the moon are all in the right places. It's time. The dry lands will sink, and the seas shall rise…"

"For the world shall be cleansed with ice and floods and I'll thank you to keep to your own shelf in the refrigerator," I said.

"Sorry?"

"Nothing. What's the quickest way to get up to those cliffs?"

"Back up Marsh Street. Hang a left at the Church of Dagon, till you reach Manuxet Way and then just keep on going." He pulled a coat off the back of the door, and put it on. "C'mon. I'll walk you up there. I'd hate to miss any of the fun."

"You sure?"

"No-one in town's going to be drinking tonight." We stepped out, and he locked the door to the bar behind us.

It was chilly in the street, and fallen snow blew about the ground, like white mists. From street level I could no longer tell if Madame Ezekiel was in her den above her neon sign, or if my guests were still waiting for me in my office.

We put our heads down against the wind, and we walked.

Over the noise of the wind I heard the barman talking to himself:

"*Winnow with giant arms the slumbering green,*" he was saying.

"*There hath he lain for ages and will lie*
Battening upon huge seaworms in his sleep,
Until the latter fire shall heat the deep;
Then once by men and angels to be seen,
In roaring he shall rise…"

He stopped there, and we walked on together in silence, with blown snow stinging our faces.

And on the surface die, I thought, but said nothing out loud.

Twenty minutes' walking and we were out of Innsmouth. The Manuxet Way stopped when we left the town, and it became a narrow dirt path, partly covered with snow and ice, and we slipped and slid our way up it in the darkness.

The moon was not yet up, but the stars had already begun to come out. There were so many of them. They were sprinkled like diamond dust and crushed sapphires across the night sky. You can see so many stars from the sea-shore, more than you could ever see back in the city.

At the top of the cliff, behind the bonfire, two people were waiting—one huge and fat, one much smaller. The barman left my side and walked over to stand beside them, facing me.

"Behold," he said, "the sacrificial wolf." There was now an oddly familiar quality to his voice.

I didn't say anything. The fire was burning with green flames, and it lit the three of them from below; classic spook lighting.

"Do you know why I brought you up here?" asked the barman, and I knew then why his voice was familiar: it was the voice of the man who had attempted to sell me aluminum-siding.

"To stop the world ending?"

He laughed at me, then.

The second figure was the fat man I had found asleep in my office chair. "Well, if you're going to get eschatological about it..." he murmured, in a voice deep enough to rattle walls. His eyes were closed. He was fast asleep.

The third figure was shrouded in dark silks and smelled of patchouli oil. It held a knife. It said nothing.

"This night," said the barman, "the moon is the moon of the deep ones. This night are the stars configured in the shapes and patterns of the dark, old times. This night, if we call them, they will come. If our sacrifice is worthy. If our cries are heard."

The moon rose, huge and amber and heavy, on the other side of the bay, and a chorus of low croaking rose with it from the ocean far beneath us.

Moonlight on snow and ice is not daylight, but it will do. And my eyes were getting sharper with the moon: in the cold waters men like frogs were surfacing and submerging in a slow water-dance. Men like frogs, and women, too: it seemed to me that I could see my landlady down there, writhing and croaking in the bay with the rest of them.

It was too soon for another change; I was still exhausted from the night before; but I felt strange under that amber moon.

"Poor wolf-man," came a whisper from the silks. "All his dreams have come to this; a lonely death upon a distant cliff."

I will dream if I want to, I said, *and my death is my own affair*. But I was unsure if I had said it out loud.

Senses heighten in the moon's light; I heard the roar of the ocean still, but now, overlaid on top of it, I could hear each wave rise and crash; I heard the splash of the frog people; I heard the drowned whispers of the dead in the bay; I heard the creak of green wrecks far beneath the ocean.

Smell improves, too. The Aluminum-siding man was human, while the fat man had other blood in him.

And the figure in the silks...

I had smelled her perfume when I wore man-shape. Now I could smell something else, less heady, beneath it. A smell of decay, of putrefying meat, and rotten flesh.

The silks fluttered. She was moving toward me. She held the knife.

"Madame Ezekiel?" My voice was roughening and coarsening. Soon I would lose it all. I didn't understand what was happening, but the moon was rising higher and higher, losing its amber colour, and filling my mind with its pale light.

"Madame Ezekiel?"

"You deserve to die," she said, her voice cold and low. "If only for what you did to my cards. They were old."

"I don't die," I told her. "*Even a man who is pure in heart, and says his prayers by night.* Remember?"

"It's bullshit," she said. "You know what the oldest way to end the curse of the werewolf is?"

"No."

The bonfire burned brighter now, burned with the green of the world beneath the sea, the green of algae, and of slowly-drifting weed; burned with the colour of emeralds.

"You simply wait till they're in human shape, a whole month away from another change; then you take the sacrificial knife, and you kill them. That's all."

I turned to run, but the barman was behind me, pulling my arms, twisting my wrists up into the small of my back. The knife glinted pale silver in the moonlight. Madame Ezekiel smiled.

She sliced across my throat.

Blood began to gush, and then to flow. And then it slowed, and stopped...

—The pounding in the front of my head, the pressure in the back. All a roiling change a how-wow-row-now change a red wall coming towards me from the night

—I tasted stars dissolved in brine, fizzy and distant and salt

—my fingers prickled with pins and my skin was lashed with tongues of flame my eyes were topaz I could taste the night

My breath steamed and billowed in the icy air.

I growled involuntarily, low in my throat. My forepaws were touching the snow.

I pulled back, tensed, and sprang at her.

There was a sense of corruption that hung in the air, like a mist, surrounding me. High in my leap I seemed to pause, and something burst like a soapbubble...

~~*~*

I was deep, deep in the darkness under the sea, standing on all fours on a slimy rock floor, at the entrance of some kind of citadel, built of enormous, rough-hewn stones. The stones gave off a pale glow-in-the-dark light; a ghostly luminescence, like the hands of a watch.

A cloud of black blood trickled from my neck.

She was standing in the doorway, in front of me. She was now six, maybe seven feet high. There was flesh on her skeletal bones, pitted and gnawed, but the silks were weeds, drifting in the cold water, down there in the dreamless deeps. They hid her face like a slow green veil.

There were limpets growing on the upper surfaces of her arms, and on the flesh that hung from her ribcage.

I felt like I was being crushed. I couldn't think any more.

She moved towards me. The weed that surrounded her head shifted. She had a face like the stuff you don't want to eat in a sushi counter, all suckers and spines and drifting anemone fronds; and somewhere in all that I knew she was smiling

I pushed with my hind-legs. We met there, in the deep, and we struggled. It was so cold, so dark. I closed my jaws on her face, and felt something rend and tear.

It was almost a kiss, down there in the abysmal deep…
~~*~*

I landed softly on the snow, a silk scarf locked between my jaws.

The other scarves were fluttering to the ground. Madame Ezekiel was nowhere to be seen.

The silver knife lay on the ground, in the snow. I waited on all fours, in the moonlight, soaking wet. I shook myself, spraying the brine about. I heard it hiss and spit when it hit the fire.

I was dizzy, and weak. I pulled the air deep into my lungs.

Down, far below, in the bay, I could see the frog people hanging on the surface of the sea like dead things; for a handful of seconds they drifted back and forth on the tide, then they twisted and leapt, and each by each they *plop-plopped* down into the bay and vanished beneath the sea.

There was a scream. It was the fox-haired bartender, the pop-eyed aluminum-siding salesman, and he was staring at the night sky, at the clouds that were drifting in, covering the stars, and he was screaming. There was rage and there was frustration in that cry, and it scared me.

He picked up the knife from the ground, wiped the snow from the handle with his fingers, wiped the blood from the blade with his coat. Then he looked across at me. He was crying. "You bastard," he said. "What did you do to her?"

I would have told him I didn't do anything to her, that she was still on guard far beneath the ocean, but I couldn't talk any more, only growl and whine and howl.

He was crying. He stank of insanity, and of disappointment. He raised the knife and ran at me, and I moved to one side.

Some people just can't adjust even to tiny changes. The barman stumbled past me, off the cliff, into nothing.

In the moonlight blood is black, not red, and the marks he left on the cliff-side as he fell and bounced and fell were smudges of black and dark grey. Then, finally, he lay still on the icy rocks at the base of the cliff, until an arm reached out from the sea and dragged him, with a slowness that was almost painful to watch, under the dark water.

A hand scratched the back of my head. It felt good.

"What was she? Just an avatar of the Deep Ones, sir. An eidolon, a manifestation, if you will, sent up to us from the uttermost deeps to bring about the end of the world."

I bristled.

"No, it's over, for now. You disrupted her, sir. And the ritual is most specific. Three of us must stand together and call the sacred names, while innocent blood pools and pulses at our feet."

I looked up at the fat man, and whined a query. He patted me on the back of the neck, sleepily.

"Of course she doesn't love you, boy. She hardly even exists on this plane, in any material sense."

The snow began to fall once more. The bonfire was going out.

"Your change tonight, incidentally, I would opine, is a direct result of the self-same celestial configurations and lunar forces that made tonight such a perfect night to bring back my old friends from Underneath..."

He continued talking, in his deep voice, and perhaps he was telling me important things. I'll never know, for the appetite was growing inside me, and his words had lost all but the shadow of any meaning; I had no further interest in the sea or the clifftop or the fat man.

There were deer running in the woods beyond the meadow: I could smell them on the winter's night's air.

And I was, above all things, hungry.

~~*~*

I was naked when I came to myself again, early the next morning, a half-eaten deer next to me in the snow. A fly crawled across its eye, and its tongue lolled out of its dead mouth, making it look comical and pathetic, like an animal in a newspaper cartoon.

The snow was stained a fluorescent crimson where the deer's belly had been torn out.

My face and chest were sticky and red with the stuff. My throat was scabbed and scarred, and it stung; by the next full moon it would be whole once more.

The sun was a long way away, small and yellow, but the sky was blue and cloudless, and there was no breeze. I could hear the roar of the sea some distance away.

I was cold and naked and bloody and alone; ah well, I thought: it happens to all of us, in the beginning. I just get it once a month.

I was painfully exhausted, but I would hold out until I found a deserted barn, or a cave; and then I was going to sleep for a couple of weeks.

A hawk flew low over the snow toward me, with something dangling from its talons. It hovered above me for a heartbeat, then dropped a small grey squid in the snow at my feet, and flew upward. The flaccid thing lay there, still and silent and tentacled in the bloody snow.

I took it as an omen, but whether good or bad I couldn't say and I didn't really care anymore; I turned my back to the sea, and on the shadowy town of Innsmouth, and began to make my way toward the city.

MARINA J. LOSTETTER's original short fiction has appeared in venues such as Lightspeed, InterGalactic Medicine Show and Baen.com. In 2012, her story, Master Belladino's Mask, won second place in the Writers of the Future contest. Her tie-in work for the Star Citizen and the Sargasso Legacy universes can be found in the Spectrum Dispatch and Galaxy's Edge Magazine respectively. Originally from Oregon, Marina now lives in Arkansas with her husband, Alex. She tweets as @MarinaLostetter, and her official website can be found at www.lostetter.net

LENORA OF THE LOW
Marina J. Lostetter

onight Lenora would destroy a reaper.

But first she had to put in her eyes.

The two globes sat nestled in a viscous solution at the bottom of a Mason jar she'd perched on the edge of her bathroom sink. She drew them out slowly, testing their elasticity with her fingers. They smelled strange—not quite rotten, but not quite fresh.

As she popped them in, a siren blared in the street next to her hotel. Lenora tilted her head, straining to hear the commotion with her single ear. *Hopefully the streets of Paris won't be filled with dirty German* boches *this evening*, she thought. That would be her luck; they'd suddenly decided to enforce curfew when her plans were ready to culminate.

The eyes bulged uncomfortably, and she had to blink repeatedly before the filthy room came into focus. A roach made its way leisurely across the porcelain basin and into a pile of dark sludge. Lenora's years in the reaper's menagerie, when she was bodiless, had stricken most memories of human sanitation from her consciousness. And now, undead, with rotten bones and shriveled bowels, why should the decay of a building bother her?

Lenora turned to the claw-footed bathtub and pulled the cracked curtain from around its edge. Beyond lay her flesh-garden.

Like insects pinned to a collector's cardstock, sections of skin lay mounted on fragments of wood in a saline bath. Small wires slithered into the tub and provided mild shocks every few moments. The flesh crawled with the energy, flexing and shivering at the stimulation.

Each stolen piece of living tissue equated another day on Earth for a Low One such as she. Another day beyond the reach of the reaper's clawing spirit.

Exiting the bathroom, she began preparations for her last harvest. With giddy, fidgeting fingers, she pulled her tobacco pouch and pipe from their hiding place between the bedsprings and lit up.

Thin smoke curled around her like a halo. Avoiding her grotesque reflection in the vanity mirror, she pulled a small chain with a rose charm from a drawer and secured it around her neck. It was a reminder that this night didn't belong to her alone. She would get her revenge and become a savior all in one glorious swoop.

Ready to leave—eager to—she grabbed her rucksack, threw on her large coat, and wrapped her face with a moth-eaten scarf.

On her way down the stairs, the night manager stopped her to gather the rent. He never made a comment about her swollen face or her mismatched features—she wasn't even sure he'd noticed. She always paid on time and kept quiet, which meant the employees had no reason to disturb her room. The francs she handed over now were stolen, like everything else she owned. Right down to her skin, everything had belonged to someone else.

She stopped on the landing to double check she had all of her things. The gun, the knife, the Mason jar, they were all there.

In her years before the menagerie, she never would have pictured herself at home with a pistol and a pipe. She'd always been a girly girl through and through; just dresses and posies, please and thank you.

The gutter smelled of piss, so she kept to the center of the street as best she could. The 'lights out at eleven' rule meant she could travel unnoticed through most of the city.

She stopped at every side street, listening, looking for the choicest victim. Someone alone, someone lost, someone weak and vulnerable.

She'd taken so many parts since the first one, she felt indifferent about the process now. The first time she'd stolen flesh there hadn't been a question of right or wrong in her mind, just an insatiable panic. She'd needed a piece. If she hadn't found one by the end of the night, her reaper, Angeu, would have reclaimed her soul. When the sun came, he would have wound his deathly-cold ethereal hands around her neck and yanked her back into Limbo.

A gruff cough rumbled out of a darkened side-street. She stopped, one hand in her pocket, the other on her pipe, and peered in. Maybe this was it. She picked out a slumping figure huddled against one wall.

Realizing her tobacco had gone cold, she struck a match and relit it before approaching. The amber glow highlighted the ridges of her skull, and she knew it emphasized the mismatch of skin to bone.

The man coughed again. She made no secret of her advance, but pulled the pistol slowly from her pouch, keeping it hidden amongst the folds of her coat.

"Salut, levez-vous." With a clipped greeting, she demanded he stand. Though her real heart lay still, its ghost pounded against her brittle ribs. "Let me see you," she directed, as though she were a German enforcer.

He took several steps towards her without a word, and she continued forwards until they were an arm's breadth apart. This close, she could smell him, and he had the most hideously familiar aroma. He stank of death. Stealing from him would do her no good. Those already standing on La Grande Faucheuse's stoop had nothing to offer.

"As you were," she said, ready to continue the hunt.

"I know what you are," he said, slurring his words.

Squinting, she looked him in the eyes; they were covered with cataracts.

"You're one of the Low Ones," he said with certainty.

She hissed, and the shriveled remains of her stomach jumped. How could he know? How could he tell?

His lips pulled back in a cracked smile, revealing teeth like chipped, yellow china.

"I'm no such creature," she denied.

"No? You are a Low One, a dead given one more day. What task did you promise to complete for your reaper—your *faucheuse*—that convinced him to let you out? What did you trade?"

She kept quiet, disgust at the memory writhing across her face. She recalled the cold of Angeu's being, something more eternal than a soul, colliding with hers, overpowering hers. It poked holes in her purity with little needles of lust and obsession.

The old man appeared to take her silence as a confirmation. "Give him something that precious did you? And what living tissue did he gather for you?" He pointed at her crotch. "A warm *moule* so you could enjoy it, perhaps?"

Appalled, she turned and hurried away. His cackling calls followed after. "He'll come for you! You cannot stay. He'll come at sunrise, just as he came for my Christine!"

Out of the alley, away from the jeering man, she rounded the corner and braced herself against the wrought-iron railing of a stoop. She'd escaped its catalyst, but not the memory. It sprang back into her mind and yanked like a fishhook through her consciousness.

She had known all along that Angeu desired her. He thought of her as his pet, a plaything. He blatantly coveted the shape and depth of her soul, and knowing this she'd formed a plan to escape his zoo. She offered herself to him, giving in to the abomination that was his unnatural craving, and demanded a day in return. In order to walk once again, her dead body needed a twinge of life, a piece of living flesh.

Angeu had not stolen genitalia for her, as the drunk suggested. He'd stolen an ear from a small girl, and had lovingly sewn it onto Lenora's entombed body, so that she could hear the sweet nothings he would whisper to her during their intimate exchange.

The next day, the one she'd been allotted on Earth, she'd risen with no sense other than shallow hearing, and no task other than her own.

And, clever Lenora, she had begun her harvesting. If one piece of stolen skin meant she had a day, what might a second piece give her?

All the time she'd been on Earth Angeu could not reach her, could not find a way to kill her because she was still more dead than alive.

But tonight he would get his chance. She was about to tip the scale into more living than dead. He would come, she counted on it. And still, the thought of meeting him again made her ill. If she had any acid left in her bowels she would have thrown up at the thought.

She caught a whiff of the wind, and suddenly Angeu was pushed to the back of her mind. There was a heavenly aroma, sweet, and *pure*. So heady, it made her dizzy. That was it, her victim. The soul smelled worthy of a menagerie.

She followed the scent like a bloodhound, fixated. Her dusty blood shifted like sand in her veins.

Lenora tracked the smell to a woman who had hurried past just moments before, walking with a briskness that revealed her fright. She clutched the fine folds of her champagne colored dress in tight fists, keeping the hem high above her ankles. She must have gotten separated from her male accompaniment, and was rushing to find a place she deemed safe.

Trailing her, Lenora felt something of her old self. The gentleness that once inhabited her spirit, before Angeu had tainted her. This woman, with her finger waves, close-fitting silk dress, high heels, and innocent scent reminded Lenora of herself. Her spirit had known no trouble, no hardship. She was the perfect prize for any reaper.

And that was why Lenora had to have her. Had to ruin her.

Reaching into her rucksack, Lenora pulled out a few more francs. She smoothed them out as best she could, and, using the sweetest voice she could muster, called after the woman.

"Miss, you dropped your money. Miss?"

The woman stopped and turned, revealing her naiveté.

Lenora caught up, and as the woman held out her hand to examine the francs, the start of *merci* on her lips, Lenora revealed the pistol. The woman yelped, but did not run. Her outstretched arm began to shake, and the rest of her body followed. Lenora marched her onto a thin side street.

"Please," the woman pleaded, "Take my purse, my broach. Let me go."

The alley walls closed in on the pair, like devilish accomplices to Lenora's dark deed. In the narrow spaces between buildings her confidence always increased; the city was on her side.

Once she was sure they were out of view of the main street, Lenora sprang. She shoved the woman to the ground, thrusting the rucksack against her victim's face in order to muffle any cries. Lenora seamlessly drew the knife from the bag. With one quick swipe, she removed the woman's left ear from her head and let it fall to the dirty ground.

The pain and the panic sent an extra shock of adrenaline through the woman, and she forced Lenora off. Holding the bloodied side of her head, she ran.

"I'm not doing this for me, I'm sorry," Lenora called. *I can't let him do to my sister what he did to me.* She raised the pistol. Her numb fingertip settled against the trigger, and without hesitation, she pulled. A deafening *pop* bounced between the stone walls.

The slug pierced the woman's back, and she jerked. One last whimper escaped her lips before she toppled to the ground. A bloom of red pooled beneath her shimmering silk dress.

Lenora retrieved the fallen ear, emotionless. She'd long ago become desensitized to the gore, and even the violence didn't nauseate her anymore. Deep down, she wished she wasn't so detached. She wanted so badly to stay amongst the living, but she behaved fully as the traveling dead.

She put the ear in the Mason jar. It sank to the bottom of the briny solution.

That was it, the final piece she needed to be completely sheathed in living tissue.

She hurried away from the body and back to the hotel. The manager didn't stop her on the way up the stairs, despite the smear of blood on her sleeve.

Throwing off her coat and scarf once she was through the door, she retrieved the jar and a needle and thread from the dresser, then entered the bathroom.

The air hummed with electricity. She examined the flesh garden, making absolutely certain every piece was alive and ready to be grafted.

She'd saved the very best parts for the garden. Everything that belonged to a pair had a perfectly matched mate. Instead of harvesting a full face like the one she wore, she'd been careful to find just the right nose, more petite than the one protruding from her features, and just the right lips, fuller than her own. Every piece of skin was smooth, young, and perfect.

She looked to the jar that contained the bloodied ear, then to the needle and thread. Here was the crux her plan relied on. Fully encased in living flesh, she was sure it was enough for Angeu to surface and claim her. All she had to do was attach the ear, and she would mimic life enough to be killed once more.

She shivered. Their bestial encounter had forged a connection between them. Every night she'd felt Angeu dogging her steps, and had sensed echoes of his thoughts. She knew instinctually the capacity and limitations of his power. It was as though she walked on a mirror, with Angeu as her reflection in Limbo. The soles of their feet seemed to be sewn together, just like the bits of her body. He longed for her constantly, came as close to the physical world as he was able. She had not felt him draw fully away the entire time she'd been on Earth, which meant he had neglected his reaping. And though he was with her at every turn, she knew he watched only her form, not her actions.

His single-mindedness would be his undoing.

Before sewing on the ear, she pulled all of the specimens out of the garden and wrapped them carefully in scraps of cloth. Using her bed sheet, she bundled them together. Once the ear was in place, she would have to act quickly. She had no way of knowing how long she had before Angeu would catch up with her.

Bracing herself for a race against time, she pulled out the ear, dried it off, and placed it against her head. Noise came rushing into her brain immediately, but she ignored it and ran the needle through the top part of the ear and the bottom part of the scalp. She hurried, her hand shaking as she sewed. Eager to be finished, she didn't care that she'd attached the appendage crookedly.

Done, she bit off the end of the thread and stuffed the remainder of the spool in the bed sheet. The needle she pinned to the front of her blouse. Taking up the sheet-sack, she threw it over her shoulder like St. Nick's toy bag before making her way out of the building.

She flew down the streets of Paris, towards Père Lachaise Cemetery. If Angeu followed her onto graveyard dirt her trap would be sprung.

Haussmann architecture, with black roofs sloping at forty-five degrees over close-set, rectangular windows, lined her path as she ran. The buildings' tan façades made the windows and doorways look like empty eyes and gaping mouths. These faces observed her, vacant and undiscerning, like funeral masks.

Her course was direct, down main streets. Every now and again she passed small groups of pedestrians chatting amongst themselves. No one noticed the small, oddly formed woman rushing across the cobbles of the thoroughfares. The sounds, smells, and sights of Paris blurred as she focused on her goal. She had to get to graveyard ground before Angeu appeared—only there would she be safe.

Nearly at her destination, she felt him rise. He was on the same street, not far behind. His presence loomed. An oppressive weight swooped over her, and she struggled forward. The feeling increased when she reached the cemetery, nearly at a crescendo, and felt like hundreds of angry violins screeching in her brain.

She made it to the cemetery entrance without being caught. The rounded tops of the entrance archway were stained yellow and brown with age, forewarning visitors of the decay that lay beyond. With a renewed urgency, she pushed her way between the stone double-doors. They were cold and heavy, draining both heat and strength from her limbs.

Now, safely inside, she had to find the grave.

But, would Angeu follow?

"Lenora," she heard him call. His voice burned her ears like acid.

Tombs, monuments, mausoleums, and headstones jutted from the ground on all sides. The white and gray marble seemed to suck up all light and heat around it, forbidding the hallmarks of life from vying for attention amongst the emblems of death. Flowers, laid on various plots during the daylight hours, had already wilted and their color had gone.

"Lenora."

She could not pinpoint his location. She did her best to ignore his advance, hurrying for the familiar grave. "You made a mistake, Lenora. You're too alive now. And if you're alive that means you can be reaped."

It also means I can stay alive, she thought.

"I'm coming for you, Lenora."

She had been right. His obsession blinded him. He wanted her, and that robbed him of his focus. Angeu didn't see the danger Père Lachaise Cemetery presented.

Dark and ghostly shapes rose out of the gloom as she passed, setting her on edge. Any of them could be Angeu. He was only playing now. Frightening her for his own pleasure.

"That was a very nasty trick you played on me," he said. His voice seemed to come from nowhere and everywhere at once. "I know I'm to blame. I gave you idle hands."

She turned a bend in the path, coming upon her destination. And there he was, with a cloak of white mist and skin that personified the absence of light, so deep his face seemed a hole—empty and featureless. He sat upon a headstone, one that proclaimed the birth and death of Rosalyn Depaul.

"You get away from her," she hissed, dropping her sack.

He stroked the headstone, tilting his head lovingly this way and that. The edges of his cloak billowed and thinned, wisps of it rolled off and dissipated into the air. "She's safely back at the Menagerie, where you should be."

"You still want me? Look, look close! You see what I've done to my soul to keep me here? It's not beautiful anymore, it's not perfect. I would be a blight to your collection. The others would laugh at you. Who would take you seriously with such an ugly specimen hiding amongst your showpieces?

"You don't want to expend the effort to keep me in Limbo. I have to slip one way or the other. Life or death. I'm spoiled; I don't belong in your soul-gallery."

He waved his black-hole of a hand. "Nonsense. It's much harder to corrupt a spirit once it's dead. You've only hidden your soul with festers and wrong doings, much like you've only hidden your decaying body from sight, obscured it with life. I just have to peel both away and you'll be mine again." He slid from the headstone, like smoke, and glided towards her.

She glanced at the headstone and its neighbor: the second marker was her own. *Here lies Lenora Depaul*, it said, *loving daughter, sweet niece, faithful sister.*

"You made a mistake," he snapped, swirling around her. She pulled her shoulders up against his foul wind, hugging herself. "You never should have completed your skin. Now you're more alive than dead and I can take you back. I can reap you once more. Didn't you think of that? Desperate, desperate girl." He stopped and spat, "Stupid."

A shiver hit her, and it was not caused by Angeu. The wind changed, grew frigid. There was another *faucheuse* about.

"You underestimate me, Angeu. Think hard, look past your arrogance. You know my soul, and it is not stupid."

"Angeu!" came a roar from the night.

He backed away from Lenora immediately, his head rolling, searching.

The air around them grew colder. Reapers flooded into the cemetery. Lenora had to crouch and rub her limbs to keep her skin from freezing.

They materialized out of the night, their physical forms rushing together like angry swarms of insects, amassing and coalescing into black figures. Soon they were all around, each darker than the next, each robed in a different kind of weather. There were ones she recognized as visitors to Angeu's menagerie, and ones she had never seen before. One rose above the rest, massive and intimidating. He wore a swirling storm of air, a tornado that ate at the ground beneath him, pulling up clods of grass, dirt, and rock. He was *La Grande Faucheuse*, the Lord of the Reapers.

"This is my reaping," Angeu said immediately, clearly afraid they'd each come to claim Lenora for themselves.

"Then you acknowledge she is yours? You admit it?" the Lord Reaper had a booming voice, like thunder bouncing between mountain tops.

Angeu placed himself between Lenora and the others, guarding his possession from his brothers' sticky fingers. "Of course she's mine. Only mine!"

Another reaper stepped closer. His garment was a wash of horizontal rain. "Do you have any idea what your little pet has done? How many pure spirits she's ruined?"

Angeu's shoulders fell, his hard stance laxed. "What do you mean?"

"I had two of them pegged for my collection once their time was up. But she tortured them before they died, she shredded their pristine souls. She robbed me of two perfect specimens," howled one dressed in flurries.

Angeu turned on Lenora, looked over her swollen body parts. "You, you stole from untainted souls?"

"How did she get out in the first place?" demanded Yama, one she recognized. He wore a sandstorm. "You must have allotted her a day, why did you not bring her back when she finished the task you sent her on?"

"He gave me no task," Lenora cried. "He traded for my *services* instead."

The group went silent, taking a collective, breathless gasp.

"You gave her freedom with no bounds?" said Yama. "She was not tied to a task, compelled to complete it? You let her do as she wished?"

"You *lay* with a reaped soul?" cried another.

They murmured amongst themselves for a moment, each angered by Angeu's recklessness, and disgusted by his depravity.

"As her owner, Angeu," said the Lord Reaper. "You take responsibility for her crimes. She destroyed perfect souls, stole them from your brothers. You know the punishment for stealing a prized reaping."

"And she ruined dozens," Yama added.

Angeu turned on Lenora. She'd tricked him again. Only on ground filled with death-rot could reapers materialize solidly enough to physically interact with one another. Only in a cemetery could one reaper be captured by another.

He raised his arms and flexed his fingers, intending to strike out and wring her decaying neck, but paused. The watchful eyes of the others made him impotent.

He glanced from each brother to the next, imploring them to understand. "No, you can't blame me." Panic sounded uncouth on a reaper. "Punish her, torture her. You can't blame me." He backed away, only to be corralled on all sides. They came closer and closer, tightening their circle. "No, you cannot take me. You cannot."

"We can," said the Lord, "And we will."

They converged on him at once, rising into the air and slamming down in a stormy pile. Lightning cracked into the sky where warm fronts and cold fronts collided, a swirling storm of ice, wind, and fire obscured Angeu from view. The air smelled of burnt ozone. He screamed a protest, denied his responsibility, cursed Lenora. Dark hands sprang out from the tempest, like black wings of squabbling birds, and the edges of their cloaks snapped outwards, flinging weather in all directions. The storm became a whirlpool, spiraling down and down, tighter and tighter until it disappeared into another realm, beyond the physical world, leaving nothing behind but the echoes of Angeu's cries.

Heat slowly returned to the night air, making it warm and comfortable in the aftermath of the reapers' cold.

Hurrying to her task, Lenora fetched the shovel she'd hidden in the bushes some nights before. She toed the blade into Rosalyn's grave, and heaved out shovelful after shovelful. Down and down she dug, until she hit the coffin. The top was wood and already rotting. She jabbed at it with the shovel, splintering it apart, then pulled the shards out of the hole until the corpse was fully exposed. Jumping into the grave, she lugged Rosalyn's gray and flaking body from its casket, then pushed it up onto level ground. The head detached from the neck, falling back against the worm-eaten lining. She tossed it up afterwards.

She pulled herself up out of the grave, then opened her bed sheet. Working quickly, but carefully, she gently removed the sections of skin from their mountings and placed them in the proper alignment on the body. She sewed loose stitches, foregoing tidiness for haste.

A reaper could only be gone from his menagerie for so long before the walls began to collapse. If he did not repair them the souls would float free, drawn out of Limbo either downwards towards death, or upwards towards life.

Before giving herself over to Angeu's desires, she'd told Rosalyn of her plan. "Choose life," she had pleaded with her sister, "Come up, I'll be waiting for you. I'll prepare everything. I'll get you out of here. He'll never touch you, I promise."

The walls of the menagerie would fall soon, and Rosalyn's spirit would rise. But if she had no living flesh to cling to, Lenora could not keep her.

Lenora worked from the bottom up, starting with the soles of Rosalyn's feet, laboring up the legs to the torso and beyond. She attached the head with a long, fine strip of neck, then affixed the scalp. Finally she began work on the face.

She felt the ground breathe beneath her, heaving upwards. Spirits were escaping the nether world. In the distance, she heard a scream. A soul had reentered its dead body, and was struggling to stay. It let out one long, blood-filled cry as it sank back down into oblivion, away from life forever.

"Just a few moments, my dear," Lenora pleaded, sewing on the nose. "Just another moment."

When she placed the lips over the exposed teeth of the skull, Rosalyn's fingers began to twitch. A sucking sound, like air into a vacuum, started deep in her chest, beneath the new flesh of her living breasts.

"Stay with me. Stay with me!" Lenora worked faster. Only a few more items to go. She dug out the flaccid, dry remains of her sister's eyes and popped in the new ones.

Rosalyn blinked, focused, and saw her. She tried to open her mouth, to speak, but something was still holding her back.

This wasn't like a reaper's gift of flesh, which was endowed with his power. If the skin was incomplete, Rosalyn would seep out of the gap and back into Limbo. Lenora looked around for what she could have missed, and saw a gaping hole on the side of her skull. She hadn't yet attached her second ear.

Her sister began to scream like the other spirit had. She reached up for Lenora, clawed at her blouse and hair, looking for a handhold to keep her in this world.

Lenora pulled herself away from the flailing half-dead and searched in panic for the lost item. It wasn't in the sheet, and she could see it nowhere on the ground.

She couldn't have gone through all this to lose her now. She refused to fail.

Abandoning the search, she returned to Rosalyn. Steadying herself, she reached up to her own newly-grafter ear and tore with all her strength. The ear ripped free, and she hurried to attach it before her sister finished her death cries.

The deed done, Lenora sat back on her haunches, and noticed the sweat her skin had produced.

"Lenora?" Rosalyn asked, her lips not yet working as they should. She sat up slowly, her bones creaking, decaying ligaments snapping, but her form held fast in its new casing.

Lenora began to laugh, and cry, though no tears fell. Rosalyn was safe, and Angeu was gone. They were back amongst the living, though not truly alive. They still had more to steal if they wished to eat, and breathe, and run with blood as life demanded.

She leaned over and hugged her sister, grateful to no one but her own hard work for their second chance. Rosalyn struggled to stand, and Lenora helped her to her feet. She took shaky steps forward, her hands wandering her body, feeling the ridges that formed the borders between different pieces of skin.

Rosalyn clearly couldn't comprehend the strangeness of her form. Continuing to explore, her hands shook as she asked, "Lenora, am I alive?" Her face displayed raw fear.

Lenora knew she was afraid of the answer, afraid that the tissues were not her own, afraid this was just a death-dream. "No, not yet," she said. "We are the Low Ones, neither living nor dead. We take from the High Ones to preserve our place." She touched her sister's nose and Rosalyn struggled to smile with her poorly stitched lips. "I'll fix those better for you when we get home," she promised. "But right now, I only have one good ear, and I need a pair before the sun rises." She took her sister's hand and led her away from their graves. "Come with me, and I'll tell you how I beat the reaper."

KATHARINE KERR has been a mainstay of fantasy sections in bookstores everywhere for the past four decades. Her best known works comprise the *Deverry* series, which began in 1986 with *Daggerspell* and spans fifteen volumes. She is also an accomplished SF writer, most notably with her *Polar City* books and many standalone novels. Her most recent urban fantasy series features *Secret Agent Nola* O'Grady, and she has edited several anthologies, written multiple short stories and has contributed gaming modules to TSR and others.

Check out her website at www.deverry.com

TRUFAN FEVER
Katharine Kerr

"We're getting an expansion team!" Angela emailed me with many more exclamation points than two, but I'll spare you. "We've got to get season tickets! Drinks after work to discuss?"

I answered yes. After I closed up the boutique I manage, I went to our usual well-lighted bar and got our usual spot in a corner among the greenery. In a few minutes Angela came striding through the tables to join me. She's a tall woman, nearly six feet, with a mane of long blonde hair that flaps behind her when she walks fast, which she usually does. She sat down and flopped a couple of pieces of print-out onto the table between us.

"Brochure," Angela said. "I printed it out just for you."

"I know I'm a Luddite." I grinned. "And I'm proud."

"When are you going to get a smartphone? So you can text. Email is so lame!"

"I can't type on those little tiny spaces."

"Well, it's those nails of yours. God, they're so long!"

"Oh, go on, call them claws. Sound like my mother. I dare you."

Since we held this discussion on a regular basis, Angela merely rolled her eyes and ordered a drink. While she sipped a murky liquid called a chocolate martini, I allowed myself one small dry sherry and glanced at the ticket prices. OMG! High doesn't begin to describe it. Still, I could scrape up the space on my credit cards, if I really wanted to.

"I don't know about season tickets," I said. "I don't want to commit to every other weekend. It's too much excitement for the likes of me."

"Rita, you need more excitement in your life." She wrinkled her nose at me. "All you do is sell clothes and read books."

"Yeah, so? I need my peace and quiet."

Angela ordered a second martini. I looked at the print-out again. This time the name of the team jumped out at me.

"Los Angeles Leopards," I said. "Okay, I'm in."

When we bought our season tickets, Angela, her boyfriend Cody, and I deliberately chose seats behind one end zone. Other friends joined us when we decided to go in costume. Yes, of course those Oakland Raider fans in their Black Hole gave us the idea, but if they could dress up and have fun, why couldn't we? Angela and Cody created orc suits—black and yellow face paint, lots of cardboard armor painted to look like golden bronze but with black leopard spots painted on, spiky cardboard helmets—you get the idea. Others in our pack chose to dress as wizards, white-faced ghouls, and just plain weird creatures, all of them with fake leopard-print fur or rosettes of spots prominent among the bits of finery.

I decided upon full leopard formal dress. For most games I wore a headpiece with the proper rounded big cat ears. I pasted cat whiskers on my face, painted rosettes on my décolletage, and wore elbow-length gloves made of gauzy leopard-print material with slits to let my nails come through. I sewed up a fake fur pair of gloves, too, for later in the season, but it's hot in L.A. during the early fall. My main costume piece was a slinky red full-length dress left over from college. Just call me Miss Leopardine Sweetheart.

For most games. Once there was this exception.

All expansion teams start out dismally, and the 'Pards ran true to form. Or maybe I should say, didn't run, because our million dollar running back fumbled more often than he scored, and the two million dollar quarterback threw perfect passes—right to the opposing teams' DBs, that is, their corners and safeties. Our defense guys mostly stood still and hoped that the ball carrier would run into them instead of bothering to go around.

Our friends often ask Angela and me why we enjoy watching football. I guess females "aren't supposed to," but to hell with that! Seeing truly bad football helped me find answers. I've always loved the intellectual side of the game, which I think of as small unit tactics, not strategy in the broad military sense. It takes a keen mind to invent ways to advance a football down the field when other tactical geniuses are trying to come up with ways to stop that advance. The calculations involve assessing the potential of both sets of players and using psychology as well as understanding the rules at a gut level so you can find loopholes in them. That first year, the Leopards' OC and DC lacked the right kind of mind. They obviously thought football involved nothing more than big guys banging into each other.

Don't get me wrong. Brutality's part of the game, too, but what intrigues me is the difficulty of implementing those carefully devised tactics in the midst of the violent action. The game has room for clever schemes, individual initiative, heroism, self-sacrifice, and buffed guys in really tight pants. What's not to like? In those first games, the 'Pards supplied mostly the men in tight pants, not enough to hold the interest of the truly dedicated fan.

When we weren't busy groaning and booing, the end zone crowd got to know each other. At first, my friends and I were the only ones in costume, but soon enough everyone in the rows down front joined us. The costumes built up slowly, a hunk of printed fake fur there, a pair of leopard-like ears there, a little orc-ish makeup over yonder, until by the October home games a lot of fans appeared in full fantasy body armor or assemblages of fake fur pieces and tattoos. Hey, it kept us all from thinking too much about the horror show going on out on the turf.

One good-looking Hispanic guy in our section held out, though he made up for his lack of costume with the amount of fan gear he piled on himself. He had official Leopard team laces in his running shoes, the official sweatpants, a genuine Leopard home-game jersey with his own name, Valdez, on the back, a training-camp-style Leopard hoodie, and an official away-game baseball cap. Thank the spotted gods, however, he never wore one of those grotesque fake wigs in team colors. His own hair was dark, short, and lustrous, and he had deep-set dark eyes. Just every now and then I'd look his way. He'd smile and consider me with one eyebrow quirked, as if he was daring me to speak to him. I never did.

Most of my friends drank beer all through the game, even though the concessions overcharged for it. I mean, seven-fifty for one lousy bottle poured into a plastic cup! As the designated driver for myself, Angela, and Cody, I stayed sober. When I'm out and about, I need to keep control of myself at all times. In fact, I did my best to drink nothing, not even water, because even though a set of women's restrooms were close by on the concourse above our section, I hated using them. When women fans drink too much, they forget to use the paper covers. They perch and they miss, if you know what I mean. Yuck!

Valdez never drank booze. He did buy nachos now and then. I knew this only because Angela ran into him at the concession stand during the game against the San Diego team. She came hurrying back and handed Cody a basket of garlic fries before she slid into her seat next to me. Through her leopardish face-paint I could see her grinning.

"Valdez asked me if you had a boyfriend," she said.

"I hope you told him no."

"I did. Hah! You're interested in him, aren't you?"

"I am totally uninterested in any male companionship, as you well know."

She made a very rude snorting sound.

"Or female companionship, either," I went on. "My life's too busy as it is."

"Oh yeah sure." Cody leaned in front of her and breathed garlic in my direction. "Live a little, Rita!"

I would have stuck my tongue out at him, but doing so would have smeared my make-up, so I didn't. "I hope," I said to Angela, "that you didn't tell that guy my name."

"Of course not." But she was grinning. "None of my business."

After that little incident, I tried to refrain from looking in Valdez's direction. But you know how it is. Try not to look at someone or something and your eyes wander that way before you can stop them. Most times when I slipped up I found him looking back. This little glance dance went on for two full home games while the 'Pards slowly, ever so slowly, improved out on the field. Not that they won a game, mind. They did come close once, only to lose in overtime when our kicker missed an easy field goal.

Finally, in late November the Leopards were slated to play on Thursday night, an inconvenient time, but that dedicated football channel had promised them a televised game to help generate interest. Thanks to that, the team sold a bunch of walk-up tickets. Everyone in Los Angeles wants to be on TV, even if it's only in a thirty-second shot of the fans at a football game. Our section with all the costumes figured to be a camera target. For a change, there were no empty seats. Valdez took his usual place on the aisle.

That night the 'Pards played a team even lamer than they were, the Ospreys, let us call them, from way up north. On the very first play, when the Leopards kicked off, the Osprey return man muffed the catch. One of our guys scooped up the ball and ran for the end zone. He reached it without fumbling. Were our fortunes were turning for the better? I felt a flash of hope. When our defense forced the Ospreys to go three and out on the next possession, the flash turned into a spark. We scored a touchdown as soon as we got the ball back. The spark became a blaze within my fannish soul.

It wasn't until late in the game that I realized I was in deep trouble. The 'Pards were leading the Ospreys by two touches and a field goal by then. Cody leaned over in front of Angela and yelled, "Feathers all over the field!"

"Yes!" I yelled back. "Yes!"

The crowd around us was screaming and roaring too loudly for eloquence. The stadium glowed with light, while overhead and all around, the dark night ruled, as if we were a pocket universe, sealed away from all the troubles on Earth. I felt myself part of a pack, a glorious troop of fans, swaying, chanting, exulting while out on the field our warriors fought on. I'd like to say they fought on brilliantly, but at the beginning of the fourth quarter they began to blow it. The defense must have been overtired, poor babies, because the damned Ospreys scored one touchdown on an interception, and then another by running the ball into and through our porous secondary. Our lead shrank to three. The screams around me changed to agony. I joined in.

By then I was sweating in rivulets. I ached all over and felt hot pain in my knees, hips, and shoulders. My joints were beginning to soften. I felt my body swelling, perceived the telltale itching that signaled fur trying to grow along my arms and down my back. *Oh Goddess no!* I thought. *Be calm, Rita, be calm! It's just a game. You can't change here! Just a game, just a game!*

Out on the field, the Ospreys were kicking off. Our return man caught the ball and swerved, dodged, ran down the field in a brilliant series of moves. He made it to Ospreys' thirty-two before their defense finally brought him down. I yelled and rose from my seat to dance because the itching had reached my butt.

I took deep breaths. I thought of beautiful meadows with views of mountains. Didn't work. I could feel my body thickening through the middle, pressing against the fabric of my dress. If the muscle mass kept building up, I'd strangle in my underwear. I handed Angela my beaded bag and yelled, "Got to go to the restroom!" She nodded and tucked the bag under her armor's breastplate while she kept staring out at the field. I sidled my way past the other fans to the aisle and ran up the concrete steps. The muscles in my legs had grown, turned strong and fierce. I bounded up those stairs. I wanted to drool. I wanted to tear off my clothing right there and then.

Fortunately, I made it to the restroom first. Equally fortunately, no one else was using it. I ducked into a stall and disrobed barely in time. My fingernails were turning into proper claws, which made rolling up my clothes difficult. I managed to open the door and puddle-jump out to the wash-up area of the restroom. On the wall above a paper towel dispenser hung a small shelf. I reached up with one aching arm and laid the wad of clothes upon it. I prayed to Bast and Sekhmet that no one found it and took it away.

From outside I could hear cheering. Had the 'Pards scored? Excitement overwhelmed me in an icy wave. I *changed*. A glance in the mirror showed me a female leopard tottering on her hind legs with no trace of ape girl visible. I threw back my head and roared. At the sound my human self receded to a little pool of consciousness floating on pure leopard mind. I dropped to all fours. She, the leopard, wanted to run. I ran, and my human nature became a tiny jockey clinging to the back of a powerful animal.

I raced out of the restroom onto the concourse, a concrete walkway that curved around that level of the stadium. As we galloped past a gaggle of male fans, they yelled in drunken appreciation. "Go, go, yeah, that's the way, girl!" They frightened her, the leopard. She bounded into the air, dropped again, ran a few steps, and looked wildly around. She raced for a yawning opening in the wall. Stairs down—she roared and flung herself onto the stairway, bounded and leapt and ran down the stairs between two sections of seats. At first no one noticed, but when she—when we—reached the lowest rank of seats, someone screamed.

"It's real!" A high-pitched voice floated over the crowd. "Leopard! Help! A real leopard!"

Screaming hurt her ears. Concrete hurt her paws. Ahead lay a green field of grass. My human mind was yelling, *no no no*, but she didn't listen. She rarely does. She ran for the railing, leapt over with no thought for the drop, landed on the wounded-warrior motorized cart, bounced off that, and ran onto the field. Osprey men in white jerseys were racing around, yelling numbers, tossing the brown leather ball that smelled of oil and dead animal. The leopard saw it as a streak of prey flying through the air. She dodged in front of their wide receiver and leapt straight up. Her fangs sank into the ball with a satisfying hiss of air. She landed on all fours just as the yells and screaming broke out in earnest. Some of the noise spoke of terror, but some of it cheered for us.

For those brief moments I knew how it felt to play. At last I had achieved oneness with my team! The leopard saw burly men in various colored shirts running away from her. She chased them, caught up with them, dodged in and around the fleeing bodies. Two men, huge apes in her eyes, grabbed at her prey as she raced by. She twisted and leapt and dodged. They missed. We galloped into the endzone to the sound of cheering and hysterical laughter from end zone fans too drunk to know better. "Touchdown! Touchdown! Touchdown!"

That's when I saw policemen, rushing toward us with drawn guns.

Is this is where I die? Oh shit!

My human desperation plus the leopard's sudden fear forced her to obey. *Drop the damn ball!* She shook her head and threw the crumpled leather right at the pair of cops. *Back to the stands!* She spun around and ran with the few players still on the field. Under their involuntary cover we angled back across the grass and reached the 'Pard's sideline before the cops got a chance to shoot. Players, refs, coaches, TV personnel—they were dashing around, yelling, waving their arms in a total panic that made it far too dangerous for the cops to fire, though I suppose that if they'd shot that lousy QB by mistake, no one would have cared much. We plunged in among the men, knocked over a bench, hit the tub of Gatorade, and with that icy shower got free of the chaos at last. Once again the leopard leapt up on the motorized cart and from there bounded onto the stairs.

The fans in the aisle seats screamed and jumped up, sidled and shoved themselves toward the middle of their sections, but the leopard never noticed or cared. By then she was growing tired, foaming at the mouth, panting, clambering rather bounding up the painful concrete. At last we reached the top of the tier. With a last growl for strength, she lunged into the opening and made it to the walkway. We trotted, gasping for breath, back to the restroom. Just a couple of yards away from the door, the bitch deserted me. I fell forward onto the concrete as a naked woman.

As I scrambled to my feet, I heard bullhorns shouting alarms and commands. A gaggle of security guards jogged around the curve and started forward. From behind them a big cat roared. I couldn't see it, but the sound echoed off the concrete. The guards turned and ran back in that direction. I stumbled into the restroom. I was sweating, exhausted, aching in every muscle. A foul taste filled my mouth from the football—leather, oil, and sweat. My make-up had run into nasty gray streaks on my neck and between my breasts.

My clothes, thank the Fur Goddesses, lay where I'd stashed them. Before I touched them, I washed my face and moistened a wad of paper towels. With trembling hands I wiped the sweat and dead make-up off my body. I heard male voices just outside and grabbed my clothes. I dressed in a hurry, then limped out to face a pair of security guards.

"Are you all right, miss?" the portly guy said.

"Yeah," I said. "What's going on? I heard all this screaming, so I was afraid to come out."

"There was a wild animal on the loose, a leopard. A really stupid move on the team's part, if you ask me. Maybe a mascot broke out of its cage. Or a prank got way out of hand."

I gasped in pretend terror. "It is gone?"

"We don't know for sure yet, but we think it's escaped from the stadium. Go back to your seat. That's probably the safest place to be. The game's been called."

"Damn! And we were winning!"

Both guards laughed. "That's a true fan for you," the skinny one said. "A real true fan."

Little did he know!

I staggered back along the walkway toward our section. At the head of the stairs I saw Valdez. He was leaning against the wall, waiting for me with just the slightest trace of a smile on his face, a little curve of his lips like a cat's. That's when I first suspected the truth, not that it took him long to confirm it. He came to meet me and offered me his arm for support. I needed the help badly enough to take it.

"Tell me something," he said, "how do you feel about jaguars?"

"Wonderful animals. Why?"

"Huh, like you don't know!"

I stared. He grinned.

"We've both got rosettes," he said, "and a common ancestor."

"I'm sure I don't know to what you are referring."

His grin deepened. "You put that dress on backwards. After you got done changing. And yeah, I do mean *changing*."

Damn! I looked down at the neckline and saw the tag sticking out. With my free hand I tucked it back in.

"Was it you who roared when I changed back?"

"Yeah. I didn't want those guards to see you." He gazed into my eyes. "For weeks now I've been smelling leopard every time you walked past me. It's been driving me wild."

As pick-up lines go, this one stank as badly as my alternate nature, but how often was I going to meet a were-jaguar, much less get to date one? If things got really exciting between us, no longer would I have to worry about losing control. If I changed, he'd just do the same. I smiled.

"Tell me more," I said.

"You're so beautiful when you run," Valdez went on. "It took every bit of will power I've got to keep myself from changing and joining you."

I sighed. Deeply. "What's your first name?" I said. "Mine's Rita."

"Esteban, but call me Steve."

So I did.

I still do, actually. Now that the Leopards are playing well, we no longer go to the home games—too exciting for both of us. The management got into enough trouble with the league as it was, thanks to my escapade. The Commissioner investigated, ruminated, and pontificated, but no one could ever prove that the team had let a wild leopard loose on the field—or a tame one, either, since of course no one ever found the actual big cat. I would have apologized, but how could I? I would have ended up in a locked psycho ward somewhere, for sure, if not the zoo.

Angela approves of my new boyfriend, by the way, not that she knows why things developed so fast between us. Steve and I see our friends at other times than the home games, so we're not missing all the fun. Besides, the TV football coverage has close-ups. We can see all the details as we lounge, side by side, paw to paw, on the sofa in our new apartment.

JACKIE KESSLER is the American author of the *Hell on Earth* urban fantasy series and is the co-author (with Caitlin Kittredge) of the *Icarus Project* superhero novels. She's had numerous short stories published in various magazines, including *Realms of Fantasy* and *Farthing*, and she contributed a story for Dark Horse Comic's *Buffy The Vampire Slayer* series. As Jackie Morse Kessler, she's penned four young adult novels in the Riders of the Apocalypse series and a traditional fantasy novel, *To Bear An Iron Key*.

Her website is www.jackiekessler.com and she can be found on Twitter: @jackiekessler

UNDYING LOVE
Jackie Kessler

The thing about demons? They're tricky. They lie, they cheat, they ignore any rules that no one's strong enough to enforce. And they're unpredictable, except for one thing: they'll always be true to their nature. No matter what, demons are evil. They can't help it; it's how they're made.

I should know. I'd been a demon for more than four thousand years. (Currently, I'm human. Well, humanish. It's complicated.)

It didn't surprise me that a demon was lurking in the alley that I passed. Lurking goes with the nefarious territory. I caught a whiff of brimstone, felt that old familiar pang of homesickness, and paused in my stride just long enough to make eye contact. First glance showed me a man in his thirties, more sexy than handsome and putting out serious "Come hither" vibes. Then his aura flared darkly, and I knew the truth of it: he was a vampire, a minor entity at best, barely qualifying as a creature of Hell.

I smiled. "Dare you to try it."

He blinked, then shrank back, hissing. I'd spooked him—all sixty-four inches and one hundred-ten pounds of me.

Heh.

Chuckling, I said, "Slink away, sweetie."

He slunk away.

I grinned as I kept walking. A stronger creature would have attacked me on the dare alone; no demon worth its ichor lets a direct challenge pass. But all the vampire had done was spit and cower. Back when I first began hunting demons that entered my territory, I would have summoned my sword and carved him like a Thanksgiving turkey. But I'd mellowed over the past year. The vampire wasn't a threat; therefore, he wasn't worth my time. So I let him go.

That's the thing I'd remember, after all was said and done: I let him go.

Five minutes later, I was in my favorite café, seated at the counter and making yummy sounds as I ate a slice of chocolate cream pie with extra whipped cream. Only a few patrons were in the café this time of night, and I didn't give a damn if they noticed my foodgasm. Some said that chocolate was heavenly. Me, I considered it one of my favorite sins.

Behind the counter, Holly gazed at my plate and shook her head, setting her large silver cat's face earrings to bob back and forth. "I swear, Jesse, if I ate pie five nights a week like you, I'd be big as a house."

"You're pregnant," I said, pointing my chin at her baby bump. "You can eat whatever you want."

"This little guy only gets healthy food." She affectionately patted her belly. In a squeak that made her sound like a cartoon chipmunk, she said, "Isn't that right, Honey Bear? You're gonna be big and strong, and that won't happen on crap food, will it? No, it won't!"

"Yet another reason I'm grateful I'm not reproducing," I said around a mouthful of pie. "I thrive on crap food."

"I don't know how you do it," she said, talking to me again in her normal voice. "You've been coming here, what, six months now? And you haven't gained an ounce. How do you keep your figure?"

"Eh, I teach dance lessons."

"Tango, Fox Trot, that sort of thing?"

"That too." Most of my clients were into the pole variety. First lesson tended to focus on walking in five-inch platform heels.

"Sounds fun!"

"It can be. Plus, I run." Chasing after demons burns lots of calories. "And a few nights a week, I take sword lessons."

Her eyebrows flew up. "Sword lessons? You training to be a samurai?"

"Nah. Samurais are warriors. I'm training to be a ninja assassin."

She laughed, and her large earrings bobbed. "Remind me not to get on your bad side."

"Get me a little more whipped cream, and I promise you'll be on my good side forever."

"Deal."

Holly whip-creamed my pie until it drowned. Death by dessert—the sort of death I could firmly get behind. Sighing happily, I dug in.

When I was halfway done, the bell over the café door jingled. A moment later, a man sidled up to the counter, making mooneyes at Holly and grinning hugely. I didn't need to see his aura to know he was madly in love with her; affection oozed from his pores. She was just as bad as him, based on her goofy smile.

"Hey, Baby Mama," he said to her.

"Hey, Baby Daddy," she replied, voice breathy.

"Missed you."

"Missed you more."

"Did Baby miss me?"

"Baby missed you most of all." She touched her belly, and in her cartoon chipmunk voice, she said, "Didn't you, Honey Bear? Yes, you did!"

Satan spare me from the love-struck and new parents. I rolled my eyes and ate my pie.

Baby Daddy said, "Ready to go?"

"Give me a sec." Holly untied her apron as she walked over to another waitress, presumably to talk waitressy things. Baby Daddy kept smiling at her, even though Holly wasn't looking at him. The expression on his face was the stuff of epic poetry, all adoration and joy. He was a man who had everything that mattered and was blissfully happy.

But that kind of happiness never lasted. I knew it, even before his aura flashed, spiking black.

I pretended I didn't see it as I scraped whipped cream from my plate.

Holly grabbed her purse from behind the counter and fiddled with an earring that had caught in her hair. It looked like the silver cat's face was trying to cough up a hairball. She pouted, "Darn thing keeps getting tangled in my hair!"

"So take it off," said Baby Daddy.

"These earrings are from you," she cooed. "I'm never taking them off! Besides, they're the closest things I'll ever get to having a cat. You and your allergies!"

"Find a cat that's dander-free, and we can talk about it…"

"Not one of those mummy cats with no hair! Cats are supposed to have hair!"

"Some people even call it 'fur'."

She laughed as she playfully slapped his arm.

In that moment, I caught her aura, too, and I fidgeted. Ignore it, I told myself. I'm just here for the pie. Any waitress could serve me pie. So what that Holly always chatted with me, always laughed at my bad jokes and shared a couple herself? So what that she'd told me she was going to name her baby after her father, who was dead for five years? So what that I knew she tended to sing in her sweetly off-key voice when she was stocking the napkins, sing a song about rainbows and lovers and dreamers? So what to all of that? Holly was just another human, in this world of more than seven billion. I didn't even know her last name.

But I knew what the auras meant.

As she and Baby Daddy walked to the door, Holly called out, "Good night, Jesse!"

I couldn't manage the lie of wishing her a good night, so I waved half-heartedly and tried to convince myself that I didn't care. I ate my pie, but all the taste had bled out onto the crumbs on the plate.

My aura reading was a flaky ability, I reminded myself; maybe I was wrong about what I'd seen.

I knew I wasn't wrong.

I stared at the smears of chocolate and whipped cream on my plate and saw bloodstains on the street.

Bless it all.

I left a twenty on the counter and ran out the door.

By the time I caught up to Holly and her man, it was already too late.

Baby Daddy was a mess of limbs on the blood-spattered ground, his throat torn out, his face and body awash in red. Next to him, Holly was in a heap, her body jerking and one hand clutching her belly as if she could save the baby within. Squatting over her, a demon slobbered at Holly's neck.

Not just any demon—the vampire from earlier that night. The one I'd let go, because he hadn't been worth my time.

My vision tunneled as I summoned my sword, a blade forged from magic and steel. The vampire didn't even have time to hiss before I skewered his brain. His body poofed away in a burst of brimstone.

On the sidewalk, Holly let out a weak moan.

I dropped my sword, and it magicked itself away to a pocket dimension. Out of sight, and all that jazz. Crouching next to Holly, I assessed the damage. One of her ears was bleeding from its ragged end, the lobe having been ripped off. Maybe that dangling silver cat's face earring had saved her from meeting Baby Daddy's fate, because instead of her neck being a mess of meat and blood, there were only two puncture marks, now weeping a viscous red.

I tore off part of my shirt and pressed the material against Holly's throat to slow the blood loss. Holding the scrap with one hand, I used my other hand to fish my cell phone from my back pocket and punch the button for 9-1-1.

"Your effort is in vain, you who were Jesse Harris."

I threw a glare at the angel, both for the sudden appearance and for the less-than-encouraging announcement, then ignored her as the emergency operator answered the call. I gave the pertinent information and hung up without offering my name. The operator wouldn't be able to trace the call to me—benefit of having a magically spelled cell phone and a witch who'd owed me a favor.

When I was done, I pocketed my phone and looked over at the angel. She was dressed head to toe in white, wearing a certain 1970s-style leisure suit that begged for a disco soundtrack. A glance at Baby Daddy told me that the celestial had already collected his soul: his corpse seemed emptier, deflated.

She reached for Holly, and I growled, "Don't."

Disco Angel frowned. It was a beautiful frown, and filled with derision. I would have been impressed if the frown had been on anyone else's face. Angels could teach demons of Arrogance how to be proud. And they tend to have sticks jammed firmly up their trapdoors.

"Don't what, you who were Jesse Harris?"

"One, don't call me that. Two, don't touch the woman. She's still alive."

The frown deepened as Disco Angel lifted her chin. "You were, briefly, mortal, and named Jesse Harris. You were, far longer, nefarious and called Jezebel. What shall I call you now, you who are a hybrid creature of Pit and Clay?"

I smiled, showing far too much tooth. "My friends call me Jesse. But you and your kind can call me Jezebel."

"As you wish, Jezebel." She inclined her head, once, perhaps in a show of respect. "As for your other request, consider it granted. I'm not here for the woman."

I glanced at Holly's swollen belly.

"Do not interfere," Disco Angel warned. "That soul longs for the joy of Paradise."

With a heavy sigh, I turned my head away. I hated it when angels were right.

There was a warm breeze, a hint of summer flowers—and then nothing but the sound of sirens approaching quickly. Disco Angel and her charges were gone, and I was left with a dying woman and two corpses, one still buried in its mother's womb.

Two ambulances arrived moments later. I stood in the shadows, unnoticed—a perk of tapping into Hell's power—as the emergency medical service crew loaded Holly onto a gurney and carried her into one of the trucks. It left, sirens screaming, in a mad dash to save her life.

The second ambulance took Baby Daddy's body. No sirens for him, just the mournful sound of a cold wind blowing in the dark night.

Unseen, I watched the police attempt to determine how Baby Daddy had been killed, and what had attacked Holly. For now, they were calling the victims "John and Jane Doe," because there'd been no wallets and no purse at the scene. A mugging gone wrong, they were saying, even though both vics had gold wedding rings on their fingers and the woman still had one silver earring dangling from her attached ear. The other earring—along with the remains of that ear—had been found a few feet down the sidewalk. Yes, a mugging gone very wrong, with no trace of the perp.

They'd never think "vampire"; everyone knew that creatures like that didn't exist.

The results of what everyone knew were in the back of two ambulances.

A muscle twitched in my jaw as I watched the police waste their time.

This was my fault.

I had the vampire earlier and let him go.

I'd seen the auras flash over Holly and her Baby Daddy and had said nothing. That wouldn't have changed anything; auras never lied. They had shown me Baby Daddy's death. They had shown me the unborn baby's death.

And they'd shown me Holly's death.

All my fault.

The least I could do now was see Holly's journey to the end.

With a grim sigh, I tucked Baby Daddy's wallet into Holly's purse, then I walked away from the police, unnoticed, and began to make my way to the nearest hospital.

~~*~*

Holly was already dead when I arrived. I knew she would be; that's why I'd gone straight to the mortuary. It had taken only a little bit of jiggling to distract the attendant, and then I cold-cocked him with the hilt of my sword. Maybe I would have felt guilty about that if I hadn't seen his aura. Naughty boy. Under other circumstances, I would have given him my phone number.

Holly was on the covered table, her skin already corpse pale. Blood and body matter had pooled between her legs, staining the sheet.

I stripped off the attendant's blue smock top and used it to scoop up the discharge that had been Holly's baby. I wrapped it up with the uniform top and tucked it under the attendant's unconscious form just before Holly's arm twitched.

"Hey, Holly," I said, rising to my full height. "You've had a bit of a shock."

For a long moment, nothing.

Then she gasped and opened her eyes. She sat up quickly—too quickly for a human—and pressed her hands to her flat stomach. As the wounds on her throat closed and her torn ear plumped, she rasped, "My baby...?"

It took less than a minute to tell her what had happened.

It took the rest of the night to console her. She probably would have kept crying and screaming even after the sun came up; instead, she'd frozen mid-wail, then fell down dead.

I managed to sneak her out of the hospital—combination of former-demon mojo, an empty laundry sack, and a healthy dose of devil's luck—and flagged down a taxi. Once my bundle was in the trunk and I was in the back seat, I opened Holly's purse, dug out her wallet, and found her license. I gave the driver her address and off we went. (In another life, I would have also pocketed the cash and credit cards. Humanity really was rubbing off on me.)

Holly lived on the tenth floor of an apartment building that thankfully had no doorman. Huffing, I dragged the overstuffed laundry bag across the lobby and headed toward the elevator bank. Dead weight, it turned out, was really heavy.

Upstairs, I used Holly's key to unlock her door, and then I pulled the sack over the threshold and into the apartment. Catching my breath, I took in the cluttered but neat living room, the cozy kitchen, the hallway that presumably led to bedrooms and a bathroom. Small place—a starter apartment, fine for two people in love with a baby on the way.

Fine for a new vampire to keep her coffin.

Leaving Holly where she was—in a heap in the laundry bag—I closed the window blinds in the living room, sealing off any chance of stray sunlight, then did a thorough window-check in the rest of the apartment. While I was pretty sure Holly would stay dead until the sun went down, I wasn't willing to risk her going up in flames in case I was wrong. Once everything was shrouded, I dragged Holly's sack into the bedroom and managed to heft her onto her bed.

Oof.

Mental note: start weightlifting.

It had been a very long night, and a longer morning. I sank onto the sofa in the living room and closed my eyes for a minute.

I woke hours later to the sound of screaming.

Lurching to my feet, I staggered down the hall and into the bedroom, where Holly, naked and unmarked by any wound or blemish, was shredding her blanket and wailing fit to put banshees out of business.

"Hey!" I shouted, "Holly, it's okay! Calm down!"

She whirled to face me, red-eyed and snarling.

"Holly," I said again, not shouting this time, holding out my empty palms. I really didn't want to kill her like I did her maker; I had enough guilt on my conscience. "It's me, Jesse. From the café. The one who eats pie five nights a week. Remember me? Great figure, training to be a ninja?"

Holly blinked, and sagged, and collapsed to the floor, sobbing.

For most of that night, I consoled her. Between losing her husband, losing her baby, and losing her humanity, she was a hot mess of hurt and confusion. I explained that she'd died and been reborn as vampire. I could have gotten into the specifics, how she wasn't a vampire in the classic sense because she wasn't a demon, but I figured at the moment, she really didn't give a damn about such things. So I went over the undead basics: Blood good, sunlight bad, predator skill-set unlocked. As I talked, she kept rubbing her empty belly. Tears left pink-tinged trails down her cheeks.

"I should have grabbed blood for you when we were at the hospital," I said. "Sorry, wasn't thinking. Want me to run out, get a few bags for you? Or I can help you learn how to hunt for your dinner. Stick to the criminals—less police interference that way."

She rubbed her belly and cried silently.

"Holly," I said quietly, "tell me what you want."

Her voice a bare whisper, she said, "My baby. I want my Honey Bear."

I gently took her hand. "Your baby's in Heaven with his daddy. They're both happy. It's a place of joy," I said, remembering the angel's words. "You need to think about you. Come on. Let's get you dressed, and I'll show you how to scare up your dinner."

But when I took her hunting, she just followed listlessly. I even let an overly testosteroned musclehead grab me and slam my head against the side of a storefront, to show Holly how to play helpless, but she didn't react at all. So I took Musclehead down with a bit of Hell mojo—bam, instant infatuation—and had him crane his neck to give Holly easy access.

She wouldn't bite. Literally.

Same thing happened with the car thief, the desperate junkie, and the politician who thought we were working girls. No matter what, Holly had zero interest in ingesting blood.

After I scared the politician into a lifetime of chastity, I spun to face Holly. "Sweetie, you gotta eat. Drink. Whatever—you need blood. It's a vampire thing."

"Don't want blood," she said dully. "Want my Honey Bear."

By now, my patience was thinner than a supermodel. "Honey Bear's dead. Give up the ghost and focus on *you*, Holly. Come on, I'll show you how to spot demons possessing the unwary. You want to avoid full-scale demons. Most don't have a sense of humor, and even more will jump at the chance to skin a vampire. Even angels will have a go at vampires, but they're more like celestial voyeurs—they tend to sit back and watch while demons get their hands dirty. Give me a demon over an angel any day."

Holly didn't reply.

For the rest of the night, she was nothing more than a shadow—following me, saying nothing, looming darkly.

I checked in on her for the next week, even made sure that her refrigerator was stocked with bags of blood so that she didn't have to hunt. Holly refused to adjust to her new life—she didn't eat, didn't speak, didn't do anything but collapse inside herself. Her form grew emaciated; her eyes were haunted. She kept rubbing her stomach, as if trying to feel the ghostly kicks of her dead baby. Had she been anyone else, I would've cut her loose. But Holly's condition was my fault. The thought of leaving her to suffer made my chest hurt. Stupid human feelings. I'd been much happier when I'd been a self-centered demon bent on debauchery.

The eighth night of Holly's undead life, I brought her a gift.

The kitten was homeless, white as dirty snow, and eager to play. It had been the noise that had drawn me to it earlier that afternoon; I'd walked into a dark alley in a seedy part of town, thinking I'd found a demon. Instead, I found the kitten, facing down a rat over the contents of a broken garbage bag. The kitten had been hissing loudly, his poofed-up tail thrashing back and forth, warning the rat to clear out. The rat, apparently, didn't speak Feline—it lunged forward to attack. In a flash of teeth and fur, the kitten jumped up and landed on the rat's back, tearing at the creature with his tiny claws.

It was the most adorable display of violence I'd seen in a long time.

I scared the rat away and scooped the kitten into my arms. He pressed his face against my ear and purred loudly. Smiling, I'd walked out of the alley and headed toward Holly's apartment. The kitten needed love and nurturing, and I knew a certain vampire who fit the bill.

"I remembered you saying something about wanting a cat," I told Holly as I presented her with the kitten. "Well, this little guy wants a home."

For the first time since her transformation, something close to life lit in Holly's eyes. A tentative smile touched her lips, and she hesitantly reached out to the dirty-white mass of fur and whiskers.

The kitten jumped into her arms and got right in Holly's face, purring up a storm as he rubbed against her mouth.

Holly laughed and spat out fur, which made her laugh even more.

It was a good sound.

I left her to bond with her kitten as I bought her supplies—a litter box, cat food, a bunch of overpriced cat toys, a scratching post. When I returned, Holly was smiling as the newly named Pounce attacked a throw pillow.

"He's perfect," she cooed.

"Well," I said, "Mr. Perfect there might have fleas. Just a heads up."

Over the next few hours, she played with Pounce and laughed as he explored his new home. When the kitten settled down to eat, I coaxed Holly to drink from a blood bag. "Gotta get your strength back if you're going to take care of an active kitten," I told her.

She finally agreed and downed a bag. And then a second. The blood fleshed her out, giving her a healthy glow that made her look nearly human. She drank a third bag and discovered that vampires get drunk when they chug. Tipsy, she chased the kitten around the apartment until dawn snuck up on her. She dropped dead on the living room carpet, her face locked in an expression of delight.

Pounce jumped onto her body, curled up on her chest, and fell asleep.

I said good night—well, good morning—to Holly and Pounce. Neither of them replied, so I let myself out.

On the way home, I stopped at my favorite diner and got a slice of chocolate cream pie, even though it was barely seven in the morning. I'd done a good deed, and good deeds deserved pie.

~~*~*

The next time I visited Holly, she told me she was ready to really learn how to hunt. When she took down her first rapist, I couldn't have been prouder.

Once she was done feeding, I beheaded the guy to make sure he wouldn't rise as a vampire. No one likes a messy eater.

Back at her apartment, Holly lounged, blood-buzzed, as I took in all of the changes she'd made in the past week. She'd bought five cat towers made of carpet, a dozen scratching posts, and more toys than I could count. And that was all just in the living room. Pounce seemed content; he couldn't be bothered to acknowledge me because he was too busy introducing a stuffed bear to his claws.

"Quite the cat house you've got here," I said.

"He likes it," Holly purred, smiling big. "Don't you, Pounce?"

Pounce did what he was named for and pounced on the bear.

"Jesse?"

"Yeah?"

"Will you hunt with me tomorrow?"

I grinned. "Of course."

"Cool."

She was too exhausted from her first hunt and first true feeding to be much of a conversationalist, so we watched Pounce play. At one point, he bounded over to me and attacked my boot, then he dashed off to slice the bottom of the window shades. A cat with attitude. I completely approved.

When the sun rose, Holly sprawled dead on the sofa. Pounce jumped onto her chest, turned around once, and fell asleep. Just a kitten and his vampire. Smiling, I showed myself out the door.

~~*~*

We hunted together for the next six nights. It took a lot out of me; being human(ish) meant that I needed my beauty sleep, but between my day job dance lessons, my various training sessions with swords and demons, and hunting with Holly, I was barely scraping by on four hours a night. I'd been tapping into my Hell mojo to help keep me going, but at this rate, I was going to crash—and crash hard. I intended to tell Holly that I was going to take a hunting break for a while, but I never got the chance.

On that seventh night with Holly, everything changed.

Outside of a nightclub, we watched the prey of the evening sneak out a back door and make her way into an alley. The girl couldn't have been more than sixteen, and dressed like she'd been partying with Liberace, all flowing sequins and enough shiny fabric to blind a passerby. I caught her aura and knew the whole story—too many drugs, too many bad decisions. She was huge, this teenage girl, but not just from too much crappy food.

Holly and I bore witness as the girl dumped a newborn into a garbage can at the back of the alley.

I thought I heard Holly gasp, just before she streaked out from the shadows. She was on the girl in a heartbeat, ripping open her throat and throwing her aside like a broken doll. I couldn't say if the girl died before or after she hit the wall headfirst, hard enough to bounce off and land with a thud in the middle of the alley.

Before the echo faded, Holly reached into the trashcan and carefully removed the baby.

It let out a weak cry—a protest, maybe, or a plea for help.

Holly cradled the tiny body to her chest. She lifted up the bottom of her own shirt and used it to cover the baby as she rocked her arms back and forth.

"Shhh," she said. "Shhh now. It's going to be just fine, Honey Bear. Mama's here."

"Holly," I warned, "that's not a good idea."

"You'll see," she cooed to the baby, or maybe to me. "It's all gonna be fine."

"Holly…"

"You have to run an errand for me, Jesse. Right now. Baby needs formula and a bottle, right away. You buy those things, right at the all-night pharmacy a block away from my place, and you bring them to me, in the apartment. We'll be waiting."

I sighed loudly. "You're not thinking clearly."

"Do this for me, Jesse. Please." Not bothering to hear my answer, she walked away, stepping over the dead teen mother and holding the baby in her arms like she'd been waiting her whole life for that moment.

This, I told myself, was really, really not a good idea.

But I still went out and bought a carton of formula and a package of bottles, plus a box of diapers. And a chocolate bar, because hey, good deed.

Back at the apartment, I boiled the bottle under Holly's watchful eye as she held the baby. She'd wrapped the newborn in a hand towel and was rocking the baby back and forth. Pounce attacked my legs playfully, but I barely scratched behind his ears before Holly scolded me.

"Can't touch Pounce and then the bottle. Go wash your hands. With soap!"

Rolling my eyes, I did as she asked. Then, following her instructions, I mixed a serving of formula and handed the loaded bottle to Holly. She coaxed the nipple into the baby's mouth. The little thing drank everything, belched once, then fell asleep in Holly's arms.

"Don't wake Honey Bear," she warned me in a ferocious whisper.

I mimed zipping my lips shut.

In her bedroom, Holly diapered the newborn—boy, as it turned out—rewrapped him in the towel, then gently set him inside an open dresser drawer. She put the stack of diapers on top of the bureau, along with more towels. The baby didn't stir; he was out cold. Being alive for a night was tiring work.

Pounce sniffed the empty diaper box, which Holly had left on the floor, then twitched his ears as he looked up at the drawer. He made as if to jump up, but Holly nudged him away with her foot.

We tiptoed out of the bedroom, but left the door ajar so that Holly could hear if the baby cried. She called to Pounce, who bounded out of the bedroom and immediately jumped inside the empty formula carton on the kitchen table.

Her voice pitched low, Holly said, "My Honey Bear's sleeping so soundly!" She beamed proudly. "I'm going to name him Jack, after my father."

"Holly," I said, "you've got to stop a minute and think this through."

"Oh, I am! There's so much to do," she whispered excitedly. "We need onesies and socks and mittens and a cap, and a baby tub and soap and that stuff to stop diaper rash, and more bottles, tons more diapers, and a stroller and a real crib, and..."

"Holly." I put my hand on her shoulder. "You can't be a mother."

She stiffened. "Of course I can. I'll be a great mother."

"You're a vampire."

"So what?" She lifted her chin stubbornly. "I can still do everything a human mother can do. Better! I won't be distracted or get exhausted. I'll give him everything he needs."

"You're dead during the day. How're you going to take care of him when the sun's up?"

"He'll sleep during the day, like me," she insisted. "I'll raise him at night. It'll be fine," she said loudly, a hint of panic in her voice.

"Babies don't care what time of day it is," I said. "What happens when he wakes up crying at noon because he's hungry?"

"Well... he'll just have to wait until dark. He can wait! It won't kill him to wait!"

"And what if he gets sick during the day? What if he spikes a fever and needs medicine? What if he needs a doctor?"

She screamed, "Stop confusing me!"

In the bedroom, the baby began to wail.

"Look what you did!" she shouted. "You woke my Honey Bear!" She stormed into the bedroom and slammed the door.

I looked at Pounce, who'd poked his head out of the formula carton. "Do vampires have crazy hormones? Because she's certifiable."

Pounce twitched his whiskers, then disappeared inside the carton. Smart kitten.

I should have left. I should have just walked out the door and never thought about Holly and her Honey Bear again. I'd walked away from much greater things, with far worse consequences.

Instead, I sat on the sofa and waited. I still don't know why. Stupid human feelings should come with an owner's manual.

Eventually, Holly snuck out of the bedroom. She looked at me, chagrined, then went into the kitchen. A minute later, she walked into the living room, sipping from a blood bag and eying me.

"He's sleeping again," she said.

"Okay."

A pause, and then she said, "You really upset me."

"Wasn't my intent."

She sighed. "Look, I know it's gonna be challenging. But parenting always is. This is something I gotta do, Jesse. I need to be a mother. Ever since..." Her voice trailed off, and she rubbed her stomach. "Since you know, I've felt empty. And the kitten is wonderful, but I'm no momma cat. I need a baby, Jesse. I need my Honey Bear."

"You have to think about the daylight hours," I said.

"I know. I know. But...for this first day, would you stay? Please?"

"Hey, now..."

"Please, Jesse? It's almost dawn. I can feel myself slowing down. Please, just for today, be here for Baby Jack? And when I'm up tomorrow night, I'll figure out a plan. Please?"

Idiot that I was, I agreed.

Holly squeezed me half to death, then made cooing sounds at Pounce until dawn came. Dead again, she fell to the living room floor.

The kitten bounded out of the carton, walked over Holly's body, and settled on her chest. He let out a tiny kitten yawn, then fell asleep. I was on my own.

Just call me Jezebel the babysitter.

I checked on the baby, who was still breathing. Mission accomplished, I climbed into Holly's bed. Seemed a shame to waste the mattress, since she wasn't using it tonight.

"Wake me if you need anything," I told the baby. Then I rolled over and fell asleep.

~~*~*

The moment I opened my eyes, I knew something was wrong. I felt too rested. Too peaceful. The last time I'd felt like that had been after a particularly vigorous session with a battery-powered personal toy.

Frowning, I glanced at the clock on the nightstand. Eight-fifteen in the morning. I'd slept only for a couple of hours, but it felt like it had been longer.

"It was much longer," a voice said from the foot of the bed.

I sat up and glowered at Disco Angel, who looked pristine as ever in her white leisure suit.

"Get out of my brain," I growled. "My thoughts are private." To prove my point, I thought of some extremely colorful suggestions regarding the angel's virginity, a number of pinfeathers, and a halo wedged in a particularly tight spot.

Unfazed, Disco Angel said, "You slept for twenty-six hours."

My eyes bugged out. "I *what*?"

"You were exhausted," she said primly. "You needed your sleep. I let you sleep. You're welcome, by the way."

My brain whirled. A full day? How could I have lost a full day? Why didn't Holly wake me? I demanded, "What're you doing here, angel?"

"My job, Jezebel."

Oh no.

I jumped out of bed and raced over to the bureau. The crib-drawer was still sticking out, but Baby Jack wasn't inside.

"He's in the other room," Disco Angel said.

I dashed into the living room, and skidded to a halt. The big window was wide open, the curtains fluttering in the wind. On the floor by the window, Pounce was curled on top of Baby Jack's body. The dirty-white kitten looked up at me, his eyes big.

"It wasn't the kitten's fault," Disco Angel said from somewhere behind me. "The curious thing wanted to see what his caregiver had placed in the drawer. When he jumped inside to explore, he landed on the baby. The infant died quickly."

I let out a sigh.

"If it makes any difference," said Disco Angel, "the baby would have died from exposure, had the vampire not claimed him. He was not meant long for this world."

"More than twenty-four hours might have been nice," I muttered.

"His soul is in Paradise—"

"A place of joy and bliss, blah blah. Yeah, heard it all before. Yay for the baby. Where's Holly?"

"The vampire went insane when the baby wouldn't wake. She shook him and slapped him and tried to get him to breathe. All that did was further break his body. In a fit, she threw him against the wall, and he landed there on the floor."

Now that I was looking, I could see the smear on the wall where Baby Jack had hit.

"The vampire was convinced she'd killed him," Disco Angel said, "so she flung open the window and climbed out. She perched on the ledge until the sun rose. She waited there for hours, unmoving. And so the vampire died and burned, with her ashes and tattered soul scattered to the winds."

My hands balled into fists as I turned to face the celestial. "You know all of this how?"

"I came for the baby. I stayed for the entertainment." She smiled serenely. "Vampires can be so unpredictable, don't you think? So much fun to watch."

People say that demons are evil, and they're right—that's what's in a demon's nature. But angels are worse. They're cold.

"Goodbye, Jezebel." The angel poofed away just before I could tell her to go bless herself.

Sighing, I walked over to the window and closed it. Ever since I'd seen Holly's aura that night at the café, I'd known she was going to die—truly die, not just some halfhearted death that all vampires go through every morning. And I'd stuck around until her journey's end, just as I'd promised myself. Maybe I'd been looking for absolution for letting that vampire escape weeks ago. Maybe I just liked Holly, the friendly waitress who'd been so impressed by my ability to eat chocolate pie and not gain weight. It didn't matter. I still felt lousy.

I need a baby, Jesse. I need my Honey Bear.

Holly had been filled with a need to love and nurture, to be a mother. But that sort of love is for the living. The closest that vampires can get to it is an undying love, one that turns into an obsession that burns hotter than the morning sun.

Sorry, Holly.

There was a bump against my leg, and I looked down to see Pounce trying to eat my boot.

"Hey, there," I said. "Need a home?"

The kitten nibbled leather.

"Give me a moment," I said to him. "Got to take care of something first."

I gathered Baby Jack's body and went into Holly's bedroom. I set the small corpse onto the bed. Crushed, empty of a soul, he didn't even look human, more like some dollmaker's idea of a baby.

I pulled out my cell phone and called 9-1-1.

When I was done, I scooped up Pounce.

"The authorities will bury Baby Jack properly," I told him. "They're good at covering things up. Let's get out of here."

Pounce nuzzled against my ear, as if he wanted to make sure that I'd have a killer kitten like him in my home.

Of course I would; the former demon in me wouldn't have it any other way.

PART IV:

Urban Fantasy

New York Times Best-selling author CARRIE VAUGHN is best known for her popular *Kitty Norville* urban fantasy series about a werewolf who hosts a radio phone-in show. She is also the author of several standalone young adult and fantasy novels and has dozens of short story credits to her name. In 2011, her story *Amaryllis* (originally published in *Lightspeed* magazine) was nominated for a Hugo award.

Visit her official site for more info:
www.carrievaughn.com

DANCING WITH THE MOUSE KING
Carrie Vaughn

Marie slipped through the alley, creeping along the boundary fence and pausing at trash cans and mounds of refuse. Breath fogging in the chill, she tried to move softly, quietly, stealthily, but it was hard because of the brace on her knee.

The Victorian houses that lined the street had fallen to ruin, their porches crumbling, their windows boarded up, their gardens choked with weeds. Not the best part of town anymore. She hardly noticed. She had a goal, and finally she found the house of Karl Drost.

Marie popped the deadbolt of the servants' door in back with a crowbar. Once inside, she leaned against the wall, taking weight off her bad leg. Moonlight came through the window above the sink and cast a silver glow in the kitchen, gleaming on the white tile floor. The place smelled unused and musty, but she *knew* this was the right house.

Movement flashed across the square of light that fell on the floor from the window. Startled, she flinched, pressed herself against the wall, and covered her mouth with her hand to keep from screaming. The sound of the door closing had shocked a mouse into rushing across the floor.

Then it was gone. Just a mouse. Nothing to be afraid of. She closed her eyes and sighed.

Moving to the hallway, she put a hand on the gun in her coat pocket.

The furniture, curio cabinets filled with trinkets, and pictures on the walls were shadows that Marie examined by imperfect, gray-white night vision. Scratching behind the walls seemed to follow her. The place must have been infested with mice. Gooseflesh covered her arms under her coat.

A light shone through the crack between the floor and closed door of a room halfway down the hall. Inside the room a voice hummed, low and creaky. The song was unclear, distracted, as if the person making the sound was preoccupied. Marie drew the gun from her pocket.

She stood for a minute, wondering if she should wait and surprise him as he came out, or throw open the door and confront him inside the room. She grew dizzy from standing and waiting, and that decided for her—no telling how long the old man would stay in there.

Slowly she turned the doorknob, pushed open the door. The hinges didn't squeak. Of course they didn't, this was Karl Drost's house, the hinges never squeaked.

He sat in the circle of light from an adjustable work lamp. His head, covered with close-trimmed white hair, remained bent over his workbench. He peered through a magnifying lens attached to a headband, positioned in front of his face. With needle-nosed pliers and a wire-like probe, he made adjustments to a mechanism set on the table in front of him. Brass gears the size of quarters nested together. The workbench dominated the center of the room. Piled on it were pliers, jeweler's picks, tiny screwdrivers, gears and wires, pulleys and motors. In addition to building sets for the ballet and opera, Drost made clockworks, toys and dolls that wound up and moved, clapped their hands or turned somersaults. Their parts—faces, fur, glass eyes—lay scattered among the tools.

Covering three walls were shelves filled with cuckoo clocks, wooden dolls, animals, and nutcrackers. Nutcrackers filled entire spaces. He'd made a new one every year for as long as he'd worked for the local Ballet. Some were white-haired, some black-haired, some blond. Some wore British redcoat uniforms, some wore German lederhosen, some Napoleonic velvet and braid. He must have kept every one that had ever been loved by the girls who danced as Clara for the Ballet. They were all dusted and well-preserved, glowing when the rest of the house did not.

She counted back a scant eight years from the last and there it was, her own first nutcracker. A black-haired doll with a tricorn hat and a cavalier coat with tails and lace, a cutlass held tight to its side. Its glass eyes stared, and it bared painted white teeth. She longed to test the handle sticking out the back, to see if it still worked. The muscles of her legs twitched, the memory of a *plié*. Her right leg felt a throb, a longing pain. She stumbled against the wall.

"Who's there?" Drost spoke with the hint of a German accent.

Marie gasped and raised the gun, hardly noticing how much her hand trembled, how shocked and wide her eyes were. She was more startled than Drost, who had the gun pointed at him. His expression didn't change as he set down his tools and raised his hands in surrender. He looked like an insect, the magnifier pointing antenna-like from his forehead.

"What is this?" he said.

"I—I—" It had seemed like such a good idea when she planned this. She'd seen what he could do, she had to make him help her

He could work magic.

She said, "You have to help me."

He shrugged a little, the resigned gesture of an old man who faces what he must. "What can I do, when you point a gun at me?"

She wasn't going to shoot him. She could hardly feel her hand. Her arm was shaking. The gun was heavy. "You have to fix me. I want to dance again."

He opened his mouth, a silent 'ah' of understanding. "Again I ask, what can I do?"

She almost laughed, and the tears started. "You can do anything! The doctors can't fix my knee—can't you make me a new one?"

"You know that sounds quite mad." He gestured at the leg brace. "What was it? Torn ACL? Destroyed cartilage?"

"Yes." Too complicated to describe last month's injury. Time and surgery might ease the pain, but she would never dance again.

"You know that is what it is to be a dancer. You accept the possibility that such an injury will end your story."

"But it happened before my story even started!" A month with the New York City Ballet. That was all she'd had before her knee shattered and the door closed.

"Put the gun down, Marie."

"You remember me?"

"You carried those three nutcrackers, the middle of the bottom shelf there. The Cavalier. The Cossack. The Prussian. I remember all the Claras."

Her hand dropped with the weight of the gun. She slumped against the wall, listing awkwardly on her braced leg.

"There, my dear. Don't cry." He removed his magnifier, stood and came to her, taking the gun as he drew her arm over his shoulder to help her stand. His body was surprisingly solid; he'd looked so frail, hunched over his work.

He would call the police. She ought to be locked up.

"Come to the sofa and lie down. You've had a busy day. Sleep tonight. We'll talk in the morning, yes?"

Limping, pitiful, she let the old man guide her to the parlor.

The living room smelled like a forest. A Christmas tree stood in front of the window. The seven foot spruce dripped with gold tinsel. Garlands of red and green beads roped it, and antique wood and glass ornaments weighed down the branches. It even had real candles set in holders on the outermost branches. How the tree must sparkle and glitter when they were all lit.

A grandfather clock, silent, stood against the opposite wall. The stage was set, she thought.

She focused on the pieces, set in their places—the tree, the clock, the nutcracker—so that she hardly noticed Drost directing her to lie on the sofa, unfolding a blanket, murmuring vacantly as he urged her to sleep.

As soon as she slept, he'd probably call the police. But she didn't care, because it was like it used to be—the tree, the clock, the nutcracker—and she was Clara, and when she woke the house would be filled with magic.

~~*~*

217

The overture began, light strains of violins. Backstage she practiced: point the toes, *plié, arabesque*. Then the dream: lights, music, laughter, once-a-year gowns of velvet and satin. Everyone smiled because the audience was watching. Marie didn't care so much about the audience; applause was nice, but it was background noise. She preferred to lose herself in the role. The Christmas tree grew, the toys came to life, and she was at the center of it all.

She dreamed of the dance, a stage awash in soft yellow light, like candlelight. She moved easily, floating. A few more steps would bring her to her Prince, who waited for her, ready to catch and hold her.

Her legs collapsed. She crashed to the floor and heard laughter. High pitched voices squeaking in harmony interrupted the music. Red eyes, whiskers, chisel-like rodent teeth appeared. The creatures scratched and chittered—

She woke lying on a sofa, tangled in a blanket, trapped. Something scratched the wall behind her; movement caught her gaze. She blinked, squinted, thinking it was only that she was tired and the sunlight through the window, shining through the Christmas tree, made weird shadows.

A quivering, furry body the size of an apricot zipped across the floor like it was on wheels, racing from under the sofa to the little space under the grandfather clock, so small, hardly anything could fit there.

Marie screamed reflexively. Only a mouse, she knew it was only a mouse. But that didn't stop her heart from racing.

"Ah, just like a woman to scream at a mouse." Drost came in, carrying a toolbox and the set of gears he'd been working on the previous night. "I should put out more traps. It is a constant battle, to keep the mice at bay in this old house." He gave her an appraising look.

Marie rubbed her forehead to keep her hands from shaking. A battle against the mice. Clara fought the mice, after the Christmas tree grew and the nutcracker came to life.

Drost shifted a footstool in front of the clock and opened the clock face to expose the innards. He started working, poking with tools and fitting the extracted gears back in place.

Marie pulled the blanket to her chest. "Are you going to call the police about me?"

"No. You're hurt, and I understand a little about desperation." He spoke in a half-distracted manner. "I don't know if I can help you. I am very busy, clearing out the mice for one, fixing this clock for another–I think I may finally finish soon. Then, maybe I can help you. If I have time." He gestured wryly at the clock.

Something rustled under the sofa, a snapping sound under a floorboard, like teeth biting through wood. Tapping noises traveled down the parlor wall. Marie held the blanket tightly, hugging herself, and drew away from the edge of the sofa. Scratching, biting—the sound of tiny claws scraping throughout the house. There must have been dozens of them. Hundreds. Nauseated, Marie put her hand on her stomach.

Drost hissed angrily and slapped at his leg. The gesture sent a mouse flying; it leapt from the stool and scampered away, a fluff of panicked gray disappearing into a corner.

The old man scowled after it. "You see, they try to keep me from fixing the clock. Vermin."

She sympathized, she did—she couldn't see a mouse without screaming. "Mr. Drost—I don't want to interrupt, but can you help me? If you can't, I'll go…"

He frowned at her, as if she were a clockwork broken into pieces on his workbench. He tapped his chin a moment, nodded. Hope rose up in her.

"Perhaps I can help you," he said. "But will you do something for me, first?"

"Anything."

"Can you trap the mice? If you are setting traps, I can fix the clock, then I can fix your leg, and all will be well. What do you think? Can you do that, with your leg hurt?"

It sounded easy. Just set traps. Clean them when they were dead. She wouldn't even scream.

"Yes. I'm just a little slow," she said.

He paused so long, and his face was such a mass of uncertain lines, Marie felt sure that *now* he was going to call the police. But finally he said, "Fine. Good. On the floor of the pantry is a bag of traps. I use peanut butter for bait. Also, there is a bottle of poison under the sink. For the ones that are too smart for the traps."

She set about climbing off the sofa, shifting her bad leg and propping herself on the good one. Eager, now that she had a quest. This was a role she could play.

Limping to the kitchen, she found the pantry and pulled the string of the overhead light. Movement streaked in all directions, now-familiar lumps of fur racing from the light into shadow.

She screamed, a sharp yelp, and pressed her hand to her chest and her suddenly pounding heart. Stupid, stupid. Horrible little things.

She started in the pantry, setting traps on shelves alongside packages of spaghetti with jagged chew marks in the corners, boxes of pudding mix leaking their contents through bitten-out holes. She found evidence of the mice everywhere, in chewed packages and in trails of little black droppings. The place ought to be fumigated.

The same evidence lay all over the house. Along cupboards, in corners, on the shelves in the library. Drost spent so much time on his clock and at his workbench that he'd let them overrun the place. The air smelled of mouse, filled with their exhalations.

She learned more about Drost along the way. Along with the wood carvings and clockworks, he had hundreds of books on topics ranging from mechanics and alchemy to Victorian pseudo-science and outright fairy stories. Leyden jars and perpetual motion, complicated locks to unreal doorways, the animation of clockworks and the granting of souls to dolls. Half the titles were in German; she didn't have a clue what those said.

Back in the kitchen a couple of the traps in the pantry had already killed mice. A tiny sense of victory–and dread, because now she had to clean up the bodies. She scooped them into a paper grocery bag and dumped them in a trash bin in the alley, then washed her hands for a full five minutes.

She made her ponderous way up the stairs, setting traps and bait in every corner. Most of the rooms upstairs were used for storage. Boxes and trunks stacked on each other, gathering dust. Pieces of sets and sections of painted flats showed Italian palazzos, island seascapes, and distant mountains. Drapes and chandeliers, faded and disused, lay piled on old armchairs. Framed snapshots faded to brown and gray hung on the walls– cast and crew photos from forgotten productions staged in other countries. Groups of laughing dancers crowded on stage, flanked by men in suits who were choreographers or patrons, or men and women in overalls and aprons who were carpenters and costumers. Marie recognized costumes and sets from *Coppélia, Sleeping Beauty*, all the classics.

She never would have looked under the drop cloth, but a mouse darted under it, and she had to set a trap there. Under the cloth, sitting on an old steamer trunk, was a scrapbook. The photos were all black and white. One was a formal squadron photo of a hundred uniformed young men; they couldn't have been more than eighteen or so. Snapshots of the same boys with their arms draped over each other's shoulders, the rifles in their hands incongruous with their youthful smiles. Khaki uniforms. Dark armbands. Swastikas. One person appeared in all the photos: a lanky, square-faced young man with close-cropped blond hair. He looked far too young to be a soldier. In the theater photos, he looked older, gruffer, and he wore coveralls and a tool belt. Marie recognized the older version. Karl Drost.

She closed the scrapbook, put it back exactly the way she'd found it, and tried not to think any more about it.

Back in the parlor, Drost was sitting on the floor, tools and gears scattered around him. He was eating a sandwich and gestured for her to join him.

"Here, eat. You've been working hard."

She settled to the floor, sticking her hurt leg out, and took a sandwich. The bread smelled of mouse, and she suddenly wasn't hungry.

She studied the grandfather clock. An immense antique, it stood at seven feet of polished mahogany, had a brass pendulum and fixtures, an etched crystal cabinet front, and a picture above the clock face. The picture, circular and meant to rotate, was stuck halfway between a scene of a gold leaf sun on a turquoise background and one of an opal moon on a lapis night. The key was slotted into its place under the clock face. Looking at the parts without homes, she doubted it would ever work again.

"Why do you have to fix the clock?" she asked.

"You will see, when it's fixed."

"Does it do something special?"

His gaze narrowed and he turned a sly smile. "You will be happy to know, I have time to work on your leg."

~~*~*

Clara's Uncle Drosselmeyer gave her the Nutcracker as a Christmas gift. That night when the clock chimed midnight, the toys came to life and the mice invaded the parlor. The tin soldiers did battle with the vicious mice and their seven-headed king. The Nutcracker, with its stiff gait and grotesquely painted head, commanded the soldiers, who were sorely outnumbered. Clara rescued the Nutcracker by killing the Mouse King with her shoe. Then the Nutcracker became a handsome prince who whisked her away to a fairy tale kingdom where sugared dreams danced in her honor.

The scratching of claws and clacking of teeth changed, becoming a clear, deep voice.

"Why do you wage war on us?"

A pair of red eyes flashed, then another, and another. Four sets of whiskers appeared, then six sets of ears, seven sharp-toothed mouths, but the creature that stalked toward her had only two legs and two front paws. It walked upright on steel-tipped claws.

"I can make you dance again," it said. It crept toward her; she flinched back. "Dance with me, Marie."

She could feel the movement in her muscles, but her limbs could not obey.

The hand that took hold of hers was thin and bony. Claws tipped the fingers.

"Dance with me," he said, and raised her hand in preparation for a waltz.

Gasping, she pulled away from the Mouse King and brushed off the shivers running across her skin.

~~*~*

Marie sat in the workshop, her leg stretched out on a second chair while Drost fitted pieces around her knee. The orthopedic brace was gone, and he worked over her sweatpants, securing metal bands above and below the knee, tightening them with little screws. Jointed metal struts connected them.

To distract herself, she played with one of the clockworks lying on the table, a Columbine dancer. The key in her back turned and her white chiffon dress fluttered while she kicked, turned, bowed, kicked, turned, bowed, over and over until the key slowed and she stopped, bent over.

Drost watched her staring at the clockwork dancer. He said, "It's all simple pulleys and springs, cords attached to clever joints. But cut one of those cords, those tendons, and it will never move again. Not so very different than you or I, yes? All you need are a couple of cords to replace the ones that broke, some extra support to give you strength."

He fit cords to the bands, crisscrossed over her knee. He attached gears for the cords to loop through, which would take up the slack when she bent and straightened her leg. They made clicking sounds when he turned them.

"How does that feel?" he asked.

"It feels the same as the brace."

"It should. We'll stop for now, so you can get used to this before we go on. I must get back to my clock." He gathered his tools as he stood. "Today is Christmas you know. I want to finish by midnight, so we can hear the chimes, yes?"

Christmas. She hadn't known.

Something snapped and squeaked at the same time. One of the mousetraps in the next room.

"I should check the traps," she said, standing gingerly.

Drost was already in the hallway, on his way to the parlor. "Yes. Vigilance. Never give them a moment's rest. The only way to win against mice is to wage war on them."

Why do you wage war on us? She hesitated, remembering dancing among tin soldiers while the seven-headed King advanced, slashing with his sword. Drost had designed the headpiece that the dancer portraying the King wore, the clockworks and effects that made the heads gnash their teeth and made their eyes glow red. She'd been so frightened of it, but in a giddy way, because it was only make-believe after all.

"You must be tired of it," she said. "The war, I mean."

"Yes. War is tiring."

She balanced on her left leg because she was so uncertain of the right. "You were a soldier. I saw some of the pictures."

He raised a brow, his frown deepening. "Not really. I was young. It was late in the war, and the army was taking children by that time. They told us we were making a better world. We believed them." He shrugged and rearranged the tools in the toolbox. "I am still hoping for a better world."

"But not like that," said Marie, a little afraid, as if the dictator himself had suddenly appeared before her.

"No. Not like that," said Drost. "Go on, check the traps."

She hobbled out of the room.

Step by step, she traveled from room to room. She'd never get used to the mice. She still let out a yelp when she saw one of them scurry across her path or dart behind a piece of furniture. Scooping the traps with their crushed bodies into garbage sacks still made her stomach turn.

In only a day, most of the traps had caught mice. But just as many remained. They scrabbled behind the walls and chewed as loud as ever. Even cans in the pantry had teeth marks, tiny rodents chewing through everything.

Drost made bowls of soup for Christmas dinner. Marie ate but didn't taste it.

"You've done well with the mice," Drost told her.

She wasn't pleased with the praise. The job of setting traps was menial and gross, nothing graceful about it. She'd come here to reclaim her grace.

She rested on the sofa, and he worked on the new mechanism on her leg, adding a clockwork array of gears and levers. His hands were deft and careful. She hardly felt his touch. She lay back and gazed at the plastered ceiling with its carved molding, glowing yellow in lamplight. Light and shadows. She heard scratching under the floorboards, a sound that tugged chills down her spine.

~~*~*

"I can make you dance again."

Dressed in a splendid cavalier costume of red velvet and gold trim, a shining cutlass hanging on his belt, the Mouse King loomed. All seven heads nodded in time to music, a pavane, a slow, exacting court dance.

Marie was barefoot. She wore not the sweet, white chiffon ballet gown that Clara would have worn, but tattered rags, rotting tulle of a color that had faded to dirt. He didn't seem to notice she was so ugly, so clumsy.

They danced side by side, not touching. Even with the brace and the limp, she could dance the pavane, moving slowly, stepping carefully. The Mouse King shortened his steps to allow for her injury.

She could almost enjoy it, if she didn't look at the thing beside her.

223

She found a ballet slipper in her hand. Stepping back, she hurled it at the Mouse King, because that was what she'd always done, what Clara always did, and she was at war. He knocked it aside with a wave of his arm.

The center head spoke. "What now, Marie? Will you poison me or crush my neck?"

"Crush our neck! Crush our neck!" the other six heads shouted and laughed.

He made a courtly bow, and offered his clawed hand again.

"Dance with me, Marie."

She could dance with him, like she might have danced with the Nutcracker Prince. She extended her hand toward his claw.

Her foot itched. Reaching to scratch it, her hand met a tiny, writhing lump of hair and claw. Then her other leg felt a sting. Mice were crawling up her legs, jumping off walls to grasp at her rags. She screamed in full-lunged horror and swatted all over her body to get rid of them. They jumped away, and their scratching and squeaking seemed like laughter.

They scampered and danced, footless things gliding across walls and floors, hundreds of them making a pattern as they leapfrogged each other and spun circles around her.

She found another shoe in her hand and threw it, then another, and another. The shoes became huge, smashing dozens of mice as they fell. All her anger at the injury, the unfairness of it all, flowed through her arm and added strength to each launch of a shoe. Again and again, she'd kill them all, she'd wage war if that was what she had to do.

The Mouse King stood watching, waiting for a toddler's tantrum to end. This aggravated her all the more. As she raised her arm to throw another shoe at him, one that would knock off all seven of his heads, he pointed with a bony finger.

"Look," he said.

Broken bodies of mice lay around them. A carpeting of mouse bodies, of fur in every color: gray, white, mottled, dusky, brown. All bleeding and twisted. Slaughter. She didn't have a scratch on her.

This wasn't war. It was extermination.

So what did that make her?

~~*~*

She started awake from more strange dreams, wracked with a sudden chill. The house had gotten cold, and she didn't have a blanket.

The lamps were off, but the room still glowed with rich light—the candles on the Christmas tree. It made a lovely scene, like something from a Victorian postcard. There was more: she heard it as a tickle in her mind, a sound just at the edge of consciousness, steady as a heartbeat.

Tick tick tick tick...

The brass pendulum of the grandfather clock swung back and forth. Drost had fixed it. His tools were cleared away. The hands read five to midnight.

Drost stood in the doorway. She didn't know how long he'd been watching her.

"You should get up. Try your leg. They'll be here soon, you know."

"Who?"

"The mice, of course. You didn't kill them all. So they will come."

The old man was as crazy as she was, which made it all right, she supposed.

Drost had also finished the brace on her leg. The device was almost pretty, an ornate contraption of brass and steel, polished and shining in the candlelight. Her gaze became lost when she tried to sort out the maze of gears, pulleys, wires, and cords that laced together.

Sitting up, she was afraid to put any weight on the leg, afraid to bend the knee in a way she knew would be painful. She stood, hopped a little, testing the weight. No pain. The gears spun and cords raced on pulleys. She walked a few steps—no limp. She held her breath and tried the positions, *plié* in third, stand and *arabesque*—

She stumbled, not because the leg failed but because of shock. She held her hand over her mouth and closed tearful eyes.

"Ah, it works," Drost said proudly.

"It's noisy." Every movement she made was accompanied by clicking and whirring, the mechanical litany of a wind-up toy clacking through its paces. Not graceful.

"What did you expect? It is machine, not flesh. Perhaps a little oil would help. But there isn't time for that now."

The clock began to chime the hour.

One, two, three... Brass tones shook the house's bones.

The clock. The tree. The strange old man who made carvings and clockworks. And Marie was the clockwork dancer that Drosselmeyer made.

All she was missing now was her Nutcracker Prince. Maybe Drost could bring the Cavalier to life. She suddenly felt like she needed rescuing.

Four, five, six...

"What's going to happen?"

"A door will open," he said. "The magic will burst upon the stage. You know that."

The mice will come.

"I don't know anything." She backed away from him, aware with each step that her leg was strong and she moved without a limp. But the gears chittered like squeaking mice.

"Oh, come now. When you asked me to make you dance again, what did you really want?"

"To dance—"

"No. The dancing is only a means to an end. I know you, fifty years in the ballet I've seen your kind again and again. You truly want to believe. You don't want to dance—what you want is to find that magic again. I know, because I want it too. To step through a door to another world."

Seven, eight, nine...

The light became blinding. She had to close her eyes. She felt the rumble of the chiming clock in her bones, as if the sound of thunder filled the sky. The light shone like a sun.

Dizziness rattled her. She gasped for breath and tried to speak. At least her legs were steady now. "The mice will come... you'll kill them—"

"*You* will kill them. I'm lucky you are here. You are better at fighting them than I am."

"But you were a soldier—"

"I did not fight in the war. No, I served as a guard. At Birkenau."

Marie shook her head. It wasn't real... all his beautiful work in the theater come to this... The music blurred to white noise, the light burned. Shaking her head, she covered her ears.

Ten, eleven, twelve.

The sound faded, the chimes dissipating. Marie's eyes grew accustomed to the glare and she could see again.

The Christmas tree had grown, just like in the story. Its branches were as big around as tree trunks; it was a redwood forest all by itself. The ornaments were castles nestled among the boughs, airships of gold wire traveling above her. Marie craned her neck, trying to see the crystal star at the top. The candles glittered like suns. The walls, the sofa, and the clock were mountains.

It wasn't that the Christmas tree grew. Clara *shrank*. Why hadn't Marie ever thought of that before?

Her heartbeat settled. She took a few steps, turning in a circle to study the strange place she found herself. Her legs were strong; she could spin and dance, even if she made noise like a clockwork, or a skittering mouse. Such a feeling of peace came over her, of rightness.

Then the mice came.

Sharp claws scrabbled on the rug. Their chittering replaced the fading sound of the clock's bell.

They were as large as Marie, their eyes at the same level as hers. Thousands of them lined the edges of the room and drifted toward her. Only her size had kept them at bay before. Now, they were stronger, larger, quicker, vicious with their teeth and claws.

They looked angry. They wanted revenge for all their slain brethren.

She couldn't blame them. She closed her hands into fists, wishing for a weapon, knowing how little good it would do. A dozen of them would pile on top of her before she could hurt one of them. And she would deserve it. She backed away slowly, hoping to find shelter.

She didn't scream.

Drost was at the base of the Christmas tree, picking at something on the trunk. Lines appeared, a rectangle of light, like the cracks around a door.

A doorway. For the Ballet, Drost had made a trapdoor in the stage through which the nutcracker doll was taken away and the dancer in the life-size Nutcracker mask and costume took its place. Fog from the smoke machine and light poured through that door. It made a gateway to another world. Or so Marie had wanted to believe, when she danced as Clara.

"Drost!" She started to run toward him, when her knee froze. She tripped and fell, unable to move her leg. "My leg—"

He held up a key, a clockwork winding key. "I timed that well."

Marie found the little square in her brace where the key would fit and wind the mechanism, tightening the gears and pulleys. Unwound, the brace was useless.

"If you want this, you must kill them all. They guard the doorway, you see."

"I won't fight your war." She ripped off the brace. Gears popped and cords sprang away. As the support of the brace fell away, pain returned.

"It will still take them time to finish you, and I will escape."

She expected the mice to rush her, dozens of them fighting each other for the chance to tear her flesh. But they didn't attack. While they glared with eyes of hate and glee, they kept a circle around her, waiting.

For the Mouse King.

Drost had just opened the door in the trunk of the Christmas tree when the Mouse King sprang at him, leaping from the hillside of the tree skirt, slashing with his cutlass, letting loose a seven-layered snarl as all the heads hissed at him. Drost fell, ducking the weapon. His head was thrown back, his eyes glazed with terror.

Dressed in a red cavalier cloak, the Mouse King loomed as he had in Clara's dream, head upon head leering down, eyes and teeth flashing.

Drost didn't have a chance. Or, Marie had thought Drost didn't have a chance. But the old man scrambled away from the Mouse King's reach. The Mouse King stabbed the sword down, and again Drost dodged.

Then Drost drew a handgun from the pocket of his trousers. The gun Marie had brought.

She only thought of stopping Drost. She grabbed the tangle of brass and steel that had been the brace around her leg. Ignoring the popping in her knee, tortured ligaments and bone scraping on bone, she stood and ran at the old man.

She swung her makeshift weapon at his face. He only saw her at the last moment. His eyes went wide, then she struck, slamming his head back. The gun fired, a heart-stopping crack. He fell. She dropped to her knees, crying in pain.

Drost writhed for a moment. Blood covered his neck, pooling on the floor. A sharp edge of steel had cut his throat.

Everyone had a weak spot. That was how Clara killed the Mouse King with nothing more than a slipper.

The Mouse King was kneeling. Marie held her breath, thinking he was hurt—it would have been for nothing if he'd been shot after all. But he straightened. His chest moved, taking deep breaths. He'd been worried too, it seemed. All the heads watched her, expressions unchanging, mouths still and eyes dark.

The Mouse King began removing his heads.

They were like masks, and one by one he set them aside. He came to the last, which fit him like a helmet, and took it off.

Before her crouched a young man. His face was slack with surprise, his dark gaze locked on her. He was a little too gruff to be handsome, his black hair was coming loose from a haphazard tie, his face was shadowed with a day's growth of beard. Slowly, a smile curled his lips.

"You wanted your Nutcracker Prince. Will you take a King instead?"

Around them, a thousand mice bowed their heads and made four-footed obeisance.

"Are—are you hurt?" she said.

"No," he said, shaking his head wonderingly. "I have you to thank for that. And you—are you hurt?"

She started crying, her breath catching in her throat. All she could do was nod.

He came to her slowly, as if he was afraid he might startle her. He knelt by her and put a hand—a claw, his hands were still the knobby paws of a mouse—on her knee.

"I have a little magic of my own," he murmured. "Enough to heal."

A warmth like sun filled her leg; the pain went away. His touch was gentle, and his face was kind.

Music swelling, the full orchestra, cymbals crashing as the set fell away and the Prince carried her to another world—

The Mouse King rose and stepped away. Then, like in a dream, he reached for her.

"Will you dance with me, Marie?"

She stood on perfect legs. She could run, leap, and fly into his arms if she wanted to. She gladly took the clawed hand that he offered. He led her to the gold-lined doorway set into the trunk of the Christmas tree, and together they traveled to the Kingdom of the Mice.

NNEDI OKORAFOR is an award-winning author and a professor at the University at Buffalo, SUNY. She is the author of several books for both young people and adults. Her novel, *Who Fears Death*, won the World Fantasy Award for Best Novel in 2011. Its prequel titled *The Book of Phoenix* is scheduled for release in 2015 from DAW. She recently signed a three-book deal with Hodder & Stoughton, which kicked off with *Lagoon* in April 2014. You can find out more at Nnedi.com

SHOWLOGO
Nnedi Okorafor

He fell from the clear warm Chicagoland skies at approximately 2:42pm. He landed with a muted thud on the sidewalk in the village of Glenview. Right in front of the Tunde's house. There were three witnesses. The first and closest was a college student who was home for the summer named Dolapo Tunde. She'd been pushing an old lawnmower across the lawn as she listened to Dbanj on her iPhone. The second was Mr. David Goldstein who was across the street scrubbing the hood of his sleek black Chevy Challenger and thinking about his next business trip to Japan. The third was Buster the Black Cat who'd been eyeing a feisty red squirrel on the other side of the Tunde's yard.

The sight of the man falling from the sky and landing on that sidewalk would change all three of their lives forever. Nonetheless, this story isn't about Dolapo, Mr. Goldstein or even Buster the Cat. This story is about the black man who lay in the middle of the sidewalk in blue jeans, gym shoes, and a thin coat with blood pouring from his face…

~~*~*

"I go show you my logo," Showlogo growled, pointing his thick tough-skinned finger in Yemi's face. All the men sitting around the ludo board game leaned away from Yemi.

"*Kai!*" one man shrieked, holding his hands up. "*Kai!* Na here we go!"

"Why we no fe relax, make we play?" another moaned.

But Yemi squeezed his eyes with defiance. Yemi had always been stubborn. He'd also always been a little stupid, which was why he did so poorly in school. When professors hinted to him that it was time to hand them a bribe for good grades, Yemi's nostrils flared, he bit his lower lip, frowned and did no such thing. And so Yemi remained at the bottom of his university class. He scraped by because he still, at least, paid his tuition on time. Today, he exhibited that counter-productive stubbornness by provoking Showlogo, hearing Showlogo speak his infamous warning of "I show you my logo", and not backing down. Yemi should have run. Instead, he stood there and said, "You cheat! You no fe get my money, o! I no give you!"

Showlogo flicked the soft smooth scar tissue where his left ear had been twelve years ago. He stood up tall to remind Yemi of his 6'4 muscular frame as he looked down at Yemi's 5'11 lanky frame. Then without a word, Showlogo turned and walked away. He was wearing spotless white pants and a shirt. How he'd kept that shirt so clean as he squatted with the other men in front of the ludo board game while the wind blew the dry crimson dirt around them, no one knew. No one

231

questioned this because he was Showlogo and for Showlogo, the rules were always different. As he strode down the side of the dusty road, Showlogo cut quite a figure. He was very dark skinned and this made the immaculate white of his clothing nearly glow. He looked like some sort of angel. But Showlogo was no angel.

He walked past two shabby houses and an abandoned building, arriving at his small flat in his "face me, I slap you" apartment complex. He wordlessly walked down the dark hallway past four doors and entered his home. It was custom for none of the flats in the building to have keys, too expensive. Showlogo had always liked being able to just open his door. Plus, no one was dumb enough to rob him, so what need did he have for locks and keys or hiding his most valued things? He slipped his shoes off and walked straight to his neatly made bed. Then he removed his white shirt, his white pants, his white boxers, too. He folded and put them on his pillow in an orderly stack. He removed the diamond stud from his right ear. Then he turned and walked out. People peeked from behind doors but not one person spoke to Showlogo or each other. Not a whisper. Unlike Yemi, his neighbors were smart.

Showlogo's meaty chest and arms were gnarled with scars, some from fighting and some from threatening to fight. Often, he'd take a small pocket knife he liked to carry, stab his bicep and growl, "Come on!" when anyone was dumb enough to challenge him. Today, however, he didn't have his pocket knife. *No matter*, Showlogo thought as he strode down the street naked. *I go kill am.*

As he walked back to the game, people watched from food stands, cars honked at him, passersby laughed and softly commented to each other.

"Who no go know, no go know. Showlogo know some logo, o."

"I hope say you body ready for him."

"Hope na man today. Not woman."

Everyone knew that if said "I go show you my logo" to a woman, it meant… something else. Either way, if you were smart, you knew to run. When Showlogo arrived back at the game he found that Yemi had finally run for his life. Showlogo stood there, vibrating his chest, every pore in his body open, inhaling the hot Nigerian air.

"Why dey run?" Showlogo asked, his eyes focusing on Ikenna who had a big grin on his face. Showlogo sucked his teeth in disgust. "Dem no get liver for trouble."

"Please, o. Forget Yemi, Showlogo," Ikenna said, laughing nervously. "Make you calm down. He ran like rabbit. Here, take." He held a stack of naira in front of Showlogo's twitching chest. Showlogo scowled at it, flaring his nostrils and breathing heavily through them. Slowly, he took the stack of naira and counted, nudging each purple and pink bill up with a thumb. The hot breeze ruffled the short tightly twisted dreadlocks on his head. He grunted. It was the proper amount. If Yemi had given too little or too much, Showlogo would have gone, found the disrespectful *mumu* and beaten him bloody. Instead, Showlogo went home and put some clothes on, jeans and a yellow polo shirt, this time. Today, his fists would not tenderize flesh.

~~*~*

Showlogo owned a farm and he farmed it himself. It was good work. He'd inherited it from his adoptive father Olusegun Bogunjoko. Twelve years ago, when his best friend Ibrahim was killed during riots between Ibrahim's clan and a neighboring clan, Ibrahim's father, who had no other children, adopted Showlogo as his son. Showlogo had been sixteen years old. Bogunjoko had always loved Showlogo. The fact that Showlogo was so strong in mind and body and refused to join any side, be it a confraternity or a clan's core membership, set his mind at ease, as well.

Showlogo's parents had died when he was very young and he already deferred to Bogunjoko as a father, so the adoption made perfect sense. Showlogo took over the coco farm and ran it with the strong attentive hand of a farmer from the old colonial times, of a farmer before oil had been discovered in Nigeria and overshadowed all other produce, before Nigeria was even "Nigeria". Showlogo was a true son of the soil and the death of his best friend and love of Bogunjoko brought this out in him.

Showlogo worked hard on his farm, though it made little money. However, when he was relaxing and not playing ludo with his friends, he was smoking what the famous Afrobeat singer Fela Kuti liked to call "giant mold", a very large joint that was thick at the end and thin at the tip. When Showlogo rolled one of his "giant mold" his friends would call him "Little Fela" and he'd smile and flex his big muscles.

Few people in Ajegunle District had not heard of the Great and Powerful Showlogo, the Man Who Could Not Die, The Man Who Could Fight Ten Men While Drunk and Walk Away Not Bleeding, The Man Who Was Not Right In The Head, The Man Who'd Chosen To Cut Off His Ear Rather Than Join a Confraternity.

He'd once jumped from a moving fruit truck just to show that he could. "I dey testing my power," he said as he climbed onto the truck, clamoring over its haul of oranges. "No pain, no gain. Na no know." He asked the driver (who'd been taking a Guinness Beer drinking break before driving his haul to Abuja) to speed down the road. When the truck was moving forty-five miles per hour, Showlogo jumped, hit the road and tumbled to the side of it where he lay for several seconds not moving. His friends ran up to him, pressing their hands to their heads and wailing about how terrible Nigeria's roads were for always taking life. But then Showlogo raised his head, sat up, stretched his arms and cracked his knuckles and smiled. "You see now, I no fe die. Even death dey fear me."

He'd thrown himself down hills, jumped from speeding danfos, jumped from the fourth floor of an apartment building, fought five men at the same time and won, been shot three times, lost count of the number of times he'd been stabbed or slashed with a knife, saved a friend from armed robbers by driving by and throwing a water bottle at one of their heads, Showlogo had even looked a powerful witchdoctor in the face and called him "shit." Some said that Showlogo was protected by Shango and loved by many spirits whose names could not be spoken. He only laughed when asked if this were true.

And of course, there was not one woman who had not heard of his massive "head office". Some said that he'd once visited a prostitute and she'd given him back his money just to get him to stop having sex with her. According to this piece of local lore, the prostitute "couldn't handle his logo". Nobody messed with Showlogo and didn't regret it. However, two days after he nearly killed Yemi, Showlogo stepped from local celebrity into legend.

~~*~*

In Nigeria, farming no longer made one rich unless you were farming oil. So, to make ends meet, Showlogo took odd jobs. For two months, he'd actually managed to hold a job at the Lagos Airport. He spent the day loading luggage into and off of planes. It was the kind of work he loved-physical labor. Plus, he rarely had to deal with his boss (which was when the trouble usually began for him at other jobs). The hours in the sun made his near black skin blacker and the loading of luggage bulked up his muscles nicely. In the two months he'd been working at the airport, he imagined he was starting to really look like Shango's son.

However, just because he kept out of trouble at work, didn't mean he kept out of trouble elsewhere.

"I pay you next time," Vera said as she got off of Showlogo's okada.

Showlogo only smiled and shook his head as he started the engine. "No payment necessary," he said. He watched her backside jiggling as she entered her flat. Vera wasn't plump, the way he liked his women. However, she was plump in some nicely chosen places. Showlogo chuckled to himself and drove off. It was always worth driving Vera wherever she needed to go. It was also a good way to end a long day at the airport.

He didn't make it a mile before two road police ruined his mood. He stopped at their make-shift roadblock, a long thick dry branch. He was shocked when the police officers demanded he pay them a bribe in order to pass.

"Do you know who I be?" Showlogo snapped, looking the two men over as if they were pieces of rotting meat.

"Abeg, give us money," one of the police officers demanded, brandishing his gun. He waved a hand dismissively. "Then make you dey waka!" He was smaller and fatter than the other, standing about 5'6 and looking like he had never seen a fight in his life. The taller slimmer one who was closer to 6'3 vibrated his chest muscles through his uniform and flared his nostrils at Showlogo.

Showlogo pointed a finger in the smaller fatter man's face. "You go die today if you no turn and waka away from me now."

The moment the taller one took a step toward him, Showlogo jumped off his okada, used the kickstand to prop it up and stepped into the grass. He glanced at the bush behind him and then at the two policemen who were approaching. There was a red leather satchel that he carried everywhere; this way, he always had what he needed. He'd wrapped the strap on the handlebars of his okada. Now, he unwrapped it, put it over his shoulder and pushed the satchel to rest on his back.

He knew exactly what he was going to do. He'd decided it as a god would decide the fate of two mere men. He slapped the smaller man across the face so hard that a tooth flew out. The trick was to open his big calloused hand wide and arch his palm just so. He grabbed the other man by the balls and squeezed, then he kneed him in the face as the police officer doubled over.

Both men were in hot pain and bleeding, one from his mouth and one from his nose, as Showlogo wordlessly dragged them into the bush. The foliage was not dense and if there were snakes in the high grass, Showlogo didn't care. Any snake dumb enough to bite him would die and he would not.

"Abeg," one of the policemen said as he coughed, his words wet from the blood on his lips. "Let us go. Dis has gone too far. Wetin na dey do?"

"I dey show you my logo," Showlogo muttered. "You asked for my logo and I go show you. Stupid set of people."

He dragged them for several minutes and neither man tried to fight his way to freedom. They had realized who he was; they knew better now. Soon, their bleeding slowed but they were bothered by mosquitoes buzzing around their heads. They stood before the trunk of a tall palm tree. Showlogo held their hands together as he looked into his satchel and brought out a coil of rope.

The policemen never spoke to anyone about how one man was able to tie two gun carrying men to a tree so well that they could not undo the knots. This is understandable because it was so humiliating. Even if it was the madman Showlogo, how could they have NOT tried to take him or at least run away? It is shameful. Nevertheless, this happened. Showlogo tied them to a tree and then returned to his okada and drove off.

The policemen were stuck at that tree for two days. No food, no water, mosquitoes and other biting insects feasting on their blood. They sat in their own urine and feces and they sang songs they'd learned from the powerful and violent university confraternities they both belonged to. And it was this singing that attracted the group of women coming from a nearby stream. Those men could have easily died there, but luck was finally on their side.

Word about the incident spread like wildfire. If Showlogo was not already a local legend, he certainly was the biggest one now.

"Why you dey ask me dis nonsense, again?" he asked days later. "I don move on with my life, o. Na thunder go fire those yao yao police." He took a giant pull off his "giant mold". He was sitting with his cousin Success T at the restaurant they fondly called "the cholera joint", a plate of roasted goat meat and jollof rice in front of him. He exhaled and grabbed his spoon with his left hand and shoveled rice into his mouth. It had been a long day of work at the airport and the food tasted like heaven. "Next time they will stay out of my way," he added, through his mouthful of rice.

"People dey talk about it," Success T said, smiling. He was the only person on earth Showlogo trusted. The two had grown up together and then lived in the same flat for years when they were older. Both even had access to each other's bank accounts. "How you dey tie them? Everyone wants to know."

Showlogo paused as he ate more rice and drank from his bottle of Coca Cola. He belched loudly and pounded a fist against his chest. "I be One Man Mopo. I no need help and no dey fight in group," he said, biting into the piece of goat meat. "You no believe me?"

"I do," Success T said. He leaned forward, the smile dropping from his face. "Showlogo, I no want make you go to jail. Those police be cultist. Their people haven't forgotten, o."

Showlogo chewed his goat meat and smiled. "Jail no be for animal. Na for human person. But don worry. Jail no be for me."

~~*~*

He wasn't stupid. He thought about it. The police always had each other's backs. And they held grudges like old women. And the fact that those two idiots who had the nerve to ask him for bribes were also part of confraternities was not good. So Showlogo decided to lay low for a bit. No partying or playing ludo outside with his friends for a few weeks. Go to work and then go home, that was the plan.

Then, the Igbo shop down the street was robbed. Showlogo held the phone to his ear as he got on his okada that evening. Hearing about the incident first, Success T had called to warn him. "Watch out, o!" Success T said. "Word on the street is that they caught the guys who did it and they said they knew you." Showlogo blinked. Time to disappear. He would stay with Success T for a day or so until he figured out a better place to stay for a while. He put the phone in his pocket and quickly drove home.

As he tried to pack up a few things, he heard cars arrive outside his building. When he looked out of his window, he saw that one of the men who exited the police car was the very police officer he'd left to die in the bush, the one with the fat wobble wobble belly. They'd arrest him and once in police custody, Showlogo knew they'd find all sorts of reasons not to release him. He'd rot in jail for months, maybe years. He escaped from the back of the building just before the police came to his flat's door.

He fled to the most hidden place he could think of- the airport tarmac. The shaded area beneath the mango tree on the far side of the strip was where the luggage loaders took their breaks. He'd once spent a night here when he was too tired to go home. Now, he sat down on the dirt to eat the jollof rice he'd bought from one of the lady vendors on his way here. He leaned his back against the tree and let out a tired sigh thinking about his flat. Would the police force their way in and ransack the place?

As he sat in the early evening darkness, chewing spicy tomatoey rice, Showlogo made the decision in the way he made every decision. Fast fast. He stared at the 747 across the tarmac. He knew the schedule; this one would soon be bound for London. It was still glistening from its most recent wash. The water droplets sparkled in the orange and white airport lights. The airplane looked fresh, new and it was headed to new lands. The sight of the fresh, "new" airplane combine with the spicy rice in his mouth made the world suddenly seem ripe. Full of potential. Offering escape. For a while. He drank from his bottle of warm Coca Cola and the drink's sweetness was corrupted by the pepper in his mouth. He smacked his lips. He'd always liked this combination.

An hour later, he bought another container of rice from the same woman, demanding that she pack it into the plastic container he normally used to carry his toothbrush, toothpaste and washcloth when he worked late hours. He went to his locker and brought out the heavy jacket he used when he worked during chillier nights.

"Success T, how far?" he asked, shrugging on the jacket as he held his phone to his ear.

"I'm good," Success T said. "I dey study. You dey come out with us tonight. Where are you?"

"Look, I'm going away for a little while. These police need to calm down. Can you have Mohammed and Yomi watch my farm?"

"Where no dey go?"

"Away."

After a paused, Success T said, "Good. I dey call you before. You hear about that kobo kobo Igbo shop? Some police dey wait outside your place. I drove by half hour ago."

"Make you no worry about me. I fine."

When he finished talking to Success T, he stared out at the tarmac as he shut off his phone and pushed it deep into his pocket. He moved quickly. It was dark but he knew where he could walk and remain in shadow. The 747 would be pushing off soon, so he had to be quick. He climbed up the undercarriage, pressing a foot against the thick tough wheel. He hoisted himself into the plane's landing gear bay. In the metal space around him were wires, pipes, levers and other machinery. He positioned himself in a spot where the wheels would not crush him and he could hang on to a solid narrow pipe. He'd have to grasp it tightly upon take off because the bay would fill with powerful rushing sucking air as the plane picked up speed and left the earth. "One man Mopo," he said with a laugh as he practiced his grip. He positioned his satchel at his back. Inside it, he carried his mobile phone, charger, a container of rice, a torch, his wallet and a few other small things. All he'd need.

Showlogo's mind was at ease when the plane began to move. In a few hours, he'd be in the United States. He'd never dreamed of going there. Nigeria was his home and the city of Lagos was his playground. But he understood change and that it could happen in the blink of an eye. He'd learned this when he was seven years old. One day his parents had been there, then the next, they'd died in a car crash. Since then he'd learned this lesson over and over. One day Chinelo had loved him, the next she was marrying his cousin and pretending she didn't know him. One day, there was food to eat, the next there was none. One day he had no money, the next his pockets were stuffed with naira and he had two jobs. One day he could buy fuel for his car, the next his car had been stolen and this didn't matter because there was a fuel shortage. He'd lived his life this way, understanding, reacting to and riding the powerful and weak waves of the universe's ocean. He was a strong man, so he always survived.

The plane taxied to the runway. Showlogo watched the passing black pavement below. Success T would keep his flat for him, maybe use it as a second home where he could stay when he wanted to be alone. Success T lived a fast life and was always sneaking away to spend days in remote hotels to get away from it all; the idea that Success T could now use Showlogo's place was comforting to Showlogo.

Of course, Success T would have to get rid of the police, first. He chuckled to himself when he thought of the police who were probably still waiting for him outside his home. They would spend weeks trying to find him. He'd lose his job at the airport by tomorrow morning and be replaced by the afternoon. So be it. He would be elsewhere.

Showlogo began to have second thoughts when the plane started picking up speed. The suction in the landing gear bay was growing stronger and stronger...and stronger. *Oh my God*, Showlogo thought. He looked down at the pavement below. It was flying by. But maybe he could throw himself out and survive. The plane wasn't even off the ground, but already he felt an end to his strength. It was too late.

Whooosh!

When the plane left the ground, Showlogo felt as if he were dying. Every part of his body pressed against the bay's metal walls. The air was sucked from his lungs. As the earth dropped away from him, his world swam. This sense of death only lasted about thirty seconds. Then his body stabilized. In the next few minutes, Showlogo marveled at the fact that he would never be the same again. Who could be after feeling what he felt, seeing what he was seeing? Nigeria was flying away from him.

As the air's temperature rapidly dropped and he pulled his thin coat over himself and thanked God that he'd worn his best and thickest jeans, socks and gym shoes. The undercarriage retracted. The clouds and distant earth below were shut away as the metal doors closed and Showlogo was pressed in tightly. "Shit," he screamed. There was so much less space than he expected. The temperature was still dropping.

He shivered. "Sh-Sh-Showlogo no go sh-sh-shake. No sh-sh-shaking for Sh-Sh-Showlogo," he muttered. Only a few yards above him, people sat in their cushioned seats, warm and safe. The flight attendants were probably about to offer drinks and tell them about the meal that would be served. Showlogo had flown twice in his life. The first was to Abuja with his parents when he was five. When his parents were still alive and telling him every day what a great doctor he would be. The second time was a few years ago to Port Harcourt, when his parents were long dead and he had business to take care of in Calabar. On both flights, he remembered, they'd served snacks. When he was five, it had been peanuts or popcorn. When he was an adult, it had been drinks and crackers. His cousin Success T told him that on international flights, there was an actual meal.

"It was shit," Success T had laughed. "For this small small plate, the beef wey dem put dey tasteless, o! If I chop am, I go die before we reach Heathrow!"

Success T wasn't exaggerating. He had been born with intestinal mal-rotation and lived on a very strict diet of seafood, fruits and vegetables and very selected starches. He could not eat fufu, much rice, foods soaked in preservatives and he could not eat most European or American cuisines. As Showlogo thought of his cousin who was practically solid muscle and scared anyone he competed against in boxing tournaments, yet could be felled by merely eating the wrong food, he chuckled. Then he shivered again. He brought out his torch and flicked it on. The light was dim despite the fact that he'd put in fresh batteries less than two hours ago.

He could see his breath as if he were smoking a giant mold. Speaking of which. He reached into his satchel and brought it out. He had to flick his lighter ten times before it produced a very weak flame. The large joint's tip burned blandly and he managed three puffs before it went out. He shivered again and his flesh prickled as he lay back. The vibration of the plane's engine shook his freezing body, causing his legs and arms to flex. He squeezed his palms and curled his feet and toes. He flexed his buttocks and straightened the tendons in his neck. Time was slowing down and he felt calm. He could see the black borders between the frames. Slowly, he ate his jollof rice, wheezing between bites. It was warm, red and spicy, heating his belly. Then he lay back and remembered nothing more.

~~*~*

As he laid on the sidewalk, the woman named Dolapo Tunde, the man named Mr. David Goldstein, and the black cat stared. Dolapo shuddered, as she grasped her lawnmower. She shuddered again and crossed herself. Then she pulled out her blue ear buds and let them fall and dangle at her thigh. Mr. Goldstein dropped his soapy sponge and leaned against his Chevy Challenger. All thoughts of work fled his mind as he tried to piece things together. The man could not have fallen from any house or building. There wasn't one close enough. No tree, either. He'd fallen from the damn sky! But Mr. Goldstein had seen photos on the net of what was left of people who jump from tall buildings. He'd seen one of a man who'd jumped from a skyscraper. The guy was nothing but mush in the road! So Mr. Goldstein shuddered, as well, for he did not want to see or even know what the man looked like underneath.

Only Buster the Cat was brave and, of course, curious enough to inspect. He padded across the road. He hesitated for only a moment and then he walked right up to Showlogo's body and sniffed the side of his head. Buster looked at the man's nose, which was pressed to the concrete and dribbling blood. The smell of the blood was rich and strong, very very strong. Buster had never smelled blood with such a powerful scent. Buster was focusing so hard on the rich bloody aroma that when

Showlogo grunted, Buster was so deeply startled that he leapt four feet in the air.

Across the street Mr. Goldstein shouted, "Holy shit! HOLY SHIT! Whoa!! He's alive! How the *fuck* is that dude alive? What the hell!"

Showlogo lifted his head and looked around. He coughed and wiped his bloody nose. He sat up, stretched his arms and cracked his knuckles and smiled tiredly. He looked at Dolapo who was staring at him with her mouth hanging open. His brain was addled, so when he spoke, the language that came out was not the Pidgin English he meant to speak, not even the Standard English he should have spoken, for he was most certainly in America. Instead, he spoke the language of his birth, Yoruba.

"You see? I can never die," he said. "Even death fears me."

Dolapo tried to reply but all that came out was a gagging sound.

"I agree with you," he said to her. "There are better ways to travel. Can you prepare some yam with palm oil for me? I have taste for that."

Dolapo stared at him for several more seconds and crossed herself again. Then she quietly responded to him in Yoruba, "God is with me! I have no reason to fear evil. Be gone, fallen angel! Be gone, devil!" She switched to English. "In the name of Jesus!"

Showlogo stared blankly at her and then he laughed. "My eyes tell me I'm in America, my ears tell me something else." He stretched his back and began to walk up the sidewalk. He was Showlogo and he could survive anything and anywhere. Behind him Buster the Black Cat followed, attracted and intrigued by the strongest smelling blood he'd ever sniffed.

JAYE WELLS is a USA Today-bestselling author of urban fantasy and speculative crime fiction. Raised by booksellers, she loved reading books from a very young age. That gateway drug eventually led to a full-blown writing addiction. When she's not chasing the word dragon, she loves to travel, drink good bourbon, and do things that scare her so she can put them in her books. To learn more about Jaye's stories, please visit www.jayewells.com

THE BLUEST HOUR
Jaye Wells

The old man takes a drag from his cigarette. Kools, menthol. The brown skin of his fingers bear yellow stains and his clothes smell of minty smoke and turned earth. "I sing to them, that's all. There's no real magic to it. Just sing a few bars and they come a runnin'."

"That can't be all," I say. "Surely there's more."

He chuckles—a smoker's sound full of phlegm. "You either got it or you ain't, son."

I lean back and cross my arms. On the table between us, my plastic cup of Abita beer drips with condensation that mimics the beads of sweat rolling down my back. It's August in New Orleans, when nothing is dry. "Then how'd you know you had it?"

The old man rubs his lip and looks at me through rheumy eyes, the whites as yellow as the stains on his fingers. "Now that part wasn't so easy."

He takes a long pull from his Kool before tamping it out on the cobblestones. We're sitting at a bistro table outside a bar in Pirate's Alley. It's full dark outside but still sultry as Neptune's daughter. A tourist family eats ice cream at the next table. The mother scrunches her nose at the smoke. The old man tips his hat to her, and she turns away, chastened.

When he gives me his attention again, I find I am breathless. I've looked for someone like this old man for what feels like decades, and now, finally, we're getting somewhere. But the whole scene doesn't feel right: the heat, the crush of tourists, the scent of cheap beer. I feel like apologizing, but he speaks before I can find the words.

"Truth be told," he begins, "I couldn't always sing. Mama used to tell me not to sing in church 'cause it sounded like the devil hisself skinnin' a cat." That chuckle again. I don't understand. The thing he does—his gift?—it has to be a terrible burden. How can he laugh so easily? "Nah, it wasn't until I met old Rambo Jones that I learnt how to sing like I do."

The questions tumble from my lips. Who is Rambo Jones? Is he a singer, too? How does it work? Where do they go?

He holds up a hand. "Tell you what, you come to the cemetery tomorrow and I'll show you."

My heart stutters in my chest. I'm not sure if it's excitement or dread. "Really?"

"Sure. Cemetery closes at sundown." He winks at me. "That's when the magic happens."

~~*~*

The next day passes slow as molasses. Inspired by my new friend, I buy a pack of cigarettes and waste time chain smoking and watching people pass under my balcony on Ursulines Avenue. It's too hot to walk around. Too hot for respectable clothes, too, so I sit in my undershirt and trousers and pretend I'm Stanley Kowalski.

Around two in the afternoon, I order room service. Steak with a side of bourbon. The meat is tough, but the bourbon is smooth. That's how I end up with the phone in my hand. I don't remember picking it up. Don't remember dialing. But I remember asking for forgiveness and hearing, "Leave me alone, asshole," before the line goes dead.

After that mistake, I sit on that balcony in the afternoon heat with bourbon burning in my gut and the phone cutting into my hand. Some part of my brain—the small, sober part—asks what the hell I'm doing, but I ignore it.

I've come to New Orleans looking for answers I'm not sure I really want. Just tired of always asking, I guess. Always wondering what happened.

I suppose people must exist who have never felt the sharp ache of loss. Probably those people smile a lot. But I don't know anyone like that. Most people I know carry a crater in their chest. The walking wounded.

I heard it said once that you never really recover from loss—you just get used to the pain. Whoever said that was a luckier man than me—or a more numb one, anyway.

I light another cigarette. Drink some more. Maybe the only way to stop the nagging ache, I think, is to become someone else's loss.

But I've managed to piss off everyone who ever might've cared if I die.

Leave me alone, asshole has become the refrain of every relationship I've had since that ice blue winter.

I try to count the years on my fingers, but they aren't working too well. I squeeze my eyes to concentrate, but instead of a calendar, I see *her.*

Those laughing blue eyes and the bright red lipstick that made her teeth seem impossibly white when she flashed that dagger-in-the-heart smile. Creamy skin that felt like silk against my calloused paws.

But that was all *before.*

Before the icy road and the drunk. Before the phone screamed at three a.m. Before my heart deserted me to play house with her in a box six feet down.

She used to tease me about my lack of faith. But she was wrong. I had plenty. Used to, anyway. Before.

But then I'd heard whispers about the Soul Singers. People who collected the souls of the dead and helped them pass over to the other side, wherever that was.

I'd resisted believing the legends at first. But then my editor had called. Deadline was looming and he needed a story.

"Soul singers," I said. "Need to do a research trip, though."

"Where?" he'd demanded. Editors are tighter than priests' assholes when it comes to travel expenses.

Truth was, I'd had no idea where to find the singers, but I'd picked New Orleans for three reasons. First, I hadn't had a decent bowl of gumbo in a decade. Second, if the soul singer piece died on the page, the Big Easy was a generous muse. And third, if any city was the love child of Thanatos and Eros, it was New Orleans, which made it the perfect hangout for people who wooed the dead with song.

It hadn't taken me long to find someone who'd heard of the Soul Singers. It's near impossible to avoid making friends in the French Quarter. And when you got a few extra clams to rub together, you can get any sort of information you want. Especially if you visit the voodoo shops. Not the touristy ones on Bourbon Street, but the real ones hidden behind wooden doors bearing discrete plaques.

The woman who'd introduced me to the old man was a voodooienne by the name of Madame Lunesta Beauregard. Her skin had been black as midnight, and when I'd walked into her shop, she looked at me like she'd been expecting me. "Be careful what you go looking for, chere," she'd said in a dire tone.

But she'd made a call and set up the meeting with the old man. Before I'd left the store, she'd pressed a grisgris bag in my hand. The red flannel pouch smelled of camphor and whisky. "For protection," she'd whispered.

I laughed at her. "From what?"

"Yo'self."

Now, I pull the bag from my pocket and watch it as I polish off the last of the bourbon. The felt is blood red in the dying afternoon light. My head feels full of static that I chalk up to the booze, but booze can't explain the grave-walking chill in my bones.

A moment later, the spell passes and I rise to shower for my meeting at the cemetery. I leave the grisgris on the ledge next to the empty bottle of bourbon.

~~*~*

The late-day sun gilds the Victorian and Georgian mansions along St. Charles Avenue. Stately oaks posture above the warped sidewalks and moss hangs over the ancient arms like the hair of mourning women.

The streetcar isn't air conditioned, and in moments I am sliding on the old wooden bench in a pool of my own sweat. The bourbon crawls up the back of my throat and the shrieks of delight from the tourists' children pound behind my eyes like an aneurysm.

I haven't been to a cemetery since that spring following that particular winter. Once the ground thawed, I had to sit next to the hole and try not to give into the urge to jump in there with her. My gut had been a cauldron of broken glass and acid. My brain, black as the bottom of that hole.

Real men don't cry. My daddy told me that when I was twelve and we were standing beside my mother's grave. That piece of advice and a genetic tendency toward alcoholism were the only two bits of legacy I'd gotten from my old man. According to everyone else, I'd gotten the rest from that Channel-scented ghost with the soft hands and the angel's voice.

My shrink said that funeral set me on this path. It's textbook, really, he said. I'm a God damned macabre cliché.

The squeal of metal-on-metal abrades my nerves. The streetcar stops at Second Street. I let the kids and their tired parents go first before hauling myself off the bench. I grab the paper bag containing the bottle the old man told me to bring and step onto the grassy median.

Lafayette Cemetery No. 1 is a couple of blocks off St. Charles. By the time I reach its broad wrought iron arch, the sun is sinking low. A few tourists mill around the locked gates, snapping pictures. I wave through the bars at a fifty-something ex-convict-type in blue coveralls. He nods and unlocks the padlocks without a word, as if the old man had warned him of my arrival.

The gates shriek open on unoiled hinges. A few of the tourists mutter complaints about my being allowed entrance. He shoos them away with a grunt. "The cemetery's closed." He slams the gate shut again and locks it before pointing me toward a shack at the far end of the closest path.

Monuments to the dead rise from the soggy earth and squat cheek-to-jowl on wide avenues coated in gravel. Silk flowers and trinkets decorate some of the crypts, but it's the moldering teddy bear on the grave of a five-year-old that makes me want run back to the refuge of the hotel's bar.

The old man steps out from behind a columbarium at the end of the row. He raises crooked fingers and tips his hat. I walk toward him on heavy legs.

"I'm glad you decided to come." He says it kindly, but I hate him for being so sure I considered standing him up. He looks down at the bag. "You brought it?"

He takes it as reverently as if I am handing over the baby Jesus. The brown paper crinkles as he pulls it off. "Four Roses," he says, nodding as if I am finally catching on. "This'll do just fine."

I grimace. When my editor eventually gets the expense report with the two-hundred-dollar bottle of bourbon on it, I'm pretty sure his reaction will be a tad more expressive.

He takes me into the small building on the edge of the cemetery. Four concrete block walls, barred windows from the outside. Inside it's not much more scenic. A small metal desk is shoved under one of the square windows and a shelving unit next to the door holds muddy boots, shovels, trowels, and other grave-minding implements.

From the deep drawer in the bottom of the desk, he pulls out an ancient-looking scrapbook. Cracked brown leather on the outside, yellowed photos inside. He flips a few pages and lands on a sepia-toned picture of an African American man sitting on the stoop of a row house. The man wears a fedora tipped to the side and a natty suit. Across his lap is a cane of some sort, but his strong posture and confident smile tell me he only uses the walking stick as an affectation.

The old man taps on the picture. "Rambo Jones." His tone is reverent.

"He taught you how to sing?"

"Didn't give me singin' lessons, if that's what you mean." A smile, as if he's made a private joke, appears on his lips. "He gave me his gift."

I frown. "I don't follow."

"'Course you don't."

"Listen—" I feel wrung out. It's the heat and the humidity and the bourbon. It's the trip all the way to the cemetery expecting to receive answers, but instead having riddles tossed in my face.

"Relax, son." The old man pats my arm. "I forget this is new to folks ain't used to the way things is."

"Then explain it to me." I drop into an ancient office chair made of green metal and cracked vinyl. It's probably older than the old man, and it squeaks when I move as if bitching about my weight.

He leans a slim hip on the edge of the desk to stare down at me. The dim light in the shack casts shadows on his angular face. "I didn't know how to sing the day I met old Rambo. But by that night? I just could, is all."

"How could he teach you to sing in one day?"

"Singing was the easy part. He just touched my throat, and then I could sing like an angel." I open my mouth to ask more, but he puts up a hand. "What he taught me—the important part—was how to call the souls with my song."

I leaned forward. "Go on."

FANTASY FOR GOOD - URBAN FANTASY

"Rambo told me his time was done. He'd been crooning for them spirits going on fifty years. He was tired, he said."

"So he passed the gift on to you? Just like that?"

The old man smiles, a bit sad. "Just like that."

I lean back and let this sink in. It can't be as easy as that, can it? "But what about God?" I blurt.

"What about 'im?"

"Where does He come into all this?" I gesture wildly to indicate the cemetery and the world at large.

"Can't rightly say. I'll know once my time comes, I suppose." There's that laugh again.

"Do you expect me to believe you don't even know where they go?"

His face darkens and I immediately regret my patronizing tone. "You ever pray, son?"

My skin tightens. I glance at the dirty floor. "Used to."

"You ever wonder where those prayers gone to?"

I look up. "To God."

"How you know?"

I huff out an annoyed breath. "Because—where else would they go?"

The old man smiles and sits back a little, pleased with himself. "Exactly."

"What about hell—what if that's where they go?"

His face darkens, as if I've insulted him. "Did your mama drop you on your head, boy? Heaven and hell? They ain't my business."

"But you said they go to God."

"*You* said they go to God. I ain't put no name on it. People was dying before that name existed and they'll keep dying when there's a new one," he says. "No, sir, don't care much for names."

I rise because his words make me too restless to sit still. "What do you care about then?" I hear the anger in my own voice but I don't care. I need answers.

"I care about singing the right song." He rises too because I've insulted him. He points a finger at me. "What do you care about, boy?"

A few pat answers spring to my tongue, but I don't say them. I don't say them because the air has tightened and the old man's eyes have narrowed, and I am suddenly painfully aware that for some reason my answer matters. Really matters.

I close my mouth and think about it. The old man watches me with an odd intensity, but he doesn't hurry me.

What *do* I care about?

Answers, I think. That's why I became a writer, right? Hoping that one day I'll find the right combination of letters and suddenly the great mysteries will reveal themselves? But that doesn't feel true enough.

Love? That's why I'm alone, isn't it? Once I'd lost real love, I'd tried desperately to replace it. Pleasant lies in smoky bars exchanged for the fleeting press of skin on strange sheets. But those meaningless exchanges of fluids felt blasphemous compared to the sacred pleasure-pain of being totally bare with another human.

I glance at the old man. He watches me with a frown, as if he can hear my answers and is judging each, ranking them. I dismiss love, too. It's the stuff of romance novels and tortured heroes and people who believe in other people.

I rub the bridge of my nose and look to the floor again. But inside, I dig deeper into my own layers. Past the polite facades and the not-so-polite ones. Down past the duty and the dreams. Down to the recesses that no one ever got to see—not even *her*. To the part of myself I kept hidden from everyone—even myself.

In that shadowed corner of my psyche, with its face pressed against the wall to avoid the light of my attention, a single word shivered in the cold. Once I spot it there, I know it is the correct answer. Unfortunately, it is also the most terrifying one.

I speak the answer in a whisper: "I care about the end."

The old man cocks his head. "Come again."

I know he heard me just fine. But I reply anyway because I need to understand it myself. "I care about the fact that one day this is all going to end. That you and I and everyone else out there will simply cease to be. It's unbearable, but also a terrible relief." I shook my head, trying to understand the words even as they left me. "I guess what I'm saying is, I care about making the time I have worth the fact it's all going to end."

Silence ticks by like heavy heartbeats. My skin feels clammy despite the heat, and a strange pressure clogs my throat. I try to swallow it down, but it refuses to budge.

Finally, the old man removes his hat and places it over his chest. The corner of his mouth lifts a little. I worry for a brief, terrifying moment that this old man is going to shame me. My ears burn and pulse, preparing for the painful bite of his laughter.

Instead, he tips his chin and says, "Good answer, son. Mighty good answer."

~~*~*

The old man leads me to the center of the main gravel avenue, which ends at the cemetery's large black gates. Sounds are muted by the tall oaks with their mourning veils of Spanish moss, as well as the tall brick wall that allows the dead to rest in peace.

The light has mellowed and every surface seems kissed by silver. The French call this time of day *l'heure bleue*—the blue hour. It's the time of day when it is neither full day nor complete night. When light and

249

shadow combine into a sweet dreamy blue-violet. According to the old man, it's also when the veil between the corporeal world and the other world is gossamer thin and easily pierced.

"It's time," the old man says in a hushed tone reminiscent of prayer.

I clasp my hands together and lower my head. I'm not sure what was coming, but I am sure giving voice to my questions would be blasphemous. We aren't in a church, but the moment feels sacred nonetheless.

"Whatever happens, stay out of the way and quiet," the old man warns. In this light, his angles have softened, but the edge in his tone ruins the effect. It seems to say that he might make jokes out of a lot of things, but not this. Never this.

A hush falls over the graves. The old man lifts his face to the sky. He clears his throat. And then...

A single note escapes from between his lips and rises into the air. I'm no music expert—I can't tell clefs from flats–but something told me this note was perfection. Crystal clear, cutting almost—painful in its beauty.

That note hangs above us even as the old man moves on to produce more. The air in front of his face shimmers until the notes become opaque points of light. Before I can recover from this shock, the lights vibrate into the shape of birds.

The light birds—thirteen of them—circle the air over our heads.

The old man ignores my shock. Until that moment, he's been singing single notes without words attached. But now, he finally begins to sing the first verse of a song I've never heard.

Oh Lord, take me down.
I say, Oh Lord take me down.
Take me down to the riverside
Where the water's cool and the shore is wide.
Oh Lord, take me down.

Like I said, I'm no music expert, but I know the blues when I hear them. As he sings, the birds fly away from the cemetery in a starburst pattern.

Take me down where the water's clean
Where the saints give blessings and the current's mean
Oh Lord, take me down.

I close my eyes and let the song wash over me. It tugs at my heart, like a magnet's pull. Or perhaps it's not my heart at all. My soul? Maybe.

When the waters rise I won't run away
'Cause we'll all be a'swimmin' come judgment day
Oh Lord, take me down to the river wide
And carry me away on your righteous tide
Oh Lord, take me down.

My limbs fill with the dark waters he's describing. I float on the air in the blue light, being swept away by the music and the magic. It seems both unreal and real at the same time. Surreal, hyper-real. Disorienting and completely grounding at once. The possibility he might be a con artist—an illusion master—occurs to me, but I instantly dismiss the notion. Despite my shock, I know the things I'm seeing and hearing are absolutely happening.

The old man stops singing lyrics and the song mellows into a sort of peaceful humming. The round sounds vibrate into the air like circles of light. The air around the old man shimmers until a corona of light surrounds his body, like the opening of a great eye.

Above the humming, birdsong reaches my ears. Over the buildings, through the deepening blue of dusk, the dark outline of dozens of black wings. Their songs fly out before them like harbingers, and I realize with a start they're singing the same melody as the old man.

As they fly closer, I realize that each bird has a small sphere of light gently clasped between its claws.

The music sinks through my skin and makes the blood quiver in my veins. The closer the birds fly, the more intense the sensation. I place a hand over my chest, as if the move will prevent my own soul from escaping.

The birds circled overhead. The lights they carry create a dizzying laser show.

The tunnel of light the old man opened earlier pulses between us. The old man raises a single finger into the air. The humming stops. The birds' song ends. For a brief, sharp moment the entire world holds its breath.

The old man raises his face to the sky and sings a single note. The sound slashes through skin and bone down to my marrow. One by one, the birds break off from their flying circle and dive toward the portal of light. When they each fly into the circle, they have the spheres of light in their claws, but when they emerge on the other side, the lights are gone.

It takes a full minute for each bird to be relieved of its burden. When the final one flies through, the old man tapers off the note. When it ends, a great sucking accompanies the portal closing in on itself.

My ears pop and the pressure in my chest eases instantly. Air whooshes from my lungs and I sag against a nearby tomb. Pressure pulses behind my lids and distorts my vision until the old man's image wavers and shifts like a hologram.

I lick my dry lips and try to sift through my fractured thoughts to find enough letters to create a coherent sentence. The old man leans heavily against a faux bois statue of a tree stump. He blinks away the tears that have gathered in his eyes. He watches me, as if waiting.

But before I can utter a single syllable, the old man's hand flies to his chest. A gasp escapes his lips.

The universal signal of distress disperses the mental fog and marshals my limbs. I scramble toward the old man even as he falls to the ground.

I lean over him and cradle his head in my arms. "Wh—"

"Shh." He's not looking at me. His eyes look past me, as if someone is standing at my shoulder. I glance around just in case, but find that we are alone. "Do you hear it?" he whispers.

"Hear what?"

His lips lift in a smile. "The music."

I swallow hard. "No," I say, "I don't hear anything."

His eyes move toward my face finally. "It's time, son."

I know immediately. I know suddenly and completely what he is saying. "No," I say, "not yet."

He doesn't argue with me. He simply lifts a single brown finger to my throat. The pad of the finger presses against my Adam's apple. Presses so hard that I begin to choke and fight. But despite his weakened state, he presses on, his face a mask of determination.

A shock of electricity passes through my throat. It expands and fans out through my nerve endings, contracting every cell, expanding every vein. My eyes open impossibly wide and I see things I never noticed before. The layout of the entire city like a map in my mind—thousands of spots of light dotting the landscape like Christmas bulbs. I also see birds. So many birds. Pelicans and cranes and swallows and crows. I not only see the souls and the birds—I feel them as visceral energy in my chest.

My breathing speeds up until I'm panting from the pain and the connection and the awareness he's forcing on me.

The old man swallows and his throat clicks. His eyes are impossibly bright in the darkness. Finally, that finger lifts from my skin, but its imprint throbs on my throat like a bruise. "Sing, son," he says. His voice is weak, gritty. "Sing."

Cold sweat coats my skin like paste. I'm stuck. I feel stuck and scared. I want to run, but I am as rooted to the ground as those tombs surrounding us. "I—I can't," I say. My voice sounds like metal scraping concrete. "I'm scared."

He grabs my hand with a surprisingly strong grip. "Sing, damn you." But before I can decide to obey or leave, a convulsion rocks the old man's body. His grip on my hand tightens painfully. His eyes—those watery, too-knowing eyes—roll back in their sockets until all that's visible is the yellowed whites.

He gasps in a lungful of air. His body arcs up from the ground. He freezes in mid-air, as if someone pressed a pause button on his life. My hand hurts and my chest is impossibly tight. I know this is the end for the old man, and it's too late to ask for more answers. Too late to do anything but hold on.

A final, loud exhalation of air escapes a split second before he body goes slack. His grip slips from mine.

Before I can consciously aware of giving my body the order, the first note escapes my lips. I hear it both from inside my body and outside, like a stereo. The sound is timid but clear. This is not the voice I have heard come from my body for the last thirty-nine years. This is a new voice that comes from the same place I found my answer to the old man's question.

Another note. This one stronger. I hold it until it rises up from my lips and shimmers in the air. I keep holding it as it morphs into the shape of tiny bird. A swallow, I think.

I'm not dumb. The old man has not bamboozled me. Sure, he pretended to want to help me find answers, when all along he'd wanted me to help him. But this feels too inevitable to pretend I didn't know it was coming. I'd left that protective gris gris bag in the hotel for some reason. I knew he was going to touch my throat before he did. And I knew before I sang my first note that it would be clear and bright and sharp as a blade.

The bird circles above the man's chest in tight circles.

"What do you care about?" he'd asked.

The end.

Hesitantly, I echo the words I'd heard from the old man.

Oh Lord, take me down.

Each note felt like a prayer. Each word, a benediction.

I say, Oh Lord take me down.

The old man lay still on the ground. His eyes stared up past the dark night sky, past the stars—to a place beyond human knowing.

Take me down to the riverside

Where the water's cool and the shore is wide.

Without conscious thought or strength of will, that portal opens in the same spot it had opened for the old man.

Oh Lord, take me down.

I continue singing all the words. I watch as the sphere of light rises from the spot in the center of the old man's chest. From the place where his heart once beat strong and true, now silenced just like his song. The bird snatches the light from the air. Then it circles some more as it echoes the melody I'm singing.

Even as the song has summoned the old man's soul, it's also gone to work on mine. It's stitching the ragged, black edges. It's mending the worn spots. Soothing, yes. It's soothing my soul.

When I reach the final line of the song—the old man's song, which is now mine to sing until I find my own song—the bird flies up into the sky. After one triumphant circuit around the cemetery, it executes a graceful dive. I hold the final note and realize it isn't just a note—it's a farewell.

Just before the bird flies through the portal, that sphere of light shines impossibly bright. Pain like an aneurysm—the pain of knowledge of eternity—explodes in my brain.

The bird disappears into the great eye of light. Two heartbeats later, it reappears on the other side without its burden.

Now, the cemetery is unbearably silent. It is the quiet of a tomb. The quiet of eternal sleep. The quiet of nothingness. Of disappearing. Of never having existed at all.

Tears flood my eyes. But not tears of mourning. Not tears of loss or hopelessness. They are tears of relief.

I know I will never return to the life of before. I won't return to the booze and the angst and the looking for meaning in words no one will read. The tears are a baptism.

I finally understand how the old man could laugh so easily. I finally know why the soul singers sing.

All ends are beginnings.

Beginnings are to be celebrated.

And every celebration deserves a song.

SAMIT BASU is well known in his native India where he wrote his first novel, *The Simoqin Prophecies*, when he was just 22. It was published a year later. Since then he has completed the *GameWorld* trilogy, all of which have topped the Indian bestsellers list. In 2012, Samit came to the attention of western readers with his superhero novel, *Turbulence*, which won an award from Wired Magazine. He has written comics and a YA novel, and he is also a columnist, screenwriter and documentary filmmaker.

Visit his official site to find out more: samitbasu.com

PANDAL FOOD
Samit Basu

There are about four hundred people in and around the pandal at midnight—just a trickle, then. I think we got around five thousand in the early evening. Good night. Busy night. But it's hardly surprising. This is Calcutta, during the pujas, of course thousands of people have shown up to worship the goddess. All right, not worship the goddess, worship each other, and food, and the fact that they made it through another year.

It's been a horrible year, which means people make more of an effort to celebrate the pujas—none of that nonsense about staying indoors and being too cool to mingle with the crowd, with all the shoving and sweat that involves. No, they're all out tonight, in their kurtas and their saris and for the younger ones, their rebel clothes, a little shoulder, a little back, a little leg. A few hours ago, they were all dancing and twirling with the crazy drummers, and getting high off the smoke and general frenzy in the air. It takes very little for people to cast off the whole city sophisticate thing and become the tribe that the pujas remind them they are.

It's the same thing ever year—the faces change a little, and the clothes change a little more, but it's always the same people at the pandal. The cursory visit to the actual idols, token worship, the ten-minute awkward stand near the auditorium where some local hero wails lustily to the sound of—well, Bollywood now, but it used to be Tagore songs. Then, the real pujas begin—they eat like starving demons, find a chair in the park, and imagine themselves sleeping with all the hot young things roaming the pandal grounds. And the food is usually greasy and horrible, but they don't care—they wake up next morning ready to do it again. That's the beauty of pandal food.

I love crowds. I've been at pandals, some years, where it's just a family affair, and there are maybe fifty people around. These are all very high-class old-school Bengali zamindar family affairs, and they're boring. This year, I'm doing a pandal in Salt Lake, which used to be a swamp, and then it was a quiet suburb, and now it's a technology hub and almost a part of the city centre. Calcutta changes every year, even though the people who leave it and come only to visit complain that it doesn't change at all. New things come and go like mushrooms, living and dying and coming back. The last couple of years, it's been phones instead of cameras, everyone's taking pictures of the same people and things they see every year and putting it up on the Internet. I guess it helps them feel alive. And it helps them pretend they've been to more pandals than they have. Saves time. Traffic is always terrible. All fourteen million

Calcuttans are out on the streets, plus many times that number from outside.

At one a.m., the lights around the idols are switched off, leaving only a few lamps and incense sticks to keep the goddess and her children assured that we all still love them. I heave a sigh of relief as the pandal finally empties, and then, when it's dark, I change into my social clothes. When I step out, into the light, I'm looking pretty good—a handsome young Bengali man in a sharp kurta. It's a classic look. Always works, always will.

The stalls are shutting down, one by one—I grab the last dirty candyfloss from one stall, shoot the last set of balloons with an airgun at another. I ride the creaky merry-go-round—it's for kids, really, but Akbar bhai, who runs it, owes me a favour or two. I know I look fairly ridiculous, a grown man on a children's ride, but I don't care. I've been working all day, and pandal management is one of the most stressful jobs in the world.

Purab and Alok arrive in half an hour or so. The pandals they're running this year are all nearby—we'd decided we'd do Salt Lake properly this year. We usually find ourselves slots in South Calcutta, where all the gorgeous women go, but Purab had insisted we try out the city's new hub. And as they enter the park and wave at me, I notice they're really giving the trying new things mission their attention this year—they've got a girl with them, a foreign girl.

"This is Claudia," says Purab, as I shake hands, awkwardly, with the girl. She's wearing a sleeveless kurta over jeans, which is usually a college girl I-can't-be-bothered-to-dress-up-but-look-at-my-excellent-muscle-tone thing, but she pulls it off.

"Claudia is from the Netherlands," says Alok gleefully. "She's new in town."

"They told me you would be the best person to explain this whole puja to me," says Claudia. "They said you know all about it."

I do know all about it. So I toss a few teenagers from the chairs they've been guarding savagely, and we sit down, and I explain the whole thing to her. How a pandal is more than just a tent with some clay figures in it. How the goddess Durga, after slaying several asurs and pulling off lots of classical dance moves, comes to her parents' house with all her kids for a few days every year. Claudia has the usual questions—who are the four gods around the main Durga/lion/asur idol? Why does Ganesh have an elephant's head? Why is he married to a banana tree? What are the peacock, the mouse, the owl and swan doing with the gods? Why are Durga's kids doing nothing while their mother, in every pandal, is so hard at work slaying the horrific green asur with her spear and her angry lion?

I tell her the stories. I explain to her that the moment every idol depicts—Durga, the warrior goddess, standing on her lion, driving her spear through the heart of the mighty asur, is more than just an action scene—it's the moment the gods really defeated their mortal enemies, the asurs, really set the foundations of the world we live in now. I've told so many outsiders these stories I've got it all down perfectly, and she understands. Like all foreigners, she's amazed at the way the whole city turns into a carnival, at the amount of work that goes into making hundreds of thousands of beautiful idols, incredible pandal tents—and how it's all just thrown into the river when the festival is done. I learn something in exchange, though—the Dutch don't really know what going Dutch means. It's not an expression they use. Ah, cultural exchange. So glorious.

"I've been to Rio during Carnival," says Claudia. "But this is something else."

"Yes, it's definitely very different," says Purab with a knowing smirk. Like he's ever been to Brazil. He definitely knows what he's planning to do with Claudia later, though. She's a lovely girl, and wins our hearts by bringing up something we've always wondered about the pujas.

"So, the gods all made this ultimate warrior goddess Durga by adding their powers together because the asur was kicking their asses at combat, right? But what had the asur done that was actually wrong? As in, why is he the villain?"

"Because he's ugly," says Alok. "And because he dared to take on the gods. So they ganged up on him. But there are tribes all over India who still think he got a raw deal—they think the pujas are a time of mourning, and actually worship the asurs. Of course most of these tribes are still living in the Stone Age."

"I wonder what would have happened if he'd won," says Claudia.

"Well, given what happened to the world after the gods won, you have to wonder," says Alok. "Maybe the asurs would have handled things better. But we wouldn't have had the pujas, so it all evens out."

"Well, I'm glad she won," says Claudia. "Girl power, yes? It would've been a pretty shitty statue with the big demon killing the young goddess. Also, this is why Calcutta women, why Bengali women are so awesome, yes? The rest of the country is all about men."

Claudia has many more questions, but we have a problem: we're all getting hungry. We've all been working hard all day, and nothing builds up an appetite more than watching other people eat. But we can't really get started until Subir gets here.

Subir makes his entrance at around three in the morning. He's fairly drunk. We're sitting around, four of us, in an empty field dotted with tacky plastic chairs. To my left, the pandal is asleep, empty except for a sleeping security guard. It's quiet, though the field seems to throb with the echoes of the day's chaos. The city is aglow, the sky grey and yellow, a dull wave of noise washing over us every now and then.

"Anyone hungry?" Subir asks, and we all groan.

"I'm sorted," says Purab, a cloud of smoke drifting from his nostrils, the orange glow of his cigarette reflected in his large, round eyes. Claudia looks at him, and there's a moment that passes between them that we all notice. Maybe Purab and Claudia might be one of those puja romances that really work out. Earlier the pujas used to be the only time in the year when young men and women could actually meet without parents breathing down their necks. It was mating season, every year, and that was really why young people looked forward to it. Now times have changed, of course, and people meet each other all the time, in the real world and in cyberspace, but the ghost of mating seasons past still lingers over the whole city. People still have puja romances. It's a thing.

"Have you eaten?" Alok asks Subir.

"Usual. Pandal food. This and that. Just got in from Maddox."

We have to pause for a bit while I explain to Claudia that Maddox square is Puja Mating Central, where you have to be seen if you're hoping to make your mark in trendy Calcutta society.

"Good crowd?" asks Alok, grinning.

"Lovely. Before you ask me what the pandal looks like, don't; I don't think I even looked at it. The girls just get hotter every year. Such fit, firm bodies they have now, and not afraid to show them! There was this one chick, my god...she could get on a lion and slay me any time. But why do you ask? You've not eaten?"

"No. I think I'm going to go find dinner now, in fact. Want to come?"

"Not if you're going South-side. Won't find transport back at this hour, and I have to be at work in the morning."

"We all have to be at work. Come on!"

"Sorry." Purab gestures towards Alok and Subir. "You want to go with him?"

"Depends where you're going," Alok grins. "I'm not hungry, but I'm up for some fun. Where will the good girls be, this time of night? Subir? You up for some romance? There's no point just hanging around with us guys, you know."

Subir doesn't say anything. But he glares at Alok, and we all laugh, though this is a jibe that gets repeated every year at every possible occasion. Subir rises and burps, indicating his willingness to leave. So we bid our goodbyes to Purab and Claudia get into my car.

As I drive off, I see Purab, shaking his head, walk into the pandal with Claudia—she'd been talking about getting another look at the idols before they left. Claudia blows me a kiss as they enter, fading into the shadows cast by the lamps in front of the idols, until they're just a suggestion of a moving shape, grey-green in the light from a huge glowing ad hoarding across the street proclaiming the virtues of some antiseptic or other.

We turn the corner and drive on. Alok's next to me, smiling a secret smile to himself as he scans the streets, marvelling at the new, flashing lights and bright colours of the city we watched change before our eyes. We're from the north, of course, and we're all old enough to remember when everything was different; when you could smell the earth and the river, when the pujas, while still a huge carnival, were about people not things, not about smartphones and Best Pandal TV contests, when the lights on the street, the decorations, were wonders to gaze in awe at. When the pujas were a source of faith and mystery. Ah well, we were younger ourselves, then, and you feel things more deeply when you're young.

"I want to tell you something," says Subir suddenly. "I'm gay."

If he expects us to be shocked, he's in for a disappointment. "We know," says Alok. "And we've always felt bad for you during the pujas— Calcutta's not really a good hunting ground for attractive men, is it? Still, at least some of them have a little muscle now. If they'd only stop wearing net-vests at pandals, you'd be ok." Subir grumbles, and is silent.

Enough conversation. It's time to eat.

At Maddox, Mating Central, we find what we're looking for—an attractive young couple wandering around in a little winding lane near the pandal. We get out of the car. They don't even notice us until we're right next to them. It's over quickly, without much of a struggle. Subir eats the boy, I eat the girl, and Alok watches, smiling, snacking on a hand. She's very tasty, though her strange foreign perfume leaves an acid taste in my mouth. Give me old-fashioned sweat any day.

It's almost dawn now. Time to go to work. We drive back to Salt Lake, and I drop Alok and Subir at their pandals. I park my car and walk inside my pandal. I clean up the smear of blood near the lamp—Purab's getting sloppy in his old age. Poor Claudia. She was nice. Did she come to India to find herself?

"Couldn't save her, could you?" I ask the Durga idol. She stares back at me, her fiery eyes unmoving. I scream at her, at the whole family for a while, ancient challenges, taunts. I wish they'd come back, fight me again. I miss them. Where did they go? Why did they leave?

But it's morning now, and the pandal workers will be here soon... I slouch up to the divine family and their pets. I assume my position, below Durga's spear, in front of the lion's mouth. I stretch my face into a mask of anger and fear, my fangs glistening in the lamp-light, my body now green, strong, well-fed. I freeze. Soon the day will be here, and so will I. Waiting. Maybe you'll come visit me, laugh at the silly asur. And I'll be watching you. Maybe I'll like you. Maybe you'll look good.

I love pandal food.

As a solo writer, KEVIN J. ANDERSON has written several *Star Wars* novels as well as *X-Files* tie-ins, and he's co-authored over a dozen novels in the *Dune* universe with Brian Herbert. He is well known for the *Saga of Seven Suns* series of original novels, as well as the *Terra Incognita* trilogy, the *Dan Shamble, Zombie PI* series and many more.

REBECCA MOESTA is the author of a *Buffy* novel and three *Junior Jedi Knights Star Wars* books. Together with husband Kevin she has written fourteen more *Star Wars* novels, along with multiple tie-ins and movie novelizations. They have also released the *Crystal Doors* trilogy together.

See more at wordfire.com

LOINCLOTH
Kevin J. Anderson and Rebecca Moesta

ll alone in the props warehouse on the back lot of Duro Studios, he made his case to Shirley in his mind, rehashing the argument they had had the night before. This time, though, he was bold and articulate, and he easily convinced her.

Walter Groves opened another one of the big crates and tore out the packing straw mixed with Styrofoam peanuts. "Not exciting enough for you, huh? You don't feel fireworks? I'm too sedate-not a man's man? Think about it, Shirley. Women say they want nice guys, the shy and sensitive type, men who are sweet and remember birthdays and anniversaries. Isn't that what you told me you needed-someone just like me? You've always despised hypocrites. But what do you do? You fall for a bad boy, someone with tattoos and a heavy smoking habit, someone who can't keep a job for more than a month, someone like that last jerk you dated, who treated you rough and left you out in the cold.

"But I loved you. I treated you with respect, drove you to visit your grandmother in the hospital, and fixed your computer when the hard drive crashed. I got out of bed when you called at three in the morning and came to your apartment just to hold you because you had a nightmare and couldn't sleep. I gave you flowers, dinners by candlelight, and love notes-not to mention the best six months of my life. 'Someday, you'll regret it. Maybe not today. Maybe not tomorrow, but soon'"—he pictured himself as Bogart in *Casablanca*—"you'll realize what you threw away. But I won't be waiting. I'm a good man, and I deserve a wonderful woman who values me for who I am, who appreciates my dedication, and wants a nice, normal life. Go ahead. Have your shallow, exciting fling with Mr. James Dean in *Rebel Without a Cause*. I'll find someone sincere who wants Jimmy Stewart in *It's a Wonderful Life*."

Scattering straw and packing material, he pulled a long plastic elephant tusk out of the prop box. The faux ivory was sharp at one end and painted with "native symbols". He glanced at the label on the box: JUNGO'S REVENGE. After marking the name of the film on his clipboard, he listed the stored items beneath the title. He sighed.

If only he could have come up with just the right answers last night, maybe Shirley wouldn't have dumped him. If only he could have been tough like Mel Gibson in *Braveheart*, confident like Clark Gable in *Gone with the Wind*, or romantic like Dermot Mulroney in *The Wedding Date*. Instead, he had squirmed, speechless with shock, his lower lip trembling as if he were Stan Laurel caught in an embarrassing failure. Walter had made no heartfelt appeals or snappy comebacks; those would have been as much fiction as a script for any Duro Studios production.

Shirley had grabbed her stuff-along with some of his, though he hadn't had the presence of mind to mention it—and stormed out of the apartment.

Sharon Stone in *Basic Instinct*. That's who she reminded him of.

The large black walkie-talkie at his hip crackled, and even through the static of the poor-quality unit, he heard the lovely musical speech of Desiree Drea. Her voice never failed to make his heart skip a beat, then go back and skip it all over again. "Walter? Mr. Carmichael wants to know how you're coming with the props. He needs me to type up the inventory."

"I... um... I—" He looked down at the box, searching for words, and seized upon the letters stenciled to the crate. "I'm just now up to *Jungo's Revenge*. I've finished about half of the work."

As Desiree responded, he could hear the producer's voice bellowing in the background. "Jungo! It's all worthless crap. Trash it."

The secretary softened the message as she relayed it. "Mr. Carmichael suggests that it's of no value, so please put it in the Dumpster."

"And tell him he damn well better stay until he finishes," the voice in the background growled. "We need that building tomorrow to start shooting *Horror in the Prop Warehouse*."

"Tell him I'll do what needs to be done," Walter said, then clicked off the walkie-talkie, though he would gladly have chatted with Desiree for hours. He didn't have anything better to do that evening than work, anyway. He was very conscientious and would finish the job.

Chris Carmichael—producer of low-budget knock-off movies. The Jungo ape-man series, a bad Tarzan knock-off, had skated just a little too close to Tarzan's copyright line. The threatened legal action had caused the films to flop, even though they went direct to video. Walter had seen one of them and thought that the movies were bad enough to have flopped all on their own, without any legal difficulties to help them along. If anything, the publicity had boosted the sales.

He pulled out the other plastic elephant tusk, then some ugly looking tribal masks, three rubber cobras, and a giant plastic insect as big as his palm that was labeled DEADLY TSETSE FLY. Walter shook his head. He had to agree about the worthlessness of these props. There wouldn't be any collector interested in even giving them shelf space. If there had been enough fans to generate a few collectors, the Jungo franchise might never have disappeared.

Near the bottom of the crate he found a rattle, a shrunken head, and another tribal mask, but these props were far superior to the others. They looked handmade, with real wood and bone. The shrunken head had an

266

odd leathery feel that made him wonder if it was real. He shuddered as he took it out of the crate.

It seemed unlikely that Chris Carmichael, a tight-wad with utter contempt for his audiences as well as his employees, would spend money on the genuine articles to use as props. Maybe a prop master had purchased them online or found them in a junk bin somewhere. Beneath the last of the witch doctor items, at the very bottom of the crate, he found a scrap of cloth that made him smile as he pulled it out and brushed off the bits of straw that clung to it.

A leopard-skin loincloth, the only garment Jungo the Ape Man had ever worn in the films-all the better to show off his well-developed physique, of course. Walter tried to remember. According to the story, Jungo had killed a leopard with his bare hands when he was only five years old and had made the loincloth out of its pelt. Apparently, the loincloth had grown along with the boy. Maybe the leopard had been part Spandex... Jungo was probably the type of man Shirley would have fallen for-wild, tanned, brawny, and barely capable of stringing together three-word sentences. Walter groaned at the thought.

Now Desiree was another story entirely. Even on the big studio lot, they often crossed paths. He saw her in the commissary at lunch almost daily-because he timed his lunch hour to match hers. She was strikingly beautiful with her reddish-gold hair, her large blue eyes, her delicate chin, and when she smiled directly at him, as she had done three times now, it made him feel as if someone in the special effects shop had created the most spectacular sunrise ever.

But Walter still hadn't gotten up the nerve to ask if he could sit and eat with her. He was a nobody who did odd jobs around the lot for the various producers. Some of them were nice, and some of them were... like Chris Carmichael. The man was Dabney Coleman in 9 *to* 5, or Bill Murray before his transformation in *Scrooged*. Carmichael had put in a requisition, and Walter had pulled the card: One man needed to clear prop warehouse. It was really a job for four men and four days, but Carmichael always slashed his budgets to leave more money in his own expense account. Carmichael didn't even know who Walter Groves was.

But Desiree did. That was all that mattered.

He gazed at the leopard-skin loincloth, hearing Shirley's words ring in his head. "You aren't a man's man. You don't let yourself go wild." He sniffed, trying to picture himself in the role she seemed to want him to play. What if Desiree felt the same way? What if all women thought they wanted a nice man but were only attracted to bad boys?

He picked up the witch doctor's rattle and gave it a playful shake, then put it down by the mask and the shrunken head. Even though she had hurt him, he wasn't the type either to put a curse on Shirley, or to transform himself for her into a muscular hunk of beefcake like Jungo. He would have needed an awfully large special effects budget to pull that off. Walter held up the leopard-skin loincloth to his waist and considered the fashion statement it would make. It looked ridiculous-even more so in contrast with his work pants and his conservative window-pane plaid shirt.

"If I wore this, what would Desiree think?" Would it convince her that he was a wild man, or would she just think him pale-skinned and scrawny? All alone in the prop warehouse, he had no particular need to hurry up. Carmichael, who never noticed anyone's hard work, had already said that the props were junk.

Before he could change his mind and think sensibly, Walter unbuttoned his shirt and peeled it off. Taking a deep breath, he slipped off his shoes and trousers and tied on the loincloth. He surveyed the effect, looking critically at his skinny chest, thin arms, white skin, and the leopard-skin loincloth. He cast a skeptical glance at the witch doctor mask. "Exactly how did I expect this to bring out the wild man in me?"

Then something happened.

His heart began to pound like drumbeats in his ears. His skin grew hot and his blood hotter. He felt dizzy and then very, *very* sure of himself. The worries and confusion of his life seemed to float away like soap bubbles on the wind. His attention focused down to a single pinprick. Everything was so clear, so simple. He had worried too much, *thought* too much, suppressed all of his natural desires. He drew a deep breath, kept inhaling until his chest swelled. Then on impulse, he pounded on his proudly expanded chest. It felt good and right.

He didn't have to worry about the prop inventory or about Shirley. She had made a bad choice, and she was gone. He no longer needed to think of her. Outside the sun was bright. He was a man, and Desiree was a woman. Everything else was extraneous, a distraction. He was a hunter, and he knew his quarry. A real man relied on his instincts to tell him what to do.

He let out a warbling call, broadcasting a defiant challenge to anyone who might get in his way. Barefoot, he sprinted like a cheetah out of the prop warehouse and onto the lot. He had seen where Desiree worked. He knew where to find Chris Carmichael's trailer. His vision tunneled down to that one focus.

He streaked past the people working on various films. Someone made a cat-call, but most of the crews ignored him. Employees at Duro Studios were accustomed to seeing axe-murderers, Martians, barbarians, and monsters of all kinds.

Chris Carmichael's headquarters were in a dingy, gray-walled trailer on the far end of the east lot. The success of a producer's films earned him clout in the studios, and Carmichael 's track record had earned him this unobtrusive trailer and one secretary.

Desiree.

Walter yanked open the door and leaped in. He hadn't decided what to say or do next, but an ape-man took matters one step at a time. He reacted to situations, without planning in excruciating detail beforehand. Instead of startling Desiree at her keyboard and the producer on the phone, he blundered into a shocking scene that would have made his hackles rise if he'd had any. Carmichael stood with both hands planted on his desk, crouched like a predator ready to spring. Desiree shielded herself on the other side of the desk, trying to keep it, with its empty coffee mugs, framed pictures, and jumbled stacks of scripts, between herself and Carmichael.

He leered at her, moved to the left, and she shifted in the other direction. She was flushed and nervous. "Please, Mr. Carmichael. I'm not that kind of girl."

"Of course you are," he said. "If you didn't want to break into pictures, why would you work in a place like this? I can make you an extra in my next feature, *Horror in the Prop Warehouse.* Ten-second screen time minimum, but there's a price. You have to give me something." Now he circled to the right and she moved in the opposite direction.

"Please, don't do this. I don't want to file a complaint, but I'll call Security if I have to."

"You do that, and you'll never work in this town again."

Before she could reply, Walter let out a bestial roar. He wasn't sure exactly what happened. Seeing red, he acted on instinct and charged forward. He grabbed the producer by the back of his clean white collar, yanked him away from the desk, and spun him around. As he spluttered, Walter the ape-man landed a powerful roundhouse punch on his chin and knocked him backward into the chair he reserved for visiting actors.

Startled, Desiree gasped, but Walter was already on the move. He bounded over the desk, slipped an arm around her waist, and crashed through the screen of the trailer's open window, carrying his woman with him. The rest was a blur.

When he could think straight again-after the witch doctor's spell, or whatever it was wore off-he found himself on the rooftop of one of the back lot sets, sitting next to Desiree, his lips pressed against hers. With a start, he drew back. Her hair was rumpled, her cheeks flushed, and she wore an expression of surprise and amusement. "That was a bit unorthodox, Walter," she said, "but you were amazing. You saved me when I needed it most."

"What have I done?" Walter glanced down at the loincloth, flexed his sore knuckles, and knew with absolute certainty that he would soon die from embarrassment. He was sitting half-naked on a roof at work and had just made a complete fool of himself in front of a woman he had a genuine crush on. "I'm sorry. I'm sorry!" He scuttled backward, stood to look for a ladder or stairs, and quickly found an exit. "I didn't mean to hurt you. Mr. Carmichael's going to get me fired, for sure."

"Who, Chris? He has no clue who you are," she said. "Anyway, I'm going to hand in my own resignation. I've had enough of that man."

"I... I need to put something decent on. I can't understand what got into me." He felt his cheeks burning. His legs wobbled, and his knees threatened to knock together. Some ape-man!

Before Desiree could say anything more, he bolted, cringing at the thought that someone else might see him this way—that Desiree *had* seen him. He was sure Jungo never had days like this.

~~*~*

By the time he got home, Walter was consumed with guilt. He felt flustered, exposed, and too embarrassed for words. He couldn't believe what he had done, prancing around the lot in nothing more than a loincloth, crashing into the producer's trailer offices. He had punched out Chris Carmichael! Then, after jumping through a window with Desiree, he had somehow whisked her off to a rooftop and *kissed her*! He was the very definition of the word "mortified." To make matters worse, Walter had gotten dressed again, called in a friend to finish clearing out the warehouse, then slunk off the lot, taking Jungo's loincloth with him. He could justify this, since Carmichael had made it clear that the props could be thrown into a dumpster.

He sat miserably in his empty apartment—without Shirley—and wondered how he could possibly make it up to Desiree. He didn't much care about Chris Carmichael. The man was a cad, but Walter himself had stolen a kiss from Desiree, practically ravished her! Considering the power the loincloth had worked on him, he could easily have gotten carried away. In the process of saving Desiree, he had proved that he was no better than that jerk of a producer.

And Walter had just left her stranded there, on the roof of the movie set. No, no, that wasn't Walter Groves. That wasn't who he really was. Though he wanted nothing more than to crawl under a rock, he knew what he had to do for the sake of honor. He had to go find Desiree and beg her forgiveness.

For a long time he stood in the shower under a pounding stream of hot water, rehearsing what to say until he knew he couldn't put it off any longer. Every moment he avoided her was another moment she could think terrible things about him. He dried his hair, dabbed on some aftershave, and put on his best dress slacks, a clean shirt, and a striped blue necktie. This was going to be a formal apology, and he wanted to look his best. Pulling on his nicest, though rarely worn, sport jacket, he rolled up Jungo's loincloth and stuffed it into the pocket. Though it didn't make any sense, he would try to tell Desiree what had happened, explain how the magic had changed him somehow into a wild man, someone he wouldn't normally be.

After dialing information, then searching on the Internet, he tracked down a local street address for D. Drea. He knew it had to be her. Gathering his resolve, he marched out to go face her. He didn't need the crutch of a loincloth or some imaginary witch doctor's spells to give him courage to do the right thing. He would do this himself.

On the way to her apartment, he didn't let himself think, forcing himself onward before the shame could make him turn back. He had to be like Michael Douglas in *Romancing the Stone*, not Rick Moranis in *Little Shop of Horrors*. Nothing should disrupt the apology. Leaving his cell phone in the car, he walked to the door of her apartment, raised his hand to knock, then hesitated. He wasn't thinking clearly. He really should have brought flowers and a card. Why not go to a store now, buy them, and then come back?

He heard shouts coming from the other side of the door, followed by a scream—Desiree's scream!

He froze in terror. What should he do? Desiree was in trouble. Maybe he should run back outside, get his cell phone and call 911. He could bring the police here, or, better yet, pound on her neighbors' doors and find someone who was big and strong. She screamed again, and Walter knew there could be only one solution. He tried the knob, found the door unlocked, and barged in. He found Chris Carmichael already there, reeking of cheap cologne and bourbon.

"Leave me alone," Desiree said. She held a lamp in one hand, brandishing it like a club.

Carmichael let out an evil chuckle. "Now that you no longer work for me, we can have any sort of relationship I want. There are no ethical problems."

She raised the lamp higher. Walter stepped forward, outraged but quailing at the idea of a fight. When Desiree saw him, her eyes lit up.

Carmichael turned.

Walter blurted, "Hey, what—what's going on here?" He wished he could hide or, at the very least, run back out of the apartment and return to do a second take of the scene. He needed to be a tough guy, like Dirty Harry in *Sudden Impact*—"Go ahead, make my day"—and the best he could come up with was a Don Knotts-worthy, "Hey, what's going on here?" He groaned.

Carmichael recognized him, and his eyes grew stormy. Ignoring Desiree for the moment, the larger man lurched toward Walter, grabbed him by the shirt, yanked his tie, and drew Walter closer to him. "You're that little freak that sucker-punched me in my office, aren't you? Where's the spotted underwear?"

"I—I—I don't need it."

"You'll need an ambulance is what you'll need."

Indiana Jones would have done something different. He would have punched the villain, starting an all-out brawl, but as Carmichael lifted him and twisted his tie, he could only make a small "meep" sound.

"You put him down," Desiree cried, and Walter's heart lurched. She was actually defending him!

Carmichael laughed again. "You can't even save yourself. How do you expect to help this mouse?" He pushed Walter up against the wall, clenched his fist, and drew back his arm, as if cocking a shotgun.

Walter was sure his head would go straight through the drywall. "Wait. Wait, please." He swallowed and drew a deep breath. "If you're going to do this, let me face it like a man. I… I'd like to use the rest-room, please."

Carmichael blinked, then gave him a knowing smile. "Oh, afraid you're going to wet yourself, eh?" He let Walter slump to the floor. "Sure. Why not? Desiree and I were just enjoying an intimate conversation. We can wait."

He glared at her, and she sat down on the sofa, not sure what to do. Walter scurried into the bathroom and closed the door, his mind spinning. Maybe Desiree kept a gun in the bathroom, perhaps taped behind the toilet tank, like in *Godfather*. But he found nothing there, and a quick search of the drawers and the medicine cabinet revealed no other weapons he could use to save the day.

He stuck his hands in his jacket pockets and his fingers brushed a patch of sleek fur. The loincloth. It was his only chance.

Walter burst out of the bathroom wearing nothing but the scrap of leopard-skin. Barefoot and barechested. His mind filled with the thoughts of a hunter. Testosterone and adrenaline pumped through his veins, and he let out a wild yell, pounding on his chest. His hair was a mess, his eyes on fire. Seeing his enemy, the producer, he lunged toward him like a hungry lion attacking a springbok. Walter felt total confidence and did not hesitate.

Chris Carmichael, who used his position of perceived power to intimidate people, faltered. When he saw Walter leap toward him, he suddenly reconsidered what he'd been about to do.

Walter let out another roar. His lungs seemed to have twice their normal capacity. "*My* woman!"

Carmichael had probably never been challenged before. A producer, even a bad producer of second-rate movies, could boss people around in Hollywood. But Walter the ape-man, wearing nothing but his loincloth in Desiree's apartment, had no doubt that he himself was king of the jungle. Carmichael turned, took several steps in retreat, then paused. Through his hunter-focused gaze, Walter watched his prey, preparing to throw himself on the man if he made a move in the wrong direction.

Desiree decided for both men, though. As Carmichael started to turn back, she lifted her lamp, and smashed it on his head. He crumpled to the carpet like King Kong falling off the Empire State Building. The rush in Walter's mind drained away, and he found himself standing naked in Desiree's apartment, except for the ape-man's loincloth. He shivered, and goose bumps appeared on his arms. "What did I do this time?" he said, looking down at the producer with dismay.

But Desiree was close to him. Very close and very beautiful. "You protected me, Walter. You saved me." She slid her arms around his waist and gave him a hug. "You're my hero."

It was not the magic of the loincloth that made his heart start pounding again. "You—you don't mind?" he asked in surprise.

"I'll show you how much I mind in just a minute." She stepped away and looked down at the unconscious Carmichael. "But first, help me take out the garbage. We'll put him in the hall and call the police." Walter and Desiree rolled the man like a skid row drunk into the apartment hallway.

Desiree closed the door, locked it, and turned to face him. Suddenly he felt as if he were the prey and she the hungry lioness.

He gulped. "I'm really a nice guy most of the time. But I can be bad, if I need to be."

"Walter, I *like* that you're a nice guy. It's the first thing I noticed about you, even from a distance. You may not have known I was watching, but I've seen you hold doors for other people, help them carry things when their arms were full, lend them lunch money, listen to what they say. Most of the time, that's exactly what women want. It's what *I* want. But women are... complex creatures. So once in a while we also like a bit of a wild man. You seem like the best of both worlds to me."

"You may never be safe," he pointed out. "What if Mr. Carmichael comes back? I don't think he'll leave you alone."

With a lovely smile, she led him to the couch and sat him down. "In that case, maybe you'll just have to stay here to protect me."

There was a stirring in the loincloth, and he felt very self-conscious. "Maybe I should get dressed in real clothes."

"No, Walter. You stay just the way you are." Desiree leaned over to kiss him.

KYLE AISTEACH is a writer, blogger, and educator based in Fresno, California. His work has previously been seen in *Cosmos Magazine, Digital Science Fiction, Emerald Sky, Stupefying Stories,* and in various anthologies. At 6'4" and 260 pounds, Kyle Aisteach is one of the biggest authors in this anthology.

For more information please visit his site:
www.aisteach.com

MAN OF WATER
Kyle Aisteach

iraquae—

I should start at the beginning…

Please forgive me if I'm confused. I've been running for my life for the past three days. At least, I think it was three days ago. Time seems unreal to me now.

My name is Baxter Small. Congressman Small. Former Congressman Small. I had fallen asleep on the sofa. I don't know what woke me, but it was just in time. A man in a Special Forces uniform crept across my living room, knife in hand.

Two tours in a war zone. The instincts are still there. I kicked the coffee table. Three meals' worth of china rattled. The soldier hesitated long enough for me to dash for the door.

As I reached the footpath across the street, I heard my burglar alarm go off belatedly. I ran—well, trotted—at my age I don't run so much anymore—toward downtown. There's an all-night coffeehouse about a mile from my house, and I kept the best pace my old frame would allow all the way there.

That late at night, only a few die-hard denizens were present. I sat down with my back against the wall of amateur art, and I thought about what to do next.

A young woman—dressed in black, with pale skin and too many piercings—moved over to me. "You're Congressman Small, aren't you?" she asked.

"Former Congressman," I said. "I'm a private citizen these days."

"Oh, yeah, I heard that." She sat down across the small table from me without waiting to be invited.

I considered the implications of my burglar alarm going off only after I had made it clear across the street. That meant the soldier had gotten in without tripping it.

"So, what are you doing now? Are you a lobbyist or something?" the young woman asked.

I had seen the soldier before, I recalled. And it made staying awake a priority. I looked at my uninvited companion, glad to have her stimulus. "No," I said. "I'm retired now."

Viraquae—literally *man of water* in Latin. The soldier was the CIA's viraquae. When I was on the Armed Services Committee I had spent some time with the handlers while we were considering their budget. I had seen that Special Forces soldier then. It was a form the viraquae frequently took when it was responding to one particular trainer. They change form based on who is around, based on what the greater need is.

Fascinating creatures, viraquaes, when they're not trying to kill you.

"Oh, well, I heard a lot of politicians do that when their careers end," my young companion said to the ceiling. "A sort of a safety net."

Most people have met a viraquae at some point, only not realized it. They're that stranger who was there for you. Just the right person at just the right time. The one who you always wished you could find to thank.

Most viraquaes aren't captive, and aren't trained killers. The CIA's is the only domesticated one I know of.

"Most politicians aren't hurting for money," I said, glancing around the coffeehouse. The more people around me the better. Viraquaes are weak in crowds. They're empathic. Crowds pull them in too many directions.

"It's got to be hell, you know," the young woman said, "working your whole life like that, only to lose it all in one election."

"It's the nature of the job," I said. After all these years, they had actually sent the viraquae after me.

"I hope your family's supportive," the young woman said. "Mine're a bunch of freaks."

I felt myself twinge. I hadn't really been paying attention as my new friend had drifted into dangerously personal matters. "Oh, right," she said. "I remember now. I read about your divorce."

I had one advantage that most other people don't have. I know what a viraquae is. The one the government owns had been captured after World War II, and was generally used in places where there was no jurisdiction or where it was important to leave no evidence. But as long as I was awake and the handler wasn't nearby, my own needs would confuse the viraquae if it got near me. It would take the form that I needed, not the form the handler needed.

The young woman leaned forward and spoke quietly. "Look, if you'd like, I've got some stuff that really helps with the pain."

It took me a few seconds to figure out what she meant. And then I laughed. I could just see the headlines: *Former Congressman Overdoses.* "No, thank you," I said.

The young woman twisted in her seat. "What's a budget clearing account?"

It was an odd question. I wondered what they were including in those blog things that her generation seemed to get its news from. "It's an account used to hold money temporarily. When a payment is supposed to go out, but there's nowhere for it to go, it moves into a BCA," I explained. "Or if a payment comes in and it's not clear what budget it belongs to, same thing. Makes the accounting easier." It also makes it easier to make money vanish in the shell game.

She tipped her head toward the back of the coffeehouse, arching her body over the arm of her chair. "Where is the money?"

A calm dread came over me as I realized.

I looked the young woman directly in the eye. "I never had it. Tell your trainer to check with the taxpayers."

"What?" she—no—it said.

German is the language of choice for handling the trained viraquae. On the several tours through the training facility I had learned the command to send it back to its jar. "Geh zu d'Haus!"

The young woman melted into a clear puddle. It flowed over the velveteen seat cushion without wetting it, and then slithered toward the restrooms in the rear of the coffeehouse.

No one else seemed to have noticed. I stood up and headed out the front door.

Almost on instinct, I went to the homeless shelter. Hundreds of people, all with terrible needs. Even the best trainer wouldn't have been able to keep the viraquae focused. I spent the night there, trying to ignore the smell of urine and the screams of my fellow humans.

The next afternoon I decided to risk going to my financial planner's office. She set me up with some traveling money, and I signed everything else over to the homeless shelter. And then I caught the next bus south. We drove all night. I even got some sleep—about thirty people on the bus, none trying to get close to me.

The next day I found myself in a dirty part of a town near the Mexican border. Prostitutes walked the streets. On nearly every corner, money openly changed hands for drugs. A graffiti artist spray-painted the door of an abandoned car. And there I was, a disheveled old man walking the streets like I belonged there.

The first gunshot sent me diving for the nearest door—veteran's instinct—my rational mind screaming at me that it was just a backfire. The fourth shot shattered the window on the other side of the door, and I belatedly realized the instinct had saved my life.

Everyone else on the street had taken cover, too. One of the drug dealers, hiding behind the abandoned car, had drawn a weapon of his own, but looked around confusedly, not sure where the shots had come from.

A husky voice came from behind me. "Jesus Christ! What're they shootin' at you for?"

I hadn't noticed the woman in the doorway when I dove in. She stood taller than me in her stiletto heels, and she wore so much makeup that the foundation cracked and sank into the lines on her face. Her outfit barely qualified as lingerie. "Begging your pardon, ma'am," I said.

"You can't be on the street," she said. "It ain't safe. Here, this is my buildin'. You better come up."

"No really," I said. "I'm safer on the streets." Again the headlines flashed in front of me. *Former Congressman Shot With Prostitute.*

"You talk sense, now, grandpa, you comin' up," she said, peeking out of the doorway once to check the street. She grabbed my wrist and dragged me up a steep, dark stairway.

We entered her apartment through a kitchenette with a water closet standing in the corner. She had just one room, with a double bed on the far wall and a lot of knickknacks cluttering the counter and hung on the walls. "Now who's out there shootin' at you?" she asked.

"Just some old friends," I said.

She moved to the wall by the bed and looked out the window as she asked, "What'd you do?"

I wasn't quite sure how to answer that. The truth was that I had returned something that they had stolen. The truth was that not every police jurisdiction thinks the government is above the law. I finally settled on, "Played their game for 25 years, and then decided to play my own."

She stepped back into the kitchenette and took a glass out of the drying rack. The old plumbing creaked and groaned as a trickle of water drained out of the faucet and filled it. She brought it to me. "You can stay here. You seem nice."

I smiled politely and took a drink. As a politician it was always more important to seem nice than to be nice.

She glanced out the window again, and began to fidget.

I was alone with her. Just the right person at just the right time. And it was between me and the door.

I folded my arms and kept my tone pleasant as I asked, "Wondering where your trainer is?"

Her jaw went slack. "Huh?"

"Geh zu d'Haus!"

She melted, but re-formed almost instantly.

In retrospect, I realize the plan was ideal. The trainer fires off a few shots in the street—he may even have been the drug dealer I saw—and the viraquae and I are instinctively drawn to each other. It probably wouldn't move on me while I was interacting with it, but once I fell asleep...

The viraquae took two steps toward me.

I focused my mind, the way they taught me to in those acting classes I took when I was planning my first run for city council. "Would you like me to tell you what I really, really need?"

The viraquae stopped, staring at me.

"What I really, really need," I said, "is to see reality, quite clearly."

I could feel my heart pounding as I waited. I concentrated. If I needed something more than the handler needed me dead...

Finally, the viraquae melted. And so did most of the decor in the tiny room. Only a small crucifix adorned the wall. I had never realized they could affect an environment, too.

Whoever actually lived here was a meticulous housekeeper. I carefully stepped around the viraquae. It squirmed on the floor like a giant amoeba.

"I don't know if you can understand me in that state," I said as I started to wash my glass, "but I fully intend to disappear. To never be a problem again. To live my life in some foreign land and never again strive to change the world."

I put my glass back in the drying rack and looked around. The viraquae pulled itself up a bit before settling back down into a blob.

"Confusing, isn't it?" I said. "Not knowing what you're supposed to be, not knowing how to be yourself." I pulled the cash I was carrying out of my pocket and left it on the table. "I'm going to leave now. What I really, really need is for you to stay here for at least 48 hours. I suspect whoever lives here needs something."

I stepped out into the hallway, locking the door behind myself—not that doing so would actually slow down a viraquae, but it might stop the handler from undoing my suggestions.

The back door of the building led out into an alley. I marched toward the sun as fast as I could go. Midday. Toward the sun is south at midday.

And I walked. Clear out of town and into the desert, remarking the whole time on the viraquae's odd choice of forms when interacting with me.

I hadn't brought any water, and even in the winter the sun baked me dry. It is winter now, isn't it? The sun set quickly enough, but on foot, I couldn't be confident I was moving fast enough to bed down safely. It had caught up with me at the coffeehouse almost immediately.

I saw a campfire. As I approached, voices carried toward me. I made out a group of about two dozen men around it, probably illegal immigrants making their way north, though the campfire was a risky move if that was the case.

I'm sure I looked like a viraquae to them—a mysterious old man appearing out of the blackness into the firelight. One spoke excellent English, and when I explained that I was heading south, they happily offered me a share of their food and water.

My Spanish is extremely limited, but even so the conversation was pleasant. I lay down against a large rock and watched the fire for some time.

After a while the English speaker leaned over to me and spoke in a voice that sounded like he was about to start a ghost story. "What do you know about viraquaes?"

I looked around. The rest of the group had gone quiet and studied us as though they could suddenly understand.

"More than most," I said. "If you've heard of them, you know more than most."

The whole group sat in rapt attention. The English speaker crossed his hands on his knees. "Do you know where they come from?"

"There are a lot of theories," I said, sitting up. "Why? Are you a viraquae?"

He half smiled as he spoke. "If I was, I would not know it."

"No, I guess you wouldn't," I admitted.

"I would be whatever I was," he said. "I would believe that I am me. My memories real. My body real. And I would not be able to tell you where I come from."

I nodded, and noticed that several of the others were nodding, too. "I suppose," I said, "that if I really needed to know, maybe you'd be able to tell me then."

"Is possible," he said, leaning back and looking up at the sky.

"Geh zu d'Haus!"

He smiled broadly. "They say they come from the stars," he said. "They say they are angels. You know what I say? I say they are men like you."

I couldn't help but laugh a little, even as I surveyed the blackness for an escape. "I'm no viraquae."

"Not yet," he said ominously. All eyes were still on me. "But you might be."

"Viraquaes live to be helpful," I said. "I'm afraid that I've spent my life being anything but useful."

He stood up and leaned over me. "You, in your heart, you want to serve. That is why you became a politician."

"I became a politician as popularity contest," I said matter-of-factly.

He spoke gently. "Then why do they send a viraquae to kill you?"

I hadn't mentioned that fact. "Obviously, I don't know enough about viraquaes," I said. I knew I should try to run, but alone, in the desert...

"Do you know your choices?" he said.

I tried to sound confident—to feel confident. "Yes."

"No," he said and raised himself up to his full height—only about five feet. He held out his hand. "You can choose to be one of us. We were men once. Men who left our bodies to serve. Men like our captive brother who hunts you. Baxter Small, you can be a viraquae."

I found myself unable to respond for a long time. It felt like my body resonated. "Is this a setup?"

He smiled. "Yes."

And it was a good one. I looked directly at him and spoke as carefully as I could. "Haven't we tried this once before? My will is too strong for you to kill me directly. Servant of two masters. So you have to convince me to just give up, or be close to me when I let my guard down."

"Not us," he said. "If you say no, we help you go to Mexico. But, Baxter Small, you can live forever. You can help forever."

I looked around. One by one, the other men in the group melted into individual viraquaes. The fire vanished. In the light of a quarter moon I could just make out the one last silhouette. "Baxter Small, what is your need?"

And all at once, I understood. And it was what I wanted.

And in that moment, I felt myself melt.

My body lay against the rock, motionless. And in a thousand directions, I could feel the call of people who needed me.

My name is Baxter Small.

You can find my remains in the desert north of the Mexican border.

But somehow, I knew you needed to hear my story.

I can't stay, though. Someone else needs me. And I have to flow away now.

PART V:

Weird Fantasy

A former US Marine and ex SoCal police officer, MICHAEL EZELL lives in California with his wife and two sons. Michael's work appears in *Stupefying Stories'* Weird Wild West edition, and two additional anthologies: *I, Automaton* and *Girl at the End of the World*.

BONES OF A RIGHTEOUS MAN
Michael Ezell

– Has the life of a righteous man been taken?
– We find that it has, Excellency.
– And what shall become of the killer?
– He shall carry the bones of the righteous man until their weight does cause his death.

~~*~*

he setting sun reflected in a million rose-hued sparkles across the surface of the Glass Desert. The slit in Traveler's eyeshades cut everything down to a thin panorama. A glittering expanse of heat glass, marked only by the crushed tracks of the Apostates' road. In those tracks travelled the wagon he'd been following for days. Weeks, really. With a start, he realized it was more like months. Wasn't it?

Through the shimmer to his right, he saw either a town, or a mirage that would lead him astray, wasting precious time.

Bands of red and purple from the western sky reflected in the glass to his left. Not long till dark. A man could wander off course at night out there. Wander into the ruptured plates of glass in the deep desert, where a simple trip and fall could easily mean decapitation, or at the least, the loss of some fingers.

Given the options, he'd take the mirage.

~~*~*

There were at least forty rough timber buildings dominated by the high rock walls of a Foundation Church. An impressive settlement this far out. Fortunately for folks so close to the Glass Desert, the Apostates considered the Foundation a group of silly children. That's the only reason that rock-walled behemoth of a church wasn't rubble and dust right now.

The shimmer he'd seen came not from heat waves, but from an immense salt lake behind the town. A foul wind off the dead water carried the steady *ka-chunk ka-chunk* of a steam machine.

Though he knew they were there, as certain as his own ribs were, Traveler still patted the pistols under his cloak. People with technology this far from the Known would have made a deal with someone powerful to acquire it. And those deals were not always written in ink.

He looked for signs of wagon tracks coming from the deep glass into this town, but saw none. Not Apostates, then. Who else would give these people a steam engine? And more's the worry, what could they possibly have to trade for it?

For a long moment, he just stood, his black journey cloak making him a twin of his shadow. Something about the foul wind told him this was not a place to rest his soul. But he'd been awake for days, or weeks,

285

or possibly months. And the straps of his burden weighed heavy on his shoulders.

He entered the town at the farthest point from the water and followed the steam engine's sound.

The few people he saw on the street openly stared. With his journey cloak, floppy hat, face covered by a breathing cloth, and his eyeshades, he probably looked like Carnon the Death Angel to them.

They all dressed in flowing lines and bright colors like Elites from the Known. Desert rubes trying to imitate the moneyed folk.

A boy of about twelve walked right up, his curiosity pure and without malice. His mother made weak noises of protest, but she was too afraid to come after him.

"Say, Mister, did you come outta the Glass Desert?"

"I suppose I did. You get many folks from there?" He hadn't spoken in so long, the words came out a little ragged around the edges.

"Nope. The Traders come across the water. We don't get no visitors from the desert side. Momma says the wagon-riders don't like folks who truck with the Traders. Say, is that a real journey cloak?"

"It is. You know about these?"

"Well, sure. Pastor Gilliam says when a man has to pay a penance, the Church gives him a journey cloak and sets him to walking."

Traveler unhooked his breathing cloth and worked up enough moisture to spit in the dirt.

"My cloak don't come from the Church, kid; I don't truck with *them*. Beg pardon, but can I ask you a question now? What sort of machine is that I hear?"

"Oh, that's the desalva- er, desaler- something that takes the salt from the water so you can drink it."

"Well, ain't that somethin'? All the way out here in the Wilds."

The boy reached out to touch the journey cloak and his sleeve fell away from a pale, bony wrist. A brand stood out on the tender skin. The scar was old. But how could that be? For a boy this age to have a scar that old—No. He was mistaken.

"That's a strange scrape on your wrist there."

The boy's hand dropped immediately.

"Oh, it's nothing. When I was small, I burned myself by accident on my mother's cooking stove."

Traveler felt the eyes on him now. Not curious, but hostile. The adults were clearly afraid to speak outright. They glared their reproach at the mother and she dashed into the street to grab the boy.

"Come now, we must go." She said.

The boy waved goodbye from behind her skirts and Traveler smiled for the first time—in how long? His life, it seemed.

Standing still reminded him of the throbbing in his feet. They longed to be out of his heavy boots and propped up high for a few hours.

Raucous laughter from inside a building down the street caught his attention. He followed this new sound through the middle of the town proper. Aside from the massive church, no structure taller than two stories, all made of solid timber that was never meant to know a desert like this.

When he reached the source of the merriment, Traveler saw a weathered sign over the door. The hand-painted symbol came from the Old Language. It meant food, board, and companionship were available here.

He entered and ignored the stares he already expected. He stepped up to the highly polished bar and removed his eyeshades. The bar and the thick oak tables occupied by the ten or twelve townies meant these folks had quite a deal going with the "Traders," whoever they were.

A stout man with long whiskers on the point of his chin stood behind the bar. "Help you, Mister?"

"Sign outside says food and lodge. I'll take both."

The dull thud of a gold coin on the bar made everyone relax. Food appeared, along with a beer that was weak, but passable. Some sort of vegetable stew, spiced with peppers and Terpin flowers, which definitely didn't grow here. He hadn't seen any sign of crops being fed with their purified water, so they must trade for every scrap of food.

As quick as the food was on the bar, a woman was at his elbow. Pale breasts rode high in the neckline of a dress you'd normally see on a saloon girl back in the Known.

"Care for some company, Mister?"

"Nope."

Her false smiled died, leaving only the hard glitter in her eyes. "Won't cost you much more than that meal."

"From the looks of your sallow skin, it'd stay with me longer, I suspect."

Now the room grew quiet again.

Did they think him a damn fool? Maybe dressing like Elites made them believe he was the rube here. A woman with the Mark was never hard to spot. Once you knew what to look for.

"What did you say, you son of a bitch?"

"Your skin. And the tinge of red around the color of your eyes. I'm no fool, woman."

"Bastard!" She shoved Traveler hard and the leather pack on his back hit the bar. Her hands were clawed to go for his eyes, but she stopped short when she heard the dry rattle from the pack. Open fear replaced the hardness in her eyes and she backed away from him.

A man near the far wall stood in the silence. He also carried whiskers on the point of his chin, but his were white, with beads of desert glass woven into them.

"I am Pastor Gilliam, the spiritual leader of this town. May I ask what you carry, sir?"

"You may."

A long silence followed while Traveler spooned the rest of the vegetable stew into his mouth. No need to let it go to waste. It was already clear that he wouldn't be given sleep here, and he needed the meal. He wiped his lips on a sleeve and downed the weak beer.

A barrel-chested man stood and slapped a long cudgel in his palm. "What the good Pastor means to say is, what exactly do you carry, desert rat?"

Bound by the spell of his journey, Traveler sighed. He swung the pack onto the bar and the movement opened his journey cloak, revealing the twin-barreled wheel-lock pistols.

He heard the metallic *click-clock* from the back of the room. Two men in opposite corners, each armed with a wheel-lock rifle. He marked them as dead and felt the hollow guilt in the pit of his stomach.

Tired. So tired. This journey had no end; the man running from him was only a spirit that lived in his mind. But he was bound. They asked and he had to tell.

"I carry the bones of a righteous man."

Shouts and screams—The good Pastor called on his riflemen.

Might as well try to out-strike a desert rattler.

The pistols appeared as if called to his hands, the left locks already cocked, according to the rules of the journey. At the rough bark of the guns, the two riflemen men fell like string-cut puppets.

Motion from the left made him twitch to the side, narrowly escaping the crossbow bolt that buried itself in the doorframe.

His last two shots took the bowman and the chin-whiskered bartender, who suddenly appeared with a black sword in his hand. Traveler had a fleeting thought that he'd never seen material like that blade, and then stars burst into his vision as the cudgel laid his scalp open to the bone.

He fell hard, dragging the leather pack below the bar with him. He used his legs to fend them off as best he could. He heard a couple of knees pop under his walking boots, but they just kept coming at him, swinging wild, clipping him now and again. One eye swelled shut and he felt his consciousness slipping away.

The whore leaned in and spit in his face. "Now you're the low one, ain't ya?"

The man with the cudgel caught him good in the ribs and Traveler knew he'd die on the floor of this inn.

Not if the pack is opened.

"Stop! Leave it be." He begged the voice in his head as much as the people beating him. But the people just laughed and continued. As his vision went dark, Traveler felt hands grab at the pack.

"Stoke the furnace in the smithy!" Pastor Gilliam shouted.

"No!" Traveler clutched the pack tight to his chest. Like a burrowing animal with a mind of its own, his right hand crept inside. His body took the punishment while his fingers slid over the dry bones, landing finally on a tiny one. Felt like a toe bone.

When he pulled the bone into view, he heard a high-pitched scream. Hard to tell if it was a woman or man.

The white symbols written on the yellowed bone seemed to force his mouth open as he read the ancient word aloud.

The word didn't rush across his vocal chords with the wind of his lungs; rather it crept out, like a vile toad, and hopped from his lips bristling with warts and disease.

They reeled back from him, already screaming and trying to claw the burning from their skin.

The man who split Traveler's scalp with the cudgel swallowed his tongue and fell dead on the spot. A throbbing power filled the air with a *whum-whum-whum* sensation. The desert-glass windows exploded outward, whirling scimitars of glazed sand slashing random people on the street.

Searing fire on his scalp as his wound healed over, and Traveler vomited his hard-won meal on the polished wood floor. Still dizzy, he forced himself to stand and gather his belongings.

Pastor Gilliam lay on the hardwood planks, his eyes as dead as the glass beads in his whiskers. The prostitute had her back to the wall, shivering with fear.

"P-please... don't kill me." She whispered.

"Woman, I'm truly sorry. That's all I can offer."

The spreading blood on her skirt registered on her and she saw the puddle on the floor. Her screams accompanied Traveler into the street.

People ran from him, leaving those wounded by the exploding windows to fend for themselves. His scalp blazed with pain and his tongue felt like someone stuffed a sock full of sand in his mouth.

But he traveled on. That was his task. Like all the other places he'd been on his journey, he'd get no sleep here tonight.

~~*~*

Shuffling through crushed glass powder in the tracks of the steam wagon again. He should have known better than to stop, should have just stilled his growling belly and kept moving.

Not long after sunrise, he thought he heard the ghosts of dead townsfolk treading through the powder behind him, but when he turned he only saw the wavering form of a lone person in the distance. Small. The boy he'd spoken to in the street.

It took most of the morning for the boy's short little legs to catch up, but they did. Traveler wondered at the lad's determination.

Finally, when he heard the boy panting not two steps behind, he spun with his pistols in hand.

"What do you want, boy?"

The boy didn't flinch, didn't back away. He just gulped dry desert air in an effort to catch his breath, and held up his wrist. The strange brand stood out on his pale skin. A double-helix design Traveler had seen before, in a book back in the Known. But this one had a star at one end.

"Well? What's this to me?"

"It's the mark of the Traders." The boy said.

He swung a small pack off his shoulders and retrieved a skin of water. He took a long, healthy pull and offered some to Traveler, who took a polite sip. Rude to turn down any hospitality in the desert. But he handed it right back to the boy. Might give him an extra day or two out here.

"So? The mark of the Traders."

"It's put on certain kids when they're little. The Traders pick which ones. I dunno why."

"Pick? Pick for what?"

The boy looked up at him with hollow eyes. "When those with the mark are sixteen, they're given to the Traders. Nobody knows, or says, why. That's just the deal the oldsters struck to be rich out here, and safe."

"They would throw their own children away for that?"

The boy shrugged. "Pastor Gilliam says— *said* that we're like the son of Ehai, offered up as a sacrifice for the good of many."

"So why are you followin' me?"

"I don't wanna be a sacrifice. For nobody. I'd rather travel with a warlock than do that, so you can cast what spells you will."

Beneath his breathing cloth, Traveler smiled. Kid had a backbone, that was for certain.

He travelled on and the kid followed without invitation.

"What makes you think I'm a warlock?"

"Folks say you killed everyone with a spell in the tavern."

"Not exactly. I just said its name. That's all."

"Pastor Gilliam says—*said* that we should always burn the dead, 'cause angels can be captured in human bones by people with evil purpose."

Traveler studied on that for a while as the two walked along in the crushed track of the steam wagon that was days, weeks, or months ahead of him.

"I wouldn't say that the things inside these bones are angels, and it ain't as simple as Pastor Gilliam made it out to be. The deed's got to be done by a strong witch back in the grand temples of the Known. And the bones have to be those of a righteous man."

"Why a witch? Can't you do it?"

The rich baritone laugh felt like poison being spewed from a festering wound. It emptied Traveler of the ugliness from the town.

"Believe me, son, I'm no warlock. In fact, some say there are none. They say only a woman can trap the life-force these bones hold, 'cause only a woman carries a life inside her."

"Okay."

After that, the boy said nothing for hours. They walked in silence until they heard music drifting on the dry air.

~~*~*

The long, twisted finger of sand ran in from the north, widening into a natural road as it went back toward its origin, showing that even the great Glass Desert can die and be reclaimed.

They watched the gypsy camp from far enough away that the people looked like shivering shadow puppets through the heat waves. Of course, they would already know Traveler was here. But he'd have no trouble from them. These bones would be the last thing they'd want to see.

Maybe he could ask them to take the boy. Their bands sometimes took in orphans. The boy would certainly be safer with them. Once he caught up with the man he pursued, there would be bloodshed. All around.

The gypsy men were waiting when the two traveling companions arrived. Casual enough, but with hands close to ornate knife hilts. One of them, the tallest, had an ancient flintlock pistol in his belt, the checkering on the grip worn nearly smooth by generations of gypsy hands before him.

He was the one who spoke. "I see by your cloak that you Travel. Will you not rest here for the night?"

Gypsy hospitality was well known, despite some old fairy tales about them stealing kidlets and such. But something about them being this far into the Glass Desert felt wrong.

His silence might be considered rude in a few more seconds.

"I hope to, friend."

The taller man smiled and waved a welcoming hand toward the small camp. Two steam wagons that doubled as living quarters for the women, and two tents staked into the sand for the men.

They shared dried dates, some hard cheese, and a wonderful stew made from mushrooms and a fat hare.

The fire burned down low and the stars wheeled overhead. The eldest male, an oldster with wispy white hair, told the tale of the Stone of God. Being raised in the Foundation Church, the boy had of course never heard this before.

He hung on every word about the world-sized rock that passed by the Irth eons ago. How it dipped just its very tip into the air of our world right on this spot, burning the sky and creating the Glass Desert. Entire oceans were moved by its pull, and newborn mountains shrugged off cities like so many fleas. And then the Stone of God flew on. Into the black. Destined to someday circle back and do us proper next time.

A peppering of questions from the boy made the wizened gypsy laugh, and he started the story over again, explaining how each part came to pass.

The jovial mood didn't touch the eyes of the other gypsies, and that wasn't lost on Traveler. He found his gaze drawn repeatedly back to a young woman, maybe twenty. She sat in the door of one of the wagons, a tiny cloth bundle on her lap. An older woman tried to feed her, but the girl would only stare at the ground. The firelight was bright enough to pick out each glittering tear as it dropped from her face to the sand.

They had to be relatives, given the similar wide noses and the green eyes. They spoke with a brogue that tasted of the far North, which only added to the wrongness of seeing them here. Best to be direct about it, even if it meant he would find no rest once again.

"I've not seen the sand this far into the Glass Desert. May I ask what brought you all the way out here?"

The conversation stopped. Not in a hostile way, but with a heavy sadness as each looked to the elder. Finally, the old man spoke.

"We have followed the red star from our homeland. When someone dies, if a red star appears, our people believe we will be reunited with the soul of our loved one if we follow it."

"And has it ever worked?"

"I have only seen a red star once before. And we ran out of land before we could sleep beneath it."

All their eyes drifted upward and Traveler looked, knowing but not wanting to know.

A red star hung above them. Feeble and faint, but clear enough beside all its burning white brethren.

His lips felt numb, but he heard his own voice say, "Who has died?"

"My child."

They all flinched. She'd walked up behind them quiet as a cat. She still held the bundle in her arms.

One of the women tried to hush the girl and take her back to the wagon, but she would not be moved. She stared into Traveler's eyes and right on through him.

"His father was taken from me by a fever when I became with child. He was born never knowing a father, and now I will never know my son."

"My lady, please know my heart aches for you. Ain't right, what happens in this life. Losin' a child is something no one should ever know."

She stared at him a moment longer, perhaps seeing a bit of her own pain in his eyes. She nodded and turned back to the wagon, but this time she didn't perch in the door. She climbed inside and blew out the lantern.

This was why they'd been so quick to welcome him. They knew his burden, the power hidden inside, squirming to get out.

He stood and excused himself. "I thank you for the meal, but it has been too long since I shut my eyes in peace. I ask for your leave."

They all nodded and smiled as he went off a proper distance on the sand and made his bedroll. The boy caught none of the tension.

Just before Traveler closed his eyes, he saw the storytelling elder showing the boy how to make a gargoyle out of goat skin and rabbit bones to watch over your garden.

~~*~*

He must have slept, surely. The stars were in different positions, and embers winked in the dark like dragon's eyes where there had once been a crackling fire. But it didn't feel like he slept. It felt more like reality just slipped for a moment, and when it caught, he was here, lying under the stars. Just as bone-tired as he had always been.

What had roused him, or brought him back to the here and now, whichever it was? A sigh? Faint shuffling?

Whispering? A whispering voice from his pack...

No. No, it wasn't that.

Traveler rose from the sand, silent as a shade. One hand held a pistol, the other, his burden in its leather pack. A wise and experienced traveler, he simply stood and listened. Watched for movement on the edge of his vision where it was easiest to see at night.

The tactic rewarded him with a glimpse of someone moving onto the widening sand, away from the sleeping camp and the Glass Desert. Traveler stepped over the boy, who had curled up next to him in the fleeting moment he slept. Past the tents and wagons of the slumbering gypsies he went, treading in the tracks of the person he'd seen.

When he rounded the first dune, he heard the sound that woke him. A soft hitching sob. He saw the girl, saw the blackness of her blood like oil in the moonlight.

The shining blade poised to strike the other wrist now—

"Stop, girl!" Traveler wrenched the knife away. He took hold of her slashed wrist so hard that her fingers turned white.

"You tryin' to doom yourself to wander in darkness with those who leave before the Maker says to?"

"I wish... to die. To stop my heart from beating so I won't feel this ache every day, every hour, every breath since they've gone."

Even with his iron grip, the blood coursed between his fingers, dripping into the thirsty sand and onto the cloth bundle in her lap. She'd struck deep and true. Traveler stared into her dying eyes, just as he had stared into the eyes of the man whose bones he carried.

Again the whispering itch inside his skull where it couldn't be scratched, couldn't be quieted.

Poor girl.Poor, poor girl.

He clenched his teeth, but a pathetic whine still escaped.

Pity to die so young. Just like Agatha.

"Stop."But weak, so weak. "Please... not her name."

Tears streamed down his face and he felt something give inside, collapsing his will, bending him as easily as a smith's hammer shapes soft copper.

His hand dug into the leather pack, and even then a last bit of his stubborn heart tried to squeeze his eyes closed against the name he would see. He knew the bone that would come from the pack. A short rib.

Through the blur of his bitter tears, the symbols on the bone danced, daring him. When he read the word, it burned his mouth and nose on the way out, the sound bursting into a brilliant light that blinded him. He fell screaming to the sand, fists screwed into his eyes, begging for the black fire to stop. The pain twisted him into a ball of flesh and bone and he felt as if he'd finally die.

Then, faint and weak... a sound that made every hair on his body bristle.

A muffled cry. Like an infant swaddled in a cloth bundle.

~~*~*

And this time when he woke, or reality caught like a branch in the spokes of a wheel, the night had fled for good.

"They left before sunrise."

"You were supposed—" Traveler's vision swam. His tongue lay in his mouth like a dried sliver from a wood plank. He retched into the sand and the boy handed him a skin of water.

"You were supposed to go with them. You would have been safe. Where I'm going is no place for a boy your age."

"That baby was alive. And the mother said you healed her wrist. But Pastor Gilliam says—said that those bones you carry only kill and maim people."

"Yeah, well... don't always believe what the folks in charge tell you. They most often look to themselves first, like everyone else."

Woozy, Traveler forced himself to his feet. Managed to stay standing. "And I told you once, it ain't me and it ain't the bones. What's in them, I can't exactly say. Them things are above my station in life."

The boy's dark hollow eyes held an accusation that wasn't there the day before.

"They said the man you follow is no more than a day ahead of you."

"What?" Traveler snatched up his belongings and made ready to leave. "How do they know this?"

"They helped the Apostate fix his wagon. His passenger's making him drive too fast, and the heat has begun to make the wheels break."

"Of course. He knows I'm behind him."

"He told the gypsies a murderer was chasing him."

"And he was right."

~~*~*

He had hoped the kid would follow the gypsies. Those short young legs forced Traveler to a more methodical pace, when all he wanted to do was sprint along the powdered glass tracks until he either caught up to the wagon or his heart burst. Maybe it was a good thing the kid was here. Except for all the talking.

"The gypsies said the sand is going to reclaim the Glass Desert someday, and the Apostates' fortress will fall."

"It's not just the Glass Desert that protects the Apostates. They have strong weapons."

"Do they have witches there?"

"Something like.Seen a painting of one, once."

The kid looked like he just opened a Solstice Day treat or something. "Wow! What did she look like? A thousand-year-old crone, a mean snake-headed creature, a warted, nasty—"

"Something tells me your mother doesn't like witches."

"Oh... yeah."

"She was none of those hideous things. Her skin was so pale, she must surely have lived in a cave all her born days. Naked as her birth-day, too."

Traveler couldn't help but grin when the kid's brows shot up above his eyeshades.

"Eyes green as jade from the Southern Tribes, flaming red hair smooth as satin, and she held a snake of reckoning and a staff of power in her hands."

"Where did you see it?"

That one almost stopped him in his tracks. He'd been talking about The Before without realizing it. And that topic wasn't open for discussion.

"Never you mind. Now save your breath for walkin'."

Before the boy could protest, in fact, before they could walk another step, they both saw it.

A shape through the undulating heat waves. Too square to be natural. But something looked wrong about it.

Traveler began to run, the pack of bones rattling against his back, breath coming in short gasps.

It was a steam wagon. Overturned.

~~*~*

The two front hubs had simply flown apart under the stress. The frantic pace overheated the metal, and the machine punished the two men riding on it.

Traveler shielded the boy's eyes from the sight of the decapitated Apostate. He'd been ejected from the pilot's chair into a field of jagged glass plates thrown up by a long-ago earthquake. Treacherous glass slick with blood. Even if the Apostates believed in recovering their dead, no one would venture out there after the pieces.

But the man he had been seeking for days or weeks or months or years laid not twenty paces away. The piece of black glass that ran through his middle was as tall as the boy and as big around as his arm.

Almost like a dream, walking up and staring down into those eyes. How long ago had it truly been since he last looked into them? The crow's-feet had been fewer, the haze of a *kabet* smoker not there, but this was him.

"I never told you to kill that man," he said, with blood on his teeth.

So rapt was he in the rage he'd bottled all this time, Traveler ignored the boy as he walked up behind them. He shouted down at the impaled man.

"You told me he was a seditionist, set against the Queen and the Senate!"

The man just giggled and coughed a bit of blood.

"Why would you tell me that? You knew what I would do."

"Then you've answered your own question."

"But why in Hades did you *want* me to do it?"

"He was to marry a woman I loved."

"Liar." Traveler spat on the glass. There was a higher purpose at work here, something greater in scope than a jealous lover.

The dying man's eyelids fluttered, and he extended a hand to touch the hem of Traveler's journey cloak.

"Set to wander the Irth until you drop, eh? Carrying the bones of that poor, righteous man?"

"I had a life, you bastard."

"Did you? The Queen's pocket assassin? Family dead and gone. What life is that?"

"I was no assassin."

"The former owner of those bones might argue with you."

Even losing his lifeblood onto the twisted desert glass, the man's words were still fired with passion.

"They took your name from you, those witches in the Senate. Burdened your mind with the spell of the Traveler. And then set those bones upon your back. Why would they place such a powerful thing in the hands of a soldier?"

"The nature of these bones makes people pursue me. It's the way of the journey."

"Exactly. And sooner or later you'll fall. Best if you fell to some small wizard out here, someone with an axe to grind. Those old crones want the things in the bones loose in the world. Out here in the Wilds. It makes them needed in the Known, gives them the power to do what they please. All in the name of protecting the People, of course."

"You. You were the seditionist."

A weak smile. "Come now, Traveler. Heal me with one of those righteous bones. Speak the word that is not a word and make me whole again."

"No."

Whispers itched in his skull.

"No, be quiet."

"What is it, Traveler? The righteous bones talking to you, telling what you must do? Telling you to help a soul in need?"

Louder, scratching and rough, not a seductive whisper—

Small fingers grabbed his hand and brought Traveler 'round like a splash of cold water.

"He's already done that." The boy said.

The man glared at the boy for a long moment, but when the youngster didn't back down, the man sighed.

"Then kill me. I've failed, so I might as well die here."

"Failed? What was your goal?" Traveler said.

"Making you chase me until the desert killed you."

"What would that have gained you?"

"The bones. Those things the righteous bones hold. I would have carried them to the hands that would do the most good with them."

"Traitor."

"And you? What did loyalty gain you?"

The boy stepped between them and looked up at Traveler.

"The gypsies said there's another strip of sand ahead. If we want to camp there before dark, we should go."

It suddenly occurred to Traveler. "Go where?"

"Well... we should tell the Apostates that their brother is dead. At the least, they'll want their wagon."

"At the least," Traveler said. He ruffled the boy's hair and they started off toward the horizon, following the Apostates' road.

"Wait! Don't leave me like this. Kill me or heal me, whichever you will. But not like this..."

The weight of one more life on his shoulders slowed Traveler's feet. He glanced back and tossed a skin of water next to the man.

"Goodbye."

He took the boy's hand and they left together. After a long while, they heard one last plea, screamed as a name.

"Davian!"

Traveler certainly didn't know that name. It made walking on that much easier.

~~*~*~*

The craggy cliffs bursting through the deep glass looked deceptively close. In truth, both he and the boy were near death by the time they arrived.

He was burdened by a leather pack of dry bones on his back, and a bundle of flesh-covered bones in his arms. The boy stopped sweating this morning, and Traveler knew he'd be among the ether-folk before sunset if they didn't find water here.

He staggered into a wide crack in the cliff and saw light on the far side. The smell of water was so sudden and clear he thought some vital workings in his brain had ruptured. Surely it wasn't–

Real.

He'd heard the Apostates had a mighty fortress in the heart of the Glass Desert, but that was a lie.

The lush valley of verdant life hidden behind the gargantuan cliffs had him slack-jawed, like a kid who just saw a conjurer turn a hare into a horse.

Orchards bursting with succulent fruit, soaring oak trees that cast inviting pools of shade, rough stone and earth huts scattered throughout. The life here was not simply healthy; to desert-burned eyes, the plants here looked aggressively alive, twisting and turning upward to take life from the same sun that was killing him and the boy.

Two men wearing sky-blue robes of Apostate Brothers approached, their long hair dyed the same midnight black. The older had discs of polished glass in his stretched earlobes, while the younger man still had the acolyte's pebble in his.

"May we offer water, food, and shelter, weary Traveler?" the eldest Brother said.

"Please." Did that dry croak form the word?

His arms unfolded of their own accord and the acolyte caught the boy. Two more young acolytes appeared and carried the unconscious lad into one of the larger huts.

Traveler's glazed eyes followed them, but his heat-addled brain was unable to form the question.

"He will live," the older Apostate said. "He is safe here."

The old man's gnarled hand touched Traveler's arm and a feeling of serenity and peace washed over his tired bones. He would have wept, had he the moisture for it.

Two young women dressed in the brown robes of Apostate Sisters came bearing a tray of meats, bread, and cheese, and a large skin of water.

Any other time, he would have been ashamed at wasting the water that splashed down his front, but all he cared about at the moment was how much made it into his belly. He drank and drank until he was sick with it.

He collapsed onto the improbable green grass and the girl who offered the water smiled at him. Fair, even with her shorn hair and the three scars of the Original Sisters on her left cheek.

"May I take your burden from you?" Her voice so soft.

A groan. That's the best he could do. He felt at the end, his death sentence near fulfilled. Finally, the weight of this would break him.

"I carry the bones of a righteous man."

The older Brother gave him a strange smile. "Do you? What was his name?"

"Barnabus Platick."

"And how did he die?"

"I killed him."

The old man stepped over to a pile of green tree branches, freshly cut and stacked near the entrance to their paradise.

"Pity. Too much hatred, evil, and fighting in this world. Not enough love. Not enough care for someone other than ourselves. Grena, will you help the man?"

The young woman, Grena, held out her hand. In days past, Traveler would already have pistols out, blazing a path of death on his way to—

Where? Where had he been on the way to, exactly? Before. Before he'd chased the man who started all this—

Nowhere. Set to walk and walk until…

No whispers.

He stopped his spinning mind and closed his eyes. No scratching whispers. No desire to keep this fair young girl with the shorn hair from lifting the pack off his shoulders. In fact, it felt like the most natural notion he'd ever had.

He handed her the pack, and in her hand it seemed light as a feather, as if the weight of his guilt had leaked out a torn seam while he'd been walking.

She took it to the Brother and he tossed it onto the pile of green wood. He called out a fire word and a brilliant jet of emerald flame shot out of the wood, roaring toward the sky. Shrieks that laid his nerves bare made Traveler squeeze his eyes shut, as the things held within the bones were burned into the open and shot into the heavens in a gout of Irth fire.

And then the flames were gone.

And so was the wood.

And so was that damned pack of bones.

Only an empty spot on the grass where the pyre had been. The Apostate released the life force held in the wood, consuming wood, pack, bones, and all. But the grass beneath was fresh as the first day of spring.

"Green witches."

"We prefer the term Wiccanites."

"How? They can't be destroyed. The things that can be held in the bones of a righteous man—"

The old man silenced him with a hand on his shoulder.

"Of all the lies you have been told, that is the greatest. Traveler… O Weary Traveler… there is no such thing as a righteous man."

That struck his heart still. All this way. All this pain and suffering.

"What have I done? The lives I took in their name."

The Apostate Brother grabbed Traveler's hand and touched him wrist to wrist, their pulses suddenly joining—

A whirling history of violence, slashing blades and acrid gunpowder in pitched battles, rooting out traitors to the throne, putting them to the blade or noose, Barnabus Platick bleeding on white sheets, the crones in the Senate leering down from their high seats, the Queen turning her face from him in ritual denial.

Even seeing all this, the Brother smiled at Traveler. "Will you stay with us, Davian? Release these things and live in this valley in peace."

They left him there with food and drink to contemplate that. He lay under the branches of a whispering oak until pinpoints of white shined in the black heavens above him. Finally, in the streak of a falling star he saw it. The truth of what he was, and where his life would lead.

After all, he was no more righteous than the man whose bones he carried across a desert.

In the morning, he'd sort out his pistols and blades. Then he would strike out for home, a Prodigal Son no one would rejoice in seeing. And like the Stone of God come 'round again, he would leave a changed world in his wake.

For the first time in what felt like his entire life, he fell into a peaceful, dreamless sleep.

STEVEN SAVILE has written for *Doctor Who, Torchwood, Primeval, Stargate, Warhammer, Slaine, Fireborn, Pathfinder, Arkham Horror, Rogue Angel, WarMachine,* and other popular game and comic worlds. His novels have been published in eight languages to date, including the Italian bestseller *L'eridita.* He won the International Media Association of Tie-In Writers award for his *Primeval* novel, *Shadow of the Jaguar,* and the inaugural Lifeboat to the Stars award for *Tau Ceti* (co-authored with Kevin J. Anderson). His debut thriller, *Silver,* reached number 2 in the Amazon UK e-charts. His latest books include *HNIC* (with Hip Hop artist Prodigy of Mobb Deep) and the novelization of the computer game *Risen 2: Dark Waters.* He is currently working on *The Harrowing,* an original epic fantasy novel.

Sign up for his mailing list to keep up to date with current projects here: eepurl.com/5TkBz

TIME'S MISTRESS
Steven Savile

"What will the clock make of me, my sweet, sweet Suli?" Immaculada wondered on her death bed.

He took her hand in his tenderly, tracing a finger along the ridge of fine bone standing out against the slack skin. "The clock adores you," he assured her. "Its love is written in every crease and fold of your flesh, lady. Do not worry about your place in time, Odalisque. You should rest."

"Flatterer," she scolded him gently, but her smile told him all he needed to know. Suli smoothed a matted grey curl away from her brow. It pained him to see her like this, so humbled by age. She chuckled at that old name, as though it amused her to be reminded of her innocence. "There will be time enough for that, my boy."

Immaculada lay back in the pillows. Sweat stains soaked into the fabric around her head like some dirty halo. He only had to close his eyes to remember her as she was the first time he had laid eyes upon her: the great beauty of her youth, the olive cast to her skin and the innocence of her deep brown eyes. He could see her now as though it were only a handful of revolutions of her precious 'clock' ago.

The old woman never referred to it as time. For her it would only ever be the clock. The rest, she had argued so many times during her long life, was meaningless. Planets could revolve, the clouds ghost across the sky and tides roll in relentlessly and they were merely mechanisms of life but the clock was different, it was a mechanism of precision. Its ticks and tocks were relentless.

She had been such a beautiful child. A miracle. The Sultan's men had brought her out of the Komark after the fighting had devastated the township. A babe in swaddling clothes. She had no name so Suli had chosen to call her Immaculada, innocence. It had seemed so fitting to him then. Eight thousand people camped in the wretched filth and squalor of the Komark, and all but one of them had died in that filth. By dint of survival Immaculada had become the hope of the poor—an innocent soul in the Sultan's court. No one wanted to remember but neither did they want to forget. There was something altogether more tragic in letting eight thousand souls slip away unremembered. So this little girl with the big brown eyes became so much more than a mere orphan.

"This line," Suli said, smiling as he traced one of the deep creases across her palm, "this was the first. Your birth line."

"Read it for me, my love. My eyes are not so good."

"Of course," he said, ever the storyteller. "Come with me to the day it all began." She smiled despite herself. "The darkest day in our people's

303

history of dark days. It began much as every day had for as long as anyone could remember—with the sounds of fighting and the screams of dying. It was worse though. The civil war had entered its end game. No one could tell you when the sun came up; the sky was black. Amid the sounds of war and terror was one note so out of place you couldn't help but stop and listen in wonder. It was the sound of a baby being born to the world. You, my sweet. No one understood what was happening at the time, of course. How could we? It wasn't until Uskafel brought you up to the palace that anyone suspected anything out of the ordinary. You were six days old by then. The big man pounded on the heavy doors and, as though in answer, the Sultan's Perpetual Motion Clock fell silent. They said it was not possible, of course. Time could not stand still, neither could the grand mechanism. The timekeeper swore and huffed and laboured, but it was useless. The clock that could never stop had stopped. The great hourly bell would never cry out again. So, of course, others took it as a sign, pointing fingers at the slaughter of the township. There gods were angry, they cried. These woeful flagellants beating themselves bloody in the main square were right, of course, the gods were angry. And why wouldn't they be? A few bands of steel had succeeded where centuries of starvation, privation and hardship had failed, but the clock had not ceased its ticking to mark the passing of the dead, far from it, it was honouring you, sweet Odalisque."

"You old fool, it was nothing of the sort," she said.

"How would you know? You were six days old. Now hush, I am telling the story, not you."

"Yes, Suli," she said, smiling indulgently.

"Now where was I? Oh yes, the clock... Even to this day the grand mechanism has never moved on so much as another second. Did you know that? In the silence of the palace no one knew what to do. They looked down at this bundle of beautiful child and listened to the absence of time, that one ever-present in their lives until that very moment, and like the clock they froze.

"It was Iminez who suggested we take you up to the enchanter. I think perhaps even then she knew, or at least suspected. It was up in his draughty minaret that the raveller divined the truth that surrounded your life. More than a few suspected the old charlatan was spouting the usual lies—the old fool was one of the many deeply affected by the slaughter of Komark—because he didn't want another death on his hands."

"You say that as though he had been asked to put me in a sack and drown me like some annoying kitten, Suli."

"And it was just so, believe me, Immaculada. The world you were born into was starkly different to the one you are leaving behind, my love. The clock may no longer tick but the thing it measures always moves on relentlessly, does it not? People were torn between wanting to remember and wanting to bury every reminder. More than anything you were a reminder. Especially when the raveller made his gambit. He took you in his bony old arms and cradled you close, your tiny lips inches from his ear. He nodded, kissed you once on the forehead and returned you to Iminez's arms. The silence was almost reverent while people waited. When finally he spoke it was to say that you were our salvation. Eight thousand souls lived on through you and only through you might we, their murderers, find salvation, and eventually redemption."

"And when you think of it now, when you see me lying here like this at the end of my story, do you see redemption?"

"I see the most beautiful woman who ever lived," Suli said. "I see the one person who ever owned my heart, and of course because of that, I see my greatest regret."

She looked at him. He had always thought she saw him like no one else ever did. She didn't see the old man he had become, but neither did she see the young man he had been. She saw the myriad of people he might have become had he made different choices, the better men, the worse men. She saw all of him, all the ghosts of choices made and choices avoided. He had never hidden himself from her. That, more than anything, was what convinced him it was love not infatuation.

"Are you trying to make me cry again?"

Now it was his turn to smile. They had been together a long time, a lifetime, and he had never seen her cry.

She winced then, the slightest gasp escaping from her broken lips. She sank back into the bank of pillows beneath her head and seemed to die a little bit more before his eyes.

"Is it time?" he asked, needing to find something to say simply to make her answer him. He wasn't ready for her to go yet. He looked over at the leather-bound book on the nightstand. His last gift.

"Patience, my guardian angel," she barely managed the words which meant it was.

It was difficult to imagine a world without her. She had always been the one. He would learn to live again, but with so few days of his own left it was hardly worth it. That was the worst part of watching her die; how it brought home his own strange mortality. Suli had lived more years than many. That was his curse, to live while those around him grew old and died. He hadn't understood it when the woman had first offered him the cup. She had said, "Drink, you will never be thirsty again," and he had taken the simple clay cup in both hands, shaking with the effort of lifting it to his lips, and swallowed the water down gulp by gulp by desperate gulp.

That woman had been his first great love. The first, he was ashamed to say, of many. But hand on heart he could swear he had loved them all brilliantly, with all of his soul.

Her name, Sati, meant truth but he never heard a word of it from her lips. That was when he first learned the irony of names. Call a giant tiny, call a snake truth. Words could be taken and twisted to mean anything, be anything, and to conjure anything. They had power, there was no denying it. She taught him that. She taught him that the world was nothing more than words, God's story being experienced by everyone all at once. Sati said it was God's story because God's was the only one worth telling. She spoke like that, as though she knew the Almighty. Maybe she did. He had no way of knowing. The woman called truth who lived in lies had taken Suli from his home, a simple hovel in the wilderness of the sands, and brought him to her palace where she had promised him eternity then gelded him. Suli the Eunuch, fated to live forever without the very thing that made eternity worthwhile. She said it was what would make his story unique. He would live out a life that, thanks to the water from the clay cup, would feel like eternity, surrounded by beauty he could never have.

It was all a great joke to the woman called truth. Sati had been the old Sultan's raveller. She claimed once to have been God's first wife. The audacity of the claim had made the old Sultan covet her all the more. Who wouldn't want to lay with the woman who had taken God into her flesh?

It had been long before the clock had ticked its first tick. Long, in fact, before the wandering chronophage had stumbled into the Sultan's palace clutching his drawings and raving in the delirium of fever that he had found God. Suli remembered the day. Some few from the thousands he had lived still stood out. That was one of them. He hadn't really understood what the chronophage had meant by God. It wasn't the deity who shaped the ground beneath their feet and put the dreams inside their heads while they slept. It couldn't be. His God was one of numbers and formula, not divinity and martyrs. Still, the woman had been fascinated, and her fascination rubbed off on Suli. Even after all she had put him through he still wanted to please her. The need had weakened considerably but it wasn't until the Great Mechanism was built that he finally broke that curious need she had instilled in him. She called it love but he knew it wasn't. How could it be? She took lovers in front of him using her voice, her moans and screams, to hurt him. Each little murmur was like a crucifixion nail being driven home into the soft parts of his flesh, each delicious moan like the meat being flayed from his bones.

But there came a point where the pain had to stop or overwhelm him completely, a point where his mind could take no more while still clinging on to his sense of self. All things have to end, that is the way of things. One had to give. In the end it turned out he loved himself more. That was a revelation to Suli. The chronophage's ramblings had been fundamental in him winning himself back. He had claimed to have found God and it wasn't her God. That made it a God Suli wanted to find. At first the chronophage refused to share his formula. It was for the Sultan only, for only one so close to the divine could dare to understand it. Of course the Sultan made the right noises, pretending that the marks on the paper made perfect sense to him and that in fact the chronophage had made the smallest miscalculation in his workings. He corrected this with a slight down-stroke of black ink and handed the crumpled paper back to the grateful chronophage who bowed and scraped obsequiously.

Suli could read. He was one of the few in the service of the Sultan who could.

He knew that the slash of black on the parchment was meaningless.

It was one of the first times he saw the vanity of the Sultan. The man could not admit weakness. Suli had no such problem. There was safety in weakness. The weak survived. All of the wisdom that claimed that the fittest and strongest survived was a myth. The weak were ignored. They were never considered a threat. The strong were forever challenged to prove their strength, to fight and kill and die. That was the way of strength. Even the very strongest, those supposedly untouchable, spent every waking hour glancing over their shoulder for the knife they knew had to be coming. The weak were left to walk in peace. It was the first great irony Suli had learned. It had been lady liar who had taught him—though it had not been a lesson she had shared willingly. Far from it, it was the first thing he stole from her. There were others, but none so valuable. He watched the way she played different people. She had a different face for each encounter. A different way of saying yes, of demurring or deferring or denying. She was fascinating, and far far stronger than the Sultan could ever have dreamed because of it. So while the Sultan lied and pretended to his court that he was some great God King, all seeing, all knowing, the woman took everything away from him. And how did she do that? She became his wife.

The Sultan had six hundred women he called wives, all charged with a single duty, to give him sons.

Such was the colossal vanity of the man, he would have a kingdom built in his own image.

At first Suli had struggled to see how the man could hope to keep six hundred women happy, but as he got to know them he realized it wasn't about their happiness, it was about his image. These women had secret lovers, secret because should the Sultan ever discover he had been cuckolded not only would their lives be forfeit, their lovers would die as would everyone of their blood. It was a heavy punishment, but it only served to make them all the more careful not to get caught, it didn't stop them from spreading their legs.

She was the only woman who refused to give him a child, and she cheated on him more than any other but somehow she did not get caught. The other wives whispered about her until she had their tongues cut out or had their eyes put out or their flesh burned until it was ugly and the Sultan couldn't bear the sight of them never mind their touch. One by one the other wives fell away until there was only the snake. Suli had befriended many of them, his survival depended upon the kindness of others and with the Sultan being unpredictable at best, downright fickle at worst, friends in his court were a must. It was the game of politics. She was good at it. He pitied the wives because without realizing it they had become brood mares and stopped being women. They simply didn't know how to deal with Suli the liar. He couldn't help them though. He didn't dare risk his own position. So he fell into the comfortable lie of weakness.

He spent his days watching the chronophage building God. That was how he described what he was doing. He was building God. God was in the machine. At first Suli hadn't grasped what he meant but day by day it became clearer. The Great Mechanism was a colossal construct. Its gears and levers, pendulums and cogs were all part of the guts of the world. They were the rhythm that everything in creation danced to. It was illuminating. Suli was a hungry student. He lurked at the man's shoulder listening to every mumble and curse as something went wrong and every slight joy as something went right.

When Suli realized she had a rival for his affections she laughed. It was that familiar derisory laugh she used to belittle him. It pleased him. It meant that he was hiding his strength from her as well. She might have taken his prick, the 'man' on the outside of his body, but she would never take the man inside.

She underestimated him.

Ultimately that was how he had been able to kill her. She had never imagined him capable of such deception. But of course he had always been capable. That was why the Sultan had kept him around, not because of his wry wit or his asexual good looks. He had killed more than once for the man, and taking the drink, sacrificing old age for this prolonged youth was a deal that worked well not only for Suli but for the Sultan and his son, and his son, and his after. He was the constant in their lives: death with his charming face.

Of course, it had been nothing more than a coincidence that his plan had come to fruition on the same day the Odalisque was brought into the palace. It was his fault that the clock had stopped. No one save for him and the Sultan himself knew the truth of what had happened. The Sultan because it was his will, Suli because it was his doing.

When he asked Immaculada if it was time he was asking so much more than: is this when you leave me? He was asking her if it was time for his final gift. Only at the very last would he open the book and show her the truth. The chronophage might have found God but it was Suli who stole him. It was Suli who had taken God out of the machine and given it the liar instead. Soon it would be time for him to share this stolen God with the woman of his heart. He longed to see her expression, to see the wonder in her eyes as it all came to life before her. What better way to leave this earth than looking into the face of the divine? He thought, stroking her brow.

It had been hard watching her grow old. Time was merciless. More than once he had regretted killing Suli simply because she must have known where the wellspring was. She had given him the clay goblet, she had made him drink the water and the water had kept this face of youth on his old bones. One sip could have bought him a decade with the Odalisque. One mouthful a lifetime.

So he had done what he had for a reason. He had stopped the clock. But it was more than just that, it was murder. He had torn the divine from the machine and trapped it within what he called the book of the world. It was all in there, every secret. And every page was inked with Suli's blood as though finally bled dry she might record the truth she was named after.

The murder had needed stealth, of course, and cunning. He was equipped for both. First he gave the chronophage plans for adjustments to his Grand Mechanism. The man had been resistant until Suli had explained that these few changes would give God a voice. That had sold him on them. It was one thing to find God but if you couldn't communicate with him then what use was it?

The man made the changes. The clock ticked on.

Suli had sent word via one of the wives that the Sultan would see his first wife beneath the great pendulum of the Grand Mechanism for he had a miraculous truth he would share with her. It was about the absence of divinity. No more, no less. Enough to capture Suli's attention and spark her imagination, and maybe just maybe fire her greed, but not so much that she would hear the lie. Then he had sent word to the chronophage to meet him beneath the God Bell at the same time. Next he bade the raveller meet him betwixt and between the Grand Cogs and requested a scribe be there to record every word. Explicitly, he was to bring his quills and parchment but no ink. The ink would be provided. His final missive went to the Sultan himself. While the old man would never dirty his hands he did like to watch his will be done.

All of these separate threads came together in a careful pattern; each triggered when it was needed and not a second before. He had the time measured out in huge booming ticks and backwards tocks. He could not hide from it.

Suli had hidden himself away and watched as the liar paced back and forth beneath the pendulum and seen her perturbed frown as the scribe hustled up with his carefully wrapped quills. She did not like being made to wait. It showed. He looked up to see the Sultan in place, obscured from Suli's position by the swing of the pendulum's mechanism, and the raveller beneath the bell. The only one missing was the chronophage. Without him none of it would work. He gritted his teeth. He hated waiting every bit as much as the Sultan's wife. Having eternity at his disposal only made him despise it all the more. Finally the little man shuffled into the chamber. As ever his eyes lit up at the sight of his great folly. Folly, Suli thought, because no matter what he might have hoped to achieve all he had actually built was one single enormous timepiece. The miracle of it was that it did not require a timekeeper to run constantly from mechanism to mechanism to keep all the springs wound tight. But in a few minutes his machine would be miraculous in so many more ways.

Suli gave the signal. He hadn't known then how it had coincided so perfectly with the hammering on the door outside and the arrival of the girl child who lay withered and old on her bed beside him now waiting to die.

The raveller whispered his invocation, and touched the metal plate that anchored the huge pendulum. Mid swing it began to buckle and twist, becoming a serpent. As it passed over the head of the liar it struck, sinking its huge fangs into her face. She screamed but Suli had expected that. No amount of screaming would save her. The scribe darted forward, dipping his quills in her torn flesh and began to transcribe the words that babbled out in agony, writing each one down on her body as it bucked and writhed, trying to shake free of the fangs. He turned her into a book of flesh and blood. Her last words becoming the testament of her body. The chronophage played his part perfectly. He fed her to the machine. He had added a metal harness, a cage that could be assembled by pulling various mechanisms and twisting certain cogs. He shackled the cage around her. Then the bell sounded, a single deep chime and the cage retreated back into the machine, taking her body back into it piece by piece until she became a part of the Great Mechanism. This was the worst of it, Suli knew, because if he was right, she couldn't die. So piece by piece she was consumed by the cogs and the wheels, she greased the axles and kept the pendulum smooth.

The scribe crawled on his hands and knees collecting the shreds of his manuscript. Later Suli would have them bound into the living book. For now it was enough to retrieve them from the machine.

He remembered the day as vividly as if it was yesterday. He emerged from hiding and found the tatters of her face. He held it in his hands wanting to believe he saw some signs of life in the ruin. She wasn't beautiful anymore.

As the doors opened and the baby was brought in Suli gave the second signal and the chronophage started the Grand Mechanism again. It lasted for three hundred and twenty seven full pendulum swings. In that time the chronophage's alterations spat out the book of the world page by page, the words of God, for want of a better description. Suli's flesh pulped and mangled until every last ounce of colour was squeezed from it onto the pages the scribe fed into the machine. He didn't know if she was dead. He didn't care. He had exacted his revenge. She would not cuckold the Sultan with a string of lovers or scheme against his wives. Instead she had become what she was born to be: the truth.

He had given the pages to the scribe and bade him to stitch and bind them. Instead the man put out his own eyes and died weeping tears of blood. None of the Sultan's other scribes would touch the cursed pages so Suli took them to an aged leather worker on the outskirts of the city. One of the wives had told him about the old man. It had been her grandfather. He had been blinded in a tragic accident in the tannery and never worked again. Suli convinced him to take up his needle and braddle and all the other tools of his old trade and work one last piece of magic, turning the pages into a book.

When he held it in his hands he knew it was a work of art, worthy of holding the truth of the world and all of the petty things of existence. He had carried it carefully back into the city. It felt strange in his hands. Alive.Hungry. He felt it pulsing. The pulse made his skin crawl. Despite that he couldn't help himself, he wanted to turn the page, to read the first truth of Suli... but it wasn't his place. This was a gift fit only for the Sultan, not for some lowly eunuch in his service.

The Sultan had rewarded him well when presented with the book. Holding the thing with a mixture of reverence and trepidation the old man had opened the book. His eyes roved hungrily down the first page but after reading it he closed the book and said he had no wish to read more. The old man looked visibly shaken. "Take it, hide it. Never let this fall into the wrong hands, my friend. Do you understand?" Suli had nodded. "The living book can never be opened. Some truths the world does not need to know," the Sultan had told him.

It was the same book that rested on the nightstand beside Immaculada's death bed.

He had wanted to tell her so much before she left him. He had wanted to confess his love—but of course he did not need to. Some things never needed to be said. They were known. He looked at the clock on the wall. The shadow had moved on. It was deep in the night now. Long past the moment yesterday when she was alive and into today when she was dead. "One last story," he said.

She smiled at him. "Make it a short one, my love." It was as close as she came to admitting she was slipping into darkness.

Which one should he tell her? Should he take her back to the day she went from whore to wife? It was a beautiful day. The old Sultan had died and his first son took his place. He knew the story of the woman and the clock, as did everyone in the palace, and he decided that this miraculous girl should be his wife. What more auspicious omen could there be than marrying the child who stopped the hands of time itself? She had been seventeen. They had taken her out of the children's palace three years earlier and with no one to shelter her she had been welcomed by Farusi the harlot. But she had always been different. The others in Farusi's house were whores, Immaculada was never a whore, she was only ever the Odalisque. She lay with a single man during her three years in the house, the old Sultan himself. That was another reason the son wanted her, to possess something his father had only ever 'borrowed.'

It didn't seem like a fitting death bed story.

Then he wondered about the birth of her own son, but that was a tale that ended in tragedy so he did not want her dwelling upon it as she left this world.

Instead he told her a story she had never heard before, a love story of sorts. His mother had told him the story of the stone. She had been given it by his father. She had told him it was enchanted. He had never really believed that. He just liked the story. "Have I told you about my father's last gift?" he asked. He knew he hadn't but he wanted to keep her involved, to make her interact because it would keep her alive a little moment longer.

She said, "No," and smiled. He loved her smile. "Is it a sad story?"

"No," he promised. "My grandmother was blind. My grandfather would come to her day after day and sit with her, telling her all about the world she couldn't see. Words were his last gift."

"I can't imagine anything more intimate," Immaculada said. He knew she was imagining it. He had heard his grandmother talk about those days before he was born so often, but he was so young he couldn't appreciate what she meant. The tenderness in her voice as she lived in those memories hurt him in some most basic of ways. Now he did. Now he knew what she was feeling was loss. His grandfather, Lukas, had died long before her, but she wasn't alone anymore, his mother, their baby girl, Poli

312

was with her. The one story of hers he remembered was about those few weeks when she could see and how she hated the blandness of the world, and how after his grandfather's death she had left Aksandria and moved across the great sea to the Komark where she knew no one but at least she wasn't surrounded by the smells and sounds that she would forever associate with her hopeless romantic of a husband. Breathing in the fragrance of Immaculada he finally understood. These corridors would never be the same again without her fragrance clinging to them. They would be forever empty.

"I am so tired, Suli. I think I will sleep now."

He looked at her and knew instinctively that her eyes would not reopen. He moved around the bed and took the book from the nightstand. "I always wanted to grow up like my grandfather, though I never knew him," Suli said. His smile was tender. "I can't imagine a more precious gift than words," he handed her the book. "I might never have been able to touch you in the way a lover could, not with my body, but if my grandmother's story taught me anything it was that lovers didn't merely touch with hands and fingers and lips, they touched with something much more intimate."

"Words," she said, still with him. Just. He realized he was crying.

He opened the book for her. He wished he could see whatever it was she saw, but instead he contented himself with watching it come alive in her eyes. He saw the blue first, the shape of the world slowly spinning in the dark pupil, then all of the other colours, so rich and vibrant. Her lips parted, not quite the death-breath. "What can you see?" he asked. He couldn't help himself.

"Everything," she said to him. "All of it. I never knew... I never... look," she demanded, tilting the book toward him but he reached up to stop her.

"Not yet. I don't want to know everything. When it is my time, perhaps, but for now I need my curiosity. Without it I might as well..." he stopped himself from saying 'be dead'.

"You have to see," she said. "This can't die with me."

He didn't understand. She pushed the book down so that it lay flat on the bed covers, rising and falling with the last shaky breaths of her chest. He couldn't help himself. He looked down at the page. It took him a moment but then he understood. The words had come alive. They rippled and twisted, lifting from the page so that instead of seeing Suli's prophecies and promises he saw the shape of the world, everything, all of it, as Immaculada had said. Only there were gaps now. Little dark shadows where she had already absorbed the truth. It could never be replaced because there was only one truth. He saw it like God. If he focused he could see closer, down to the hills and the cities, and closer down to the streets. But as his attention closed in he started to hear them. At first it was just a constant wash of noise, but it began to break up slowly, fracturing into individual voices—and he could hear them, every last one of them. Not the words from their mouths. The ones inside, the secrets they never shared with the world.

Somehow the raveller's magic and the chronophage's machine had combined to open up the world to him. He understood why the Sultan had closed the book. Suli's attention was naturally drawn toward himself in this world. He could feel his consciousness rushing toward Komark, toward the Sultan's palace, and inside it, the Odalisque's chamber.

And then he could hear her.

She looked at him across the pages of the book of truths and all he could hear was her voice inside his head saying "I am frightened. I don't want to go there without you."

He knew where there was. And he didn't want her to go there alone, either.

And then, the more frightened whisper, "Oh god, there's nothing..."

He looked down at the woman lying on the bed and realized she was gone. He reached down and felt her throat for the flutter of blood still pumping through her body. There was none. But he could still hear her inside his head.

"I can't see," she said. "Suli? Suli, my sweet, where are you? I don't want to be alone."

"You're not alone," he said, but he had no idea if his words reached her, wherever she was.

He didn't understand how the book's magic worked, what part of it was Suli, what was the raveller manipulating the threads of the world and what was the God the chronophage had found and harnessed with his endless machine. He didn't need to understand. For once he only needed to experience.

"Suli? I can't see you."

The book contained everything. It contained the world. The world was God. It was all in there. Every thought, every joy and every sorrow. They all came together into the body and mind of God. That was the truth. God did not make the world. God was the world. There was no heaven above, no hell below. The world was all.

She was a part of it, she always would be. He was a part of it and always would be. They were both parts of God, aspects of divinity.

"Talk to me," he said, urging her to keep that link between them.

"Suli? I can hear you, my sweet, sweet man, but I can't see you. Hold my hand. I am frightened."

He took her hand in his. It was cold. He felt every deep crease the clock had worn into it over the years. "I am here," he soothed. "I will never leave you." It was that kind of rash lover's promise he could never hope to keep. Everyone leaves. That was the truth. But as he said it he knew it was true in ways he had never understood before. He would never leave her, just as she would never leave the world, because they were a vital part of everything. They didn't simply cease to be.

She was gone as much as she would ever be gone, and here as little as she would ever be here again.

He realized then that Suli had robbed him of far more than his cock. She had taken his place within the great mechanism of the world from him. He would only ever be Suli. He would never be anything more. Now his tears were for himself.

When he looked down at the book he saw that the pages were empty. The bloody words gone, the vision of the world gone. In its place were blank pages. She had absorbed it all. She had taken everything inside her. It wasn't gone. It couldn't be. He was still alive. Still standing in the same room, holding her hand, listening to her voice inside his head. It wasn't gone.

"Immaculada," he said, calling out her name.

She must have heard the panic in his voice because suddenly it was her that soothed and reassured him. "Shhhh, I know," she said, over and over. "I know. Don't cry for me, my love. I can feel it all. I can hear everything. It is all here in the darkness. I am not alone."

But he couldn't help himself.

He cradled the dead woman in his arms and carried her through the corridors of the Sultan's palace for one last time, breaking his heart as he turned every corner with her for the last time. He didn't know where he was going until he was there, standing beneath the pendulum of the Grand Mechanism.

Suli didn't realize what he heard at first, the tick-tock and whirr of the gears in the guts of the machine, then the bell chimed, struck by the huge hammer just once, and he saw the body in his arms and the smile on her dead face, and it all started to make sense. He knew it had to be something to do with the book, that in reading it the Odalisque had somehow let time's divinity back into the world. He didn't understand how or why, and yet again it wasn't something he needed to understand. He was nothing more than her eunuch, why should it be important that he understand anything? He wasn't a raveller. He wasn't the chronophage who had found the truth. He wasn't even Suli, the woman who had given her blood and bones to be the voice of God. He was nothing more than a man. A craven coward of a man, a schemer, a survivor. He wasn't even a hero with a magical blade or a destiny to fulfil, he was just a man.

He stood there beneath the huge pendulum curiously comforted by the slow regular tick tock tick tock as it moved from extreme to extreme over his head. Time had begun again after all of these years.

It was time.

The chronophage had been right all those years ago, he had discovered God. Now it was time for Suli to give her back to the clock just as all those years ago he had given another woman he loved to it.

He laid her down gently. He couldn't see for the tears streaming down his face but he found the lever that released the cage.

She didn't scream.

Why would she? The clock had been kind to her. It always was.

The late JAY LAKE won the John W. Campbell Award for Best New Writer in Science Fiction in 2004, and since then he was astonishingly prolific in multiple genres. He wrote ten novels, hundreds of short stories and he edited the *Polyphony* anthology series for Wheatland Press.

In 2008, Jay was diagnosed with colon cancer, and in May 2014 he passed away. His frank and brutally honest blog has given his fans and admirers a unique window into his journey, and everyone should read it.

www.jlake.com

LITTLE PIG, BERRY BROWN
AND THE HARD MOON
Jay Lake

Little Pig sat in the thin-leaf tree and watched Mother Sun dance upon the water. She-of-the-Sky made silver sparkle in the creek below the bear fur that wrapped the girl in warmth. Little Pig smiled, but folded her laughter within—noise out of place could bring a hungry cat.

Stick, Little Pig's only toy and best and greatest friend, opened her tiny carved mouth. "*Child, child, sitting in a tree, what sort of furry fruit do you be?*"

Little Pig swallowed another laugh, though her body shook and swayed against the thin-leaf's bark. "Silly Stick," she whispered, then put her friend within her own mouth for silence and safekeeping.

~~*~*

Later Brother Spear returned from his hunt with her mother and the rest of the clan to fetch Little Pig down from the safety of the thin-leaf tree. He was covered in mud and sweat and blood that stank of the Tusk Beast, breath steaming in the evening as the stars cut away his heat in tiny ribbons to feed their secret jealousies. His glittering eyes were narrow-closed, but the axe of his anger did not seem held high for Little Pig. She hugged to his chest as he carried her home, and kept quiet as a nesting mouse, still sucking on Stick and wishing she could ask her friend about the fire in Brother Spear's face.

Soon enough she found the reason, when they returned to the Hard Moon Camp.

Her clan had different camps for different moons. Each was in a place that drew good fortune from the cold skies and sheltered the People from whatever harmed them most in that season of Sister Moon's journey through the year.

The People's Hard Moon Camp was in a shallow bowl atop a bluff near the Biggest River. The bowl was for luck in saving enough food for the Ice Moon and Dying Moon camps soon to come. The bluff kept the People above the animals in the scrub forest surrounding the Biggest River. As they crossed the ridge, she smelled blood, and saw that this night there was fire, big as any prayer-fire, meat on drying frames spread before the flames. Close to the fire, Oldest Woman and Broken-Eye knelt next to someone wrapped in too many furs.

Like the last grub in the sack, Little Pig thought, lonely and unlucky. None of the People should be so sad.

"Stick," she whispered, risking noise as Brother Spear made his quiet way down to the warm light. "Who is it?"

319

"Child, child, clutching tight, count the People here tonight."

Brother Spear touched her back with his hand, signaling quiet, but she had Stick's advice now and made good. Little Pig wasn't very clever with numbers, but she knew names, and so she sang the list of the People in the voice only she could hear, behind her ears, looking for each one as she named them.

Oldest Woman, hands so bent
Sleeping Sister, dreaming much
Broken-Eye, sees only night
Walks On Rock, feet too big
Berry Brown, mother of my heart

There she stopped, for she did not see her mother anywhere. Little Pig was hungry then, for Berry Brown had always fed her. Little Pig was frightened then, for Berry Brown had always comforted her. Little Pig was worried then, for Berry Brown had always protected her. Berry Brown belonged to Little Pig the way Mother Sun belonged to Daughter Sky.

Brother Spear stopped at the feet of Berry Brown, who was wrapped in the three magic furs and head close to the fire. "I have brought the child," he said. Little Pig felt the rumble of his voice where her head lay against his chest. She held Stick close.

Berry Brown had made Stick for her, carving her friend with a black-stone blade and the patience of rain, lending her breath into Stick's mouth, kissing Stick's hurts. Little Pig's eyes salted like summer-killed meat, as she clutched her toy tight enough to make Stick squeak and shiver.

Oldest Woman took the bear fur robe from Brother Spear and greeted Little Pig with a tiny dry kiss upon her forehead. Then she made Little Pig stand with her close to the fire, next to Berry Brown's face, a soft little hand wrapped inside a trembling old one.

"Who lies before us?" Oldest Woman asked. Her voice was not unkind, but Little Pig knew Oldest Woman could crack rocks with her will, and not even Boar Killer with his temper and his huge muscles would argue with her.

"Child, child, before the fire, answer all Oldest Woman desires," whispered Stick, squirming in her hand.

"Berry Brown." Little Pig stared at the unmoving eyes, lost in the sweating face like leaves in the creek. Her chest shuddered. "My mother."

"What has happened to her?" Oldest Woman asked.

"I do not—" Little Pig began, then stopped.

"Child, child, Berry went hunting, did not hear the Tusk Beast grunting."

Oldest Woman made a soft noise, inviting Little Pig's next words to come out of her mouth.

Little Pig closed Stick to her chest, just as Berry Brown used to hold Little Pig. "She was hurt by the Tusk Beast, wasn't she?"

A squeeze of the hand. Then: "What will become of her?"

Little Pig waited for Stick to speak, but the toy was silent. Oldest Woman squeezed her hand again. *What was she supposed to say?*

"She is my mother." Little Pig's voice was as slow as her thoughts. "She will not leave me behind."

Oldest Woman bent and whispered in Little Pig's ear. As she spoke, Little Pig could feel Stick straining to listen. "Berry Brown has gone beyond the reach of my hands' skill or the depths of Broken-Eye's wisdom. We cannot make her whole. Still, she might come home for you, child. But you must ask the Hard Moon and the sharp stars if this can be, and what words will bring her back."

"I will speak to the moon," said Little Pig.

Oldest Woman released her hand, brushed her hard, crooked fingers across Little Pig's shoulder. "Go find your way, then."

~~*~*

Little Pig climbed up toward the rim of the Hard Moon Camp's small round valley. She took one of her paths, not the People's trails, so she could visit her special places. The Hard Moon was not so old that she had lost the light. She touched her crystal rocks, the oldest bone, and the brown anthill. Stick always liked the special places, sometimes talked about the magic that dwelt in each, though right now Stick seemed to be silent. Thinking, perhaps. Mice scuttled away from Little Pig as she walked, while an owl sailed overhead, wide-winged and vigilant. Had the night-hunter come to take the last of Berry Brown's spirit away?

She almost ran into Brother Spear. He sat cross-legged, still covered in blood and muck, making tiny sparks as he chipped at the edge of his spear point.

"I am sorry," he told Little Pig without meeting her eye.

She thought about that a moment. "You did not hurt Berry Brown."

More chips of the rock. "I led. Success is mine, failure mine."

"There is meat by the fire, for the Ice Moon and the Dying Moon." Little Pig knew this without turning to look, as the dank blood smell lay upon the entire valley.

Brother Spear finally lifted his chin to her. "There is no magic. Only spear and blood and bone. Tusk Beast took Berry Brown in trade for itself. Blood for blood."

"Child, child, Brother Spear is wrong, Berry has not yet sung her last song."

Little Pig squeezed Stick, a gentle hug of thanks and reassurance. "My mother is alive," she told Brother Spear, touching his knee with her free hand.

A smile ghosted across his face like a crane in the mist. "Go on. Follow Oldest Woman's magic. Ask the moon. I only know the spear. It feeds us but it takes away as well."

"Like the Tusk Beast. Spears are our sharp teeth. You are the strong hand."

He bent once more to his work. Little Pig gave Brother Spear back his silence and moved on to talk to the moon.

~~*~*

She picked a tree that some great storm had driven down, and climbed the mossy, rotting trunk to sit among the insects and the tiny plants at the top. The perch gave her a view of the Hard Moon Camp and her mother's body—a tiny dark smear before the fire circle when seen from here. If she faced away from the flames, the sky ghosted above her. The knives of the stars glittered sharp. The Hard Moon was beginning to rot and grow lean, and hungered already for the bed at Daughter Sky's western verge. To the north was the faint, dull glow of the Ice Wall.

"What shall I do, Stick?" Little Pig held her toy up in the moonlight. The tiny eyes squinted. The mouth pursed as in thought. Stick's long wooden body twitched in Little Pigs' hand. Then she smiled, ivory bright as any bone from the sand pits of the Biggest River.

Little Pig had never seen Stick's teeth before.

"Child, child, ask the moon, she rules over every doom."

She kissed Stick. Stick kissed back—another first!—though it was a sting, like the bite of a tree ant, rather than the gentle press of Berry Brown's lips. Then Little Pig set her legs apart, as Broken-Eye did when he was called to wrestle spirits from the weed smoke. She spread her arms wide, as Oldest Woman did when asking questions of the southern wind. She titled her head back, as Brother Spear did when calling to the wolves and bears and cats. Stick clung to her outstretched hand, and the Hard Moon swam at the top of her upward gaze.

"Sister Moon," Little Pig said quietly. She did not feel a need to shout. No voice was great enough to reach the moon if the moon was not ready to listen, and any voice should reach if the moon had turned her face to hear. "I have been told three times to speak to you. A thing thrice-told is a thing true through and through. Tell me if Berry Brown may live. Tell me what I can do to make her whole. Tell me what magic there is under your cold light."

She listened a while, to the whisper of the wind in the thin-leaf trees, and the call of a distant nighthawk hunting insects, and the puzzled, nervous snorts of the deer moving through the scrub brush.

Sister Moon made no answer, but Stick twisted in Little Pig's hand.

She listened more, to the rustle of the mice scavenging under cover of darkness, and the mutter of the Biggest River remaking its bed every moment, and the faint ringing of the night's cold pouring off the Ice Wall to the north.

Still Sister Moon made no answer. Still Stick twisted, twitched, demanding attention.

She listened a third time, to the faraway scream of some animal caught up by great rushing feathers, to the cough of a hunting cat, to the scrape of claws on rock.

A third time Sister Moon made no answer. She was silent as she had ever been, edging through the sky toward her meeting with the western horizon.

"What is it, Stick?" Little Pig asked, feeling no hope.

"*Child, child, you have grown, lay me down and walk alone.*"

"No!" she shouted, then swiftly sat to wait in silence. She had made far too much noise for being this distant from the fire and the rest of the People. A cat could come, or a wolf, or even one of the mountain teratornis. Stick twitched but held her peace.

After a time, as the trees creaked and the breeze brought a musky scent of furry hunger, Little Pig whispered urgently to Stick. "You are my friend. Berry Brown made you for me. I cannot leave you behind."

"*Child, child, think what she did, when Berry carved me from a stick.*"

"You're *Stick*," hissed Little Pig. "You watch over me when I am alone. You're always close when the People are far. You protect me."

"*Child, child, your mother is in me, and I am part of what she could be.*"

Little Pig studied Stick's eyes. They were wide open now, a deep, shining black just as Berry Brown's had been. *Were*, she thought as her stomach lurched. Just as Berry Brown's were. The tiny teeth gleamed ivory-bright, and Stick's narrow cheeks had rounded.

"So you are her, and she is you?"

Stick twitched. A nod.

"I could keep you. Hold you close. Never let you leave. You'd always be with me!"

Then Little Pig's eyes were drawn back to the fire down within the bowl of the Hard Moon Camp. Berry Brown lay still upon the ground. Oldest Woman stood beside her, shadow bent and shaking, waiting for Little Pig to return.

She could keep Stick close, always have her mother. But at the same time, Berry Brown would lie by the fire, unmoving and cooling. Like a stunned doe with the slaughter-knife trapped in her throat, leaping up unexpected into the forest to bleed out her pain until the People ran her down again and completed her life.

Or Little Pig could lay down Stick—her toy, her friend, her companion, the always-touch of Berry Brown—and let the Tusk Beast's work be finished.

"I understand what Oldest Woman meant for me to learn from the moon," she said.

Stick lay quiet, as if knowing what was to come. Crying, Little Pig found her way back down the hill toward the firelight, scarcely noticing the bright eyes which watched from above. They were of the same night that had taken Berry Brown away from her, and so she gave them none of her concern.

~~*~*

Walking toward Oldest Woman, and the rest of the People who watched in shadowed silence, Little Pig could feel years settling upon her shoulders. Though she was still seasons from her own bleedings, she could not be a child when Berry Brown's place among the People was empty.

Her eyes were dry when she passed out of darkness.

Oldest Woman's voice rang with the authority of rock splitting water. "Have you asked the Hard Moon what might be done?"

Little Pig stroked Stick. "Yes, I have." She looked around the fire, where the eyes of the People gleamed little different from the eyes of the beasts around the outer ring of the Hard Moon Camp.

"And what answer did Sister Moon give you?"

"Silence," said Little Pig. She raised Stick above her head, turning slowly so that everyone might see what had become of her toy. If they could see it. "Silence, which told me everything. Silence, which told me that no matter what we do the sky circles onward and the seasons of the moon pass just the same. I can no more ask Sister Moon to turn back Berry Brown's time than I can ask her to turn back the Ice time or the Dying time."

Oldest Woman stared a while at Little Pig, then smiled. It was thin smile, quick as a lightning stroke, but Little Pig saw it come and go, and like looking at lightning, was blinded for a moment. "And now that Berry Brown is gone where the skill of my hands cannot follow, where Broken-Eye's wisdom cannot lead, what will you do for your mother?"

Little Pig squatted on her heels next to Berry Brown and touched her mother's pale face. The skin was chill, the eyes never moved even as her hand passed before them. She tugged the furs aside—bear, wolf and cat—and lay Stick down in the bruised skin between Berry Brown's breasts. Stick smiled at her, showing not only the new teeth but a tongue and mouth within, far pinker than the black blood which had dried upon her mother.

"I give Berry Brown back the toy which she had made for me," Little Pig said slowly. "I will not be a child anymore, now that she is gone. My mother needs her spirit returned so that she can travel into the lands beyond the horizon where Sister Moon goes every night."

"Woman, woman, letting go, your mother's love is bright as snow."

With those words, Stick became stick—a bit of wood slashed in a few places to make something like a face, worn from endless handling, tips softened where an infant had suckled on the wood in her hunger, split where a toddler had grown her teeth, worn where a child carried it everywhere. Little Pig looked at the bare and damaged wood and wondered what gifts of her mother's remained to her.

~~*~*

Oldest Woman gave Little Pig her new name, to help her take her mother's place among their little clan. Trembling hands blessed her before the fire, Oldest Woman speaking of the mothers who had birthed the People just as the mountain streams birthed the Biggest River. Little Pig was set upon her own journey toward motherhood, following Berry Brown's path.

Now Youngest Woman, she held Brother Spear close as he wept his sorrow. The tears helped her mother's spirit move onward. In his turn, Brother Spear dug a grave, that Berry Brown might sleep deep enough to stay out of the claws of cat or wolf during the Ice Moon and the Dying Moon to come.

"I will work alone to set the rocks," she said. Three days later, Youngest Woman laid the last of the stones upon the cairn. Berry Brown and the old, chewed stick now rested beneath. Youngest Woman spread leaves and soil between the rocks, and found the secret seeds of flowers for the days of the Bright Moon to come, even though the People would not be camped here then.

She stood silent beneath the pale sun, the ice wind plucking sweat from her head and hands. In that quiet moment, her mother came to her, carrying Stick. "I did not think it would be so beautiful," said Berry Brown in a voice made of the wind sighing in the grass, the buzz of insect wings, the creak of trees on the distant hills.

Stick nodded.

Youngest Woman returned the nod. "The toy you made for me carried me through my years of need, mother. May it carry you through yours."

Berry Brown smiled, her mouth a glimmer of beetles' wings and shiny pebbles and light on water. "As you will carry me onward through the journey of your heart."

"Always," said Youngest Woman, but she was speaking only to herself and the uncaring sky.

There was time before she had to lay the evening fire for Oldest Woman, and the rest of the People were out gathering garlic and onions.

This was what she knew that day: just as the streams become rivers, daughters become their mothers, and in turn make more daughters to spread like rain upon the land. She owed her daughters-to-come the memory of Berry Brown, the wisdom of her mother, and whatever more she might glean from her own life.

And so Youngest Woman went looking for a stick. With Stick had come stories, comfort, safety. Love. She might as well start practicing to carve now. Then she would be skilled enough when her time came to make a toy to carry her own daughters through the years.

The Times once called MICHAEL MOORCOCK one of "The 50 greatest British writers since 1945". This legendary writer and editor has thrilled fans for decades with tales of *Elric, Corum, Hawkmoon, Jerry Cornelius* and even *Doctor Who*!

Visit Moorcock's Miscellany: www.multiverse.org

THE GRENADE GARDEN
A JERRY CORNELIUS STORY
Michael Moorcock

I

In his padded jerkin and Mongol helmet Jerry might have been part of some 19th century horde were it not for the bandoliers of 9mm cartridges criss-crossing his body, the AK-47 with its well polished stock carried on his back, the belt of magazines around his waist. His other weapons, a GTA lance and a curved scimitar, were at his side.

Jerry had, like the Cossacks before him, adopted the costume and customs of his traditional enemies. Even his style of riding his energetic little horse was borrowed from the Uzbeks. That was the secret of survival in this age of split-second branding. He who shifted his identity first won the fight.

"Oh, bugger. Look at that!" His sister Cathy, almost identically dressed and mounted, pointed ahead. Four Chinese main battle tanks had appeared in the Everest foothills. They had been hoping for a lift up the mountain.

Behind Jerry his band, stinking of gun oil and wet down, stirred uncomfortably, scanning the skies.

"These days you're no more than a pawn in a V-game." Shaky Mo Collier stroked his long mustachios and lifted big brown eyes to the info flickering across the inside of his smart shades. "Don't you think your destiny depends on a roll or two of dice thrown by some isolated nerd in Sacremento?"

"We've got the world they always dreamed of." Seated sideways on her uncomfortable wooden saddle, Miss Brunner switched her own helmet to info-mode, then to kindle. She wanted to finish 'The Heat of the Day' before they started mixing it up. The Uzbeks had perfected the art of the cavalry charge against armoured vehicles and mobile guns. "We're making it real for them again."

Catherine Cornelius removed her cap and shook out her golden curls. "Is your saddle giving you piles? Frankly, I don't think Kashmir's worth it. I'm tired of these primitive sepia landscapes and the smoke of war. Couldn't we put in for *Hollywood Omelette*?"

"Red tape, darling." Miss B touched up her lipstick. "We were due to transfer a month ago. But I must say I'm getting suspicious of your brother's motives." She regarded Jerry's back with a certain coolness. Maybe he's enjoying himself?"

"Oh, he's always done that," said Catherine indulgently. "He knows how to make the most of a situation. I wish Una were here."

Miss Brunner closed her compact with a jealous snap. She would never understand their love.

II

From a fairly safe slope of Windermere Shaky Mo Collier gave a sigh of relief as he looked down at the flat, black surface of the lake. No wonder Wordsworth had never captured the profound bleakness of the place. Only Coleridge had come close. Romantic poets simply couldn't help themselves when it came to cold reality.

Mo looked over at Frank Cornelius who had grown horribly depressed since Windsor. Frank's skin had taken on the colour of old lard. He had always been the weak link in the group. What was the point in bringing his bloody Humvee with them? Hauling it had exhausted the drays and made the Scots irritable. They had no patience with horses, let alone armoured vehicles. If you couldn't walk it or run it, it wasn't worth going. Trixiebell Beesley thought it had to do with vanity and their knees revealed by their kilts.

"Well," thought Mo, "all that showy tartan won't do them any good in Northumberland. Here, they made a virtue of khaki. Dragging a Blackberry from his tunic pocket he dialed London but they were engaged.

He looked up at the ridge. Ranks of highlanders with plaids, shields, basket-hilted longswords and AK-47s came marching down towards the lake where boats were to take them across. After that it was only a short march to Liverpool where the American marines waited to join them.

III

Bashi Mahmoud rolled himself a massive spliff. His tiny sparkling green eyes regarded Jerry with amused relish.

"You've seen the Egyptian pyramids, eh? And the Empire State Building and all those other great monuments? My friend, you are a cultural monster!" The Bashi handed over the joint. "What is your best memory?"

Jerry was bound to admit his fondness for Derry and Thoms' Famous Roof Garden. It had survived many incarnations since the late 1930s. He had loved those moments above the Kensington traffic drinking a cup of Darjeeling while the children played in the Tudor Garden and looked for flamingoes.

"Maybe Holland Park on a summer afternoon in the years before we had to simplify our history in order to sell it."

"Long ago?"

"It doesn't seem like it." Jerry had lost track of his ages. His father's memories had married so quickly with his own. One chip and it was all over for identity as he knew it. He wondered if everyone experienced it the same way. Especially when siblings shared the same parental information. The end of the generation gap.

General Mahmoud was relaxed and ready for battle. He had only bonded successfully with Mo Collier and remained a little wary of Jerry and the others who did not share his joy of battle. Having split from the original horde during the second siege of Vienna, he still wondered if he had made the right decision, especially since Bishop Beesley, who had persuaded him, was now leading a group of his own ex-churchmen on a raid of the Cadbury's factory in the Wirrel and was no longer even in radio contact.

Miss Brunner had quickly tired of the Mongol's love-making which was conservative and only conventionally cruel. Her evident cooling interest had depressed him and made him more than a little self-conscious until he had smoked at least one spliff. Frank Cornelius was sympathetic but all his attempts to bond had struck the Bashi as creepy and insincere. Of old Cornelius's children, he was the only one unwilling to marry his parent.

"OK." Jerry unrolled the big Ordnance Survey map on the camp table. "Shall we go over this again?"

IV

With the walls of York successfully breached and the city looted of its valuables, Jerry and the others decided to make for Harrogate. "I could do with a bath." Jerry shot a fastidious cuff. "And what's happening to people? Any ideas?"

He and his sister rode stirrup to stirrup and side by side in affectionate companionship. Behind them, against a pearly blue sky, black smoke made lazy shapes, reminding him of the landscapes of some previous youth.

"Do you have any regrets?" Catherine wanted to know.

"I'm not really sure. Maybe we should have given Kashmir a bit longer. What do you think?"

She shrugged her lovely shoulders. "I'm still a little shocked at the Dali Lama. Who could have believed him? I suppose I'm getting too old and tired." She had been in severe pain since a couple of days earlier when she discovered Frank had smoked her supply of Fentonyl patches. The expedition was proving far less fun than expected.

She couldn't believe it. It was like Paris all over again. She had no chance of finding a decent supply of pharmaceuticals until they got to Rugby. There, too, at any rate they would at least be able to change horses.

For his part, Frank knew he had fucked up. Usually he was able to rely on his sister for her sympathy. Now, if Jerry decided to let him suffer, he would have no chance of ending it except for a bullet in the head. Frank felt profoundly sorry for himself. So far he had failed to transfer the blame to any other member of his family.

Sulking, he dismounted and walked behind them. "I need a holiday. Can't anyone see that?"

V

Mo was the first to spot the drone squadron come darting and dancing over the horizon. Seven of them in elegant formation, leaving neat, white vapour trails as if grazing the fabric of the sky.

The Uzbeks began to whoop and cheer, unshipping their ATM lances and priming the big grenades. Somewhere in the mountains of Colorado a pilot was beginning to wonder what he was up against. Mo was glad to have the chance to show him.

Behind the drones bounced a bunch of PJ40 Main Battle Tanks, their caterpillar tracks moaning and clanking. Coordinated from nine thousand miles away the drivers' helmeted heads dropped down in unison beneath the heavy steel hatches.

"This is where we show those bastards what they're up against." Mo unlimbered his RPG launchers and got his twin Ak-47s into position before popping a toffee into his mouth. He had the vague idea that this action would redeem him in the eyes of his brother and sister back in Derby. He began to whistle through his teeth.

By tomorrow it would be all over. Already he could smell the cordite smoke. Better than Viagra, he thought.

Was anyone catching this on social media?

VI

Major Nye looked up from his desk. His was a temporary rank assigned by Whitehall until something better could be found for him. He recognized Jerry and his expression grew immediately more amiable. "Hello, old son. Long time, no see, eh? How's your mother?"

"Knocking along, thanks, Major." Jerry sat down heavily and lit a Sullivan's before offering the box.

Accepting, the old soldier took time to light it, regarding Jerry through pale blue eyes. "Many thanks, dear boy.

Jerry needed something to perk himself up. The sooner he got home to Blenheim Crescent the better. Ladbroke Grove had never felt more comforting.

Behind the major the Thames was covered in a slick of oil and ash flowing slowly down to the sluggish sea. Half of London was down, taken out bit by bit by Texan drones in a frantic reaction against any nation not sworn to back that State's bid for independence. Parts of the city were obliterated while others were untouched, giving the impression of a patchily over-exposed print. Jerry had an uninterrupted view from Canada Dock to St Paul's. Why the Texans had abandoned their vendetta against England for imagined wrongs was as mysterious as their reasons for beginning it. Britain had been the first to reopen the Texan Republic's Legation in St James's.

As soon as one was available, Jerry left the office and took a Number 15 along Whitehall, heading west. By the time he got off in Ladbroke Grove and headed for Blenheim Crescent he had spotted a small shadow overhead. Who could be delivering a package already?

When he reached his steps the Royal Mail drone had dropped off his gift-wrapped parcel. He dragged it up to his front door and through into the hallway. An early birthday present. He hoped it wasn't another Remington 38.

VII

"Oh, we grew up wiv them buzz bombs!" Mrs Cornelius raised her glass to Colonel Pyat. In the full dress uniform of a Don Cossack hetman, he had just entered the room. He glanced around self-consciously, only brightening when he recognized her. He began to push his way through the party to where she sat in the filthy old armchair she liked to call her throne. "You got used to 'em in no time. We did. I missed 'em when they stopped. Life got dead boring."

The party reminded her of old times. Jerry's guests were always interesting. But she wasn't enjoying herself as much as usual.

"You 'aven't bin the same, love, since you came 'ome," she told him. "You miss Caff, don't yer?" She put out a plump hand to stop him before he crossed the room to say hello to Miss Brunner, severe in her charcoal three-piece and pearls, on the arm of Bishop Beesley in all his mitred glory. "Yore not stuffin' that bitch?"

Jerry reassured her. "Mum. Didn't you know there's a war on?"

"Now you're just tryin' to make me feel better," she said.

Bishop Beesley reached five fat fingers towards the tray of Mars Bars Jerry offered him. Miss Brunner leaned forward to present a tight kiss on both his cheeks. "Mr Cornelius. We heard you'd been in Kabul."

"There's no money left in reconstruction," he said. "They were doing so nicely, too. Hamil sent his love."

"He's still alive, is he? What a sweetie. She glanced around the crowded room. "Doctor Rymer, Doctor Swann, Doctor Nikola?"

"Doctor who?" Bishop Beesley bit into his Mars. "The right place for a stroke or something?" Light brown dribble lined his chins.

333

"Any time." Jerry winked. He was feeling flirty since his return to London. He had his identities back. With luck he might soon be in work. The population was low enough these days. It couldn't be long. He remembered the 1940s when every newspaper had fifty pages of job ads. He had grown sick of science and codes. Even architecture had no longer engaged him. The Crow had proven no better friend than the Raven. Some past! Then Cathy had told him she was pregnant. At first he had disliked the triplets. They grew on him naturally. Nonetheless it was tiring keeping track of all those personae. But that was the modern world for you. Too many options. Not enough choices. After all, he had decided to go this way. He couldn't really complain. That said, he was pretty pissed. Black holes. Dark matter. Something was happening to the multiverse. Time radiated erratically. They all regretted Pera. What had they done?

With a sigh he rejoined the party.

"We can only rely on ourselves, these days."

"You said it, Mr C."

"Do I know you? Or me, is it?"

Cathy and Frank came in at last. As usual Frank looked angry and baffled but his sister waved cheerfully.

Jerry felt himself perking up. Say what you liked there was still something exquisite about finding yourself and your sister at the same time. Radiation made you like that. He put it down to his Catholic background.

Or was he Jewish?

VIII

Hampton Court, a pile of ancient terra cotta and snaking green vines, remained handy for the river.

"It always seemed too small for Henry somehow." Catherine slipped her exquisite hand from her brother's and stepped carefully on to the gang-plank. "Libraries. Tennis courts. And yet..."

"It must have towered over the Windsors." Jerry acknowledged the guard of honour assembling at the other end of the plank. "I wonder why they decided on us. We always seemed so marginalized."

"Sometimes that's why." She raised an expert hand in its white cotton glove. And waved. "You know very well you're enjoying this. Remember when they put you in an episode of Doctor Watt?"

"Who?"

"Why?"

"I've wondered. Believe me."

"I do, Jerry. Really."

On the well-tended shore Major Nye appeared, saluting, at the head of his bear-skinned redcoats.

"Are we," Jerry wondered, "prisoners or pensioners."

"Or all three," said Catherine.

Jerry was concerned. "Which came first? The egg or the egg? Are we putting this down to Radiant Time?" She could be losing it. He had a feeling this was going to be like Cornwall all over again.

Maybe Professor Hira was right and all they were mere echoes of echoes.

Somewhere a bell began to toll.

"Isn't that sweet," she said. "They're playing *Greensleeves.*"

"I knew it." Jerry took a tighter grip on her hand. "Too many bloody narratives."

Major Nye saluted.

"Civil war, old chap. But not as we know it. If you're lucky you'll have a chance to write your memoirs."

IX

"Every little picture has a story of its own," sang Major Nye. "Every little picture tells a tale." He added, "Sometimes a good many more than one. Are you feeling all right, old boy? Those fragmentation johnies can... Feeling all right? Are you? Old boy?"

"Never better." Jerry checked the board of the Bushwhacker main battle tank. "Do you have a separate bass control on this thing?"

"We're a bit primitive at our end of the world." Major Nye sipped his canned bitter. He shuddered. "Believe me, old chap, we're not proud of it. Now then, have you two talked this over? Who's going to be King and who wants to be Queen?"

In the rear Cathy said sweetly: "We thought we'd take turns."

Major Nye checked his watches. "We can probably sort all that out once were up and running."

"Can you smell something?" Shaky Mo poked his head down through the hatch. "Can you smell anything?"

"Not yet," said the major.

X

The sky was awash with fluttering black flags. At the head of every squadron of Cossack and Uzbek cavalry was a scarlet tank. Hovering over the tanks were PJ40 fully-armed battle drones and in a large Duesenberg staff car sat the King and Queen of London ready to lead their loyal army against the might of the Welsh Pretender.

Shaky Mo, festooned with all the latest materiel, rode up and saluted. His long moustaches moved gently in the wind. He offered them a rather self-important salute. "It's been a pleasure," he said. "Sincerely, chief. Chiefs."

Jerry and Cathy acknowledged his courtesy.

Engines began to rev the length of the ranks. "We're off," said Jerry. He checked for radiation. "Let's get this war on the road."

It was always a relief to feel that first rush of adrenaline. Life was getting sweet and simple again.

CARMEN TUDOR writes speculative adult and young adult fiction from Melbourne, Australia. Her stories feature in various international anthologies and can be found in *Miseria's Chorale, Cellar Door: Words of Beauty, Tales of Terror,* and *Spirited: 13 Haunting Tales.*

For more about Carmen, please visit her site:
www.carmentudor.net

SAND AND TEETH
Carmen Tudor

J dreamt last night that the New City's walls tumbled down. With the morning sun came no real belief that the dream was just an illusion. The sight and sound stayed with me until I could trace the horrific destruction one stone at a time.

Hauling the urn of water onto my shoulder, I trudged past the younger carriers. They hadn't yet learned that every return to the reservoir was calculated, timed, and tallied at the end of each quarter. Their weak muscles quivered as they lifted the earthenware urns, and although I had no plans to enlighten them of what their futures held if they didn't meet their quotas by quarter's end, I pitied the slack-kneed shuffles of their stilted steps. They would learn soon enough.

The coarse sand burned with the sun's heat. It was nice at first, early in the morning, but now in the afternoon blaze my cracked heels sank into the sand with each step. I surged forward and ignored the spot on my shoulder where the base of the urn broke my skin. If I didn't think about it, it was almost the same as if it wasn't there at all. A cry from behind me stilled my steps. Turning slowly, I took in Rubena, the newest carrier. Her urn lay in the sand before her. Any water it may have been carrying had disappeared and a small, darkened patch of sand was all that remained. She couldn't have been older than eight or nine—the same age I was when I was brought here. Rubena cried loudly. She watched the other girls walk past her and glanced back past the dam to the catchment. She was asking herself if it would be better to pick the urn up and continue to the reservoir as if nothing had happened. I shook my head at her and turned. I didn't wait to see if she caught my meaning; I had my own quota to meet.

The New City's stalagmite spires rose ahead of me. One more mile to go and I could remove the urn from my shoulder. The walk back to the catchment would be the sweetest part of the day.

The loose sands of the outer island abutted the gritty limestone road of the New City. I smiled at the thought that no one would have ever guessed a channel separated these two provinces. My people's generation—the best, I'd heard—had perfected the art of structural engineering. The ground below my sandal was firm; the limestone pavers were entirely seamless.

The reservoir was now in sight. Approaching the inlet conduit, I nodded to Head Mother. She stilled her scales and appraised me, my muscles, my form, as I lowered the urn. She marked down the weight and sent me on my way. The incredible lightness of the urn brought joy to my heart. My raw shoulder pulsed and although the pain was there, it was enough for me to lift the tunic from the skin and let the air and sun at it.

Once I was back on the island, the sand immediately seeped into my sandals. The familiar heat reminded me of the other girls. Of Rubena. Her lack of skill was obvious. Her pretty features wouldn't be enough to gain favor with Head Mother if she wasn't bringing an adequate amount of water into the New City. Other girls trotted past. Some were older, some younger. None of them, I knew, were as fast as I. They ignored me now. They were all thinking it, all appraising me as Head Mother had. Soon I would receive my orders to leave the island and the water-carrier duties for my new life. It thrilled me and terrified me equally.

Eventually I spied Rubena's slight form. She carried her urn in front of her with her arms wrapped around its curved belly. Her legs bowed outward at the knees and her little feet sank into the sand. She was losing time simply for not following the most basic carrier instructions.

"Stop," I said.

She halted her steps so suddenly the water in her urn sloshed about and spilled out over the lip. She quickly placed her tiny hand over the opening.

"When you carry it that way the uneven weight of your steps drags you down. Has no one told you this already?"

She nodded.

"Lift the urn."

Rubena held tighter.

"Lift the urn to your shoulder." I demonstrated with my own.

She set her own urn between her feet and lifted the sleeve of her tunic to show me her shoulder. It was bruised, but the skin remained intact. The memory of my first weeks came flooding back. No one had told me to quicken my steps—I'd done that of my own accord.

"You must," I told her. "You must carry it higher or you will never…" What could I tell such a young child? How would I explain her dismissal? I tried again. "When you carry it on your shoulder, place your scarf over the opening. Otherwise the heat of the sun will evaporate the water as you walk."

She stared back blankly.

"The sun will slowly dry all your water. Take your scarf and cover the opening of the urn."

The little girl picked up her urn from the sand. She wrapped her arms around it and stumbled forward. I called "stupid girl!" as she walked toward the New City, but I knew she wouldn't turn or even listen to me again. Her jerky movements and ineffective walk were all she was interested in.

When I got back to the catchment I put my urn aside and drank greedily. The cool water was like balm to my burned and blistered skin and I stayed a while to bathe my wounds.

~~*~*

Head Mother collected me in the night. While the other girls slept, I lay awake calculating my quota and if I had succeeded. I had, of course. Not only had I worked hard to boost my strength as a carrier, but I'd also noticed an increase in my rations. An extra scoop of grain or a larger portion of bread had found its way to my bowl nearly every day. That only ever happened to the chosen girls, those destined for the motherhood. It was no surprise when Head Mother reached a hand out to my cheek and woke me with her touch. The other girls slept soundly and it was only for Rubena that I lingered and spared a quick glance.

Knowing I wouldn't need my scarf any longer, I dropped it onto her outstretched arm as I passed. She may not require it now, but there would come a day when she would need it. Not to shield her water from the sun. For that, she had her own. I knew that Rubena would run. Young and impulsive, she would drop her urn and course through the flying sand. Then she could take my scarf and cover her eyes, her mouth. She might even have a chance. I could have reported her. I could have made known my reservations. They would have been documented and she would have been restrained. I thought of all these things as Head Mother led me away. Instead, I curved my fingers tightly around Head Mother's and let her take me to the New City.

Things were so different after that night. So very different. We walked in silence until the sand met the limestone. Our grainy soles rasped against the paved road with each step forward. Listening to the sound, I sang along by grinding my teeth. That, the rasping of sand and teeth, would make the memory real enough to store away. That was the sound of freedom, I told myself. That was the sound of no more miles to go. Head Mother and the others were kind to me. They fitted me in robes and when I held back the blood-stained tunic, they recognized my shame. I had never known it was possible to share one's shame, but here in the quarters, the others lifted their robes aside and showed me their scars. Dressing my wounds, they tended to my care and it was Head Mother who sat behind me and combed the knots from my tangled hair.

At dawn I watched in rapture as the sky changed from deep, fearful gray to amber and gold. Rubena and the others would have already been filling their urns and making their journeys to the reservoir. Was it likely, I wondered, if the little girl had ever really seen the sun rise?

"Vaune?" Turning, I found Head Mother waiting for me. She'd spoken my name aloud. Those two, low syllables were foreign-sounding to my ears. "Dragonina says it is time." Head Mother spoke kindly. Her voice was softer than my own. Practiced. I hoped that in time I too would sound like she did.

"Let us go," I replied. I held my head high, just the way Head Mother carried hers.

The snake pit cave was a thing often heard of but seldom seen. I knew this well, but it was with childish trepidation that I approached the ceremony. Head Mother's descent was a thing of celebration and so when I shed a tear, I raised my face to the sun and let it burn away the evidence as it would. The heat was good and real; the heat reminded me of what I had been and what I now was, but it vanished as I entered the darkness. Taking my vow as head mother meant representing the carriers of the New City to Dragonina. If I displeased her, I was letting down my people. I had never let down anyone in my life. Surely I would not start now.

~~*~*

Head mother duties suited me well. Presiding over the carriers made me a proud member of the society, and the New City continued to prosper just as Dragonina had envisioned. Vaune, the simple carrier, could not have fully appreciated the aqueduct that fed the New City's secret gardens and nourished Dragonina's men. As time passed and I familiarized myself with the intricate network of pipes and tubes of the irrigation system, I grew to love the New City. Every day as I weighed the urns I felt a sense of peace that was only eclipsed by the fear that it wasn't to remain. The time would come when I too would relinquish my position and celebrate my descent. But surely it was a good thing, a right thing, to remain as head mother? My training of the young carriers had tripled their efficiency and the reservoir's volume was at half capacity for the first time in our generation. Dragonina had personally told me how pleased she was with my position as head mother. It was the way she had said it, however, that gave me pause for concern. Her eyes had lingered, I'd thought, on my arms—not nearly so sculpted as they had been when Head Mother had appraised my form.

A carrier was before me. The look on her face was neither serene nor in any way as pleasant as a carrier's demeanor should be. I'd kept her waiting as her glistening arms hugged the urn in front of her. Her dark brows rose with impatience and she wiped her perspiring cheek against the scarf around her neck. How Rubena had been employed all this time without remonstrance or transfer had entered my mind on more than one occasion. Her insolence alone should have seen her dismissed, and as I weighed her urn, her gaze swept over my arms as Dragonina's had. Did she notice that I was not as I once had been? A spot of pity touched her look, but only momentarily. There was a fire in Rubena's eyes. She could never take my place as head mother, I thought. Her heels digging into the

342

hot sand would see to that. Evidence, it was, that she had little care for authority or what was right.

"Your shoulder!" I called as she walked away. Her urn swung from one hand, back and forth as a pendulum. Go ahead, I thought, and drop it. Let it fall to the limestone road and shatter to pieces for all I care.

The obstinate girl came every day to weigh her pitiful urn, and every day she'd throw me a look as if to say, *Aren't you getting quite fat?* I continued to take down her weights and until Dragonina came to me herself, I thought things would remain the same indefinitely. But it was not to be so. I was weakening. Holding a quota book was not the same as hauling the New City's water, and wasn't I getting quite fat? It was time. Dragonina was so very pleased with my service to the New City. The date for my ceremony was set. And I was to select the new head mother.

All the carriers would envy me. They would talk quietly among themselves and speak of my descent. How they would imagine the details and muse over my coming ascent, fathom the privilege. They would be as I had been. And they would hope. Only one would know, as I knew, that she would be plucked from the obscurity of a carrier and given the role of head mother.

The old path of coarse sand still led to the catchment. It had been so long since my soles had felt the grating rasp of sand, and yet not so long as to dim the memory. The gray sky seemed to hang low above my head as I walked through the night. One more mile to go, I told myself.

The carriers slept with the ease only hard workers know. Their muffled breaths filled the small space and as I stepped over limbs and scarves, hair and sandals, I questioned what was the right thing to do. My feet stopped short of trampling an outstretched arm. When my gaze looked to the girl's face, I was surprised to find a pair of open eyes studying me. Rubena, the stolid girl of disapprobation, the infidel in my midst, lay awake as I myself had.

I nodded to her as I did at the inlet conduit. She smirked and I read something in that look that said, *So, your time has come.*

"Rise," I told her. She regarded me curiously and remained still for so long that I thought her obstinacy would at last see her dismissal. But she sat up and rose from the floor. She followed me out to where the now cold sand crept between my toes and she followed where I walked.

"You lie," Rubena whispered. "You cheat on the numbers." I said nothing and kept walking until Rubena grabbed my hand. "Why?"

"Silly girl."

"I? Silly? They will throw you to the snakes, and it is I who am silly?" She laughed and the sound of her voice so reminded me of old Head Mother's that I grew cold and stepped back. "We could run."

I always knew she would run. I simply hadn't anticipated that she would have lasted until motherhood, that time would have ticked on for so long for her.

"We could run," she repeated. "Dragonina is no longer pleased with you. It is your ceremony because she is no longer *pleased.*"

"You do not know what you say." I turned from Rubena and walked in the direction of the New City.

"You are a prisoner just as much as I. Just as much as every other carrier."

I turned and struck Rubena on the face. She skittered back in the sand and touched her cheek.

"You can control the weights in the number book, but you cannot control the carriers' thoughts. Nor their talk."

Rubena's voice was no longer pleasant. The discord of her words struck my ears harshly.

"Dragonina knows this. She knows that you lie. She knows that you cheat and keep a rebel in the society."

"You are not a member of the society," I replied.

"Not yet. But when the dam bursts, there will be no separation. The island and the city will be as one. There will be no carriers; the girls will enter the New City."

I struck the girl again. She would be dismissed instantly if word reached Dragonina that the dam's integrity had been questioned.

"Vaune." Rubena's tooth had cut her lip. She wiped the blood from her face with the short sleeve of her tunic. "We could run." She grabbed my hand and pulled me along with her carrier's strength. I stumbled forward and preparing to fall into the sand, let the girl carry me away from the New City. My protests and demands went unheeded.

The dam that had protected the catchment for our entire generation had never shown a crack, never chipped a pebble loose. It would remain as long as the New City would. If Rubena thought otherwise, she was mad. As if divining my thoughts, she spoke.

"We know things. A simple explosive is all that is needed. The destruction would be magnificent."

My tears fell readily. If Dragonina learned of this conversation, I too would be dismissed. I would be released as head mother and sent away from the island. My ceremony would be canceled and there would be no descent. The snake pit was disappearing and as my tears fell I cursed myself for my childish emotions. Letting down the carriers and the people of the New City was infinitely worse. It was unspeakable.

"Run!" Rubena ran faster and dragged me along behind her. Her grasp on my hand never softened. My feet skimmed the surface of the sand. For once my soles felt bare against my sandals. Was this what it was to fly?

Soon we were not alone. Others joined us as we ran. Their feet flew across the sand as ours did. My cries were silenced by the laughter and shouts of the girls. The melee and the din to them was the sound of freedom. Rubena slowed just as I felt I couldn't run any farther. My lagging steps had slowed us down for the last mile of the run, but seeing her now told me she wasn't displeased. Her face was radiant with joy.

"You don't have to watch."

My lungs burned and I couldn't speak.

"You can turn away." She placed her hands down upon my shoulders and turned me from the catchment in the far distance. There was not enough light to see anything and I marveled at what the girls could all be looking for on a night such as this.

A warning cry rang out. And then, before I could do anything to stop it, the sky exploded with light.

Rubena and the carriers shouted. Tears streamed down their faces as an explosion rocked the steady and impenetrable wall of the dam. The roar reached us even where we stood, and although we couldn't see, we heard all as the wall came crashing down. I fell to my knees.

~~*~*

Not one of us had ever reached the border of the island. The anticipation of not knowing what to expect, the fear and excitement, pervaded the air as the sun rose. The girls' steps slowed. As the sky turned from gray to gold, and then to amber, and the indefinable hues only I as head mother had seen, each one witnessed her own personal freedom. It wasn't sand-rasped-teeth, and it wasn't a number scribbled incorrectly for reasons even I could not name. It was the sky above marking a new time, and it was a world away from the motherhood and the carrying of another's water. It was one more mile to go. My own fears hadn't diminished. All I could think about was what had become of Dragonina and her men. I thought of the writhing snakes and the earthenware urns all smashed—every one. I thought of limestone degrading and flawless seams materializing in the afternoon blaze.

Rubena squeezed my hand. "This is where the rain falls," she said. "Wait until you hear it." She turned her face upward. "Just wait until you hear it." She let go of my hand and ran across the sand. I didn't know where she was going, and I knew she didn't either. It was very clear from the look on her face as she'd smiled up at the sun that she didn't care. This was the real road to freedom for her. And for a reason I couldn't name, I would follow her there one step at a time.

A winner of the Writers of the Future contest, DAVID PARISH-WHITTAKER writes for the steampunk series *Space 1889*. He has written tie-in fiction for the upcoming game *Dragon Assault* by Symbiant Studios and *Europa Universalis* by Paradox Development Studio. His short fiction has also appeared in *Every Day Fiction*. Besides fiction, he writes videogame reviews and analysis for *Bag of Games*. By day, he's a captain for a national airline. In previous incarnations, he has been a naval flight officer on the carrier based Viking jet, traffic watch pilot and aerobatic instructor. He lives in San Diego with his dog Molly and his horse Rocinante. He likes to play harp, screw around with small planes and joust.

You can find out more at parishwhittaker.com

THE SEAS OF HEAVEN
David Parish-Whittaker

I was there when Marianne first sang the fish into the sky, so I suppose one could blame me for not stopping what happened. I know I do. Survivors are allowed the solace of guilt.

I first met the girl as she was wandering the shore like some would-be Byronic heroine, hair down and her excessively white dress stained with the oily sea spray. I'd dropped by to court her older sister, albeit without any real hope or interest. The damnable mercury treatments had brought my bout with Cupid's pox down, but the attendant hair loss and diminished ardor did little for my temperament.

"The fish are dead," she said without looking at me.

Well, yes. They were floating in great bloated cakes, rising and falling with the surf. Oddly, they didn't wash up on the shore. But the scent still burned your nostrils.

"No use fretting about it. They've no doubt gone on to a better place," I said, scratching under my scrub wig. Abating or not, I still itched to the point of burning. "Miss Arland, correct? Shall I escort you back home?"

"Does it matter?"

"It depends on whether one is indifferent to the difference between an abattoir and a drawing room. I'm told the tea is typically better in the latter."

"How can you joke? This is all the fault of you and your mines."

I sighed. Her sister had warned me. "The waste needs to go somewhere. That's why it's called 'runoff' instead of 'stays put'. But don't worry yourself. The ocean is vast, dear girl. As the saying goes, there's other fish in the sea."

"I wouldn't expect you to care," she said, sneering theatrically. "Those mines make you rich."

"And give the former fishermen work."

"They had work! But because of you, there's hardly any fish to catch. They had a good life before you came."

"Tell that to the families who starved whenever the fish found somewhere else to summer." I had no idea why I was arguing with this witless girl. True, even my languid libido couldn't help but toy with the notion of seduction. The innocence of youth and all that. But even so, she clearly had an unfortunate fondness for talking.

Marianne was staring at me with wide, puppyish eyes. "Somewhere else to live. That's it."

"Excuse me?"

"How to save the fish. I need to tell them to leave."

"Shoo fish!" I said, waving at the water. I shrugged. "Didn't seem to work. Of course, they're all dead. Makes one deaf, I believe."

She shook her head. "Not all are dead, not yet. Come with me." She tugged at my sleeve. I was bored enough to follow.

Marianne took me to a broken down pier I'd forgotten about. As she'd said, the fishing fleets had long ago left for kinder shores. The surf surged around the pilings, keeping the water there thankfully clear of the dead fish.

She walked to the end of the pier and spread her hands out, her dress flapping in the sea breeze. I suspect she was aping a romantic painting she'd seen at some gallery or another. I've always maintained that little good comes from the education of women, and she wasn't proving me wrong.

Then she sang. I want to say something dismissive about the childishness of her voice, thin and high without a trace of proper vibrato to it. And if I'd been subjected to it in a drawing room while her proud and over-painted mother fanned herself in self-satisfaction, I'd have been reaching for my flask to numb the pain.

But here, it was right. The sea itself provided the necessary bass for the lightness of her voice. And Christ, it made you yearn, without telling you what to yearn for. For a man, eh, maybe it made one regret all the years of willful lovelessness, manifesting in tawdry nights that brought only sickness.

Mercury might burn out the blood, but it did little for my soul. But then again, what could one do?

She sang without words, but with all too much meaning, damn it. As I twisted my mouth to curse at her, the water boiled.

And the fish flew into the sky.

They hung there in a shimmering silver school, twitching one way and another, darting a hundred yards away, then two hundred in the opposite direction. They swirled around us without touching.

I watched them with wonder, but no shock. I'm not sure why I was so willing to believe what I saw. Perhaps, like the fish, my hopes for salvation allowed me to ignore reality.

And then they were gone.

When she stopped singing, I felt lethargy settle on me like the depression that follows coitus. I couldn't speak. Breaking the silence seemed almost sacrilegious. And for the first time in as long as I could remember, that mattered to me.

"Why not the sky?" she said, smiling as she turned around. "It's even larger than the sea, and the birds use so little. I told them it was all right for them to leave the water. That's all I think they needed. Permission."

I swallowed until my throat was moist enough to speak. "They were staying out of a sense of obligation?"

Marianne nodded. "Don't we all?"

I found myself oddly angry, but the mood was quickly replaced by confusion. "How on Earth did you do that?"

"Voice lessons. Mother ensures practice, speaking of obligation."

The anger returned. "You know what I mean. How do you know all this? How do you sing to fish, let alone get them to pay attention?"

"I walk the beaches, and I listen. It's a dying art." She smiled again, this time with an attractively sardonic curl to her mouth. Perhaps there was some hope for the girl, after all.

~~*~*

It was some time before I saw her again, perhaps a year. I was out surveying the moors where my fleet of fishing balloons was working. There were a few schools of minnows nestling at the base of the hill, but most of the fish preferred to swim about in the clouds, hiding in them like aerial reefs. But that wasn't anything that a bit of ingenuity couldn't overcome.

I watched as a fishing net descended to the ground, stuffed full with a catch of wriggling fish. More herring, I noted with disappointment. We'd been catching them far too easily, flooding the market. I'd just have to have them pickled and stored until the prices rose again.

Preoccupied with these thoughts, I didn't notice Marianne approaching. She may have said something, but I'd been plagued with ringing in my ears. For me, the world was filled with wind chimes that I had no way of silencing. At least my fevers weren't as bad. I still felt warm, but they no longer burned.

"I should have known you'd turn this to your own ends," she said, her sharp voice cutting through the chimes.

Filled with surprised annoyance, I turned to see her in yet another thin white dress, hands akimbo.

"Aren't you happy?" I said. "The miners you pitied are now back to fishing. But with far more efficiency than before."

"But they're still dependent on you."

"What can I say? I'm good at seizing opportunity." I waved at the sky, filled with brightly colored balloons chasing fish-infested clouds. "I owe all this to you."

She attempted to glare, but it was far too half-hearted. I knew I'd struck a chord there. She turned away from me to watch the minnows working their way through the tall heather. I could see her shoulders shaking, though I couldn't hear her crying.

Thank God for small favors, I suppose.

A vague feeling of guilt settled on me. I won't pretend I was fond of her, for all her fashionably frail prettiness. I try to dislike people who don't like me, as there's nothing more embarrassing than unreturned affection. Still, I didn't want the girl sobbing away on my account. She was an innocent. Corruption might flow through my blood and liver, but I found unnecessary cruelty tawdry at best.

And after all, she had helped me. Whether she liked it or not.

I touched her shoulder to get her attention. She spun away from me, her wet eyes narrowing.

I cleared the phlegm from my throat, perhaps too loudly. "Listen. These fellows spend all day in the sky, enjoying fresh air and sun. I might not pay them as much as you'd want me to, but they aren't starving. I challenge you to visit them and their families. You'll see nothing but chubby children swarming about the local row houses."

Her eyes opened, at least in a literal sense. "You actually call upon your fishermen?"

"Well, no," I said.

She rolled her eyes.

"It's simple logic," I said. "Fishing isn't easy. If they were malnourished, they'd be falling from the skies along with their nets."

She pursed her lips in apparent thought. "You feed them the fish?"

"Too expensive to waste on them. Your flying fish are a delicacy."

"You're lying. You'd be the first to feed them the trash fish."

Damnation. I'd best tell her the truth, I thought. Else she'd draw her own conclusions. Conclusions that could bankrupt me.

"Not lying," I said. "Not exactly, I should say. The fish, they're tasty enough. Absurdly so, in fact, as if they were the perfect example of what fish should be."

She actually smiled at me. And that made me happy. Looking back, I think I wanted her approval right then. I'd been feeling guilty. And if I could get her to say I was right, her of all people, I'd be absolved.

"Perhaps they were purified when they left the ocean for the skies." She clapped her hands like a little girl. "They're fish angels!"

"Never tasted an angel," I said. "But if they've left the sins of the world behind beneath the waves, they've also left far too much substance."

She knitted her brows in confusion.

"Those who only eat sky fish waste away," I explained. "The fish are food in form and flavor only."

"They're poisonous," she said, anger hovering behind her voice. "And you still sold them."

"Not poisonous. Just not very nutritive, that's all. I've no problem selling them to the toffs. The average gentleman could stand to lose a few stone, after all." I stroked my chin. That might actually be a selling point. The truth might not bankrupt me after all.

A fishing net landed wetly nearby, sending the pungent scent of fish cascading over us. Taking to the air hadn't abated that scent, but its character had changed somewhat. It smelled almost like bread.

She shook her head. "It doesn't matter, does it? The way you fish, they'll all be gone in a year or so. You are far too efficient."

"Thank you. But you're wrong there, too. Damnedest thing, but the schools seem to replenish themselves every week or so. I could wipe the sky clean, but soon they'd be out cluttering it up again."

She made a little "o" with her mouth. "They return to the skies after being eaten, that's what's happening. It would explain why people starve eating them."

I felt myself frown. "After they've been cleaned, fried and presumably chewed thoroughly? Look up there at them," I said pointing at the sky. "Not a speck of batter or drop of vinegar to be seen up there."

"It's miraculous, yes. But I believe in miracles. Don't you?"

"Don't care."

She strode towards the net. It was swollen like a balloon itself, the fish swarming about inside it in a great floating, pulsing mass. She began to untie its lead weights.

"Whatever you're doing, stop it," I said.

She hoisted the net over her shoulder. It was almost as large as her. But as delicate as she was, she carried it with ease. I think the fish were helping.

"You won't stop me," she said. "I'm going to take some of your catch to the village to feed the fishermen's families."

"You want to starve them?"

"They'll still have their daily bread to fill them. But they deserve more than just sustenance."

"Those are my fish, damn it!" I stepped towards her, my fist raised. I could feel the fever rising in me as the ringing in my ears raged like an orchestra's timpani.

I couldn't hear what she said, but that was irrelevant. As she said before, I wasn't going to stop her. It's one thing to avoid charity; it's another to interfere with it. My immortal soul was doubtlessly stained beyond recognition, but one never knew.

Dropping my hand to my side, I watched her walk away towards the slums where the fishermen lived. She looked so purposeful as she passed over the moors through the cloud-dappled sunlight. I can't say exactly what I felt, but it may have resembled admiration.

It was her idea, of course. But I have to wonder, was it my touch that made everything go wrong? Am I so incapable of kindness that simply my allowing it perverts it? If so, then it's just my nature. I can't be blamed for it any more than a hedgehog can be blamed for his quills.

And if that's a lie, at least it comforts me.

~~*~*

It was early winter when I visited her in the deserted tenements by the docks. With no people to chase them, the fish had settled here. Long schools wove in and out of empty doorways and broken windows like yarn through the loom of some maniacal weaver god. The sunlight splashed over them, making the sound of bells echoing down the streets. I trudged along, disturbing the rayfish on the cobblestones. Each click of my boots spat thick red lines through the air. I'd been seeing sounds of late, the latest symptom of my ongoing rot. But I didn't mind. It let me see what I couldn't hear for the ringing in my ears.

And the fever kept me warm through the loneliness of winter. I sometimes wondered where everyone had gone. The remains of their starved bodies should have littered the streets. But instead, it was as if everyone had packed up and left on holiday just before they died.

Come to think of it, that was close to the truth.

I arrived at the flat she had moved into over her mother's protests. Pushing a sea turtle away from the doorway, I headed down the dark hallway to her room. At the end was the glow from the solitary lamp she'd left burning.

The bedroom was filled with the iron scent of stale blood mixed with a familiar bread-like smell.

"You've been eating the fish," I said. "You need to eat real food."

"It wouldn't do any good, not anymore," she said from the depths of her bed. "The fish are filling enough. I'm not hungry at all. In fact, I feel quite content."

"You're still starving."

"I just want this to be over."

I could tell that she'd tried to make herself presentable for the visit, but the pile of bloody handkerchiefs by her bedside told me that her fight with consumption was coming to its inevitable end. Even by the weak light in the room, blue veins were visible underneath her far too pale skin. She'd cropped her hair like a nun. The last time I'd visited, she'd told me she was going to do that. Her daily toilette had become too much work.

"I brought you a flower," I said, pulling a white rose out of my jacket.

"The house of York?" she said. I could see her words trace themselves in light golden lines in the dark of the room. "Are you casting me as Richard the Third, crippled and mad?" I was glad to see she could still smile. I couldn't.

"It reminded me of you," I said, handing it to her. "Beautiful and pure."

"And likely to wither away over the next few days," she said. She began a coughing fit, throwing off waves of yellow green light as she ushered me away. She managed to put the rose down on her bedside table.

"It's a lovely flower," she said, done with her coughing for the moment. She glanced at me sideways. "Why are you treating me so kindly?"

I shrugged. "We're practically the only people left around here. Thought we might as well get along."

"And I'm dying."

"That too."

"I'm not sure I want your pity."

"It's my pity. I'll do what I like with it." I glared at the shadows in the room. "The hell with the doctor's orders. I'm opening the curtains."

"Don't."

"You need light and fresh air. The sea breeze smells clean these days."

"Not like when I first came here, passing out magic fish like a conceited St. Nicholas." She shook her head angrily as she propped herself upright with the bed pillows.

"You were trying to help," I said. "You had no way of knowing they'd abandon their normal food. None of my customers stopped eating."

"No one else lived in the squalor they did. I'd shown them the promise of better things."

I snorted. "Pearls before swine. Again, not your fault."

"But it was! I had no right to give them what I gave them."

"I let you take those fish, remember?"

"I was speaking of hope." She picked up the rose and examined it. I could see flecks of blood on its white petals. "Despite what you think, I'm not pure. The doctor said it was the miasmas of the docks that brought me low. But he's wrong. Consumption is a good name for what I have. My sin consumes me from within."

I laughed without color. "You? Name one sin of yours that would warrant dying."

"Pride."

I threw open the curtains. The sunlight howled like a choir of angels, bringing me to my knees as I covered my ears to shut out the sound.

I felt her hand on my shoulder.

"Thank you," she said, whispering over the din. "I couldn't face the light by myself."

353

"Why not?"

"I can't give myself permission. I needed you."

I didn't have to ask her what she meant. I knew. She was staring out the window at the sea.

"It's all right," I said. "No one will hold it against you."

She kissed my forehead with sticky lips. "I'll need help."

Taking the rose from the nightstand, she leaned on me. We tried to walk together, but it was too awkward. I took her into my arms and carried her instead.

Her body weighed nothing, even less than I would have supposed. As I carried her down to the docks, I held her as tightly as I dared. I was worried that she would float away with the wind and the fishes.

If she said anything, I couldn't hear it for the choir of angels singing wordlessly and unseen. If her words drew themselves in the air, I couldn't see it for the bright light of the wind.

I held her upright at the end of the dock as she stretched her arms out, facing the surf. The sea spray covered us, soaking through to the skin. Her nightgown stuck wetly to her sides as she fought for breath.

I kissed the back of her head, feeling the fever flow out of me. Then she was still. I released my hold on her, letting her slip into the waves before I could smell the stench of death or see her sightless eyes.

I turned my back on the ocean. The crash of the surf brought no light with it, and the angels were silent.

I live in an empty world. The town stays abandoned. Marianne's mother left years ago to stay with her daughter and grandchildren. Or perhaps she's dead. I wouldn't know.

I haven't seen the fish since Marianne went. The sky is a large place, so perhaps they are somewhere else. They must be. Angels can't die.

The fever left me with Marianne. I see without hearing, and listen without light. There is no magic in my world, not anymore.

This morning, the sea was calm, as it had never been before. I took a rowboat out and saw what I knew would be there.

Beneath the surface, there was a shining city, filled with smiling fishermen and their laughing wives. Chubby cheeked children ran through the streets, playing the games that children know and adults have forgotten.

I stood up in the boat for a long time, watching. But I didn't have the courage to leave my world.

Besides, I didn't see her there.

As I rowed away, a single white rose floated to the surface next to my boat. Watching it drift over the still water, I felt myself smile for the first time in a long time. Then I turned the boat around and rowed home.

When I close my eyes in my nightly attempts at sleep, I see the rose just as I left it. In all honesty, I prefer the visions to the rose itself. If I'd brought it home, I'd have been forced to watch it die and rot away. Instead, I remember it in all its beauty, perfecting it with the hazy recall time brings.

Keeping it in my memories, I make it an angel.

COLON CANCER - SIGNS AND WARNINGS
The Colon Cancer Alliance

Colorectal cancer first develops with few, if any, symptoms. It is important not to wait for symptoms before talking to your doctor about getting screened. However, if symptoms are present, they may include:

- A change in your bowel habits, including diarrhea or constipation or a change in the consistency of your stool
- Feeling that your bowel does not empty completely, rectal bleeding, or finding blood (either bright red or very dark) in your stool
- Finding your stools are narrower than usual
- Persistent abdominal discomfort, such as cramps, gas, pain, or feeling full or bloated
- Losing weight with no known reason
- Weakness or fatigue
- Having nausea or vomiting
- These symptoms can also be associated with many other health conditions. Only your doctor can determine why you're having these symptoms. Usually, early cancer does not cause pain. It is important not to wait to feel pain before seeing a doctor.

When to see a doctor:

If you notice any symptoms of colon cancer, such as blood in your stool or a persistent change in bowel habits, make an appointment with your doctor.

Talk to your doctor about when you should begin screening for colon cancer. Guidelines generally recommend colon cancer screenings begin at age 50. Your doctor may recommend more frequent or earlier screening if you have other risk factors, such as a family history of the disease.

http://ccalliance.org/colorectal_cancer/symptoms.html

About the Editors

JORDAN ELLINGER has been called a "standout" in a starred review in Publishers Weekly. He is a member of SFWA, a first place winner of Writers of the Future, and a graduate of Clarion West. He has collaborated with internationally best-selling authors like Mike Resnick and Steven Savile, is the Executive Producer of *Hide and Create*, a weekly podcast on writing, and is a professional editor, having worked as Executive Editor at *Every Day Publishing* and on the *Animism* Transmedia Campaign. His film, *Tender Threads*, won the jury prize at Bloodshots Canada and was screened by master of horror, George A. Romero.
Jordan's website is at: www.jordanellinger.com

RICHARD SALTER is a British writer and editor living near Toronto, Canada. He is editor of the *Doctor Who* anthology *Short Trips: Transmissions* and the shared-world apocalyptic mosaic novel *World's Collider*. He has two dozen short stories in various anthologies including *Solaris Rising* and *This Is How You Die: Stories of the Inscrutable, Infallible, Inescapable Machine of Death*. His debut novel, *The Patchwork House*, will be released December 9, 2014 by Nightscape Press. He is currently working on a second horror novel and a fantasy trilogy.
See more at www.richardsalter.com

CPSIA information can be obtained
at www.ICGtesting.com
Printed in the USA
LVOW04s1539020616

490960LV00017B/960/P